I cut my thumb and let one drip plunk down into Will's tea. I whispered a thrice-blessing against the surface and offered the mug.

"You put blood in it," he said, eyeing it suspiciously.

"To quicken the magic."

Wincing, Will said, "Drinking tea with your blood in it . . . basically goes against everything I've ever learned. About diseases. And cannibalism. And . . . religion."

"Blood is the element that makes my magic work. If you're squeamish, I don't know if I can help you."

Walking around the table, I held my hand out to him. "Blood is the conduit of magic. It is the house of power." He very gently took my hand and ran his thumb over my palm, examined my fingers one by one. I shivered at the touch, and my eyes fluttered closed of their own accord until Will pressed lightly on the tiny cut I'd made.

I drew my hand back, and then rubbed the cut thumb against my fingers. "It's just the way things are. Necessary to the magic. You have to sacrifice something to gain something."

BOOKS BY TESSA GRATTON

THE BLOOD JOURNALS
Blood Magic
The Blood Keeper

THE UNITED STATES OF ASGARD
The Lost Sun

the BLOOD KEEPER

TESSA GRATTON

BLUEFIRE

Text copyright © 2012 by Tessa Gratton
Cover art copyright © 2012 by Hilts

All rights reserved. Published in the United States by Bluefire, a division of Random
House, Inc., New York. Originally published in hardcover in the United States by
Random House Children's Books, New York, in 2012.

Bluefire and the colophon are registered trademarks of Random House, Inc.

Visit us on the Web! randomhouse.com/teens

Educators and librarians, for a variety of teaching tools, visit us at
RHTeachersLibrarians.com

The Library of Congress has cataloged the hardcover edition of this work as follows:
Gratton, Tessa.
The blood keeper / Tessa Gratton.— 1st ed.
p. cm. — (The blood journals)
Summary: Teenager Mab Prowd is perfectly content to practice blood magic on the
secluded Kansas farm where she's lived all her life until one of her spells taps into a
powerful, long-dormant curse and she finds her magic spinning out of control.
ISBN 978-0-375-86734-7 (trade) — ISBN 978-0-375-96734-4 (lib. bdg.)
ISBN 978-0-375-89769-6 (ebook)
[1. Supernatural—Fiction. 2. Magic—Fiction.] I. Title.
PZ7.G77215Blk 2012 [Fic]—dc23 2011049532

ISBN 978-0-375-86487-2 (trade pbk.)

Printed in the United States of America

10 9 8 7 6 5 4 3 2

First Bluefire Edition 2013

FOR SEAN AND TRAVIS,

THE BROTHERS I GREW UP WITH,

AND ADAM,

THE BROTHER I FOUND.

the BLOOD KEEPER

ONE

This is a love letter.
    And a confession.

TWO

MAB

The last thing the Deacon said to me before he died was "Destroy those roses."

I stood before them at dawn, the sun behind me turning the red petals into fire, and I lifted my knife.

For five weeks I'd tried to kill them. I'd attacked with a trowel, and a heavy shovel, digging at their roots. They'd thrashed with furious life, cutting my skin and flinging drops of my blood against the ground.

Then I'd set them on fire with a flick of my wrist. But the twisting vines refused to burn. My blue and orange flames danced along their leaves and thorns while the wind rushed all around, tossing fire toward the forest. I'd had to extinguish it before the entire hill caught alight.

Next I'd lain down beside them under a full moon and listened to their whispers. All night long the stars wheeled overhead and I felt the earth cracking and shifting underneath me as it turned.

Mab.

Mab, the roses whispered. *Free us.*

I rolled over and pressed my cheek into the dirt. I grasped

one of the rose vines until the thorns pricked through my skin. Pain and magic spilled from my palm and into their roots, and Arthur's voice echoed in my memory: *All the blood is yours now, Mab, all the beauty of the world. Take it.*

Shoving off the ground, I backed up toward the edge of the garden until my heels hit the wooden vegetable box where baby tomatoes grew.

The next day I asked Donna if she knew anything about the roses, and she only explained about pruning and mold and fertilizer. I called Faith, who lived in town, and she said one of the reasons she moved her family off the blood land was because Hannah woke crying and blamed her nightmares on the roses. And Granny Lyn, whose garden it had been until she died last autumn, had never allowed any of us to tend it without her.

There had been a secret planted under my bedroom window all my life.

I knew I should have spent my time creating a spell to burn the curse away, to turn the roses into ash and spread the pieces on the wind and on the river.

It's what Arthur told me to do.

But that isn't what I chose.

Here, at dawn, with my knife poised over the seven-point-star tattoo protecting my wrist, I stood facing the garden, and beside me lay a man-sized doll created of mud and bone, so that I might ask the roses a question.

A scratching on the window gable behind me drew my

attention to the large crow perched there. "Morning," I whispered. "Is Donna still asleep?"

He ruffled his feathers in an affirmative shrug.

"Where are your brothers?"

He chucked his head back and barked. Eleven more crows leapt out of the forest at the edge of our yard. Their wings flapped in unison as they swooped low overhead, washing me with damp spring air. I could feel hair curling against the back of my neck as they raised the humidity.

The flock landed around me in a semicircle, not too near the roses, their heads cocked at the same angle. One hopped forward and tapped his beak against the jar I'd set on the grass.

Inside was the heart and liver of a deer that would help give life to my doll.

Nine days ago I'd built a trap marked by runes across a well-traveled deer path, and finally, yesterday, there'd been a young buck caught in the circle. He was unable to free himself from the lines of magic weaving through the trees, and his delicate hooves stomped the ground. I stood against a walnut tree, shoulder pressed hard enough into the bark that it tore at my skin through my shirt. The buck's antlers were just beginning to press up through his head, tiny nubs of velvety bone. He stared at me with his black eyes, snorted, and reared back as if to challenge me.

"Thank you for what you're giving me," I told him.

I'd pricked my finger and clapped my hands together. The spell sucked the breath from his lungs.

That had been the cleanest part. I used Arthur's old hunting knife to slit the buck's belly and drag out the bloody insides. They spilled onto the grass as slippery as fish. His blood caught in the creases of my palms, and I rubbed them down on his still-warm neck.

I took the heart and the liver, tucking them gently into an old glass gallon jar. I twisted closed the lid and painted a star rune on top with the deer's blood. Then I closed his eyes and ran my finger along his short black lashes.

"May you find grace," I whispered.

And I left him for the vultures and coyotes.

Since then, blood had drained out of the organs to pool in a sticky mass at the base of the jar. The crow tapping it was probably hungry. I *tsk*ed at him, and promised frozen berries after the work was finished.

As the crow backed off, flapping nearer his brothers, I pierced my wrist with the tip of my knife and let three drops hit the ground. "I feed you, Earth, that my magic may come full circle," I told it, and jammed the knife into the dirt. Then I crouched beside the doll I'd made.

It was shaped like a man, with branches for bones, mud and decaying leaves for bulk, and wax to shape the smaller features like hands and mouth and eyes. I'd plucked rose petals to form a pink mouth, to give the flowers voice. If my doll could stand, it would be taller than me, with wide shoulders and room inside the cave of wooden ribs for courage and passion and laughter.

But for now it was only shadows and earth, tucked beside the thicket of roses. A doll without a string to pull.

I swallowed the pounding of my heart and knelt beside it. The scent of wet feathers and muck filled the air. An earthworm struggled to the surface of the doll's chest, where a tiny puddle had formed during last night's drizzle. I pinched the worm in my fingers and tossed it over my shoulder.

One of the crows snatched it with a snap of his beak. He ruffled his neck feathers and hunkered back down.

Water soaked into my skirt at my knees. I pushed sticky hair off my face, and I dug my hands into the doll's chest.

I parted the ribs and scooped out mud as delicately as possible. It plopped into a pile beside me. Unscrewing the lid of the gallon jar, I reached in and withdrew the heavy deer's heart. Tacky, cool blood smeared between my fingers. Gently, I placed the heart in the center of my doll's chest. It smelled sweet and raw. "For passion," I said.

Next came the liver, which I put beneath the heart. "For courage," I said.

I buried the organs with chunks of black earth and closed the ribs. My hands hovered over the doll as I paused. This was my last chance to stop, to simply follow Arthur's final instruction and destroy the roses. If only I'd questioned him then, pushed for details, but I'd been so overwhelmed by the thought of losing him, his order had barely filtered through. My loyalty warred with curiosity, and guilt with the knowledge that if I was to be Deacon in truth instead of only name, I had to understand this problem Arthur had handed me, and not just obey blindly. He'd raised me to question, to think for myself and do what I felt was right. I couldn't make that decision without exploring the magic twisting through the roses.

The crows flapped their wings, and water rained down on me and the doll.

They were in accord.

There was a metal bucket under the downspout running off the Pink House roof, filled with collected rainwater. I scooped some out and rinsed my hands. Three more crows flew up to land on the gutter, and shifted from foot to foot, their claws scratching and feathers ruffled.

With my clean hands, I grabbed a box of sea salt and shook it out in a thin circle all around myself, the doll, and the sprawling rosebushes. The grains of salt spilled through the sparse grass, glittering violet in the spare dawn light.

Kneeling next to the doll's head, I pulled an old antler out of my magic bag, smooth and polished from years of use, and sharpened to a needle-fine point. I put the tip to my wrist, where moments before I'd cut with the knife. The tattoo was a spiral and seven-point star, a rune of creation. I pressed the antler point into the hollow center with practiced ease, into the already raw wound. The quick strike of pain vanished into a tingle of magic as a thick drop of blood welled on my wrist. Holding it over the line of salt, I whispered three times, "By my blood, bless this circle," until the single drop fell into the salt crystals and the energy circle snapped into place like a vacuum seal.

My ears popped.

The crows cried out in a chorus. I hoped we wouldn't wake Donna as I pulled out of my magic bag the remaining ingredients I needed.

First I uncorked the vial of bone dust and spilled it into

the palm of my left hand and spat into it. Mixing with my fore-finger, I leaned over the doll's face and drew a line of gray down the wax forehead. "By bone, I summon you," I said.

I took up a thin strand of my own yellow hair, blessed in sunlight and sage smoke over the past three days. I pressed it crosswise over the gray line of bone mud. "Hair of the living witch, I summon you."

With a deep breath, I used my antler-needle again, to prick all ten of my fingers.

My hands on fire with energy, I held them up toward the crow perched on the gutter. Blood trailed along my fingers in thin lines, collected briefly in my palms, and scattered in rivu-lets down my forearms. The crow cocked his head and peered down with one dark eye.

"Come to me now, my friend," I said. The crows had worked magic with me for nearly five years now, helping to channel and shape my power with their own.

He snapped his wings out to their full width, so that his long primary feathers caught the edge of the morning sun and shone violet and blue.

"Reese," I said. "Thank you for the sacrifice."

He spilled off the roof and I caught him. His wings beat softly as his instinct to right himself, to fly away from me, kicked in. The feathers brushed my face like kisses.

I grasped him in my hands. I could feel his heart rushing in his small chest, could feel the burning magic pass through my bleeding fingers and into his feathers. Slowly, he stilled himself. I held him against my chest and stared into his nearest eye.

Tiny feathers spiraled around it, tinged brown. They looked so soft I wanted to run my finger along their edges.

His beak parted and he sighed. It wasn't a crow sound at all.

"By my blood and this sacrifice, I summon you," I said loudly. In a swift motion, I pushed him against the doll's chest, swiped up my antler-needle, and drove it through his small crow body. Pinned him into the mud of the doll.

Wind shot up in a column of air. The roses whipped around, and Reese's eleven remaining crows screamed in a single voice.

Scrambling, I dipped my finger into the fresh blood streaming from the crow. I painted it over my lips in two swipes, and I leaned over the doll's head. "Be alive," I said against its rose-petal lips. "Be alive." I cupped my hands around its head. "Be alive!"

I kissed it, and breathed my air into its mouth.

The earth below me shook. The doll's mouth moved against mine, tearing at my breath in an endless stream.

I jerked away, pushed up to stand over it. The living crows flew a tight circle around my head, weaving so close their wings tangled my hair.

At my feet, the crow pinned to the doll spread his wings up to the doll's shoulders. I held out my hands; rose roots and leaves snaked up from the ground, twisting over the doll into a thick, dark skin. Its fingers twitched. Its waxy face moved into an expression of pain.

It opened heavy eyelids to reveal the chunks of turquoise I'd embedded for eyes.

"Hello," I said. "I am Mab Prowd. Take this gift from me and tell me your name."

The doll sat up, crow still pinned to its chest with the white antler. His wings drooped. Blood slunk downward into the doll's lap.

It reached for me with a waxy hand. I allowed it to touch the hem of my skirt, still slightly breathless at the tingle of magic still coursing through my veins and pressing at the tips of my fingers. Laughter tickled in my stomach because of what I'd done.

My doll bent its knees and climbed to its feet. Every moment its skin hardened further, becoming smooth and light. It blinked at me with turquoise eyes. It flexed its hands. Muscles shifted under that skin, and its mouth was red with lips and tongue. Hair sprouted like black grass, and ears blossomed out. Nostrils formed themselves. Nipples. Everything growing and real, exactly as it should.

Here was a real, living man, with my friend's crow body staked to its heart.

"Tell me your name," I commanded.

The doll parted its lips; a harsh rattle sounded.

The crows screamed again and dove at it angrily, raking claws against its head. The doll swung with its thick, still-forming arms, knocking away one of the crows. The whole flock cried out, whipping around in a storm of feathers.

I faltered back out of their way.

It reached for me again, walking with a stilted shuffle. Step. Step. Closer to me, its chest and shoulders lifting with breath, in rhythm with my own. It opened its mouth and sighed, causing the soft wings of the dead crow to shake.

Then it said, "Mab."

I smiled and touched its wrist, curling my fingers around it in welcome. But it leapt forward with shocking speed. Its arm slammed my chest and I fell back, stunned, sliding through the salt circle and breaking its binding power.

The ground twirled under me. I saw the blue morning sky high overhead, shimmering through my dazed eyes.

The doll's footsteps thundered through the earth as it raced to the north.

THREE

WILL

Five weeks ago I saved Holly Georges's life when a freak earthquake knocked her out of a tree and into a lake.

This lake.

With the truck door wide open and the radio blaring, there was just enough noise that I didn't feel stifled by the hugely open sky overhead. It was about two hours past dawn. Clouds the color of orange sherbet scattered up there. Already the air was muggy. And way too quiet.

My German shepherds, Havoc and Valkyrie, bounded through the tall grass at the edge of the muddy beach, yipping and frolicking like the year-old pups they were. The heat didn't bother them, though it was already making me sweat. I tugged off my T-shirt and wiped it across my face before tossing it to the ground. Next went my running shoes and my socks, until it was just me in my track pants, and the lake.

Wind hit hard and sudden, rippling the surface of the water and grabbing my short hair. Havoc froze, nose up, and Val spun in crazy circles, her tongue hanging out of her teeth. I laughed at her and clapped my hand onto my thigh. "Here, girls," I said, and they ran at me. Val knocked her shoulder into my leg, nearly bowling me over, and Havoc put her head in the palm of my hand. I scratched behind her ears.

The wind ran away west, ripping at the tall grass. Closing my eyes, I imagined looking down at the rolling hills from a bird's eye. Pinpointed my location, then focused out until I could see the interstate just south of me. There were the sprawling suburbs creeping away from town. The Kansas River winding loose and undirected. The green summer trees all hot and bright under the sun.

It was a trick I used to orient myself so I never got lost.

Val charged into the lake, interrupting me with cool water splashed everywhere. I smelled the mud and silt, the sunbaked grass, and for a moment I was back there, just after the earthquake. Diving again and again into the murky water, running my fingers blindly against the slimy bottom, lungs burning, desperate to find her.

I dreamed about it at night. Of the sick moment I realized she hadn't come back to the surface. The shock of relief when I finally, *finally* grasped her ankle. Those long, horrible moments shaking onshore, hands covered in mud and water and blood from the gash on her head, while Shanti did CPR and all our friends crowded around whispering and touching hands and shoulders, leaning in. The sound of their breath pressed into my bare skin, pushing me down.

I'd wake up choking.

With Havoc at my side, I waded into the lake where all my bad dreams came from, hoping to bury the fear back under the mud.

It was ridiculous, I knew, but I couldn't tell Mom and Dad. Mom would blame herself. Dad would think it was some deficiency. And it sure wasn't the kind of thing I felt like telling Matt or Dylan about in the locker room before practice. Instead I'd looked up on the Internet different theories about conquering nightmares, and most had agreed that if you confronted the root of the dream head-on, you had a chance of letting go.

So here I was. The water soaked my pants, dragging them down. I tightened the drawstring and walked out farther. My feet slipped in the silt, slime squishing up through my toes. The sun beat down on my shoulders and I rolled them, trying to relax. Then I pushed out into deeper waters. Havoc held back, staying where she could touch the bottom. When I was near the middle of the small lake, I stretched out onto my back and shut my eyes.

Tiny ripples lapped at the sides of my face, and the sun glared red through my eyelids. I floated, fingers splayed, knees bobbing up. I kept my chin tilted and imagined miles of dark water under me instead of a mere thirty feet. There were bluegills stocked in the lake. Maybe some other kinds of small fish. A few weeks from now, I'd be swarmed with mosquitoes.

With my ears submerged, I could hear the high, muffled ring of my own blood running through my body and the flap of waves under my hands. My breath was a dull roar.

According to the Internet, I was supposed to invoke as many details as possible in order to relive the moments of my so-called trauma. It was easy to let my mind turn back to that afternoon. We were hanging here because it was part of

Matt's uncle's property, on the first Saturday hot enough for bikinis: mostly the guys from our soccer team and some girl-friends. Around dusk I was on the dock with Holly and Matt's girlfriend, Shanti, fiddling with a blow-up raft. Austin, being a dick before anything else, snatched Shanti's writing notebook out of her bag to see if there were love notes to Matt inside. She was so pissed she leapt at him with one of the foam noodles, and he flung the book as far down the beach as he could, where it crashed into the branches of a wide-slung tree.

Holly caught my eye to grimace. I laughed and offered to give her a leg up into the tree. I thought of her thin beach dress fluttering in the breeze. The little flashes of thigh made me keep my eyes on her hands as she reached and reached. I'd been impressed by her strength as she hauled up higher, and then surprised when she called down, "Stop shaking the tree, Will."

Only I wasn't. I leaned into the trunk, palm flat against it, and felt the very small trembling. Just as soon as I noticed, the whole ground bucked like someone snapping a beach towel. Holly's cry of panic was crowded out by the yelling and shocked laughter from the dock and beach. I fell against the tree as the shaking worsened, and called Holly's name as she slipped. Her head snapped against the branch just before she hit the water.

The earth stilled, except for the wind and screaming birds. Matt called, "Shit, Will, you okay?"

It had happened so fast. The rest of my soccer team was crowing about how awesome the quake had been, and even Shanti was laughing, soaked from ending up in the lake with Austin. Rachel tossed her a towel and I turned back to the water. "Holly?"

Nothing.

I stared at the ripples where she'd gone in. It was shallow; she should've been able to stand. Without another thought, I jumped into the cold water.

The quake had thrown up mud and silt. When I opened my eyes, they burned and all I saw was murk. I dove again, running my hands blindly over slimy mud and rocks, crawling across the bottom of the lake. Again and again into the muddy darkness. My fifth dive I caught her ankle in my hand, and relief forced the air out of me in a blast of bubbles. Lungs burning, I dragged Holly up and toward shore, standing as strong as I could with her in my arms. We burst out of the water, me coughing and Holly dead weight. Shanti was screaming and met me, half taking Holly and helping to spread her out in the grass.

"Call an ambulance!" somebody yelled as Shanti scooped her finger into Holly's mouth. I leaned on my hands and knees, shaking, while Shanti did CPR she'd learned for babysitting. Tears spilled down her cheeks, and I saw blood seeping out of Holly's head, soaking her hair and the damp shore. It was thin and pink on my hands. I dug my fingers into the mud and—

The sharp barking of my dogs broke the memory.

I flailed up, splashing my eyes, and treaded water as I tried to see what they were up to. Both dogs stood on the beach with their tails to me, hackles raised and ears back as they stared into the nearby woods.

Swimming toward shore, I called, "Here, girls, what's wrong?"

Valkyrie glanced at me, but Havoc growled. A low growl, the kind you feel before you hear it.

My toes touched ground just as the thing emerged from between two trees.

What I saw sucked the breath out of me.

It was a man—or a man-shaped *thing*—crawling with leaves and twisting branches, dripping mud. Its face looked like melted candles, except for the bright blue rocks where eyes should have been. Impossible.

I ran out of the water to my dogs, gasping. "Hello?" I said, telling myself it had to be a man, somebody in a costume or something.

The head jerked toward me and the blue rock eyes *saw* me.

Havoc charged, and Valkyrie followed instantly.

The thing reached down and batted Havoc away like she was a piñata.

"No!" I yelled, running full out.

It let out a strangled, bubbling cry and focused on me with its stone eyes. Then it lifted a stumplike foot and moved to crush Val.

I threw myself at it, a flying tackle. I hit hard, and all my breath was slammed out. We went tumbling. It smacked down on top of me, and I felt something jab hard into my sternum. I yelled again. Mud packed my nostrils and dropped chunks into my mouth. I spat, trying to shove it off, but the thing was heavier than a dozen midfielders. It stank of rot and pennies and wet dog. We rolled together, me choking and straining with all my strength. It was slippery and hard to get ahold of. It shoved its fingers into my mouth, ripping at my jaw. I bit down, and spat mud. It flailed and I pressed my elbow into its neck and twisted. Suddenly I was on top. I shoved down with all my weight. The thing jerked but remained under me. I stared at it, gasping for breath. My dogs barked and growled from either side.

It felt like a man but softer, with a wax face and a gaping mouth. Black feathers covered its chest, and a white piece of antler stuck out where its heart would be. One of its arms had torn off and twitched nearby.

It breathed. A great, shuddering breath, full of mud, and a rose petal fluttered up out of the tear of its mouth.

I bent over it, spitting muddy saliva. A rose petal fell out of my mouth, too.

My fingers were slick with mud, and sweat ran down into my eyes. My chest was tight, aching where the antler had struck me. Valkyrie whined, but Havoc growled. Pure relief made me light-headed. She was okay. "Hey, girl," I said.

The mud monster bucked, nearly tipping me off. I slammed forward, pushing my hands into its shoulders as if that could keep it down. My hands slid a half inch into its loose body. Made my stomach heave.

I swallowed the nausea. It wasn't real. It was only—only . . . What *was* it?

Too strong, that's what it was, I thought as it jerked again. I grasped the antler in one fist. The mud monster roared. Startling back, I tugged, and the antler popped out with a sucking sound. The thing under me shuddered.

I threw the antler aside.

The monster went still, just a pile of human-shaped muck, slowly sinking into the earth as though we rested on quicksand. But I didn't sink.

For a long moment I just knelt there, staring down and wondering if I was crazy—or just dreaming that I was here. My breath heaved under sore ribs, and my body shook with adrenaline. I could've crawled out of my skin. Flown away. I suddenly craved oranges. They'd been halftime snacks at soccer games when I was ten.

Valkyrie nosed at the waxy residue caking the ground. Havoc pushed her head under my empty hand.

The wind brushed over my bare back, and from behind me a girl said, "You killed it."

FOUR

WILL

My dogs jerked up and ran barking for the tree Holly'd fallen out of last month. Their barks were playful and excited now. I shakily got to my feet. My shoulder blades prickled as I turned my back on the remains of the mud monster.

The girl who'd spoken straddled the lowest branch of the tree. She sort of blended into it because of cargo pants and a green tank top that revealed arms covered in green and brown markings. They might have been tattoos, might have been finger paint. Black boots that looked uniform-approved dangled down on either side of the branch like anvils. In one hand was a small patchwork bag, and in the other a hunting knife. Awkward-looking goggles covered the upper half of her face.

I swallowed a sudden urge to laugh. It was that edge of adrenaline and shock turning the whole situation absurd. Mud monster, girl with goggles in a tree. Obviously.

Both Havoc and Val started barking again.

The girl jammed the knife into the branch. She shoved the goggles up over her forehead, pushing tangled yellow hair away from her face. "Are you all right?"

Pressing a hand flat against my stomach to get ahold of myself, I smiled widely up at her and wondered how far down the yellow-brick road I'd come. "I think so. I'm Will."

The girl's eyes narrowed and a breeze tossed her curls across her neck. It made the whole tree dance around her. Like she was part of it, grown out of the branch like a colorful fungus.

As I stared at her, something like awe simmered up from my toes.

"I'm Mab Prowd," she finally said. There was something dark as grape juice smeared across her lips. And several small sticks poked out of her hair. Before I could ask what was going on, a crow landed on the branch just above her. Then another. They held their wings open.

She glanced at them and nodded. Three more of the big black birds swooped down from the left, batting their wings enough to blow air at me. They landed on a fallen log.

I felt uncomfortable. As if the ground was about to start shaking again, with Mab Prowd as the focus of it. Everything spinning out from her. And I couldn't tell if that was a good thing or a bad thing. Was I gonna pass out? Dad would love that.

Valkyrie sat back and wagged her tail against the ground. Her tongue lolled out. Havoc pushed her shoulder heavily against my leg. I dug my fingers into her ruff. My dogs didn't mind Mab, and that was the best sign I could get.

"They trust you," she said, as if she was using them as a sign, too.

"Yeah." We stared at each other for another long moment.

I spat again, wanting the taste of blood and mud out of my mouth. "You know . . . ," I began, half turning my head toward the monster. "You know what that was?"

Swinging one leg up over the branch, she dropped her bag to the ground. It plopped into a bush. Carefully, she lowered herself down, jerked the hunting knife out of the tree, and let go. She landed in a crouch, then tucked her knife into the fallen bag.

I expected her to deny everything. So when she said, "It was a dream of roses," like that explained everything, my mouth just sort of hung open.

Mab passed me, going to crouch beside the remains of the monster. It was blood, not grape juice, smeared across her lips. The roaring in my ears rose in pitch.

I turned, not really wanting my back to her. Her expression, as she studied the monster, was ferocious. I was glad she wasn't looking at me the way she stared down at it.

Several crows pushed off the tree and landed around Mab. They hopped nearer, wings open, and I realized that it had been a dead crow nailed to the monster's chest with the antler I'd pulled out.

Val and Havoc nosed closer to Mab, Havoc snapping at one of the crows. It flapped its wings at her and clacked its beak. I hung back, watching the scene play out as if it was a movie. A horror movie.

With both hands, Mab dug into the thing's chest. Branches snapped, and she dug out huge handfuls of mud. The chunks that slid down her arms left a trail of bright red.

And then Mab pulled out a glistening hunk of meat. A heart. *A heart.*

I widened my eyes, and wasn't sure if the earth was shaking again or if it was just me.

She whispered something, stood up, took the heart over to the bag she'd dropped out of the tree. Mindless of her filthy hands, she dug out a box of salt. And dumped a good stream of it over the heart. Tiny white salt crystals stuck to the flesh, melting in, and others trickled to the ground.

Fear tightened around my ribs. I stepped back once, and then again. Toward the lake. My foot slid on the silty shore. I needed my shoes and shirt, and to run for the car. Nothing made sense about this situation, and it couldn't be real. I hadn't actually come out here to fight my dreams but was still trapped in a nightmare. That had to be it.

But.

But Mab whispered over the heart and it shriveled. It dried and shrunk in her hands, and the rest of the mud monster shrunk and crumbled, too. Her lips moved surely; her hand held the heart without disgust or fear. There was something too real about her.

"Bound to the ground," Mab said. She fisted her fingers through the shriveled heart, and it fell to dust at her feet.

I had to get away. I opened my mouth to tell Mab good luck and goodbye, but she shut her eyes and her whole body swayed. She listed hard to the side. Like *she* was about to faint.

Leaping across the distance, I caught her just as her knees gave out.

Weariness streamed through me into the earth. My legs trembled and the blood-sight glasses were so heavy my head bobbed like a sunflower in the wind. I tumbled, but the boy caught me in a sun-warmed embrace.

Will. He'd said it was his name, offhand and without any assumptions that it would mean anything to me. But names do matter. *Will.* Willpower was the thing that held all my magic together: it mattered most of all.

I blinked up at him, clutching at his bare shoulders. His face was close enough to mine that I could see his pupils contract like magic, as the sun emerged from behind a cloud.

The light dappled his skin.

He was my age, with hair cut short against his skull, and he held himself easily, even in the midst of his confusion. A typical summer farmer's tan darkened his elbows and forearms, even though it was only half into May.

"Are you okay?" he asked.

I drew a long breath, examining the way it passed through my body. My limbs felt heavy, running with thick, tired blood. The tiredness melted my flesh, and I looked down at the remains of the doll. The moment it ran off the blood ground, it had begun its slow deterioration from so-near-human back into this ruin. My vision narrowed in to it, graying with fatigue. Because the circle had been broken, I'd expended too much energy without taking any back; I needed food and my own land for healing. "I only need to get home," I said. "It's just south of here."

Will's hand found the small of my back and pressed there,

a grounding heat. He'd somehow known to remove the antler from the doll, and he knew just where to support me. He said, "You sure? I can call somebody, or drive you or take you to . . ." He paused as though he were unsure of himself, yet he kept his arm around me, like a piece of warm wind and sunlight.

"Please let me go," I said again, wondering if I'd need to ask a third time, if Will was subject to rules like that.

But he said, "Okay, Mab."

"Thank you." I smiled, imagining the way Arthur drew people into his confidence easily, with just a relaxed gesture.

"Can you stand on your own?" he asked, hand still on my back.

I drew in another long breath and pushed off his hand. "I think so. It's been a trying morning." One of his dogs nosed at my fingers and I scratched behind her ears where the fur was thin and soft.

"That's Valkyrie," he said, letting me go and holding out his hand to the second dog. "Here's Havoc."

"Did he hurt her?" I had not been directly behind the doll because I'd had to change into proper forest-hunting clothes and grab extra salt. And so I'd run out of the trees just in time to see the doll slam into Will.

His face darkened, and he crouched down, ruffling both hands in the dog's heavy fur. "I think she's all right."

"She will be with you, I'm sure."

Something strange flitted across Will's expression before he offered me a smile.

"I should go," I said.

"Me too." He glanced at the remains of the doll and spat on

the ground. I recalled the taste of its breath, when I'd kissed it into life.

He opened his mouth as if to ask me again what it was, but instead he tilted his face up to the sky, where the crows spiraled slowly as vultures. He shook his head and laughed softly. "It's impossible."

The crucial moment had swung around again: Would he let this go, believe me that it was nothing? Or would it be caught in his memory like a match, sparking again and again in his dreams? I pulled him to his feet, heaving with the strength I had left. We faced one another, and I touched his shoulder with a hand that was sticky with blood and mud and had already left streaks staining his bare chest. "It is impossible," I said softly but firmly. Spreading my fingers out, I pressed a nearly perfect handprint into his skin. "And not important. You don't need to think about it; it won't hurt you or anyone. It's gone. Fading like it never existed."

The sun was behind him, shining all around his head so that his hair turned into an auburn halo and his face was only shadows. For a split second he seemed exactly like the doll, muddy muscles and formed-wax grin. But then he shook his head, dispelling the illusion, and said, "Right. Impossible."

I took the few steps toward where my magic bag lay under the sweeping willow branches. As I tucked the bag over my shoulder, I glanced at Will again. "Thank you, Will. I owe you. Remember this: my home is two miles south off the county road there."

"Two miles. Got it."

"If you ever need anything."

"Yeah." He was staring at me, tracking my every movement with his eyes.

All the goodbyes I knew were formal and full of God and blessings and charms, and I wasn't certain he'd even remember me. People were so good at dismissing anything that didn't make sense, and I was positive I did not fit into Will's world. So I merely said, "Go with grace, Will."

I turned my back to him, focused on walking in a straight, steady line. Crow shadows scattered across the grass as the birds flew after me.

FIVE

The first time I saw you, I was seventeen. I climbed down out of the train, and there you were on the platform, leaning a slim shoulder against the brick station building, your hands tucked into the pockets of your slacks. I thought, Here is your future, Evie, *and isn't he handsome?*

Then Gabriel stepped around the corner and doffed his fedora. The cut of his suit and his polished shoes made you fade, and you didn't seem to mind. He met me with an outstretched hand and I accepted it, setting my suitcase on the platform. "Little Evie Sonnenschein," Gabriel said as he tucked my gloved hand into his elbow and pressed it there. "Welcome to Kansas."

It had been four years since I'd met him in my father's parlor, but if I'd had to say, I'd have admitted not a thing about him had aged or changed. Still slinking and smiling as if he'd walked out of an MGM studio, still with his hair waxed and shining, his fingers soft, and the mysterious tattoos peeking up his neck from under the stiff collar of his shirt. He nodded at you. "Here is my cousin Arthur, who is our benefactor, you know. Our landlord." Gabriel smiled sharply at you, and I was surprised to hear your name. I'd expected Arthur Prowd to be old, not so near my own age with pretty blue eyes and a quiet voice.

"Miss Sonnenschein," you murmured, pushing off the building. Instead of offering your hand, you bowed. You had no hat, and your moon-pale hair was tucked behind your ears. You were missing a jacket, as

well, despite the sharp chill in the air, and your shirtsleeves were rolled up over tan forearms. I liked your wrists and imagined you twisting them to conjure shapes out of smoke or to cradle a bird in the basket of your hands.

"Thank you, Mr. Prowd," I said, "for giving me sanctuary."

Together the three of us went to a ten-year-old Pontiac hunched alone in the dirt lot, its grill rusty and one of its round headlights cracked. You went to drive, and Gabriel gallantly offered me the passenger seat, taking my suitcase to the rear with him.

The sun was setting before us in vivid stripes of pink and red as we drove through empty hills to what would be our home. You steered with your arms loose and eyes ahead. I held myself still, for all I wanted was to press against the window and stare as the brown and silver land scraped past. It was the end of autumn, most trees devoid of leaves but for the desperate brown stragglers, and the few farms we passed clutching near to town had harvested already. Squares of cut wheat glowed like gold in the sunset, and I saw three deer lift their heads at the grind and pop from the car.

I'd been here for fifteen minutes and never wanted to leave.

Gabriel leaned up from the back, creaking the old leather seat, and asked how my ride had been and if any persons in Chicago were familiar with our blood. I assured him that no, all my family was dead and there were none of my school friends who knew enough about me to be trusted with those secrets.

You nodded gently but did not glance my way. I surprised myself by how much I wanted you to look at me.

"Damn, but it's cold," Gabriel said, slapping the back of my seat in consternation. "Yesterday, Evie, it was hot enough to swim. You'll get used to the confused state of Mother Nature out here on the prairie."

"Chicago isn't so different, Mr. Desmarais." But I was chilled, even in Mother's old tweed coat with the high fur collar.

"I can offer you my coat," Gabriel said, seeing my shiver.

I smiled and slipped a tiny quill out of my pocket. Tugging my glove off one finger at a time, I focused myself, breathed three times deeply, and said, "I can keep myself warm."

With a prick of my first finger on the sharp point of the quill, I snapped fire into my palm. The ball of flame hovered there, warming the cab, and as Gabriel gasped and then laughed, I noticed you finally look, and just the corner of your mouth curled into a smile.

SIX

WILL

I grabbed drive-through doughnuts on my way home.

The plan had been to go out to the lake and get rid of my bad dreams, be back in time for church before Mom had to nag. Maybe even catch a nap before Ben got home.

Turned out I was covered in mud and blood, about fifteen minutes later than I meant to be, and instead of my nightmares going away I was probably going to be dreaming about strange girls in goggles and monsters who wanted to eat my dogs.

Total FUBAR.

I pushed the gas pedal, eyes peeled for cops.

Hopefully, Dad would be close enough to a good mood because of Ben that the doughnuts would push him over the edge. And Mom liked them enough she might not mind missing church. My truck filled up with the smell of sugar instead of mud, and the alt station I'd been listening to went to commercial. I flipped over to classical, turning it as loud as it could go. I'd left the prairie and river valley mostly behind. Newly built houses popped up in identical cul-de-sacs on both sides of the road.

Our neighborhood was the color of a wasps' nest, and just

as uniform. Every house was one of five basic designs, with differences that didn't go beyond certain paint colors and allowable yard art. Clean. Sterilized. Not the kind of place I could even think about a mud monster. Or a very, very weird girl. Who'd put her bloody hand on my chest and said, *It's not important.*

The more I thought about it, the less it seemed to matter. Like they say: out of sight, out of mind.

I turned the music even louder. Everybody on our block was used to me bringing the bass, but not on a Sunday morning. I didn't cut the sound down until I rolled into the driveway. The front door opened the second I turned off the car anyway, as if Mom had been stalking at the window.

She waited for me on the small porch, in pressed slacks and a violet blouse.

All I could smell was mud and sugar, sticking to my sweaty face. I plastered on a smile, hoping to charm her so that I didn't have to lie.

"Hey, Mama!" I said as I opened the door, and I charged at her, arms spread as if I'd grab her up in a great big, filthy bear hug.

Her eyes widened and she held out her hands. "Oh no you don't! William Sanger, stop!"

I froze with my hands up and curled into claws. Slowly, I lowered my arms and tilted my chin down so that, from the height of the front steps, all she could see were my big brown eyes.

Mom rolled hers. "Oh, Will, what have you been doing?" She glanced over me at the truck.

"Out getting doughnuts?" I offered. "They're fresh and hot."

"Did you have to ford a river?"

"To the land of King Donutus, where Val and Havoc fought valiantly against the . . . um . . . Evil Lord Food Pyramid."

Laughter slipped out of her, and I relaxed. If she laughed five times a day, I was winning. Today, my goal would be ten, one for every month Aaron had been gone.

She said, "Well, Sir William, get yourself cleaned up."

"Yes, ma'am." I jogged back to the car and dragged out the flimsy pink doughnut box. "I need to take the dogs around back and hose them down."

As I gave the doughnuts to Mom, she carefully avoided the mud smears my hands left. Her eyelashes fluttered, and she glanced down at the cartoon doughnut printed on the box before drawing herself up and smiling. "Oh, Will. I suppose we have time for doughnuts, too, if you hurry yourself up with the dogs. Church starts in forty minutes."

"I thought it started ten minutes ago?"

"We're going across to Reformation instead, since you're so late."

"Why bother?" I glanced at the house like it might tell me what was going on.

She put a fist on her hip. "To thank God your brother's home safe."

I marched the dogs through the garage to hose them off before herding them to the fenced-in kennel that took up one quarter of our backyard. Tried not to think about Ben coming home. I wanted to see him, sure, but I'd have almost rather been as far away as I could get. High overhead with a bird's-eye view for real, watching from where I couldn't be seen so that if the phone rang and it all went to shit I could fly away.

Val ran for a blue and black rope she kept in her empty food bowl. She batted it against my hand and I grabbed it. We tugged for a moment. The strain pulled at the bruise hardening on my chest. An unfortunate reminder of the impossible thing I'd seen this morning.

Havoc pushed Val aside, and they snapped at each other. I wished I could ask them if they remembered the creature, too. If they could confirm or deny what I thought I'd seen. Now that I was home in the backyard, it wavered in my memory, like my brain was trying to make sense of it and the only way was to pretend it hadn't happened.

I focused on my girls again. They were sisters, and just over a year old. Aaron and I had picked them out from a litter in Tonganoxie and trained them for weeks. *So you'll have them to keep you out of trouble when I'm gone,* he'd said. Of course, he'd meant gone away to school. Mom had been horrified at the thought of two giant dogs dragging mud through her living room, and I'd spent all my money from last summer to buy up enough wood for the kennel. Building it had kept me occupied for the first week after the funeral. That and Googling what the restrictions were for moving dogs to Australia.

I dropped to my knees and the girls came immediately. Val whined and Havoc snuffled at my ear. I wrapped an arm around each of their necks and buried my face against Havoc's smelly ruff. I thought of the mud thing throwing itself at her, of the terror ripping through me as I leapt. Of slamming into it, of its taste in my mouth, choking my throat. Of that girl holding the heart in her hand, and the salt falling like diamonds, making the monster crumble.

I tasted blood on my tongue and spat into the grass.

It hadn't been real. It couldn't have been. I'd been water-logged from soaking in the lake. This was some weird post-traumatic thing, because of Holly almost dying out there.

But compared to what was coming this afternoon, I almost preferred a monster.

MAB

It was warm under all the trees, despite the shade, as I made my way along the unpaved road that wound up the hill to the Pink House. The crows hopped from branch to branch, or glided silently over my head. I kept my feet moving steadily along one of the tire tracks that cut through the thick mud. My boots squelched, and the slow pace and difficulty sucking each foot out of the mud kept me focused. All I wanted to do was strip down, climb into the tub, and fall asleep in a hot, bubbly bath.

I thought of Will's face, all angles and surprise, as he pinned the runaway doll down. It was such fortune that he'd been there, to catch the curse before it trailed too far, or too near civilization. I hadn't expected it to be such a risk to summon up that spirit from his prison of roses. He—it—had been stronger than I anticipated, and the hunger to understand why and how and when he'd been planted in the rose roots gnawed more sharply than ever at my ribs. But now I'd never know! The creature was dead, released from the roses by possessing my doll, and torn from that when Will pulled out the antler holding its heart in place.

When I was rested, I'd have to go back and gather as much of the wax and ingredients as I could, to bring them home and experiment with the remains. Perhaps some would be useful in other avenues, or at least for warding lines to scare the rabbits away.

Only a few yards from the crown of our hill, I stepped off the road and closed my eyes.

The forest sang with deep magic, hidden just under the green. So it was because we lived and worked here: blood witches imbuing the earth with our power, and in turn drawing out the natural magic in the world in a constant recycling of energy. For a hundred years the Deacon had used this place to grow strong, to hold a stable space for any who needed our magical aid. And it showed through the magic in the trees.

Holding out my hands, I walked slowly on. Orange sunspots and cool blue shade flickered in the darkness behind my eyelids, but I could see well enough with my fingers. I reached out, my hands brushing against leaves. Because I was the Deacon, every caress, each glancing touch, drew magic. My skin drank up all the forest offered. It skimmed up my wrists and arms to coil in my chest. Gentle, sucking power, familiar and beloved.

The tiny cuts on my arms and hands knitted back together under this deluge of magic; the bruises blossomed into yellow and faded away. My steps sped up and I opened my eyes, picking my way strongly and carefully through the forest.

I was unable to stop the smile from curling across my face. My forest, my magic—it poured through my blood, and the pure, heady bliss washed away my disappointment. Instead my spirit flew.

As I broke through the trees and into the clearing where the garden and house waited, the crows sprang up and flew for the porch. Half landed on the eaves, and the other half dropped down toward the garden around the west side. Donna lifted her head from beside the sweet-pea stakes—on the opposite side of the garden from the roses. Her wide-brimmed hat flopped back, and she smiled at first, but it faded quickly as I trudged nearer.

"Are you all right?" she asked, pushing off her knees and coming at me, concern stretching to the corners of her face. She couldn't tell that under all the mud and streaks of blood, I'd already healed myself.

"I'm all right. Just tired."

Donna's garden-green eyes scanned the runes I'd painted up and down my arms. "I'd assumed you were only out for your seven-day binding and got sidetracked by something shiny."

"I was—was experimenting. With ways to get rid of the roses." I pulled my shoulders back and tried to affect the same airy confidence Arthur was so good at. I'm sure it sat on me like feathers on a cat. "It didn't go as planned, but I'm fine."

She brushed a thumb under my eye and studied me with a calm nonexpression. She had her hair in braided pigtails that hung straight along her neck, making the thin wrinkles pulling at her eyes look like smiling lines instead of age. When she'd arrived here seven years ago, I'd only been ten, and her hair had been shaved away. I remembered sitting beside her on the garden bench and running my fingers over the soft fuzz. "Why is it gone?" I'd whispered. She said, "I have to use the razor for something." She always wore long sleeves, even in the sticking August weeks, so I'd only seen the rows of jagged scars striping up her forearms one morning when she'd washed her hands in the well.

I was twelve when her hair was long enough that she could pin bits of it back from her face. Then she, Arthur, Granny Lyn, and I had done a small ritual at the blood ground, burying and binding the razor forever. It had been her very last spell. Donna still wore long sleeves and rarely smiled, but her flowers and vegetables grew full and sweet.

"You'll figure it out, little queen—they're already looking pretty devastated," she said, glancing toward the center of the garden, at the mess of mud and petals where I'd knelt that morning. "Why don't you go take a bath? I'll make breakfast, since I assume you skipped, and tea."

"Thank you." I hefted my bag higher on my shoulder and headed for the house. I wished I could tell her everything, about the doll and Will. But I would never confess to Donna that I'd trapped and killed a deer, that I'd used bone dust and my own hair to create a living doll. She wouldn't understand, because although Donna was a blood witch, just like me, she refused to use her power. Arthur had taught me it was a gift, that it was who I was. Donna believed it was more of a curse we had to control.

We walked up the porch together, and a couple of the crows darted in through the open kitchen window. Donna ignored them but to brush one off the counter, and reached for the kettle. I watched her a moment. Her motions were always so certain and gentle, as if the world around her was a delicate thing.

"Mab?"

I blinked. "Sorry. Just thinking."

She watched me from the stove. "You looked like Arthur for a moment."

Hearing her say it helped me free myself from the sudden stupor. Mother used to tell me that Arthur could rule the world if he wanted to. I believed her because of the way he whispered to trees so that they would weave their branches together and shelter us from sudden rain, how he carried me on his back to check the wards every day, found broken birds and gave them life again, put a hand on Mother's wrist and all her anger drained away. Anyone who could take Mother's shaking and transform it into peace could surely tame the whole world. So I walked like him and practiced his gestures, frowned when he frowned and memorized everything he said. I listened to my blood and the secrets it told my heart, and I promised myself I would someday be as inseparable from nature as Arthur was. That I could hold the keep as strongly and peaceably as he did.

I hadn't expected to have to prove it so soon.

But as I climbed the stairs to my bedroom, I smiled. Donna had seen him in me, and for once I hadn't even been trying.

WILL

No matter how much gum I chewed, seconds after spitting it out the taste was back. Mud monster. I might as well have been sucking dirty pennies all morning.

As soon as we got home from church, Mom began ordering us around as if she was the drill sergeant instead of Dad. I didn't see any clutter or dirt, but Mom pointed at shelves to be dusted, stairs to be vacuumed, ceiling fans with tiny cobwebs between their blades. I said Ben wouldn't notice a spotless house if it bit him on the ass.

Dad clapped me on both shoulders and told me to man up. To stop aggravating my mother. That Ben had been in arid mountains for a year and yes, by God, he would definitely appreciate some clean floors. Then Dad disappeared into the kitchen and returned with an apron. He threw it at my chest, ruffles and all. I tied it around my neck and watched the flowery folds spill down. Mom tied it around my waist. A tiny smile brought out the dimple in her cheek. She brushed her hands down the material and arched her eyebrows at me.

A sweaty hour later, we'd done everything we could. I discovered that dusting the ceiling was a great way to ignore unbelievably weird memories.

Mom still stood in the center of the living room with a pinched forehead. I took her hand and sat her down in the breakfast nook. Dad made her a mimosa. He didn't make one for himself, and I half wished he would. He hadn't had a drink in over a year. Mom offered me a sip to calm my nerves, but a quick glance at Dad had me grinning and promising I wasn't nervous at all.

Dad's phone rang just then.

Mom and I paused as he slid it from his pocket.

His tight mouth stretched into a smile as he answered. "Afternoon, Marine."

Mom came to clutch my hand. We'd stood right here in the middle of the kitchen almost a year ago. While Dad talked on the phone to the police about Aaron.

But now Dad laughed. The sound rolled through Mom, tightening her fingers. "I'll get in the car in about forty-five minutes, son. How's spaghetti sound?" He nodded, still smiling, and when he hung up he turned to us. "Ben sounds great. He's boarding his connecting flight in Cincinnati, and"—Dad stepped forward and took Mom's other hand—"spaghetti sounds great."

We'd all known it would. Ben had emailed from Kabul two months ago saying he was craving it.

"Maybe we should all go, greet him the moment he gets off the plane," Mom said.

I groaned.

Dad snapped a glare at me but only said, "Let's have our reunion here in our home." He walked into the living room, and we heard him fiddling with the CD player. A moment later, the low-key Sinatra that Mom loved followed him back into the kitchen. He bowed formally to her, shoulders sharp and hands folded like he was wearing his dress blues. Mom laughed and put out her hands. He swept her into a gentle dance.

It was nice to watch. Really nice.

I started pulling out spaghetti ingredients and stationed myself at the chopping board. And used every chance to pop small chunks of onion into my mouth. Raw onion was pretty nasty, but it got rid of the mud monster longer than gum.

The sauce was simmering when Dad left for the airport. Mom took off my apron. She hummed along with Sinatra and pulled me into a dance with her. She'd taught all of us to dance a little bit, so it was no chore keeping up. I took over the lead, swung her out. Mom laughed and said, "You're not nervous, are you?"

I spun her. In the tight kitchen, it wasn't easy. The spaghetti sauce needed stirring, smelling up the room with tomatoes and fennel. When she turned back, Mom put her hands on the sides of my face. "Will. You don't need to be."

"He's my brother. I'm not nervous." I removed her hands. "But I should stir the sauce."

Her smile tilted a little. Enough to make it sad and proud at the same time. "Everybody's hero," she murmured as I backed away and turned to the stove.

MAB

I fell asleep in the bath and dreamed of the doll. It squished its clammy wax fingers around my throat and squeezed. I bit my lip, but no blood spilled out. I scratched at my arm, and when the skin peeled back under my nails, it was dull and yellow and bloodless. The doll's jagged mouth pulled into a smile.

I jerked awake, sloshing water out of the claw-foot tub. It was tepid, and my skin was wrinkled and waterlogged. There was a strange scraping sound, and I turned to find a crow crouched on the tank of the toilet. He hopped down onto the pale green tiles and walked stiffly over them, his head bobbing as his claws slid gracelessly over the slick floor. When he reached the wall below the window, he flung himself up to the sill. Warm, humid air blew in, ruffling his feathers and tangling the thin curtains. He squawked at me, flipped his tail, and jumped into the sky.

I heard him yelling at his brothers, and then the slam of a car door. We had visitors, and the crows had come to wake me.

As I stood, water streamed down my back from my hair. This wet, it fell past my waist, all snarled and heavy. I hadn't meant to get it wet before picking out the tangles, but I'd slipped down in my sleep. I toweled off and wound my hair up into a messy knot, then stepped into my room and found a clean summer dress that was yellow like the sun. Granny Lyn had pieced it together last year from bits of an old sunflower flag.

A voice called from outside, and I walked to the open casement window. In the pebble driveway, covered in crows, was a moon-silver SUV shiny enough to attract them even if they hadn't known the owner.

Donna's son, Nick, stood next to the driver's side of the SUV, hands on his narrow hips, staring down at the splatters of mud that caked the entire bottom of his car. A few enterprising splashes streaked all the way up to the door handle. He slid a thin cell phone out of his rear pocket and snapped a photo of the dirty SUV.

Leaning out over the casement, I called down, "Nick!"

Twisting in place, he grinned up at me. He wore his standard tight T-shirt with a vest, jeans, and his favorite porkpie hat, which he tipped in my direction. "Hey there, babe." An exaggerated grimace instantly followed the epithet. "I mean Deacon, ma'am."

I smiled. "We weren't expecting you! I'll be right down." I waved and spun away before he could respond.

And in the middle of my bedroom, I paused to take a huge breath and pray that his girlfriend, Silla, wasn't with him. After the parting we'd had last month, I couldn't bear to think of her finding out I'd sacrificed one of the crows this morning.

In moments I was down the stairs, dancing barefoot over the creaky spots. As I passed the kitchen arch, I gathered myself up, remembering I wasn't a kid anymore, I wasn't just rushing to say hi to an almost-brother. I was the Deacon, welcoming a wandering blood witch home.

The day had spun up into a hot one, with sheer clouds pulled across the bold blue sky. As I stepped down off the front porch and walked smoothly toward Nick, I let my smile reflect the brightness of the day.

He'd moved to the rear door of his shiny SUV. All the crows landed on top of it, clutching at the metal runners on the roof. I drew nearer, saying, "What brings you to Kansas?" because he never, ever came only to visit his mother.

The look he cast me was grim, and I froze. Nick was also never grim: he teased you even when he was yelling at you. He pulled open the rear door and reached inside. A boy fell out with a startled grunt, landing on the warm grass at my feet.

"I've brought you a curse to lay in the ground," Nick said, resting his fingers in the boy's hair.

WILL

By the time Ben and Dad drove up, I'd decided the mud monster and the taste of blood that came with it were all in my head. There was no other possible explanation. I was letting this taste get to me because I'd rather have the huge fantasy of a mud monster distracting me from what was really about to happen: my family sitting down for our first dinner without Aaron.

Mom and Dad and I had gotten used to the dynamic, to eating at the bar in the kitchen so that it wasn't quite so obvious. But with Ben coming home, finally, we had to sit at the dining table. Had to eat at place mats and pretend to be fine.

We'd set the table with the presidential dishes—for when the president visited, of course—and real silver. Mom had made a salad, and I'd concocted a lime and pineapple punch that probably nobody would drink but me, but it looked fancy in the crystal pitcher.

The dogs started barking in the backyard, scrabbling at the wooden side gate. We heard the car door slam. Mom went to stand in the hall, and I waited just behind her. When they pushed through the front door, I thought, suddenly, what if it wasn't Ben who walked through but Aaron?

But then there was Ben, who I hadn't seen in the longest year of my life.

He swept in and picked Mom up so she could hug him right. His eyes pinched closed and his fingers bleached out where he pressed them into her back and shoulders.

She kissed him and smoothed back his hair. She wiped tears off her cheeks and smiled at him so brightly I could see it reflect off his face.

I hung back, feeling like a kid. Trying not to think about Ben in his uniform at the funeral last summer. Better this, now:

just my older brother in jeans and a shirt, seabag hanging off one shoulder. Looking at me.

"Hey, Will," he said.

His skin was different, darker, maybe. His hair the same buzz cut that always made me want to grow mine out. He was skinnier and bulkier at the same time. My brother and not my brother. It took me a second too much to react. His outstretched hand hung there too long.

Dad pushed in and said, "Are you hungry? Dinner's ready."

Ben grinned. "Smells amazing, Mom."

"Will made the sauce." She squeezed my shoulder and I nodded fast. We piled into the dining room before anybody could be more uncomfortable. I went to the kitchen and grabbed the sauce. Dad said the blessing. Mom thanked me for such a lovely meal. I managed to say, "I'm glad you're home, Ben." And I meant it, too. We sat opposite each other, and if I ignored the empty place next to me, it was almost like everything was normal. I could throw peas at him, and he could reach under the table to kick my shin if he wanted.

Dad asked how his traveling had been, and Ben said smooth. I was pretty sure they'd had this conversation in the car already and only repeated it for our benefit.

While we ate, Ben launched into a long story about one of the NCOs in his battalion at Camp LeJeune, who, during boot camp a few years back, had bribed his fellows for their leftover brass off the shooting range to make into a sculpture for his mother. He'd been caught with it all, of course, and lost leave privileges to visit her. Among other things. Ben hedged around those other things, knowing Mom didn't like to hear all the details.

I laughed at the story, which got a frown from Ben. "Wasn't it supposed to be funny?"

"It's ironic," he answered.

"Irony is funny."

"Boys," Dad said, before we even had a chance to argue.

I shrugged an apology at Mom. She smiled at me, hiding it from Ben with her mimosa glass. Dad and Ben swapped a few more stories, eying me frequently with this look that promised it was my turn next. That soon I'd know about spitting constantly but never getting the grit out of your teeth, about kill blossoms and kill zones. The more they talked the more the air seemed to get heavy, pressing in on my shoulders and souring my stomach. Mom noticed I'd only been swirling my noodles instead of eating them and said, "Maybe we should talk about something more pleasant."

Ben and Dad shared a mysterious look and fell silent.

Although I could hear Sinatra floating in from the sitting room and the tick-tock of the old ship's clock hanging behind Dad at the head of the table, now it was *too* quiet. Silverware *tink*ed against plates, and I could hear myself chew. It was weirdly like the sound of the mud monster's face dissolving.

Into the silence I said, "Do you believe in . . . supernatural things?"

Ben looked at me like I was flat-out insane. Dad frowned. Mom stared at the table next to me, where Aaron used to sit. My breath exploded as I realized what they all thought I meant.

I started to backpedal, but Ben mouthed at me, *Shut up, asshole.*

Dad cleared his throat. "Will. We all . . ." He frowned again. One of his hands was flat against the table.

"Yes."

It was Mom. She smiled sadly at me and repeated herself. "Yes, I do."

Even though I'd been thinking about a girl holding a heart in her hand and a monster falling apart, I pretended I'd only been thinking about my dead brother. To make everyone feel better, I slid a smile toward Ben. "He'd have laughed at your shell casing story, too."

"That doesn't mean it was funny," Ben said caustically. But then he smiled a little back at me.

The tension bubble popped, and we all managed to finish eating.

MAB

Nick sat at the table with his legs sprawled and kept running his hands over his head as if determined to rub out all traces of hat hair. Donna poured tea into glasses, her hand tight around the pitcher's handle. Whenever Nick was here she drank so much tea I expected the whites of her eyes to wash brown. The tiny cracking sounds of rapidly heating ice filled up the kitchen, and they reminded me of the snap of the doll's wooden bones.

I flattened my hands against the table, put my chin on my wrist, and stared over the expanse of polished wood at the strange little boy. His knees were drawn up to his chest and his shins pressed against the edge of the table. Right there beside him were the gouges my cousin Justin had cut into the wood with a fork. The boy's eyes were drawn low, and his hands covered in tiny burn scars.

"I'm Mab," I said quietly. "Do you have a name?"

"He won't tell me," Nick put in.

I ignored him and focused on the boy. I'd asked Nick not to tell me anything about him, preferring to hear it from the boy's mouth. He was perhaps ten or eleven, with skin the color of fallen oak leaves. Dirt crusted his ears, and his curling hair needed a good wash. I said, "I was named after a tiny fairy queen, and my mother used to tell me a story wherein Queen Mab met a boy named Peter who had thought he was a fairy. And when he learned he was not, forgot how to fly. But he asked Mab to return his magic to him, and she agreed. May I call you Peter?"

The boy looked up at me with startling green eyes. "Pan," he said.

My grin peeled away from my teeth before I could stop it. "Pan is a more magical name," I agreed. "It's like mine, only upside down and backwards."

Pan flashed a smile there and gone so fast I wouldn't have seen it if the echo of it hadn't hung about between us.

Donna set down a glass of tea. "There's water if you prefer, Pan, and I can make eggs or toast or even soup," she said, as if it had always been his name.

"I definitely brought you to the right spot, partner," Nick drawled, running his fingers through his hair again.

"We're always the right spot for lost things," I reminded him.

He glanced at his mom's long sleeves, then back at me. "Right."

"How long are you here, Nick?" Donna asked as she hunkered down to dig her favorite skillet out from under the oven. Her voice was swallowed by the cabinet, likely on purpose so that she didn't have to meet his eyes.

"Only through the night. I've got to get back to Columbia to help Silla get ready for graduation. Right after, we're packing up and heading for Oregon, where she got into some master's program for folklore studies."

"You're going with her?" Donna shut the cabinet, her voice dry as old paper.

"You bet." He shrugged like it was the most obvious thing in the world. Which it was to everyone but his mom.

She stood beside him, her brow furrowed in a way I recognized from when I used to paint blood runes on all the kitchen drawers to keep the ants away, no matter how often she told me she found it disturbing. "All the way to Oregon, Nicholas?"

He twitched at his full name. "I'm not staying behind."

"What will you do? You still don't have your own degree."

"No worries, Silla's gonna keep me barefoot and pregnant."

"This isn't a joke. You've spent so long just traveling around."

Nick leaned forward, and his lips performed a fascinating little curl full of disdain. "Don't pretend like you have a say in my life, *Donna*."

She stared at him, and I wondered if he noticed the way her fingernails cut into her own palms. "I only want what's best for you."

"Now you do," he said. His voice was more casual when he added, "When Mab goes to college, you can use all those mothering skills you finally decided were worth putting into action."

I tapped a finger on the table to get Pan's attention. His eyes were round as he stared at Nick with a hint of anger in the corners of his mouth. "Want to meet some friends of mine?" I whispered.

Pan slunk out of his chair in a boneless fashion, and I held out my hand. He took it, and after grabbing a big loaf of raisin bread I'd baked yesterday, we left.

Outside, the sun pushed down. I stood in the middle of the front yard and broke the bread into pieces. The grass tickled the tops of my bare feet. Several of the crows gathered around, and I offered Pan half the chunks to scatter for them. For the other crows, I threw little pieces of bread into the air. They darted down from their lazy, gliding circles to catch the bread in beaks or claws. My tosses arched high, almost like I was juggling. My arms knew the patterns, for I'd fed the crows this way since I was twelve. Soon all the birds were in the sky, taking turns in an intricate pattern as I ripped bread and pitched it, again and again.

"What are they?" Pan asked.

"This is Reese." I spread my arm out in a wide gesture, glad he knew there was more to my crows than appeared. "He used to be a boy like you, before wild magic transformed him into crows. Each of them is a piece of Reese. He's my friend, and a protector of this land and everyone on it. Now that he knows you, he'll keep you safe, too."

The crows called out in unison, one loud, merry bark.

Pan didn't seem afraid, relaxing enough to sink onto the ground with his legs crossed under him. He reached out a hand to the nearest crow, which hopped toward him, wings out. "Hi," Pan said quietly.

I held still, watching, wondering how much of our magic this boy knew, and hoping it wouldn't take long to win enough of his trust that he'd tell me his story.

"Nice," Nick said from behind me. I hadn't heard him come down the porch or the slap of the screen door.

One of the crows immediately flapped up to land on Nick's shoulder and nuzzled the flat of his beak against Nick's cheek. Nick scratched under the crow's left wing, just as the crow liked best.

I asked Nick, flicking my finger back toward the house, "How's Donna?"

"Fine. I just hate it that she knows me so well."

"She should. She's your mother."

Nick grunted under his breath, and the crow on his shoulder flew down to Pan. The boy had a pink pebble from the driveway, and he threw it for them, in a sort of fetch game. Nick and I stood side by side to watch. I hoped he wouldn't notice there was one fewer crow than usual, so that I didn't have to lie to him. Or to Silla. "Is she still mad at me?" I asked quietly, annoyed that I sounded meek.

"Oh, well." Nick pulled at his earlobe. "She's too busy to be angry."

"In other words, yes."

"You did say some shitty things."

The way his eyebrows drew together, I knew he took her

side. But then, he always did. I tilted my chin up. "So did she. I'm not my mother, and it isn't my fault the crows chose to stay here with me. She's the one who always tried to force him to—" I stopped because I didn't want to argue in front of Pan. The boy pretended to ignore us, but the slight lean of his head gave him away.

We fell into silence again, watching. Three of the crows flapped their wings, arguing over the stone they'd fetched for Pan. As if they were three different minds, instead of part of a whole.

"Does he seem less . . ." Nick paused. "Less human? Than he used to."

I wove my fingers together in front of me. "Sometimes."

"I just remember he used to follow conversations—he'd watch us, and one of the heads would move between us as we talked so that it was like he was at a tennis match or something. I haven't seen him do that in a year."

I said, "It doesn't mean he isn't listening. Maybe he's better at it now, at following only with his ears."

"Yeah. I'm sure that'll make Silla feel better," he said with a sarcastic edge.

"He knows his name," I offered, quietly.

Nick lowered his voice. "I'm not sure that one does."

My eyes went to Pan, holding his palm out with the pink stone in its center, waiting for two of the crows to decide which would pluck it up. If he didn't know who he was, he'd come to the right place. We made new lives here, as the crows themselves could attest.

SEVEN

WILL

I was avoiding sleep and nightmares by fighting electronic half-lion monsters online with my soccer team's keeper. The sound track to a battle scene from some epic movie blared from my iPod. The TV showed a UK vs. US game recorded from the last World Cup. And two upright fans shoved air at me with mutual whirs. My can of Dr Pepper was nearly empty. I needed another. Weirdly enough, the sweet carbonation masked the coppery taste in my mouth better than anything else. It had bugged me all day, it and the bruise on my chest. At least the bruises had to be touched to irritate. But this taste stuck with me, waiting to grab my attention again from around every corner.

The TV suddenly shut off, popping a level of sound, and I spun around in my computer chair.

Ben had closed the door behind him, and after setting the TV remote back on top of the monitor, he leaned a shoulder against the wall. "Want to kick the ball around?"

"It's dark out." It was after ten p.m. And I was hot and wanted to just sit in my room with all the noise and melt.

"So? You guys used to play out there till midnight if they let you."

Yeah, Aaron and I had. But when Ben left for the academy, I'd barely known how to dribble. I just stared back at him, not sure how to say, *You aren't Aaron.*

The epic movie sound track burst into some serious bass action, and Ben frowned at it and turned it off. He leveled a Superior Officer stare at me. "Get off-line so we can talk."

"About what?" I twisted my chair back around to face the desk and winced to see my player down half his life since I'd looked away for two seconds. One of the undead lion-monsters had nearly ripped my arm off.

"Come on, Will. I don't know how long I'll be home."

Gritting my teeth, I nodded. I clicked on Matt's icon and told him I was off for a bit, then put my computer to sleep. Ben had moved to my bed and was shuffling around the open text-books and loose-leaf papers sprawled over the summer quilt. "Dad says you're getting a B in Spanish."

Great opening line, Ben. I shrugged. "And in English, and a C in History if I don't bother to memorize seven thousand dates for the final. So?"

"What's your GPA?"

I jerked my shoulders in a shrug. "Low three something. I get As in all the science and math classes, okay?"

"You need a decent class rank to get into the academy."

The only sound for a long moment was the whir of the fans. My tongue tasted like yelling, and I thought suddenly of Mab's fingers squeezing that heart. I said, "I'm not going."

Ben shoved his neck out. "Don't be stupid."

"I don't want to go to the Naval Academy, Ben. There are other things in the world."

"You want to go to some state school and then join up through the OCS? Please don't tell me you're thinking of ROTC." He spread his hands as if he was clutching a giant ball between them. And probably imagining it was my head.

I leaned back in my chair, stretched my legs, and tried to look unconcerned. Why hadn't I just gone outside to play soccer with him? The last year had exploded all the things I'd thought I wanted, but Ben probably couldn't understand that. He hadn't done anything unexpected in his whole life. I was not prepared to argue about my lack of ambition and upending four generations of Sanger family tradition. I cleared my throat. "I'm thinking of traveling. Like to New Zealand, actually. Somewhere different. And college later. When I know what I want." Ben was turning green. "*If* I decide on the Corps, sure, I can always go to Officer Candidate School after I get a degree."

"You're just saying this to piss me off."

"I'm not applying to the academy. That's a done deal."

Ben crossed his arms over his chest. He was only wearing a T-shirt and jeans, but it was like I could see the ghost of his dress uniform hovering over him. "This little rebellion is because of Aaron?"

I stood up, probably proving his point. "No. It's because I don't know. Sorry I'm not as perfect as you, but I just don't know."

"You're afraid of it."

It was almost a relief for somebody to call me a coward instead of a hero, just because of Holly. We hadn't talked about the earthquake yet. Today was all about Ben. Not me and my not-heroics.

When I didn't reply, Ben shook his head and adopted a baffled expression. "You've always wanted to join."

"Have I?" I wouldn't have called it want. More like assumption. "I don't know. I've been thinking about it for a while, and I just don't know."

"It'll be good for you. I love it. Dad loves it—it's what you're meant for, Will."

"You talk like I'm some long-lost heir or something. It's just a job."

Ben's arms tightened, and I imagined I could hear his muscles creaking with tension. "No," he said through his teeth. "It isn't. If you're going to be a baby, fine. But don't pretend what Dad and I do isn't more than that."

"Then don't pretend you give a shit about playing soccer with me in the backyard. Don't pretend you have any motive other than recruiting another Marine." I knew as I said it that it wasn't fair, but didn't care. My chest was tight, like the bruise there had dug into me and pulled.

"Do you have any respect for anything?" Ben demanded.

"I know that Aaron should've been in some fancy engineering school learning how to build spaceships, and instead he was going halfway across the country to fix Humvees."

"That was his choice."

"Yeah. You keep telling yourself that."

"So you'll just make the opposite choice no matter what?"

I hunched my shoulders.

"Will, just . . ." Ben stepped forward. "Promise me you won't make a bad decision based on Aaron. Or because you're afraid. It's okay to be afraid—you should be. But you can't let it cripple you. You're a Sanger."

"I'm not afraid." I jerked forward, grabbed my soccer ball from the carpet, and stomped outside to kick it alone against the backyard fence.

MAB

The sun scorched the western horizon as I hurried down the south face of our hill, past the sunflower field, to my silo. It was a great, hulking tower made of orange tiles, four stories tall, with a rusty ladder striping one side and a tree growing out the roof.

I climbed up through the violet twilight, avoiding the rotten rungs and rusty nails, glad I'd remembered to change into a camisole and loose pants. At the top, I swung myself over the rim and into the shade of the redbud tree. It spread its wide, heart-shaped leaves over the silo like an emerald cap.

Wind blew from the north, tugging at my hair and making the bells that dangled from my tree shake with music. There were the chimes, too, made of river reeds, and long, bright ribbons that fluttered in the wind, old bracelets, and tiny pillows filled with lavender and rose petals.

From the bag hooked over my shoulder, I withdrew a tiny star I'd carved months ago out of firewood and covered in silver sequins. Pan had chosen it out of my box of charms.

The tree was covered in such charms. I'd made them myself, or with Arthur and Granny, shaping them out of clay or wood into the kind of magic I wanted here: warmth, abundance, safety. Some I'd hung for whimsy and laughter, and some represented people who'd passed through our gates. There was a butterfly for Granny, a howling coyote Arthur had made, a flock of tiny bluebirds for Faith, a plastic soldier Nick had brought, Silla's blue theater mask and Justin's pewter moon, a toy ax for Eli, three kinds of fairies for Hannah, and a bright red apple for my mother.

I stared at it, at the chunks of red glitter still clinging desperately to the skin of the apple.

My mother's name was Josephine Darly, and when I was young, I thought she was the best creature in the world. I lived for the great smile she only offered when she saw me after a long time away, for her sharp nails trailing gently against my scalp as she washed my hair. For her cool voice singing to me about my father's bones turning into coral at the bottom of the sea. My last memory of her was seeing the moonlight catch the white flower embroidered on the shoulder of her dress as she ran. Like a mountain lion, all control and power, away from the house, from me, over the lawn, toward the forest, until she was just a brief orange flash between dark trees.

Until she was gone.

And the day I grew up was the day I found out she wasn't the best but possibly the worst. That when she left me that night, she went out to kill two people, and turned their only son into crows.

I reached up and took hold of a branch of the redbud tree, then tied the blue ribbon of Pan's charm to a twig. When I released it the branch snapped up and the star bounced, throwing flecks of light everywhere.

Silla, who was the only part of her family left living, had killed my mother for her crimes and bound her into the ground hundreds of miles away. Josephine's bones were the bones of a faraway forest, now and forever. Then Silla had come here, bringing her brother-who-was-crows; her boyfriend, Nick; a suitcase; a handful of questions for the Deacon. She'd come for help with the magic, and with the hope that Arthur could return her brother into the body of a man.

She hadn't expected to find me, a girl with familiar eyes and the same lioness hair, with blood under my nails and a laugh as wild as my mother's.

Standing at the lip of my silo, my toes digging into the sparse grass, I spread my arms out to catch the wind.

The silo stood at the base of the forested hill protecting the Pink House, and in all other directions there was nothing but gently rolling fields of long-forgotten wheat and prairie flowers. Besides the county road cutting across the east, there wasn't a neighbor or single touch of civilization for almost three square miles. It was only me and the world here.

And sometimes, the crows.

They always seemed to know when I came. Even now they approached, and I lifted my hand to wave, spreading a smile for them.

In the end it had not been Josephine who came between Silla and me. She knew I couldn't be responsible for what my mother had done, and I knew my mother's fate had only been magic balancing itself the way a fire will cleanse the prairie.

No, the center Silla and I spun around and around, as fierce and angry as tornadoes, was only the crows.

From the moment I'd seen them, cutting a smooth line against the sky, I'd known they were unique. I'd felt the power humming through them, and given them a lock of my hair within moments of their landing in the tree around me. They moved as one, they spoke as one, and when the stiff primary feather from the bravest of them brushed against my face, a thrill of magic burned through me as if I'd cut my chest open and sung a spell for fire.

They lived with us, with me, here where it was safe, and Silla came back to learn between semesters of college, trying to cram years of practice and spellcraft into only a few months. She was focused and determined and nearly kept up with me, especially when it came to magic that might lead to saving her brother: possession and regeneration and transformations. Silla fixated on what—on who—the crows had been, but I fell in love with what they were. New and perfect: all the strength of a blood witch, transformed into flight. As the summers passed, we both became more powerful, but it was my magic the crows slowly linked into, each one a finger of my power, each becoming a piece of my intricate familiar.

Silla didn't understand that until last month, when Arthur died.

We stood shoulder to shoulder, in front of the spill of violet flowers marking Arthur's grave, and she said, "It's over, then. The Deacon is dead, and the new Deacon has no interest in undoing her mother's curse."

I frowned and glanced toward the crows weighing down the branches of Granny's linden tree. "The crows aren't interested, either."

"You don't know that." Silla stepped away from me and pointed sharply at them. "My brother wanted to live. He wanted to go to school and be a farmer, he wanted our family's land, and to grow up and get married and have, like, a half dozen kids, Mab. You never knew him. You can't know what he would have wanted."

"I know what he wants now, and that is magic and flight. You don't know who he is, because you never listen to him."

"He can't talk, Mab, he's *crows*. Don't you see? I've spent so much energy just to be able to hear him talk again!"

"But not for him." I leaned in on my toes, to make myself as tall as she was. "Only for you. You've only ever done any of this for you. You're selfish! *You* want Reese back. *You* want to turn him into a man again. You, you, you. Did you ever think why Arthur didn't clap his hands and create Reese a new body? He could have, you know, he could have done that in a half a day—my God, I could do it myself in three! But Arthur did not give Reese a human body no matter how many times you begged, because *Reese never asked*." I stumbled back, surprised at my own vehemence.

And Silla, who I'd always admired for the way her barrettes matched her cowboy boots, for the smooth polish on her nails and the graceful way she drew runes; Silla, who made me feel, with my unkempt hair and holey jeans, like nothing so much as an explosion; that Silla's face cracked open for the briefest moment and she said, "And so Josephine has taken everything from me."

The silence then was a hole in the world, deep enough to

draw Nick and Donna out of the house to observe the final wound.

In that moment, I only thought about my mother's pride and boldness, not any of the horrible things she'd done. I drew myself up, and wind from all around pushed hair exactly like hers back from my face and shoulders. I said, "Reese was not taken away from you. You lost him."

Her eyes glared past me, flicking among all the crows, and as one they raised open their wings as if about to leap into the sky.

"Let's go, Reese, come home with me," Silla said, turning away and walking smoothly toward Nick's SUV. "Nick," she snapped, and I saw him grimace at Donna and dash around to the driver's side. He only glanced at me, a look that was half apology, half irritation, as he turned the engine over and slammed shut his door.

Silla climbed up so that she stood halfway into the tall car, one hand gripping the silver bars on the roof for leverage. "Reese!" she called.

One crow called back, a single, echoing cry.

We all waited. I only watched, my heart racing so fast I thought the blood might pop out of my fingertips. The crows perched behind me, and I felt their strength tingle against my back.

"Reese." Silla's voice was quieter now, though firm.

I heard the wind in the leaves and the solemn sound of crows settling in. They were not jumping into flight. They remained. At my back.

And it broke Silla's heart.

It was no wonder she hadn't called to invite us to her graduation. And no wonder Nick wasn't too happy with me.

And now the crows flew overhead in a sunwise circle, sharp black silhouettes against the sky. I felt my spirit lift in my chest as I watched them; despite my dark thoughts, I was lighter and wished to step off the edge and float with them, to fly joyous circles and laugh rough and raw.

As the world darkened into shades of gray and purple, I crouched and pulled out my sharp bone blood-letter. The crows landed in the redbud, shaking the bells and wind chimes into merry, discordant song.

It was as much the Deacon's responsibility to tend the blood family as it was to protect the land. My charms, one for every person marked by our magic, were here to remind me of that. Arthur had been loved by everyone, and so easily gained trust and respect. I had to try much harder not to say the wrong thing, or to put people off by my wild nature. I forgot to wipe blood off my mouth before going to the library, or left squirrel bones tied in my hair for the farmers' market. I allowed a doll of earth and roses to run rampant, and left muddy, bloody handprints on the chest of the boy who stopped it.

I forgot that most people value human life over a crow's.

The hardest thing I had to do as Deacon was to remember I was part of a family.

As always, I turned to magic for help. Under the shadows of my redbud tree, I pricked my tattooed wrist: the shock of pain shuddered through me, and I welcomed the rush of power that tingled just behind it, filling my body and raising goose bumps on my arms.

With my blood, I marked my forehead, my heart, my palms, and the soles of my feet. I spread out on my back, making a five-point star with my head at the top. "I bind myself," I said, blowing the words up to the first stars that glimmered through the curtain of purple sky.

"To the land I bind my heart," I said. Above me all my charms dangled, dancing in the breeze. They were my family, tied to my tree, and my tree rooted deep in the land.

"To the land I bind my head." I thought of Arthur, enveloped in a hundred purple flowers, part of the land forever. Of Granny buried under her linden tree.

"I bind my hands, that I may work for the magic and for the land." I thought of Donna and Nick, wishing I could bind their hearts as a mother and son. And I thought of Silla, who was as much a part of this family as me but always thought she was alone.

"I bind my feet, that my every step be for the blood land, my every dance weave life between the earth and myself." Now there was Pan, to be shown the patterns of magic. To be healed.

"Finally, I bind my dreams." The crows flapped their wings, pushing warm, sticky wind down onto me.

With the blood-letter, I broke the skin over my womb, where the roots of my magic grew. I took a finger and drew lines spilling out from it, a star of blood over my belly.

I said, "I bind myself."

I was the center.

EIGHT

You'd built the farmhouse yourself, just after the First World War: a two-story wood and brick home with an attic and storm cellar, at the top of a wild hill. I settled quickly into the bedroom in the northwest corner, and from my window I could see the whole of the front yard, stretching untamed from the porch to the ring of oak trees crowning the hill. There was plenty of space for a garden. Vegetables and herbs, I thought. Perhaps some roses.

The three of us ate dinner that evening, a meal I insisted on cooking. You already kept the kitchen tidy, and plenty of butter in the larder. I whipped up a goulash with the last of the paprika from my grandmother's hoard, wrapped in an old handkerchief she'd had straight from her own mother. Both you and Gabriel ate until you nearly popped your buttons, and I remember thinking it was kind of you, regardless of how well you truly liked my food.

We gathered in the parlor with hot applesauce and cream, me on the delicate sofa and you and Gabriel lounging on rugs near the fire. The space filled with warmth, and although I felt the sorrow and loneliness of losing my family still crouched in my heart, your gentle eyes and Gabriel's crackling energy soothed it.

"What do you want here, Evie?" Gabriel asked as he set aside his bowl and leaned back onto both his hands. In the firelight his slick hair glinted like oil.

You touched his wrist with just a flick of your fingers, and he shrugged one shoulder. "She isn't offended, Arthur," he said.

"No, I'm not." I took in his relaxed posture, and the way you, too, seemed to have softened into the room, with your boots off and your back reclined against the arm of the sofa. "It's your home, and of course you should know what I want." I bent and unbuttoned the ankles of my shoes, slipping my feet out and tucking them up under me. You followed the motion with your eyes, and Gabriel grinned as he stretched like a cat.

"He never told me what you wrote in your letter," you said, finally.

I spoke directly to you: "My older brother died in France, and my mother of a weak heart last year. Father vanished a month ago, and the authorities suspect he was robbed and murdered. I performed what magic I could to find him, and he is not to be found." I sighed as prettily as possible. "There was nothing for me to do but pay his debts, which were few to my fortune, and seek work. I remembered Gabriel from a visit just after the war, that he'd mentioned living here in Kansas where there is always work for a strong man and land all around. A city, perhaps, would be better suited to a young girl needing a place, but he spoke of the prairie with such"—here my eyes strayed to Gabriel—"such hunger and pride, it invoked the first desire I'd felt since Father disappeared."

Gabriel's smile curled deeper and he leaned forward. "Creating desire is a particular skill of mine."

His insinuation made my eyelashes flutter, and I focused on keeping my hands relaxed in my lap. I raised my chin and said, "My girlfriends and the headmistress of my school warned me of coming to two men, no matter how I insisted we were related. I indicated the relation was much closer than it is." I had no idea if our mutually powerful blood suggested there was any truth in the claim, but it had worked with my would-be protectors in Chicago.

You said with quiet assurance, "It was well done, and no lie. In the eyes of God, certainly, our blood is connected."

I was able to meet your glance, glad to hear you voice the connection I felt already. "I did allow," I admitted, shakily, "that if they do not have news of me within the month, to send the authorities here to you, to say you had no doubt done horrible things to me."

Gabriel laughed again and got to his feet. "I like you, Evie. You have the courage of a blue jay—yelling and beating away birds five times your size to protect what's yours."

"And you do not need protection from us," you added. "You're safe, Miss Sonnenschein, here."

I allowed myself a smile. "That is what I need, and all I want in addition is to be busy. To build a garden, perhaps, and cook and sew and learn the land. For now."

All during the train ride from Chicago, I'd held dear the hope that you would offer me a home, knowing it was temporary. While I grew and learned, while I found my happiness again. After a few years I would take the train to Kansas City for college, would find a calling beyond the garden, then find a good man and raise my own family.

But already those imaginings were breaking into little pieces. Every time you looked at me, a shard of my old dreams fell away.

You would not let me clean the kitchen because it was my first night, instead dragging Gabriel in to help you. As the two of you banged around, as Gabriel lifted his voice in an old French song I could not understand, I walked outside into the darkness with the handkerchief of ground paprika.

Cold wind brushed the trees together, making me shiver in the thin blue dress I'd worn under my coat all the way from Chicago. It was darker than any night I'd ever seen, and the stars sprinkled across the sky like spilled salt. I rolled off my stockings and shuffled through the high, wild grass to the southwest corner of the house, which I thought would be best for my garden. Here there would be both shade and sun, where the hill cut down steeply enough that the trees didn't grow too near the house.

Kneeling, I dug into the cool earth with my fingers, sifting through the loamy soil. There I set down my grandmother's mother's handkerchief, with its little bits of paprika dust. I spilt three drops of blood over it and buried it all with a short prayer that it would settle my spirit and make roots for my heart.

NINE

WILL

I dreamed about crazy-sharp rose thorns and struggles in the dark. When I woke up, sweat stuck the sheets to me. My mouth was a wasteland, and my chest ached. I stumbled to the bathroom. I rinsed and brushed and swished Listerine—twice. I was rewarded with a few minutes free of it, but by the time I finished my shower it was creeping back with a hint of blood. So was the quick memory of a rose petal falling out of my mouth onto the messed-up face of a mud monster.

I tried not to think about that. Couldn't have been real. It was only dreams. A new twist to my Holly nightmares. But I barely bothered drying off before pulling my lips back to check my tongue and gums for cuts. Maybe I'd actually been bleeding just slightly since yesterday morning? But there was nothing cut that I could see, and no tender spots as I poked around.

Maybe it was a head injury.

What if I had a tumor or something and it was making me taste blood and imagine crazy girls fighting off mud monsters? I turned away from the mirror and took deep breaths.

Back in my bedroom, I powered up the computer while I pulled on clothes. The Internet wouldn't be the most accurate place to find medical info, but it could give me an idea.

I started on one of those symptom tracker sites and put in "metallic taste" and "furry tongue," which felt true. The site told me I might be constipated. I laughed, because that definitely wasn't the case. Other options: medical reaction (no kidding), antibiotic use (not that I knew of), or poisoning.

I scrubbed at my face with my hands. It was just a dumb Internet doctor site, so I shouldn't let myself get worked up. But I stuck in one more potential symptom: "hallucinations."

That was the scary one. More potential conditions popped up on my screen. Drug abuse. Three different kinds of epilepsy. Schizophrenia.

I shoved away from the computer and rolled my shoulders. "Don't get worked up," I ordered myself, and clicked on my stereo. A heavy-metal mash-up blasted through my bedroom. It shook its way through my skull and overpowered the fear, making it hard to breathe.

Forcing myself to sort of sing along, I hurried through the rest of my morning routine, ignoring the taste of blood poking at my tongue.

MAB

First thing in the morning, I found Nick feeding the crows bits of burned bacon on the front porch. The sunrise was well under way, the morning air surprisingly cool on my bare arms. He fed them from his fingers, one piece, one bird, at a time.

His bag leaned against the front tire of the SUV; Nick had only been waiting to say goodbye before heading out.

"Morning, Mab," he said, holding out the plate of bacon. I

sat beside him on the steps and tied my hair into a knot at the back of my neck.

"Did you sleep well?"

"As I ever do on that sofa." When I'd retired last night, Nick had stretched out in the parlor with his hat over his face. No wonder he was the first person up, when I remembered him sleeping until noon in the past.

"No bad dreams?"

"No dreams at all."

I glanced toward the garden, where the roses curled in tight knots. It had been a full day now since I'd released the curse from their roots, since it had gone careening away in my doll. Today, I supposed, I should go gather the pieces of it and give the perished curse a proper binding. It was certainly what Arthur had meant when he told me to destroy the roses: not the plants themselves, but the curse. Once the curse was dealt with entirely, the roses themselves would be only harmless flowers. I glanced around the house to where the garden sprawled in all its lush glory. The multicolored buds and the tangle of leaves made me think of Granny Lyn crouched beside them for hours, digging into the ground with her sharp trowel, plucking individual leaves and dotting others with her blood to keep away blight and bugs.

"Are Donna and the kid still sleeping?" Nick asked, tossing the final crumbs of bacon into the grass.

"Yes." We'd been up late after I came home from the silo, watching an old Disney movie about a living car. Pan had fallen asleep in a mess of old quilts, and Nick had carried him up into Arthur's bedroom. I'd peeked in this morning to find him curled into a ball at the very foot of the bed, pillows entirely abandoned. "Where did you find him?"

"Arkansas. I was driving up from New Orleans—you know, the Perrys?"

I nodded. The blood kin scattered all over the country, in small pockets and family strings, and the Perrys were my cousins.

"I'd gone down to pick up some stuff they had for Silla and was eating lunch at this antique market full of deer heads and porcelain raccoons, just off the highway, and that charm Silla made for warding against curses got hot in my pocket." He paused, started to add something with a playful lift to his mouth, but stopped and sighed as if he was disappointed. "I asked around, found out there were lots of stories about witch-fire in the woods nearby and birds falling dead out of the sky. The usual stuff. I picked a spot, dove into the woods, and basically made a beeline for the kid, like I just knew where to find him. He was alone, holding fire in his hands, waiting for me. Said the trees told him I was coming and that I'd take him to his sister." Nick eyed me. "Your mom have any other kids you know about?"

The idea tightened my intestines but expanded my heart at the same time. "No," I said. "But the Deacon is everybody's family. Did he have anyone at all?"

Nick edged closer to me. "I asked him, and he said his father lived in a cabin next to the river but that we should please just leave. I didn't like it, but when I tried to go for his dad, the kid lifted up his shirt and . . ." He wiped his hands on his jeans and then got off the porch. He walked through the gathered crows, causing them to flap and bark at him, to hunker down in the pebbled driveway. "Here, Mab."

I joined him, enjoying the massage of the tiny smooth stones on my bare feet. Nick used his finger to draw a complicated symbol into the pebbles. "This was carved into the small of his back."

"A black candle rune."

"Whatever you call it. I know what it's for."

I could tell Nick wished he didn't know. Two years ago, Faith's husband, Eli, had known a woman being stalked in Kansas City, and so Arthur and I had spun together a powerful charm to turn the man away, to bend his desires off of Eli's friend. We'd used a black candle rune on an old walnut tree, tying the charm to its life instead of our own, and within nine days the leaves had fallen dark and twisted and dead.

Tracing my finger over Nick's rune, I said softly, "His father did it?"

"Yeah."

"I've never heard of a witch using another person for a familiar like that."

"Glad to hear it, because I was a little afraid you'd say it was no big deal."

I glanced sharply at him, the words pinching. "You were?"

Nick winced. "Just a little. Sorry."

"It's good you brought him," I said, standing up and walking farther out into the yard, where the morning sun was high enough over the caps of the trees that it hit me full and warm in the face.

"It's what you do." He joined me, tipping his hat to shade his eyes.

"What *we* do," I corrected. "And we won't stop even if we're in Oregon, will we?"

Nick laughed, sharp and loud. "No, I guess not."

"Good." I faced him and put a hand flat on his T-shirt, just over his heart. "Our family spreads all across the continent, Nick. Donna might think distance changes that, but I know better."

He squinted down at me, brow furrowed under the brim of the porkpie. Once, he had told me, *You're nothing like your mother,* and even though I knew he was completely wrong, his saying it made me love him. "Okay, Mab." He took my hand off his chest but held it as he pulled me back inside to avoid further sensitive talk. "Maybe we should go make some bacon fit for human consumption before they wake up."

As we went, I glanced up at the window over the kitchen, where Pan slept, and sent up a silent prayer that the magic of the black candle rune was already broken.

TEN

The first days I lived with you, I helped prepare for winter. You and Gabriel repaired the fence around the horse pasture, though you had no horses, and took turns summoning winds to blow through the barn in order to find and plug all the leaks. There was plenty of cleaning in the house, and I mended several blankets as well as marking out the boundaries of what would be my garden in the spring. I chipped away at the cold earth to plant a few winter bulbs, and helped you clean the chimney.

When you took me into town to purchase stockpiles of feed for the chickens, I became Gabriel's niece, because he looked almost old enough for it. I suggested buying up all the late autumn fruit we could find, because I knew how to can it so that we'd have sweets for Christmas. "You'll be indispensable," Gabriel said, fingers pressing into my shoulder as he hugged me against his side at the grocer's.

I used the last of my money to buy a wool dress and sweaters, as well as a strong pair of boots. Things more suited to a farm than my pleated skirts and ankle shoes. Gabriel insisted on a pair of seed pearls for my ears, and when I demurred, he said loudly enough for others to hear, "Let me spoil my poor niece in her time of tragedy." I was trapped and gave in.

It was you I watched, always, for cues. I paid attention to the men you spoke with for more than two words, and was sure to introduce myself to their wives. You tended toward the simpler men, the farmers, while Gabriel haunted those with watches in their pockets and thoughts on the latest movies.

At times I could not understand how you and he shared a life. You seemed so different from his brazen ways. Voice quiet, eyes steady, hands reaching out only when you knew what you wanted. Gabriel laughed and shouted greetings to those he knew, touched everything, flitted about like a boy—or like a king. You both seduced the town—he with charm, and you with certainty.

But one afternoon that first week, I stomped down toward the barn to ask one of you to kill me a chicken because it was about time I learned to use the old iron oven. And there the two of you stood in the meadow beside the barn, facing one another. Both of you shirtless despite the cold, slate sky above. You focused intensely on each other, hands forward and palms out but not quite touching.

There I saw Gabriel's tattoos: magical patterns of intricate stars-within-stars ranging from his neck down his back and chest, swirling around his arms. Some were gray and old, others sharply black and red, completely new. They layered over each other as though he'd had different sets done and redone every few decades of a very long life. It was my first clue that you were both older than you seemed.

And you, you took my breath away. Your skin was pale from the elbows up to your collarbone, and pink from the cold. Long muscles shifted with every motion, and I put my fingers to my lips because I wanted to touch you, to discover if you were hot or cold, smooth or rough. My whole body flushed, and just then the two of you opened your mouths and said, Bind.

Magic leapt from the earth, snapping through me and all the air. I swayed with the immensity of it, reached out and gripped a tree to remain standing.

The hill trembled and all the forest danced. The burn of magic swept around, tingling under my skin.

It settled down, sudden and fast as hail. My ears popped. Gabriel grasped your hand and tilted his head to the sky with a wide-open laugh.

You closed your eyes and shuddered so violently I saw it from my distance. The land was bound with your magic, safe and secure from—I did not know. Anything? Everything? The overwhelming sense of security made me smile.

Until I realized that a great spell had just been performed, yet neither one of you had spilled any blood. You two were connected in ways more intimate than magic, and together your power dimmed the sun.

ELEVEN

MAB

On the third morning Pan woke up in Arthur's bed, I waited on the threshold. He'd had three days to sort us out, to decide if he could trust me, to learn the dialect of our trees. I hadn't asked him any questions about his past, about his magic or his father. I had only let him be a boy in a new house, eating and drinking and sleeping, touching all the walls and getting his feet under him. Nor had he volunteered much.

But last night, Donna had tucked him in and come slowly back down the stairs. "Those burns on his hands are self-inflicted" was all she said to me, her eyes focused on the wallpaper over my shoulder.

"I'll take him with me for the seven-day binding in the morning," I said.

And so I did. "When you're ready," I said to him as he stretched out of the roll of blankets stuffed at the foot of the bed, "come outside. I want to show you what we do here."

He came out with a bag of frozen blackberries, wearing only a thin boy's T-shirt and a pair of drawstring pants I'd hemmed Monday evening. He looked at my bare feet and wiggled his toes in the grass. "Donna said the crows like these berries best," he told me, scanning the gray sky for the birds.

"She was right." I held out one hand and he took it. Together we plunged into the forest, making our way down the northwestern face of the hill to the Child Creek. Overhead, rippling gray clouds hid the morning sun, keeping the shadows down and all the forest quiet with anticipation.

We walked along the banks of the creek, both of us splashing into the water and hopping on smooth river rocks. I tore open his bag of frozen berries, and Pan dropped them behind us. After a few moments, the crows appeared, darting down out of the sky to snatch up the frozen treats. They argued and laughed loudly, batting at each other and making Pan grin.

When the berries were gone, we'd just come around a curve of land, and the western meadow spread out before us in shades of pink and purple. Under such a steel sky, the colors shone harder and bolder. These were some of my favorite days. I said, "Every week I make my way all around our land, to rebind the magic, to keep down the curses that have been planted here over the decades. To reintroduce myself to the trees."

Pan didn't respond, but I could tell by the way his hands went still that he was listening.

"Did anyone ever mention to you the Deacon?" I asked.

Pan paused, staring out at the phlox and violets, the morning glories and wild columbine. He reached down and plucked a cluster of pink vervain. Turning, he offered it to me. "The blood keeper, is what Dad called ya."

With a smile, I accepted the flower, glad he'd decided to engage. "Yes, exactly. And that is what I want to show you. If you'd like to see?"

"Yes," he said, eagerly.

We continued north, the crows flying peacefully overhead, and followed the Child Creek to where it met the Mighty Creek and formed an arrow of land. A line of honey locust trees closed off the triangle, making it a natural place for protection and binding magic. A twisted old oak tree spread low, thick branches from the center, and all around it the ground tingled with power. One by one, the crows landed in its upper branches, folding their wings in and nestling down.

"This is the blood ground, Pan." I stepped barefoot onto the earth. Little grass grew here, and the oak roots wove up and down, like a netting to keep the blood ground tied together. I found one, stepped up onto it, and held out my hand to invite Pan up as well. "It's where we bury curses and chaotic magic too dangerous to be loose."

Pan jerked free of me.

"Oh no." My heart kicked, and I barely managed not to grab him. "No, Pan, you aren't a dangerous curse, no matter what happened to you. I didn't mean that at all."

He backed warily to stand in the creek, using the flowing water as a barrier. "Then what?"

"I want to show you what I do, so that you know I can help you. That you're safe here, because we don't do bad things. We keep in—in harmony with nature. With God."

"My dad says our magic is from the devil, and God doesn't care."

I tried to think of what I'd want to hear in his position but wasn't certain; I'd always been loved and told I was special and strong and part of God. I balanced on the root of the oak tree, walking toward the trunk. There, I placed my hand against the rough gouges of bark. "Pan, God is everything beautiful; that's what my father used to tell me. And sometimes that beauty hurts, sometimes it overwhelms us, but it's always magic."

"Was your dad the blood keeper before you?"

"Yes." I let my eyes flicker shut for a moment. "He wasn't my birth father, but he might as well have been." I'd always wished it was so.

Pan walked through the creek nearer to me but stayed so that the water ran around his ankles. He was a small golden thing amid all the green and gray, with his autumn-oak-leaf skin and copper-dark hair. Like he'd grown up out of the forest. I felt so clearly in my bones that he belonged here, I didn't say anything. He'd believe me. He'd understand this was where he needed to be, too. After a long moment watching, he said, "Show me."

Allowing myself a smile, I went out to the line of honey locust trees and pressed my palm into a bundle of thorns. Some of the spikes were as long as my hand, clustered in angry bunches up the trunks. The sharp points cut into my skin in five places. Cupping my hand, I began a circuit of the blood ground. Blood gathered in my palm, and when I completed my circle I let five drops fall.

Three times I circled the ground, three times I dripped my blood into the earth. Magic teased at my feet as I walked, and I sang a song about safety and peace. When the last drop fell at the end of my final circle, the ground trembled. I walked straight to the oak tree and pressed my hand against it. "Bound through seven nights and seven days," I said.

My hand flared hot, burning against the rough bark. I took

it back and wiped the streaks of excess blood off into my hair. Now my skin was whole, though pink and tender. I walked straight into the Child Creek near Pan, letting the cold water run around my ankles. The stream pulled all the dirt and loose grasses from my toes, its natural magic cleansing me of the blood ground.

"Now we walk the land," I said, my voice low and full of vibrant magic.

Following the flow of the water, together we made our way in a mile-wide circle around all the land. I stopped six times, resetting boundary magic and wards to bind our land back into itself. To remind it again who I was, what it was.

Pan did not interrupt the whole time, only watching me with his bright eyes, or waving at the crows that hopped along branches beside us or flew circles overhead when I set down magic. They echoed the patterns of my runes, and I think Pan could see it, too.

Nick had called him a kid, and I supposed being only ten years old made him so, but I remembered being that young, being enamored of the tingling feel of the seven-day binding. I hoped Pan was falling in love with it as I had. That whatever he'd known before paled and shrank in comparison to this here.

When the binding was done, my fingernails pulsed with my heartbeat, and so did the clouds in the sky. In streaks of sunlight, motes of dust bobbed at the same pace as my blood. I laughed at the crows teasing each other and put a hand against the smooth white bark of a gumball tree. It tickled my palm, and I heard the forest hissing my name as wind rushed all around us.

Pan held out his hands, fingers splayed, as if he might catch it. "How did that feel?" I asked him.

He shook his head as if words failed but suddenly fisted his hands, grasping the tendrils of wind. "I liked it."

I waited.

"The trees did, too," he said, crouching and touching a silver-barked birch. "They're whispering your name." His smile faded and he set his forehead against the trunk. "But they don't like it when I touch them."

Stepping softly, I went to Pan and put both of my hands on his back, just between his shoulder blades, where his wings would grow if he had them. "We can change that."

"It's my blood."

"Let me try."

He shivered and turned around, sinking down to curl against the birch tree, arms around his knees. "My mama called me Lukas," he said so softly I had to lean in.

I held out my hands, palms up, so that he could see the star tattoo on my left wrist and the snaking spiral on my right. "I swear to you, Lukas, I'll make it so the only magic marked on your skin is the kind you want there."

Hesitating only a moment, he reached out and grasped my hands with his.

WILL

I came home on Wednesday after practice to find a shiny new soccer ball in camo colors sitting on my pillow.

Ben.

I'd ignored him for the whole twenty-four hours since our

fight. Monday evening at dinner, it had dawned on me that Dad was being his usual quiet and reserved self. So Ben must not have said anything to him regarding our little discussion about the Naval Academy. Half of me was grateful. The other half wanted to yell it at Dad myself, because Ben sure didn't owe me any kind of filial loyalty over his duty to tell Dad what a screwup and traitor to family tradition I was.

I dropped my backpack on the floor and palmed the ball. As peace offerings went, this was a little backhanded. But there'd been a time I'd gotten a kick out of playing with him. Running for my life, choking on laughter as he chased me across a flat field of grass. That must've been in Maryland, where we'd lived when I was about five. He'd always catch me and grab one arm and one leg and then spin around, flinging my body into the air and yelling these high-pitched war cries. We'd spin and spin until I thought I'd puke. Ben shouldn't have been strong enough, but I was never afraid. And Aaron, who'd been six in Maryland, had been just too big. That made it our game, mine and Ben's. He used to tell me I was the stealth bomber, so I had to be silent while he swung me or the enemy would know we were coming. But I could never be quiet.

He'd left when I was only ten, off to fulfill his part of the Sanger destiny. Same destiny Aaron had followed to his death. The one I couldn't force myself into.

I sighed loudly, and instead of showering took Ben's ball out to the backyard. I fed and watered the girls, but they knew what a soccer ball meant and totally ignored the kibble. Dribbling the ball lightly on my own, I got them to chase me across the yard. They took turns darting in to trip me, and I worked hard to stay on my toes. I laughed as I danced around them, and Val made her little barks that always sounded like she was laughing with me. Havoc slipped between my feet—she had the winning ratio of success compared to Val—and I fumbled, going down hard enough that my chest contracted where that faded bruise still hung on. I spread out with my face to the sky, laughing, as both dogs swarmed me, licking my face.

"We could use her on the front lines," Ben said, coming up so that his shadow blocked the late-afternoon sun. I squinted at him as Valkyrie leapt up and put her front paws on his stomach.

He gently shoved her off and held a hand down to me. I took it, and he hauled me to my feet.

"Thanks," I said, hoping he knew I meant for the ball, too.

"Sure. Mom gave me this today." Out of his jeans pocket he pulled a folded-up newspaper article.

I groaned.

It was the special insert the local paper had run last month after the earthquake. With a picture of me from last season's soccer team and Holly in her cheer uniform.

The interviewer had come to dinner at the house. Mom made pork chops and Dad gave me his favorite tie to wear, then I had to answer questions like *What were you thinking when you dove into the water, William?* which was like asking what I thought when I poured my cereal this morning: *Nothing. It's just what you do.*

That answer made the reporter downright gleeful, and she called me "Will Sanger—Homegrown Hero" in her article. Like I was a vegetable.

That was when the guys on the soccer team began calling

me Hero when I passed in the hall at school, and my locker was plastered with copies of the interview. I don't know who decided to hand around Superman stickers to slap on my back when I wasn't looking, and I wouldn't have thought any of my friends were smart enough to think of a plastic laurel crown. And yet there it was, waiting on my assigned desk in History.

Mom and Dad were the only ones who pretty much took my so-called heroism for granted. Like they knew who I was, so what I'd done hadn't surprised them. I stared at Ben now, and braced myself. I had no clue how he was going to react.

"Strong work, Will," he said.

I let my hands fall to my sides. And shrugged. "It wasn't . . ." I didn't know how to explain that I knew it was important but that it also hadn't been a big deal.

"I get it." A small smile pulled at his mouth as he tucked the article back into his pocket. "Proof that heroism is in your blood."

"Oh God." I backed away and bent to grab up the soccer ball. "I see where this is going." I told Havoc and Val to go eat their damn dinner.

"I'm not kidding," Ben said, dodging the dogs as they ran around him toward the kennel. "You might be in denial, but your actions speak more loudly. Admit it."

I bounced the ball onto one knee and focused on keeping it in the air with only my knees. It took rhythm and balance and concentration for it not to go flailing off. Ben jumped around and snatched it.

"I get that you're scared after what happened to Aaron. I do. But you can't let it dictate what you do with your life."

"That isn't it."

"Then what?"

"I don't . . . know." It was hard to meet his skeptical eyes. "I just don't want it."

"You used to." Ben said it with total certainty. And was right.

"I don't anymore." I focused on the camouflage ball under his arm.

"Because of Aaron."

"I guess." I thought of that moment in the kitchen last year, when it got so quiet and Mom said, *Yes, this is Mrs. Sanger,* then dropped the phone. When we turned on all the TVs and the radio just to make the quiet go away. Ben hadn't been there for that. He couldn't understand. I couldn't explain.

He shrugged with fake casualness. "It sounds like fear to me, and I don't believe you're a coward. Not my brother."

I ground my teeth, and turned the grimace into a smile. "Wanna play?" I asked, pointing at the fence. "That post and that post are the edges of the goal. Bet you can't score on me."

"If I do, you answer me honestly."

Crouching and ready to guard my goal, I said, "And if you don't, I get to ask something."

"Deal."

I watched his shoulders, the way his chest aimed, as he dribbled in. He wasn't too great and totally projected his shot. I caught the ball with a hard slap and held it up over my head. Ben acknowledged defeat in a single tight nod.

Clutching the ball to my side under one arm, I said, "Okay,

Ben. You're so into the Marines, you're so sure I'll love it. Why? Why do you love it?"

His face scrunched for a brief moment, then he said, "Being part of something bigger than myself."

"Bullshit, you sound like a commercial." I stepped in. "Honest, remember? What's so great about being in it? Why is it better than anything else I could do?"

Ben sighed. He glanced off, and the corners of his eyes wrinkled. Everything about him went still, and I wondered where he was in his head, what he was thinking. When he looked back at me, I saw something in his face I never had before. It made me feel like a coward, just like he said.

"Trust, Will. I can't even explain what it feels like to be in this alien place and all you have is yourself and the man at your back. You're not thinking about it, because you don't have to. It just is. It's so strong there's nothing to say."

My brother's whole face was quiet and intense. I shook my head, because I didn't understand. But I believed him.

"That's all I've got," he snapped, and pulled away.

He marched for the back door. I wanted to say I believed him even though I didn't understand, couldn't he do the same for me?

But my mouth wouldn't open, and the screen door slapped shut behind him.

TWELVE

It was rare for me to be alone with you. We both had enough to do while the sun shone, and by evening, Gabriel would be there, too.

I did not mind him, and found him entertaining and useful and kind. I never doubted he would keep me from harm if anything threatened. He was usually the one to find me, to seek me out and ask how I was adjusting, how I fared on the prairie. "Well," I always told him, and "I love the drama and colors here."

It was true, and his laughter approved, but what I loved most were the moments you decided to smile. Before it appeared on your mouth, it sparked in your eyes, where the corners tightened, and slowly the amusement seeped down your cheeks and over the tip of your nose to find a home on your lips.

When you were weary from a long day in your barn, or covered in dirt and dust from the hay meadow, I heated water for your bath, and made tea that often Gabriel drank before you were ready. All the tiny things I did for you, he thought I did for him. How could I have known then? I was too focused on you.

One evening I baked a roast from beef you'd traded with another farmer for, and tuned the radio so that it played low, delicious jazz. You were upstairs cleaning, and I hadn't seen Gabriel since the afternoon, when he'd announced he was running into town because it was surely going to snow us in overnight.

The kitchen smelled of cloves and onions, and I was warm and happy, alone in a chamber of light, while outside it was dark and dangerous. I turned the dial of the radio as one of my favorite songs began: "Our Love Is Here to Stay."

With myself, I danced slowly around the kitchen, eyes closed, one hand against my stomach and the other held out for my invisible partner. I hummed, filling my head with gentle vibrations, singing random words when I knew them.

And then there was heat at my back, and a hand over mine, sliding around my stomach. You danced with me, smooth and soft, from behind. Your breath against my temple, smelling of lavender soap and fresh wool. My voice hitched and I couldn't even hum after that, but only sway and step as your body suggested, your hips against mine, your chest on my back, your hand in the air with mine, nudging and drawing me to and fro.

Then Gabriel clapping from the entryway shocked us both out of the song—a different song, for the first had passed on I don't know how much earlier.

"Bravo, my darlings," he said, clapping lazily still, as he came in from the cold, letting his bag thump onto the kitchen floor. "Don't stop on my account."

Gabriel moved to the sink and washed his hands, but you and I remained like statues beside the table, your hand on my stomach, my fingers tight around yours.

He opened his mouth and began to sing, looking at us over his shoulder in a teasing way, eyebrows up to egg us on. Daring, almost, and for a slight moment I wondered if he was jealous.

You stepped away from me, and I smoothed my dress. "Roast is nearly done," I murmured, going straight for the oven. It was hot standing beside it, but I was glad it might hide my blush.

Immediately, you began to ask Gabriel if his drive to Topeka had been uneventful, and if he'd found the right piece for the well pump. His answers were slow and lingering, and as I dressed the plates and watched through the corners of my eyes, I sensed you were speaking another language, buried in everyday talk. You were having an entirely different conversation than the one I was privy to, and it sounded like you'd been having it for ages.

Everyone would judge you to be nineteen or twenty, and Gabriel maybe twenty-five. But your heavy looks, his layered words, the tone of how you spoke, and the way he touched your shoulder spoke of so much more. Not only age, but experience and depth of emotions.

The thought that you were lovers skittered through me, and I rejected it, not out of reason but out of selfishness and fear. There had to be something else, I insisted, and I reached into my memory for stories my grandmother had told me of men of our blood who used the magic like the angels, never to grow old.

I clung to that, to the dream that you did not love Gabriel but had only known him for lifetimes. That the reason I'd expected an aged Arthur Prowd was because you were old, you simply didn't look it.

That was far more palatable to me than any other thing.

Oh, Arthur, I was young, which led me to be so right, and still so wrong.

THIRTEEN

MAB

The path to cleansing Lukas of the curse his father had set upon him was a slow one. Because he was young, because I had never worked with a human being as my subject before, we both were more comfortable with a careful pace.

I explained everything as I went, telling Lukas stories of other curses I'd seen, set into mammoth tooth fossils or bound into the foundation of a house. Most of them Arthur had understood, and showed me piece by piece the methods for binding them or dismantling them—all of which included destroying the thing itself or binding it in its entirety. Neither of those options were available to us, and of course we couldn't simply strip the black candle rune from his flesh.

Thursday all I did was study it. Lukas lay in the sun in a circle of salt, shirtless. The black candle rune ran across the small of his back, a sprawling spider with intricate curls and precise angles. His father must have bound him down with ropes, or knocked him unconscious. I did not ask, and Lukas gave me almost no information about the person of his father. But he promised there were no marks lower than his hips, which made me grateful his father may have been evil but perhaps not perverted.

Donna hid in the house, and I wondered if seeing a young boy who'd been abused by the magic made her remember things about herself and Nick she'd rather have left forgotten.

I made an exact sketch of the rune, detailing how Lukas said it felt when I touched it, or when I cast the protective salt circle around us and he grimaced. It helped if I pricked his finger and we grounded his blood into the earth first.

Though we hardly did anything, that evening he was exhausted. And so Friday, we left off his blood, instead focusing on the less intense but more immediately rewarding task of kitchen work.

Lukas turned out to be an excellent assistant, rolling crusts well and paying strict attention to the heat of the oven. He helped Donna make tarts, little meat pics for the crows, and two trays of cinnamon rolls. It softened her, and she obviously enjoyed telling him about the natural magic in cooking. "Transformations occur without the need for blood or incantations," she confided, shooting me a smile.

I wasn't too proud to agree, though I used blood in my baking. But I was baking charms, not food. I cooked little wheat cakes with lavender and rue that would give sweet dreams as well as stave off allergies; boiled milkweed down into a tincture that I mixed into honey for a lozenge against coughing; soaked wild echinacea root for tea; prepared boneset for oil infusion against aches and fevers. I added drops of blood to all of it, quickening the power. My home remedies were guaranteed.

Timers weren't involved in mine, for the sweet smell of perfectly boiled milkweed, the crackle of properly dried oak leaves, and a tiny dash of honey on my tongue were all I needed to know when my work was done.

I'd been aiding Arthur and Granny in charm-making for as long as I'd been alive, and the smell of flour and mingled blood and herbs made me go to Granny's old radio and turn it to a station that played old-time jazz. I didn't sing, but the rhythm of the music helped me keep away my missing them.

Lukas bit into one of the raspberry tarts, and the filling dripped down his chin. I had a sudden sharp memory of my mother drawing her finger along my chin, wiping away a sticky line of honey that she then popped into her own mouth to lick up with a grin. "Let's get out of here, pet," she'd said, brushing away Granny's protests as she dragged me upstairs to my bedroom. Her suitcase spilled open from the foot of the bed, for she always stayed with me when she was here, curled around me at night like a turtle's shell.

Mother had pulled the shutters closed and the curtains, too, tucking away every bit of sunlight until the bedroom was gray, and the scarves on the ceiling dull shadows of their usual color. She lit the fat candle on my bedside table, then sank onto the rag rug, curling her feet beneath her, and patted the floor. "Come here, Mab, I have something for you."

As I joined her, curious and tense because she rarely gave me gifts, she drew a narrow box out from under the bed. Polished dark wood, it was plain and elegant, and sealed all around with a line of wax. I breathed in quickly, the only sign of my surprise. That box had not been under my bed three nights ago when I shoved a bundle of nettles in the far corner for protection from ghosts.

Mother caressed the lid, scratching her nails against the smooth wood. "I made this for you, and it's to be our secret." She reached for me and tucked hair behind my ear. Her own blond curls were trimmed just under her chin, always behaving the way she told them to with oil and spray.

"A secret?" I'd never kept secrets from Arthur.

Her smile was knowing. "Arthur wouldn't mind, but that wife of his . . ." Something I didn't understand flickered through her eyes. "She would be appalled, Mab, and take it away, blame me for corrupting you." Mother laughed. "But you're old enough now for trouble. Not here, of course, with Arthur. But off his land, there are monsters that wear masks of men, and they will want you—you're my daughter, and women like us attract it." Her eyes unfocused and she looked through me, to some distant past or memory I couldn't reach. "Power in our veins, the will to use it. They'll always find us and try to take advantage."

I touched her cheek, and she blinked out of her memory. "So, here are weapons for you." With her thumbnail she broke the wax seal. The lid opened with a puff of cinnamon-smelling air, and I leaned into it, shivering. Tiny vials lined half of it in rainbow colors, there were braided ribbons, and a thin silver dagger.

To me it seemed nothing more than a simple beginner's kit, but Mother explained to me what the vials contained—they were no basic ingredients, like salt or ground quartz. No, there was purifying vesta powder, the poisonous yew crystals, and blinding sand. A clear bottle of belladonna. Rust-red carmot, which Arthur had told me of but I'd never seen before—the delicate potion made from blood witches' bones that would let us live young forever. Mother had braided the ribbons with bits of her own hair to make them strong as steel, and with the silver dagger she cut off strands of my hair. Together we braided it into the ribbons, and into pieces of her hair. She pricked my middle finger and told me to squeeze painful drops onto each of the cork stoppers so that my blood would diffuse into the potions and powders.

We huddled on the floor of my bedroom, me and my mother, tying all the dangerous spells inside that box to my power, to my spirit, until they could never be used against me, but only toward my protection. I remembered how Mother's breath fell soft and warm on my cheek, and the smell of her magic as she kissed my finger to heal it. In the dim light, with a single flickering candle, my bedroom became a secret underworld for that afternoon hour, filled with dark and delicious magic.

It was everything opposite of this bright kitchen, where Donna and Lukas and I made bread and charms, where Granny Lyn had danced and Arthur had lifted me once onto the table to hang Christmas streamers.

My mother was gone, and I better understood now that she'd been one of those monsters.

But even she had never used me the way Lukas's father had used him. She wouldn't have spent time contemplating how to break the black candle rune, or studying it. My mother would have gone straight to Lukas's father and cut out his heart to break the curse.

I almost regretted that wasn't an option for me.

WILL

Friday after school, I crashed out onto the soccer field.

I'd been warming up on the track when something light and soft hit the top of my head and fell behind me. A red practice jersey.

"Hey, Hero, up for a scrimmage?" Matt jogged up alongside me.

I scowled at him but slowed down, feet beating steady on the soft rubber track. "Yeah, sure."

Matt flipped his head to get his mop of brown hair out of his eyes. He was constantly jerking like that, and it reminded me of a nervous horse. We all told him to cut the hair off, but he liked the way it flew back when he ran, and claimed the ladies did, too. "You sure? You look kinda spent."

"I'm good." It wasn't exactly a lie, given that the blood taste had faded over the last few days and the headache I'd sported all Wednesday was just a dull, normal thing. I hadn't been sleeping too well, with mud monsters prowling in my dreams, but that was nothing new, and nothing I was going to talk to Matt about. I was fine. To prove it, I jogged back to the fallen shirt and grabbed it up. I stripped off my T-shirt and replaced it with the sleeveless jersey. Matt was wearing a blue one. I eyed it and said, "You think your side'll kick my ass?"

He nodded, then had to flip his hair out of his face again. "That's the plan."

We headed off the track for the far end of the school grounds. The soccer field needed to be mowed, and a few places had been worn down to dirt in both the goal boxes.

About ten guys were waiting, kicking balls and yelling back and forth. It wasn't our season, but most of the team didn't play other sports. We spent the whole year practicing—unofficially when we had to. Soccer was a fall sport, and in a month or so Coach Bryson would be on us for real, every day, for hours. It was gonna be tough finding a summer job that I could ditch by three every afternoon. Hopefully, that landscaping thing one of our strikers had going with his neighbor would pan out.

Matt and I quickly chose our teams, and we divided up to either end of the field. My fellow Reds clapped my shoulders and asked what strategy I wanted to try. Since we only had six men to a team, I decided we'd forgo a keeper and play purely offensive. Matt was the team's keeper, so we'd have to attack hard and focus on getting the ball past him. I'd stay back to sweep and put everybody else forward. It was a risk, but with Matt as their captain, they'd be sure to hold heavy on the defense.

Since I'd dressed for running on the track, I hadn't bothered with cleats. It was only a scrimmage, though, and it hardly put me at a disadvantage. The sun beat down on us. Sweat plastered the mesh jersey to me. I was laughing and yelling in equal parts, focused on the wider movement of the field instead of just the ball, since I had to strategize when to push forward and when to hang back or give up my center position momentarily.

Although winning the game would mean glory and not having to take the dirty jerseys home to wash, I was mostly just happy we seemed balanced. It was gonna be an awesome team next year. By the end of twenty minutes, we'd only managed to slip one goal past Matt, and my Reds hadn't let the Blues get near enough ours to score. I noticed a few of the cheerleaders, headed up by Matt's girlfriend, Shanti, stretching out near enough that they were mostly watching us. No wonder Matt took a huge diving leap to block a goal that landed him hard on his left shoulder. He bounced up and tossed the ball at Dylan, his winger, who'd been hanging way right and managed a clean break up the side of the field. I ran at him, met him straight on, and tried to swipe the ball away. He spun and his shoulder knocked into me. I slammed to a stop, foot on the ball, and momentum twisted us up and we both went down.

I hit the ground totally unprepared, all my breath jarred out of me. My ears rang, and I put my arms out to my sides as if I could stop the earth from spinning if I held it down. Dylan was laughing next to me, and rolled to his side to stand. He held a hand down for me. I shook my head, which was a mistake.

A second later the whole team was crowded around me. I gasped, "Fine. I'm fine. Just dizzy."

"Sanger, shit!" Matt shoved through. "What happened? Your lips are, like, blue."

"Yeah, I'm sorry, man." Dylan crouched next to me.

"No, no." I pushed up to sit, swallowing bile that burned its way back to my stomach. My throat felt raw, and I could taste blood again. "Probably just the heat." That was bullshit, though. I'd lived in Okinawa, which is a tropical island. This was nothing.

Matt took my arm and helped me up to my feet. I swayed

to one side. "Why don't you guys run some drills while I get him to the side."

A few hands patted my shoulders, and I started moving with Matt. Something thin and hot drained out of my nose before I could snort it back up. I coughed, and felt the drip hit my chest.

"You're bleeding, man," Matt said in a hushed breath.

I put the back of my hand against my nose. "Seriously?" Sure enough, my skin came back with red staining the creases. I leaned my head back and pinched my nose closed. No wonder I tasted blood again.

"Should I call somebody?"

"Nah, I'll just . . . I'll just go shower and go home. Lie down. I'm fine."

"You sure?" He looked dubious, and used a hand to wipe his hair up off his forehead. His face was flushed with effort, from playing in the humid afternoon. Everybody was hot, but not everybody was fainting.

"I'm sure," I said. I smiled. I was good at smiling.

Matt nodded. He jogged back to the field. I turned and found Holly waiting. Not pale and covered in bloody water. Just normal, in her blue cheer uniform.

I stopped smiling. "Hey," I managed.

"You okay, Will?" Her eyebrows lifted and she met my eyes, calm and steady. Nothing like the embarrassment I was feeling rather acutely showed on her face.

About ten feet behind her the rest of the cheerleaders clustered. I hadn't noticed Holly with them before, probably because she'd been out of all practices since the earthquake. I'd forgotten to look for her. From Shanti's expression, I got the distinct impression Holly'd been sent to check on me.

She pursed her lips and glanced back at the cheerleaders over her shoulder. I snapped out of it. "Yeah, Holly, I'm good."

"Can I get you water or anything?"

I stared at her. And inexplicably thought about that girl in the goggles. Mab. Holly was so different from her. The cheer uniform, for example. Sharp and pleated, in our school colors of black and blue. Holly's hair was short now, because they'd cut some of it to put the stitches in, and carefully styled to cover the worst section in the back. "I'm good," I repeated.

Holly hesitated, one hand smoothing the perfectly flat material over her stomach. Her fingers fidgeted.

I jerked my gaze back up to her face. "Are you okay?" I asked, stepping nearer. I felt like I was hulking over her, though I'm not that big. Could never play football. She wasn't tiny, either. It wasn't physical, in other words.

"I only wanted to know if . . ." She paused, and I was struck again by how calm her face appeared. That hand was her tell.

Warm blood hit my upper lip, and I caught it with the back of my knuckle, grimacing. "Sorry," I mumbled from behind my hand.

Holly's mouth pinched up, and she nodded quickly. "You should take care of it. I'll talk to you later. Soon."

I took two steps around her, my instinct to push, to find out what she needed. "Holly?"

Her eyebrows arched up again.

"You all are manning the sport booth tomorrow morning, right? Down at the farmers' market?"

"Yeah."

I tilted my head and tried out a smile despite the gross state of my nose. "I'll talk to you then, then."

"Okay, Will," she said, wincing at my face. She covered her mouth, but I saw the smile in her eyes.

FOURTEEN

It was Gabriel I asked, because you still called me Miss Sonnenschein, even two months into my stay, even when it was the longest, darkest time of the year and we were trapped, the three of us, together in the house.

I followed him into the blisteringly bright snow an afternoon in January, tears streaking down my face from the glare of sun on the brilliant white landscape. "Gabriel," I called, air sharp as needles in my throat, so that he might slow down. My boots held out the cold, but in six inches of snow I couldn't keep up with his strong strides.

He did stop, and held out a gloved hand for me. Mine were encased in mittens I'd knitted myself. The freezing wind pulled out red even in his face, and his hat was pulled down low to shield his dark eyes. I gripped his hand and walked with him down toward the barn.

"How old are you?" I asked.

Gabriel laughed. "You have a guess, do you not?"

"Old," was all I said, pulling his arm so that he would let me stare up into his face.

His mouth slid into half of a smile, and he shrugged one shoulder. "Yes, darling Evie. Very old."

"And so is Arthur."

"Nearly as old as me, but not quite."

"Tell me." I reached with my free hand and put it against his cold cheek. "Tell me, Gabriel, everything."

Gabriel tilted his head so that he kissed the rough palm of my mitten. I felt his hot breath seep through the wool and shivered. He said, "Not everything, my pet. But some."

Together we continued to walk, keeping our blood warm, through the trees. Snow whispered between the naked fingers of the forest, cold kisses on my cheeks, and Gabriel told me that both of you were more than three hundred years old. That he'd met you when you were my age, in a place called the Mohawk Valley in what is now, but was not then, New York State. You'd traveled together for decades, teaching each other magic, hunting out other men with your power in order to trade knowledge with them, discovering alchemy and everlasting life. You taught him to turn leaves into silver and draw rubies from the mountains; he showed you how to possess living creatures and to grow fruit from a barren tree.

Gabriel told me that even when you spent years apart, always you returned to each other, like geese flying south in November. He mentioned adventures he'd had without you, in the Indian Wars, during the Gold Rush, in Alaska and Florida, along the Mexican border, and when Las Vegas was only a fort in the desert. He told me about your various apprentices in the last century—Philip the doctor, Laura Harleigh who transformed herself into a swan, the sister and brother Jessica and Deitrich who traveled the South with you, healing during the Civil War.

And your wife. Who died in 1908, just before you came here to Kansas. Her name was Anne, he told me, intimately, too, as if he'd been there for all of it. As if he offered me a secret.

It was an hour or less that we walked together, down the deer path toward the barn, but his every word, every new bit of story buried me, making the snowflakes that tumbled down from the sky into heavy lead. My shoulders ached, my nose was dry and freezing, and my eyes cracked with the effort of holding back tears.

What hope did I have to win just your attention, much less affection? I was a silly little girl, and there was nothing I had to tempt you, who had lived so long, into loving me.

That night when I brought you a cup of hot cider with honey, your finger brushed mine and I nearly spilled it all down your shirt. You smiled absently and thanked me. Going to the sofa, I curled up under a blanket as Gabriel read to us an article about Cyd Charisse in Parade magazine. Your sketchbook rested on your lap, and you drew images of women dancing. I could barely focus on Gabriel's voice or the flickering fire or the needle in my hand as I tried to sew up a hole in one of your shirts. All I could think was that the faces of your dancing women must be faces you'd known, women you'd loved decades before I'd even been born.

I'd never have believed the truth.

FIFTEEN

MAB

The sun hung heavy just over the roofs in Faith and Eli's neighborhood when we pulled into their driveway Saturday morning. We had a little less than an hour before the opening of the market downtown, but the long table we used as our booth resided among Eli's tools in their back shed. I'd spent the drive down planning my morning: After helping Donna to set up, and once the shops downtown opened, I had a list of errands to run. To the Community Mercantile for the goat's feet I'd requested, the tea shop, and a jeweler who carried raw rubies in particular.

Lukas said, "It looks so normal."

Donna laughed quietly. "We don't have to be strange."

I was halfway across the too-tidily-mown lawn when the front door opened and Eli poured out with little Hannah clutching his hand and Caleb slung over his shoulders.

Eli paused on the narrow concrete steps leading out of the ranch house. He tried to speak, but Caleb's grubby little hand flailed too near. Eli had to curl an arm up to catch the boy, both of them roaring as he rolled Caleb down off his shoulder, plopping him onto the ground. Hannah let go and waved at me.

She and Caleb, after he picked himself up off the grass, ran at me, and I knelt for a hug. I put my face between their heads. Caleb I'd only known from a distance, because he'd hardly been born when they moved. Hannah, though, I squeezed tight. I'd changed her diapers and been the one she came to in the middle of the night when she dreamed the roses wanted to steal her away.

It had been those dreams, of course, that had convinced Faith to take her children off the blood land.

"Hi, Mab," Hannah said, and Caleb already had his fist tangled in my hair.

Eli crouched. His beard needed a trim, and it was difficult to see what his lips were doing. "My turn, cretins," he said, dragging them away from me. Hannah stayed near, waiting in her quiet way, but Caleb took off for Donna.

I closed my eyes at Eli's light kiss on my cheek. He was twice my age, and smelled like a proper blood witch: all copper and spicy sage. It was just like Arthur, and the bite of missing him made me hug Eli tightly. His scent slipped through my nose and settled like home in my heart.

"Good morning," he said, giving me a true smile as he pulled us both to our feet.

"We have someone to introduce you all to," I said, offering my hand down to Hannah. "Is your mama up?"

"We have pancakes," she said. She was only five, but already graceful like Faith.

From behind me, Donna said, "Here's Lukas, Eli. He's new out at the farm."

Eli nodded. "Pleasure to meet you, Lukas. I'm Eli, this is my home, and these are my children, Caleb and Hannah. If you're a friend of Mab and Donna's, you're welcome here."

The strangely formal speech had Lukas licking his lips, his eyes darting from Eli to Caleb in Donna's arms and back again. I'd explained how Eli and Faith had the magic in their blood but, like Donna, weren't much of practitioners. Not for reasons like hers, but because Eli preferred using his hands, and tools man-made, and Faith thought magic for its own sake was superfluous. She reserved it for necessity. But they both wanted their children to learn the power, because it was part of their birthright. Lukas had decided in the car that that was better than his own dad. He held out a hand to Eli and said, "Hi."

They shook like grown men, and then Donna swept over the moment, saying, "You go on in with Mab, Lukas, and I'll get the table loaded up and then we'll sit for a few minutes."

"I'll help," Eli said, and when Donna passed me Caleb, they went around back.

I hitched Caleb onto my hip, pulled a strand of my hair out of his mouth, and asked Hannah to take us inside.

Their little ranch-style house was one story, clean as a whistle, with the kitchen directly down the short hall from the front door. A house with the hearth in the center had been Faith's only requirement besides an air conditioner, I remembered her saying. She was from Michigan, a far-flung branch of the blood family, and singularly unused to our Kansas summers. She'd left home at eighteen, searching for God, and found Arthur instead. He'd taught her what he knew, helped her change her name to Faith, and introduced her to Eli.

She greeted me with a strong hug after I put Caleb into a high chair. The buttons of her overalls pressed cold against my collarbone. "Hi, Mab." Her smile slid halfway off her face, and she leveled her small brown eyes at me. "How is it, Deacon?"

"Good." I paused, covering the thoughts of my broken doll with layers of imaginary dirt and leaves. "As can be expected."

"I'm glad. You haven't called, and I've hoped that meant you were doing all right."

I nodded, glancing past her to the bar, where there was more syrup on the counter than there was in the glass jar. Hannah had climbed up onto one of the tall stools beside Caleb, and helped him with his sippy cup.

"And who's this?" Faith asked, smiling at Lukas. We'd put him in a clean shirt, but it was too big for him. Getting him some clothes of his own was another errand for the day.

"I'm Lukas," he answered himself, reaching around to catch Caleb's cup as it spilled off his high chair.

"He's family," I said, knowing it would be all Faith needed. I hoped it would sink in with Lukas, as well. This was our family, and we would all help him when he needed it.

"Pancake?" she offered.

"Pancake!" Caleb cried around the cup Lukas had returned to him.

"How could we resist?" I sat on the third stool with Lukas on my other side while Faith moved to the oven and pulled out a stack of pancakes staying warm on a serving tray.

We ate, and I told Faith Nick had stopped by, and that he and Silla were leaving for Oregon. Eli came in with Donna, and she accepted apple juice and a pancake. Caleb clapped for his dad to pick him up but was dragged to the sink instead for his whole arms and face to be washed of sticky syrup. It was loud, and I stopped chewing to let the familiarity wash around me. Lukas had barely touched his pancake, and watched everything with those darting eyes of his. I wondered how long he'd been alone, just him and his dad.

Hannah touched my hand and then reached around me to tap Lukas on the wrist. "Look," she said and held up her thin finger. A blue Band-Aid with cartoon characters I didn't recognize wrapped around it.

"Have you been learning magic?" I whispered, bending close.

Hannah nodded solemnly, but a tiny smile pressed the corners of her mouth.

"What kind?" Lukas whispered, leaning in conspiratorially.

"We woke up a flower, didn't we?" Faith said, moving back to the counter as Eli toweled Caleb's face dry.

"Resurrection?" I asked Hannah.

"It only hurt a little bit," the girl admitted.

I kissed her finger and said, "It has to, or the blood doesn't matter."

Donna set her plate down. "Everything beautiful hurts just a little bit." It was one of Arthur's sayings.

"Can you show me fire again?" Hannah asked, making her eyes big.

"Fire's dangerous," Lukas said softly. I noticed his hands were tucked into his lap, so that no one might see his scars.

"It can be," I agreed. I leaned back so that I spoke to both Lukas and Hannah. "But think of water. Water feeds our thirst, and yet can flood us or drown us. We need it, but it is also dangerous. Did God give us water, and the devil make us drown? I don't think so. The danger doesn't come from the water but from us. From how we use it and how we let it use us in turn."

Lukas pressed his small fists into his thighs.

I gave Hannah a tiny smile. "I have to go to the market this morning, but when we bring the table back, we'll go out and I'll help you. Any color you like."

"Blue," she said immediately.

"Blue fire, the best kind."

"We should get going so we set up before opening," Donna said from the sink. She was loading her plate into the dishwasher while Faith wrestled with getting Caleb's dirty shirt off and Eli washed the frying pan.

Eli walked us out to the car, and once Lukas was buckled into the backseat, he caught my elbow. "Donna said he's got some curse in him."

I pursed my lips and glanced through the window at Lukas; he had his hand on the glass, staring up past me to where the crows picked at some garbage rolling down the street. "Maybe."

"Anything we can do?"

"Not yet. Be yourselves."

Eli put his hand on my shoulder, weighing me down with comfort. "You'll find the truth," he said. "I know you."

"We will." I opened the passenger door.

As we drove away, Eli lifted his hand.

Donna said, "It's about ten minutes to downtown. How

are you doing, Lukas?" She'd been concerned the noise of the Waller house would be overwhelming for him.

He didn't respond, and I looked back to find him staring with his face pressed to the window. I craned around and saw the crows winging fast to catch up, all eleven in a double V formation. Not at all crowlike. Silla had called them cursed, too, like Eli had Lukas, but I didn't believe it. Reese lived on, free and flying, and it was possible whatever magic Lukas's father had linked into him was just as open to interpretation. I hoped that was the truth.

One evening I'd heard Eli and Arthur and Granny Lyn arguing about truth on the front porch while I practiced runes on scraps of paper with crayons. Eli said, *Knowing is the path to truth.* Arthur thought listening was the path, and Granny Lyn that it was love.

I wondered what I believed.

WILL

It was easy to find the cheerleaders at the farmers' market. At eight a.m. they were the only people younger than thirty. Everywhere else were aging hippies, robust farmers, grown-ups in jogging shorts, and about fifty kinds of dogs on leashes. The vegetables did look really great, and I was tempted by a booth with seven different colors of honey. I'd thought honey was all the same. But my hands were full of cardboard coffee cups, so I kept walking for the booth where the cheerleaders sold T-shirts with our star logo and star-shaped cookies.

Each sports team was taking a couple of Saturdays over the summer to sell the shirts and whatever baked goods we could come up with. Proceeds went to a college scholarship fund set up by the parents of two football players who'd died in a car crash last year.

The cheerleaders all wore the T-shirts themselves, a nice size too small, and white short shorts. Attracting plenty of customers. Probably they should be here every Saturday.

Kate saw me first, and she nudged Shanti, who came around the booth with a smile. "Hey, Will. Matt with you?"

I handed her one of the trays of coffee. "Nope. I brought coffee for the effort."

"Really." She narrowed her eyes like she always did when she suspected Matt of something. Her lids were dusted with gold glitter that Matt said made her hot as a Bollywood princess, but it got all over everything. "Well, thanks."

I glanced behind her at Holly, who was counting change for a woman and her fluffy poodle. There were only four cheerleaders, and I hadn't thought of a plan of action beyond bringing coffee. "Need help?"

Shanti gave me a pitying look. "Yes, it takes more than four competent cheerleaders to sell cookies to the hippies." She took the second tray of coffee and put it on the corner of the table.

"Does it take more than three?" I offered my best charming smile.

Holly thanked her customer and, before Shanti could answer, slid around to my side. "Hi, Will. Thanks for the coffee."

Shanti said, "Three will do just fine."

"Great." I waited.

Holly's eyes flickered to Shanti, and they shared one of those moments of silent girl communication. Shanti's shoulders twitched in a tiny shrug, and Holly put her hand in mine. "Let's go."

It took a second for my feet to catch up with hers. Her hand was warm, not at all like the cold, wet ankle I'd first touched in all the dark water. She didn't hold on long, though. Just until she paused at a wool booth to sift through scarves. I stood there, watching her, wondering why I was there. She wanted to talk to me, to say something. I felt like I owed her some time at least, even though I'd been the one who saved her, so probably most people would say it was the other way around. I sure didn't think so.

The day she'd come back to school, I remembered waiting all morning like there was a sniper target between my shoulder blades. Waiting for the ball to drop. At lunch, she was there with her friends, with our friends, and I sat next to Matt while she pretended to eat the chips out of her lunch bag. Shanti'd teased her about the high-fructose corn syrup in them, and Matt had punched me on the shoulder and said, "Will's here, she doesn't have to worry."

She looked up from the wool scarves then and I saw her eyes, muddy brown like the water had been. I thought of my hands with her blood on them, the watery pink blood, and at the same time we said, "I'm sorry."

We wandered toward the booths with hot breakfast. Just to have something to do I bought a piece of fry bread to pick apart. There were rickety benches and plastic card tables there, and we sat down. Trees at this edge of the parking lot gave us some shade, but it was plenty warm. People walked everywhere, chatting like old friends, poking at asparagus and avoiding the warm exhaust from the all-natural meat booth's refrigerator. I could see the cheerleaders' booth from here, doing better business with the cookies than the shirts. Maybe seeing the girls in their own shirts was reminding buyers they'd never look that good.

"I'm not sorry I'm alive," Holly said. It was the first thing she'd said since our mutual apology a few minutes ago, other than the no when I'd asked if she wanted some fry bread.

"Good." I squinted. A ray of sun had pushed through the trees behind us and glittered off her gold earrings. It flashed in my eye.

"I'm just sorry you have to put up with all that bullshit at school." She sat with her hands clasped in her lap, watching the passersby with her usual calm.

"It wasn't important. Not a problem."

"It is; you're doing it because of me."

"I don't mind," I said. I tore off a hunk of the flat fry bread. It was dark gold and stretchy.

Holly sighed sharply. "I do mind. Not about you, I mean, but . . . about the big deal. My mom got a call yesterday morning from a representative from some talk show. They want to have us come talk about near death and Kansas earthquakes." She said it fast, in one breath. "That's what I wanted to tell you yesterday. My mom thinks I should do it, but I'm tired of it, and I didn't do anything."

I was glad I hadn't actually tried to eat the bread. It was hard enough keeping the wince off my face without chewing, too.

"Did they ask you?" She touched my wrist and then pulled her hand away.

"No. Not that I know of. But I'll say no, if they do."

Her smile was instantaneous. "Oh, good. I didn't want to abandon you to it alone."

"Thanks. I, uh, I'm sorry, too." I hurried on as her smile faded fast. "I know everybody's treating you differently. Like you're still . . . delicate."

"Yeah." Holly stared at the table. She began picking at the plastic seam with her fingernail. "I feel like it, sometimes."

I looked at her pretty lips, at her brown-gray eyes that were the same color as the lake. "I don't think you're delicate. You survived a concussion and almost drowned."

"Thanks to you and Shanti."

"Okay, it was a group effort. We all rock." I grinned at her, wanting her to feel better. Less like she was going to break.

It got a light laugh out of her. "We do," she agreed.

We sat for a moment, both of us watching the people. I wondered if everybody thought they were weaker than they were. Except Ben, of course. I almost rolled my eyes at myself, and then a dazzling bit of yellow caught my attention.

There, about five booths down and across the lane from the cheerleaders, was Mab.

I pinched my eyes closed and wondered if she'd still be there when I looked. Except for the taste in my mouth and nightmares all week—choking on rose vines, sinking into thick mud—I'd done a great job not thinking about last Sunday morning.

When I opened my eyes, there she was.

Her hair was braided back at her ears. It fell behind her and reflected the sun like a mirror. Her table was covered in little glass jars and vials, piles of soap, and cloth bags tied with multicolored ribbons. A woman in long sleeves and a straw hat sat back in a folding chair. Next to her was a mixed-race boy about nine or so, cutting one of the bars of soap in half with a tiny knife. Mab leaned over him so that free strands of her hair fell around her face, and pointed at something in the soap. Whatever it was fascinated the kid.

"Do you see that booth over there," I asked Holly, "with the sign for Prowd Charms?" It looked like it had been painted by a toddler.

"Yeah." Holly tapped her nails on the table. "God, that's the Prowds. The girl, Mab, she came to try out for our softball team once, a long time ago. I thought she was going to attack Kate with the bat. And she didn't like the rules. I mean, it's kind of a stupid game, but she didn't even try." Holly laughed. "Why?"

"Oh." I shrugged and stuffed a piece of fry bread into my mouth around the sudden taste of mud. It was greasy and warm. "No reason," I said as I swallowed.

"They live out—out by Matt's uncle, actually." Her voice lowered as though she was talking to herself. "Some old cult, I guess. Homeschool all their kids."

"A cult?" I thought of Mab with the goggles over her face and the knife. And cutting the heart out of the mud monster. In that moment, it was all real.

"You should ask Kate. Her grandma used to have tea with Mab's grandma sometimes, I guess when they were kids. Kate says her grandma says the family's been on their land since after the Civil War. As long as there's been a town here, really, and you know there's Prowd Street over across from Highway 24. Same family."

"Huh." I watched Mab tell two men in creased jeans something she obviously found distasteful. She crossed her arms and put on a very poor imitation of a welcoming smile. I realized I was grinning.

"I should get back to the booth, I think," Holly said.

I shoved the fry bread away. "Sure."

As Holly and I walked past the Prowd Charms booth, I glanced at Mab and found her staring at me, too.

MAB

It was nearing fun to teach Lukas all about the ingredients I put in the charms, and why some made you clean and others made your bruises heal faster. He asked quiet questions, and sometimes Donna put in her two cents, while the sun beat down and gradually heated up the whole black parking lot. I noticed Lukas seemed to draw more attention than Donna and I ever did on our own. Probably it was how earnest he looked as he counted out change, or the delight that swept his face when one of the hundred leashed dogs squished under the table to lick at his fingers. That all certainly made the market more enjoyable for me.

I'd just finished explaining the difference between our cold tea and our fever tea to a very sweet woman who had a stroller with twins when I saw Will Sanger walking toward the booth beside one of the girls from the high school table. Her T-shirt was so tight I could see exactly where her bra was across her back, and her shorts might as well have been underwear.

He turned to me then and smiled, and I started to smile back.

"What're you staring at?" Lukas asked.

Donna said, "I believe that's the girl who fell into the lake during the earthquake."

"What?" I broke contact with Will to frown at her.

She put a hand to her forehead to block the bright sunlight. "Yes, it is, and the boy who saved her, too. Will Sanger."

"*What?*" I snapped back to look at Will, but he'd moved on, just his back to us. They arrived at the high school table, and Will said something to make all of the girls laugh.

Donna said, "Her name is Holly, I think, and the boy dove into the lake for her when she fell in. Saved her life, the paper said."

My entire body quivered, and goose bumps raced up my spine to scatter down my arms like tiny insects. "That happened," I whispered, "during Arthur's earthquake?"

Donna nodded.

Even under the warm May sun, even without a wind to pick up our sweat, I was so cold. I thought of Will at that little lake just past our woods, slamming the homunculus down, tearing out its antler. The little lake. "At . . . at that lake on Mr. Riber's land?"

"Yes, Mab, are you all right?" Donna touched my shoulder, and Lukas, too, put a hand on my elbow. Their skin was so much hotter than mine.

Closing my eyes, I drew in a long breath, cursing the black

pavement under my feet that kept me off the earth, cutting the energy of the planet away from me. I hated being in town, with its grid of roads like a web holding the world prisoner. I focused on the heat of the sunlight, on the voices all around, the distant hum of traffic from the interstate, laughter and birdsong and my family's hands on me. "Yes," I said, opening my eyes. "I'm perfectly fine."

Like the last drop of blood that seals a spell, I found Will's face through layers of crowd. I looked at his smile, at the play of light on his skin, and felt the snap of magic completing itself.

WILL

I was complimenting Lacey's star cookies and explaining with a half-full mouth that I had to run to meet my brother for a late breakfast. "Yes," I said to Shanti's pointed glance at the empty cookie bag in my hand, "I'm gonna eat more."

She opened her mouth for whatever retort, but instead her mouth just stayed open. She and Holly, Kate, and Lacey all stared behind me with mixed looks. Kate and Lacey even shifted closer together, like they were grouping up against attack.

It was probably the pug in a princess costume I'd seen wandering around.

But when I turned my shoulder to look, it was only Mab.

She stood with one hand up at her ear. Frozen in the process of tucking her braid back.

"Hi, Mab," I said, surprised. I smiled. "You know . . ." I turned to the cheerleaders, who stared at me now. My smile faltered. Holly narrowed her eyes at me, and I said, "Mab and

I met, um, while I was out hiking, out on the prairie north of town." As if I had to explain.

Which I did, since ten minutes ago I'd let Holly go on like I had no idea who Mab was.

Disappointment became a polite smile as Holly turned to Mab. "Hi. Did you want some cookies?"

All the other girls turned their smiles back on, like it was a cue. "All proceeds go to the Mars and Kemp Scholarship fund," Shanti added.

Mab squinted her mouth like she didn't understand the English. "No, no thank you. I just"—she looked back at me—"I wanted to ask Will something."

"Sure thing," I said.

But Mab tilted up her chin. "Alone." She washed any sign of uncertainty off her face and waited.

Everybody waited.

I was trapped in a little pocket of girl politics.

Slowly, I nodded. "Okay. I have to go meet my brother, so if you can . . . walk with me?"

Shanti said, "Thanks for the coffee," a bit too sweetly, but Holly caught my eye and waved her fingers. I didn't think she was mad.

But it still felt like I'd just made a choice.

"Do you need to tell your mom?" I asked as Mab and I headed out of the market.

"That isn't my mom" was all she said. Unlike Holly, Mab ignored all the booths around, making her way clearly through the crowd. I dodged an old couple in matching Kansas City Chiefs T-shirts and caught up. Her hair fell everywhere, barely restrained by the little braids behind each ear, and her summer dress hung loose from her shoulders to just past her knees. She was barefoot. I nearly tripped over a wiener dog when I noticed. On this pavement the bottoms of her feet had to be, burning. And filthy.

She got to the street, only glancing at a busker with a fiddle. She smiled at him and then asked me, "Which way?"

"Um." I looked up and down the road. "Left."

We crossed and headed through a wide alley painted with bright murals onto the main drag. Either side of the street was lined with shops and restaurants, old lampposts and small trees. The buildings were tall and narrow, mostly brick. It looked like a modern Old West town, and I had a sudden memory of when we first moved here, of Aaron geeking out because the whole place had been burned down in eighteen sixty-something, during the Civil War.

Mab walked to one of the concrete boxes that surrounded the trees. She climbed up onto it and stepped in, balancing on the thin roots. Her shoulders relaxed. I hadn't even noticed how stiff she'd been.

"You don't like the city," I said. I sat on the concrete.

"It's horrendous. At least they let *some* trees grow." She reached up and brushed her fingers along the undersides of the little oval leaves. "It would be better if they built with wood." She perched next to me, leaning her hands back into the roots and dirt. Cars drove past, sharking the parking spots all up and down the street. A crow cawed, and I glanced up to see one perched on the edge of a fake balcony right overhead. Only one, though. I looked all around for the rest of Mab's friends.

She inhaled suddenly, like cocking a pistol. "Will, why were you at the lake on Sunday?"

"Uh." I smiled at a family of four walking past us on the sidewalk. The little boy stared at me and waved a grubby hand. When they'd passed, I told her what I hadn't told anybody. "I was having nightmares about it."

"About the lake?"

"Do you remember the earthquake a few weeks ago?" My voice went all hushed, as if it was a secret. A secret that had been in the newspaper.

Mab only nodded. Her eyes were so blue. Like, animation blue.

"I was at the lake for it, and Holly, who you met back at the booth, she fell in. I dove in and found her." I rubbed my hands slowly together, focused on the hissing sound they made. "My dreams are about that. Diving through muddy water. Not being able to find her. That kind of thing. I thought maybe if I went to the lake and, like, purged the memory, I'd be able to sleep." I ran my hands through my hair, rough on my skull. "Guess that sounds ridiculous."

But when I looked at Mab, her face had gone all loose and happy. "I don't think so at all, Will. I think you were exactly right."

"You do?"

"You were meant to be there. Your dreams drew you to the lake that very morning. And so we met." She said it matter-of-factly. Not like it was full of destiny and New Age woo-woo. "Our paths connected."

I stared. There was dirt smeared on her forehead. And that

hair. So bright she'd never be missed at the bottom of a muddy lake. I thought of her jumping out of the tree with goggles on her head. Of the heart dissolving in her hands. It made my nightmares flash past. All mud and roses and sharp cuts on the palms of my hands. I winced.

"Will?"

"Yeah, I'm just . . . fine." I smiled, pushing to convince her it was nothing. It *was* nothing.

Mab touched my chest, exactly where the antler had jammed into me. Where there'd been a pale bruise for six days.

Her fingers were cool through my T-shirt. Just like when she pressed her bloody hand against me and told me it was all impossible.

I grabbed her hand suddenly. "It was real. Not impossible."

To my shock, Mab said, "It was a homunculus."

"A what?"

"A man's body that I created of earth and gave life."

I stared at her.

Mab waited. She pushed hair over her shoulder.

"Are you serious?" I asked.

"What do you think it was, if not the thing I say?" She tilted her head, and the crow on the fake balcony cawed. It flapped down, and a woman jogging with earphones in gave us all a wide berth. The crow landed in the tree next to Mab and tilted its head just like hers. I stared at it. At its glossy black feathers. At the dark brown eye that stared right back.

"Will?"

"Uh." I looked at the cracked concrete. *The mud monster.* What did I think it was? How could a thing made of mud and branches and rocks and feathers and a bloody heart be real? What else could it be? An alien? Government conspiracy? There wasn't anything more believable than what she'd said. Slowly I lifted my eyes to hers again. "I guess I think it was a homunculus."

The smile she offered back made me glad we'd walked away from the cheerleaders.

I smiled, too, and we stood there like we had nothing better to do. A car door slammed, and I jerked. "I gotta get to Ben. Um, thanks, Mab. For telling me."

Mab turned my hand over and drew an invisible circle in my palm. "You were meant to know."

SIXTEEN

All through the winter I ordered myself to let go of my infatuation. To work, to appreciate the stark beauty of our prairie winter. Crows nestled in the trees around the house, red cardinals and their dour mates, too, along with the robins and sparrows and blue jays I fed with bits of seed meant for the chickens. They were spots of color against the silver, white, and sometimes liquid blue of the sky. Their songs were like bells in the wind.

Gabriel spent days at a time away from us in the city, where there was jollity and company, he said, and plenty of alcohol to keep him warm. He tried to take me with him once, but I told him he was ridiculous to think having his niece around would have anything but a nullifying effect on his revelry. He insisted and cajoled, but I couldn't have left you—the thought of you alone in the wild, part of nature yourself, was too delightful to my imagination.

You would go out into the winter and blend in, all white and gray and blue, vanish for the entire day doing I knew not what. Other days you remained in your bedroom, sleeping, it seemed, or doing something so quiet I never heard you move. I peeked in once, on a day so still I could hear ice cracking, and you lay on your bed so deeply unconscious you hardly seemed to breathe.

I cooked or tended to the wash and upkeep of our few warm clothes, and many afternoons I read from the surprisingly large library you kept along one wall of the parlor. Collected magazines and old periodicals, books by authors both modern and old. There was little poetry, though, which I missed from school.

I was alone but never felt lonely, especially with the radio and the birds, with the hope that any moment you'd come downstairs to join me, or come in from the cold and let me take care of you.

One evening I heard you singing under your breath, "Our Love Is Here to Stay," as you unbuttoned your coat near the front door. I remembered the feel of your hand against my stomach.

I told myself it was hopeless, but walked straight to you and began to hum along. I offered my hands, and you took them. We waltzed through the house, and I tried not to think of all the years piled on your shoulders, or your wife and the children you'd certainly had before.

I closed my eyes and felt the warmth of your hands, pretending we were only a girl and a boy, simple, oh-so-normal, and free.

SEVENTEEN

MAB

The encounter with Will left a residue of wonder against my skin, shielding me from the hard concrete and asphalt of town. It coated my tongue and made me smile at the shopkeepers more brightly than they were used to. Mr. Meldon, who sold me raw rubies, said I was looking mighty pretty, and Pamela Ann in the tea shop asked if I had a new beau. I did my best to answer mysteriously. On the drive back to Eli and Faith's house, I taught Lukas a simple song, and we sang it in three parts with Donna, around and around, until Donna put her hand on my shoulder gently and smiled with approval.

We grilled free-range chicken in their backyard, and I kept my promise to show Hannah blue fire. I danced it over my fingers while she stared in awe. Lukas huddled his legs up to his chest, but he did not move away, the brave boy. After dinner Faith had to say my name three times when she wanted me to run inside for extra napkins, I was so lost in my thoughts. When I returned I surprised them all with rare extravagant magic: blowing a gust of wind around the yard to ruffle the row of petunias against the back fence and light the mosquito-warding incense that hung from the trees.

"Someone is in a delightful mood," Faith said, patting hair my wind had loosed back behind her ears.

"She made a new friend today," Donna put in, eying me.

I put on a lofty smile and joined the adults at the picnic table. Hannah was busy showing Lukas the plastic dinosaurs in the sandbox. "We'd met before, so it's hardly new."

"A young man, was it?" Eli pretended to frown, but there was a teasing lift to his left eyebrow.

"It's nothing!" I insisted, but caught myself too late, thinking of Will's bare shoulders and the quick way he dispatched my doll. The pull of his smile in that moment he chose to believe me.

"That's not a nothing look on your face," Faith teased.

I shrugged and reached for Caleb to haul him into my lap for a shield. They took pity on me as I buried my nose in his sticky baby curls. He smelled like barbecue sauce and, I imagined, was in the process of smearing it all over my dress. I let him twist his little hands in my hair and whisper secrets I only half understood. And I thought about the pattern underlying the past month of my life. Since Arthur died, since he shook the world and knocked a stranger out of a tree. Since Will Sanger rescued her but gave himself nightmares that drove him back out to that lake on the exact day I chose to unburden the roses. That he was there at the right moment, come full circle, to delay the doll long enough for me to arrive, and without instruction sensed that he needed to remove the antler binding it all together.

And here we'd met again, and even beyond that, Will had looked into my eyes and chosen to see the magic.

This was more than a full circle, it was a woven pattern that wasn't complete. I didn't understand it, not yet, but that was my favorite time: when everything was new and filled with potential. *Here are the pieces of a great spell, little queen,* Arthur might have said. *How will you fit them together?*

I had not the faintest idea but only knew that whatever happened next, Will was a part of it, and it would be exciting.

WILL

My mind was full of crazy things while I sat across from Ben and Mom and Dad. They'd all three come, instead of just Ben, and we ate at a breakfast place full of local art and self-serve coffee. The conversation went on easily without me. Then Mom took us shopping. By which I mean we trailed after her from art shop to bakery to antique toy store. I quietly followed, thinking of Mab.

When Mom and Dad headed into yet another store, Ben stopped me. "Isn't there that train park right up the block?"

"Yeah."

"And we parked right around here," he said, dragging me along. When we got to the little two-hour lot, he opened the trunk to pull out two plastic grocery sacks. Tossed me one, a challenging smile plastered on his face. I caught it against my chest and dug in. Marshmallow guns. I grinned. The guns were just PVC piping in an L shape that you shot mini-marshmallows out of like blow darts. They looked like the kind of thing Aaron and I would've cobbled together out of crap in the garage.

"Let's go down to the train," he said, jiggling a second sack full of marshmallows. "I guarantee I'll kick your ass."

"Better yet," I said, "we take the car home, load up the girls, and head out to Clinton Lake. For real war."

"I don't think you're ready for that, kid."

"You're doomed. I know the park way better than you."

"I get Havoc on my team."

"She'll never work for you."

"I have my ways of getting her to talk," he said in a crappy Russian accent.

We let Mom and Dad know. Then it only took about fifteen minutes to round up the dogs and drive out to the park.

And Ben had stuck bacon treats in his pockets. Valkyrie was an instant traitor.

The guns, with their biodegradable bullets and silent fire, were perfect for sneak attacks and running around out in the forest. The marshmallows doubled as extra treats for Havoc and Val, though I wasn't sure they were that great for their digestive systems.

It was over an hour of sneaking, climbing trees, avoiding the hordes of Saturday-afternoon hikers and bikers and picnickers, before I thought about Mab or Holly or the mud monster again. Or that I was having an awesome time with Ben. That we hadn't argued. And that Aaron wasn't hiding in the next grove over.

The guns were surprisingly hard to load, especially while running, and for best accuracy you only loaded one marshmallow. I chose to stuff in five or six at a time, going for dispersal instead of aim, but Ben turned out to be a stellar sniper. His weakness was Val—she couldn't be quiet and gave away his position every time.

We finally died of our million marshmallow wounds, collapsing beside the girls near a stretch of gravel meant for an RV hookup. I sprawled with my arms and legs out, choking as I gasped for air, my diaphragm sore from laughing and blowing my gun. The sky wheeled overhead, all bright blue and white clouds. I imagined I was up there, bird's-eye, wind slamming me around. I looked down at the state park, at the edge of the lake with all its fingery inlets, and the dam and the highway back to town. There I was, lying beside my brother, both of us sweaty and grinning, Havoc and Valkyrie panting with their legs splayed everywhere in the grass.

My breath evened out, and I closed my eyes. I thought about Mab and how she'd been so tense in town. Out here was more her: wind in leaves, lapping water on the other side of the trees. Insects buzzing. Ben's breathing, the harsher pants of the girls. Val's tail thumping on the ground. The whole world was loud if I listened.

And apparently also full of a whole lot of things I didn't understand.

"What are you thinking about so hard?" Ben asked.

I didn't open my eyes. The sun was a hot red glow through my lids. It warmed my face, drying the sweat at the neck of my shirt.

"You've been quiet all day," he continued. "You can tell me."

"Just . . . weird things. There's been a lot going on, and I don't really know what to believe."

"What kind of things?"

I shrugged, grating my shoulders against the hard ground. The grass was thin here. "Just stuff. I'm not sure how to explain."

"So. You don't need advice."

"No." I opened one eye and slanted it at him.

"It's a girl, isn't it?"

My laugh startled Havoc, and she pushed up and came to lie closer to me. I put my hand on her ribs and patted. "Yeah, I guess it is."

"Tell me about her."

I opened my mouth, but nothing came out.

Ben said, "I know a woman. Her name's Lauren, and she's a combat correspondent. We haven't had a date or anything, and I don't know how it'll all arrange itself. But I know it will. Someday."

"That sounds crazy."

"I know." He laughed, too. "It is. But every time I look at her, I have this feeling of . . . it's like peace and chaos at the same time."

Leaning up onto one side, I studied Ben. He was really trying here. Like we actually knew anything about each other. Or were supposed to. "Mab's not . . . I don't know if it's like that," I said. I hadn't really been thinking about her that way. There was too much else surrounding it. The *homunculus*. The dreams. Those weird crows. Her being so different from everything else in my life. A colorful piece of total insanity.

Okay, maybe it was like that.

I said, "I don't know what to do."

"Trust it."

I rolled onto my back again. As if it was that simple. High up, a tiny airplane left a perfect line of white through all the jumbled clouds.

EIGHTEEN

Spring came with tiny green buds and thick air. I dug into my garden, planting peas and carrots, tomatoes, and sunflowers, then smaller boxes I filled with herbs for cooking and magic.

The prairie woke slowly from the winter, and I felt, too, as though I were waking up. I walked the land on my own, while you shut yourself up into your barn with whatever projects a two-hundred-year-old man favored and Gabriel got himself involved in the electoral race in Lawrence. He brought home flyers and asked me to make tiny knit flowers to give away at campaign rallies. I obliged until I realized he was spelling them with tiny flecks of blood to be more than just pretty prizes. It was the first time we truly fought, he and I. It was ugly, and I'd never had my heart race so violently. And it drove him off the land for a month, do you remember? He was so furious he rented rooms in a boarding house along the Kaw.

One morning I was breaking ice off the well by dropping the bucket again and again, in order to water my young garden, worrying that this sudden frost would kill it all before it had a chance to sprout, and there you were suddenly. You took the bucket and said, "The flowers will like running water better than this." Together we walked along the Child Creek, and you filled the bucket with fresh, tumbling cold water. You carried it for me up the hill to the garden, and we parceled it out, going back to the creek three times. When we finished, you settled back onto your heels. "This smells like life," you said.

135

I pointed out the different plots, the herb boxes, and told you which were for eating, which for magic. For the first time, you asked me a question: "I don't see you touch the magic often. Why not?"

For someone who breathes magic, it must have seemed strange how I avoided it. "It's a tool, isn't it?" I said, hoping not to offend you. "When I need warmth but have no stove, I make fire. When I need to find something and my eyes don't see it, I search with blood and a mirror. When I need protection from things stronger than me, I make an amulet. If I don't need the magic, I don't use it."

You studied my face, and said, "That is wise, Miss Sonnenschein, but I believe it makes you miss much of the beauty in it. You do not need a sunset, you do not need music, and yet both things make life more than just eating and sleeping. We can survive without dancing, we can survive without love." Your eyebrows lifted and my breath caught in my chest. "Yet who would want to?"

My fingers shook, and I dug them into the earth, into the row of baby peas. I slowly nodded, and said without looking at you, "You're right."

"The magic is in your blood. It's a part of you, and there is nothing wrong with exploring its beauties, beyond practical necessity."

There was something new in the edges of your voice, and I glanced up. It was laughter, playing at the corners of your mouth.

I wanted more than anything to kiss it, to catch your amusement with my lips. But afraid to startle you, or lose the moment, instead I smiled and asked, "Will you show me your favorite beautiful thing?"

Your eyes widened, as if I had finally surprised you. And you promised that when you could, you would.

NINETEEN

WILL

Almost exactly a week after I tackled the mud monster, I stood in the driveway with Ben. Hot sun pressed down on the shoulders of my dress shirt. I wanted to loosen my tie before it choked me. Ben leaned his elbow on my shoulder. His eyes kept going to the basketball hoop hanging five feet over the roof of the truck. But we'd dismissed the idea of shooting after a brief discussion of the possible repercussions of getting sweaty before church.

Better to suffer boredom until Mom popped out of the house.

Plus, I wasn't sure I could move that fast.

I rolled my head to stretch my neck muscles. Overnight I'd had dreams about roses clogging my throat until I couldn't breathe. Since waking, I'd been vaguely light-headed. Probably just from sleep deprivation.

"You good?" Ben asked, lifting his elbow off me.

"Sure." I shrugged. Closed my eyes against the hard sunlight.

Ben hovered. I peered out through one eye to find him studying my face with a bit of a glare.

I closed my eye again. His finger pushed into my shoulder, shoving me over.

Dizziness turned my stomach.

"Your face is all red," he said. He gripped my arm. "I think we should go back inside."

The sun pounded down.

"Will."

It sounded like Ben had moved away—like half a football field.

"*Will.*"

I shook my head. Blood roared in my ears.

He touched me, sliding a hand around my back. Said, "You're on fire," and pulled me toward the house.

Looked like it was gonna be my fault we missed church again.

Roses held me down. My mom brushed hair away from my head. Murmured about a fever, and then the roses pulled tight. Thorny vines circled my neck. I struggled. They piled blankets on me. I told them I was hot. Too hot.

Sometimes I knew I was dreaming. Other times I couldn't tell if Aaron was sitting on my bed, or if it was Ben. A second woman danced around my bedroom, arms out to waltz. She bent over me and smiled, tried to coerce me up to dance with her. "This is my favorite song," she whispered.

The walls of my bedroom crawled with roses. They clung to the ceiling, digging their thorns in deep. The red flowers nodded at me, all at the same pace. The beat of my heart. Vines swarmed over my body. My mouth was full of petals. I coughed and they floated up. I leaned over the side of the bed and Mom was there, clutching my shoulders, saying my name.

I gagged on flowers, and puked into a bowl Mom lifted off the floor.

She rubbed my back and helped me lie down again. I fell asleep.

It was dark when I shot up out of yet another nightmare. I'd been drowning again. This time in thin, cold mud.

A tight band of pain hugged my ribs. They wouldn't expand enough for me to get a solid breath, and I stared up at the popcorn ceiling. It was bare. No roses anywhere. Just my room. The alarm clock said it was 1:43 a.m.

I ordered myself to relax. Took stock of my physical situation.

The fever was gone. No sweat. No burning up inside. My head vaguely ached, and I was thirsty. My muscles were sore, but not too bad. Overall, I felt pretty good. But I was wide awake. And smelled sour.

My vertigo was gone, too, so I made it to the dark bathroom without any noise. In the shower, I just let the not-too-hot water drip off my nose. When I was out and had turned on the light to brush my teeth, I studied myself in the mirror.

Shadows under my eyes and a pretty tired stoop in my shoulders.

And holy crap, the bruise from last week, from the antler jamming into my chest, was darker.

I shut my eyes, flicked the lights off and on, and looked again.

It wasn't just shadows or me being wrecked. I touched the dark blotch, and it didn't hurt from pressure. But I felt it, inside. Like it was a weight pushing in on me. And the edges of the bruise, which had been yellowing before, reached out purple again. Like a fresh bruise. Could I have hit it again? Was it an infection?

Leaning in, I carefully examined my chest. Ran my fingers over it, looking for a cut. It wasn't like I could get a staph infection from a bruise.

That I knew of.

Maybe it was time for more Internet research. Either that or telling Mom, which seemed like a crap idea. She'd get all upset. Take me to the hospital.

What I wanted to do was call Mab.

Which seemed kind of dumb. What was she going to do? Kiss it and make it better?

Before I could stop it, that's exactly what I imagined.

Mab, standing in front of me, leaning down and kissing my bare, messed-up chest.

I shut my eyes again. And got out of the bathroom.

MAB

In my dream, it had rained for three days, but there was finally a break in the storm, and so the crows and I raced outside to enjoy it. Water splashed up my calves as I dashed around the front yard, arms out, laughing with them. The sun shone on a million droplets of water, clinging to blades of grass and leaves, to the flower petals, to the roof—even to the air itself. The drops glittered and winked. I caught them up on my fingers and set them on my tongue, tasting the magic. Crows batted through the trees, splattering their wings, drawing out more glistening drops that sparkled like black diamonds.

But only ten crows darted overhead. Considering the one I'd sacrificed for the doll, there should still have remained eleven. I turned in a circle, hunting for the missing bird. "Where have you flown to?" I called.

As if in response, the entire flock took off down the road, flying swiftly toward the front gates. I ran after them.

The land rose up around me, reaching fingers of magic to caress my face and out-flung hands. I closed my eyes and let the trees guide me, relaxing into their embrace and trusting completely that they would never let me fall.

Mab. The whisper came from all around me.

I was soaked to the skin, my dress plastered against me, mud and grass splattered up my legs. Trees bent around me, my feet never touched the ground, and I flew as genuinely as the crows. Wings made of flowers and leaves spread away from my shoulders.

Mab.

It was the forest, calling my name in the voice of the roses.

I was wild and wonderful, and when the doll strode out from between two elm trees I opened my arms. It embraced me and kissed me. I clung to it, mouth wide and welcoming. Vines and roses wrapped around me, weaving us together, as the doll lowered me down to the wet, warm earth. I laughed and kissed it. I wrapped my arms and legs around its strong body.

As it kissed my neck, I whispered magical words, cleansing

words, and the vines and earth fell away until all that was left was Will. Whole, fresh, and naked as if he'd been reborn.

And I woke up, alone in my bed, pain in my shoulder from a crow perched there, cutting deep into my skin with his claw.

I panted, hands flat against the mattress, body reeling. The other crows stared at me from a circle, perched on my shelves, on the windowsill, on the foot of my bed. My tongue tasted like the forest, and my heart had wings. Moonlight played across the dry black feathers of the crows. I swiftly counted: only ten. That part of my dream was true.

Tossing off the thin sheet, I darted out of my room and nearly tripped over the shattered body of the eleventh crow. Its beak was open wide and its feet mangled. I cried out, floating down to my knees as if still dreaming. Through tears I saw feathers spreading out in a trail behind it on the hardwood floor.

And Lukas, sprawled half in Arthur's bedroom, half out, his face squeezed in pain and blood seeping through the back of his white T-shirt.

I threw myself to my feet and scrambled to him, hitting the ground again hard. "Lukas," I said sharply, touching his face with my hand. His cheek was alive with heat, and the smell of burning skin suddenly overwhelmed me.

Lukas's hands were smoldering.

I yelled for Donna.

Little lines of orange fire played over the boy's fingers, flaring in a familiar pattern. The palm of his hand was a mirror image of the edge of the black candle rune, and I suddenly understood why there were so many burn scars on his hands: Lukas had tried to fight the magic with his own. His father's spell powered up, and Lukas tried to burn it away.

From his own body.

Donna ran up the stairs. "Mab?"

"Bring blessed water, and a knife."

She pushed past me and the circle of silent, watching crows to the bathroom, while I spat into Lukas's palm and rubbed my saliva in a spiral. "Be cool as the rain," I murmured, biting my teeth together as the spit steamed off his skin and the tip of my finger burned.

I grasped his other hand, sweat pricking along my backbone. We had to stop the burning before I could even turn to the rune in his back. Donna fell to her knees on the other side of him, a bowl of blessed water sloshing as she set it down.

Before I could take the knife from her other hand, Donna slashed the back of her wrist too deeply, and dripped blood into the already blessed water, to make it more potent. Shocked at her decision, I unrolled the thin strips of bandages she'd brought, laying them out and ready.

If we could have turned him over, it would have helped, but his T-shirt was sticking to the small of his back now, and his breath was ragged. I couldn't wait.

Donna realized it the same moment I did, and said, "I can do this part."

I tore back to my room and pulled Mother's box out from under the bed. Heavy and unwieldy, it kept me from having the dexterity to dance around the mingling crows with it in my arms, and I yelled at them to move, knocking two of them out of my way. The box was sealed with wax, and I grabbed Donna's knife to break through.

The lid opened with a puff of cinnamon-smelling air. I grabbed the vial of vesta powder, a black and red ribbon braided with a long piece of my own hair, and a sharp scalpel. I whispered the chant for holding down the heavy magic I kept locked in this box, letting it fall shut as soon as I could.

Cutting away the bottom of Lukas's shirt, I lifted it off the bleeding black candle rune. He whimpered, and Donna took up a lullaby as she wrapped his hands in blessed water. I let his blood flow more freely, and with the scalpel swiftly cut a binding rune into his skin just above the spidering candle rune. I scattered vesta powder into my palm and cut open my tattooed wrist, knowing how much it would sting later, although this scalpel was too sharp to feel now. I mixed my blood into the fine white powder, then drew it over the bleeding rune I'd marked on Lukas's back. He struggled, and I pressed him down. Donna held his wrists while I wound the braid of ribbon and hair around his belly, then tied it off with a triple knot. I cut myself again, hard enough to make a heavy flow, smeared the blood between my hands, and clapped both bloody palms onto him, marking my fingers and my blood in a red shadow over the top of the black candle rune. "I bind you by blood, by earth, by knots. I bind you in my hands, I bind you," I whispered.

Lukas sucked in a huge breath and then stilled.

The hallway was dark and silent, with only the rustle of crow wings and Donna's humming to mar it. I sank back against the wall, my insides atwist and my tongue still burning with the spell.

TWENTY

As the earth warmed that year, I paid attention to your magic, and Gabriel's, more closely than I had before. I saw that you used it constantly. More than just breathing it, you touched the trees in the morning, and their branches bent in, as if they wished to share it with you. Gabriel listened to them, and closed his eyes throughout the day—before, I'd thought he was only pensive or privately laughing. But no, he was hearing the voices of the trees. He saw me catch him at it and said, "They know more about dreaming than you or I."

I glanced out the kitchen window on a warm afternoon, when the front meadow was pale green and yellow with dandelions. A streak of red caught my attention, and I realized Gabriel lay prone in the middle of a patch of clover. Dropping my dough, I rushed out, falling to my knees beside him. "Gabriel?" I touched his shoulder, and then his forehead. His face was still as death—as when you spent all day in your bedroom. It was not sleep, nor death. I leaned down and put my cheek to his chest. His heart beat but slowly, and he breathed once for every twelve of mine.

Fear scoured through me, and I rocked back, hugging my knees against my chest. The sun behind me turned my shoulders hot, and sweat gathered under the heavy knot of my hair. But I didn't move. I had no idea where you were, and struggled between running to find you and not wanting to abandon him. "Gabriel?" I whispered again.

The hill's oaken crown shook, bright green leaves whispering back at me. Overhead, the sky was blue with a hundred thick white clouds, pressing down, the lovely afternoon suddenly ominous, watching me and listening to my every breath.

I touched Gabriel's forehead, but he was cool, his face relaxed and youthful. Quite handsome without the slick, wary smile.

His eyelashes twitched, and he turned his face into my palm. "Evie," he said, his hand coming up to grasp my wrist. "Are you crying?"

Not knowing I had been, I reached up and caught the drops of water on my cheek. "I was afraid. Are you well? What happened, Gabriel?" I leaned over him and slid my hand beneath his neck to help him sit.

A small laugh spilled out of him. "I am fine, Evie! I was only out of my body."

And then you were there, rushing out of the forest and coming to sit beside me. You put your hand on my back, and between the two of you I felt suddenly safer and yet caught in the middle of a maelstrom. There was no room for me.

Together you tried to teach me to leave my body behind, to fling myself up into the clouds and fly as a hawk, or to chase in spirit the deer who grazed in our most western meadow.

Gently, you unbuttoned the collar of my dress. I barely breathed, with Gabriel near behind me and you, so careful not to touch my skin. I focused on your eyes, though they remained low on my collar. The short curve of your pale lashes teased me. Oh, Arthur, how I wished we were alone in that moment, that you would look up at me, or lean in to kiss my neck.

Gabriel said, "Breathe, Evie," a quiet chuckle behind his voice. He was bold enough to put his fingers on the small strip of my bare shoulder.

I released the breath I'd been holding as you pushed aside only the very top of my dress and said, "There is nothing to fear."

You cut your finger and drew a spiral over my heart with your blood.

It was hot and thrilling, a tether from my spirit to my body, a spiral path to follow up and again back down. I could do it, I could let go and slip up with you, could dance beside you and Gabriel, all of us crows playing between the low clouds. You led us from body to body, and Gabriel then drew us into the trees. The earth was quieter and stranger, with no mind of its own but only broad feelings, interconnected lines of power.

I drew us safely, softly back into our own bodies. You laughed breathlessly and Gabriel clutched at our hands, while I lay, nausea spinning in my belly. You said that would fade as I became used to the changes, as my body learned. But I said, "No, I don't think I want to do it again."

Gabriel leaned up on one elbow, and you sat up, cross-legged like a boy, frowning sadly. "Why ever not?" Gabriel asked.

I gazed past both of you, up at the blue sky, and remembered the thrill of flight, the peace of the trees. "Because I can feel those things from here." I rubbed my hand over your spiral of blood, dry and cracked against my skin, and put that hand to the earth. Magic gathered in my palm and diffused into the dirt. The grass trembled and turned golden all around me, the wind swept my hair across my face, and I heard the planet turning, creaking, breaking, and changing, as it did every moment of every day. "I belong in this body; I was born into it. I'm part of the wild just as I am."

I looked at you both, and Gabriel smiled his patronizing half smile, then smoothed back his hair with both his hands. You watched me, the frown fallen away, but I could not discern your thoughts. You were, then, such a mystery to me. Maybe you were thinking back to our earlier conversation, when I said the magic was a tool and you told me I was missing the beauty. So I touched your knee and said, "I do not have to be a cloud in the sky to see all the colors of the sunrise. My eyes, my heart, my mind—they appreciate much a crow cannot."

TWENTY-ONE

MAB

I slept through all of the morning, exhausted from the binding spell I'd performed on Lukas. By the time I did wake, it was late in the afternoon, and I was famished. Downstairs, Donna had hot tea ready for me. I sank down and breathed in the fumes, glad for the willow and ginseng and basil I smelled. They would rejuvenate me, filtering through my body with light energy to make up for the long night. Maybe I'd be able to heal the stinging cuts on my wrist that pulled every time I shifted my hand.

Donna put cold chicken and cheese and oat crackers in front of me, and I ate voraciously. She sat beside me and asked, "Do you know what happened?"

Through crumbs, I said, "Only that his father must've pulled on whatever dark spell he attached to Lukas. I don't know why the crow . . ." My eyes trailed to the cedar box sitting on the counter beside the coffeepot. "I should try to find out. Have you seen the rest of them?"

She pointed at the ceiling. "They're holding vigil on the roof, most of them right over Arthur's room."

"Good." I felt mightily better with food and tea heating my insides. "I looked in on Lukas, and I think he's all right for now. Sleeping. The binding held, but binding is only temporary."

"It doesn't have to be." She leveled me with a mother's look.

"It does. Binding that spell bound his own magic, too, and even if he doesn't want it now, which we don't know is the case, he might one day. There must be a better solution."

"Plenty of people get on every day without this blood, Mab."

I sipped my tea and stared at her over the rim but said nothing. Donna sighed, shaking her head, and pushed to her feet. She dumped her own tea into the sink and said, "I'm going to go into town and get some pills for him. He's got a fever, and we're out."

Frowning, I tried to think of an argument against it, but there weren't any. The magic holding down that black candle rune was complicated, and we couldn't afford to distract the flow of his blood with our usual healing remedies. Medicine would have to do. "Just no blood thinners."

"They might not be a bad thing," she said as she rummaged through the fridge and pantry. "I'll stop and get some beef, too, for a good stew. Enough so we don't have to go out again soon."

I stood up and tugged on her long sleeve. "Thank you," I said.

Donna straightened up, a nearly empty box of cereal in hand. "For?"

"Last night. Your magic."

Her breath eased out of her, melting her stiff shoulders. "Can't ignore my feet if I want to get across the street, now, can I?"

I laughed just a little, and she touched my shoulder. "You figure out what we can do for that boy, and I'll help you when I can." And Donna squeezed me before heading toward the hall.

I heard her lift the station wagon's keys off the peg near the front door and head out.

Nibbling on a strip of chicken breast, I went and placed my free hand on top of the dead crow's box. The wood was warm, tingling ever so slightly with power.

That was two crows dead in just over a week: more than in the whole year before. I rubbed a circle against the wood. They died sometimes. Of fighting with blue jays, or once, in a storm, one of them broke his wings trying to fly inside. We'd burned the poor battered bodies, and I'd scattered the ashes from the top of my silo. And yet Reese had always found replacements, additional crows to fill out his flock.

A tiny pinched feeling in my stomach made me set the chicken down and clutch up the box instead.

This time, part of me wondered if they'd find any new wings.

WILL

I spent most of Monday on the sofa with Ben, heels on the coffee table, watching a string of movies. He picked an old favorite: *Nightmare on Elm Street,* which made my skin crawl because of recent events. Halfway through, I shut it off. But he didn't want to watch any action movies, either. He wouldn't admit it, but I was pretty sure it was all the shooting that turned him off. By the time we'd settled on and made it through five episodes of a *South Park* marathon, Mom believed I was going to live. I hadn't had a temperature all day or vomited since Sunday afternoon. To prove the vertigo was gone, I spun in a circle for her. And I didn't mention the bruise on my chest. Or the slight headache rooted behind my eyeballs.

Convinced, she ran out for groceries, promising to be home by the time Dad got off work. Ben offered to go with her if they could stop at a video store to pick up something decent to watch. I told him that in the twenty-first century we stream movies through the Internet. He said they'd done that in Afghanistan, but he hadn't been aware that Kansas was so caught up.

Before we devolved, Mom dragged him out the door and I was on my own.

I stood for a moment in the middle of the den. Quiet pervaded the house. Mom's car rumbled to life, and I listened as they pulled down the driveway. I couldn't hear anything.

My options were: turn on the TV, radio, or my iPod before the noiselessness got to me; call Matt; or go outside and crash around with the girls. I picked the last. Changed quickly into track pants and a T-shirt, then headed out back. I jogged across the yard to the kennel. "Hey, girls," I called. Val barked back, her high-pitched happy bark. It took a second to knock back the lock, then fling open the door. Val's tail whipped and her jaw hung open in a grin. I reached out to pet her. The muscles around my ribs pulled uncomfortably.

A growl stopped me.

Val's tail drooped, and both she and I looked right, to where Havoc stood with her legs wide, her ears back, and her lips pulled up over her teeth. She growled again.

At me.

"Havoc." It wasn't a strong response, but my voice couldn't push past the shock clogging my chest. "Hey, Havoc."

She growled again, her fur bristling. Valkyrie whined.

"Havoc!" I snapped, lowering my voice and straightening my back. "Sit." I chopped my hand down through the air.

Her growl only strengthened. I stared at her, remembering when Aaron and I had gone to pick the puppies up. All ears and tongues, they'd been rolling in this massive pile of brown and tan and black inside a playpen made for toddlers. Five of them, all females. Barking their tiny little barks, and one of them growling so high and cute it sounded like a bumblebee. Their mom lolled on the grass next to the pen, worn out but with her jaws open in a grin. Aaron had knocked his elbow into mine. "Dig your hands in, find out who bites."

I'd knelt and reached into the pen for the growling puppy. Lifting her out with my hands around her ribs, I'd put her against my chest and stared down into those black eyes. Her growls tickled my palms.

"That one doesn't like anybody," the breeder was saying. "She just growls and growls, though surprisingly shows no other signs of—"

But Havoc-the-puppy suddenly stopped. Her ears popped up and she stretched her neck forward to sniff at my mouth. I laughed and blew gently at her. She shook all over, then curled up in my hands and fell asleep. I hadn't put her down until we got home over an hour later.

Now she was full grown, a hulking, sprawling beast of a dog who'd never so much as considered disobeying me. Who'd leaned into my thigh the entire four hours of Aaron's wake while Val huddled in a corner.

I knew I should grab her ruff and force her to the ground,

should push in and remind her who was pack leader here, but I couldn't move.

Valkyrie hunkered down, head between her paws, and shifted her eyes from me to Havoc. "Val," I said, slapping my thigh. "Come."

Neither dog listened.

I tried again, but even I could hear the uncertainty in my voice. "Havoc?"

She jerked forward, barking. It was like a punch in the gut, and I fell back. Havoc followed me, her bark getting angrier. I got out of the kennel as she took a swipe at my hand, and skidded over the grass to grab the door and swing it shut. It clattered into place and I threw the lock, put my back against it. Her claws scratched the wood as she slammed herself up. The wall of the kennel shook, but was solid. I closed my eyes, gasping for breath. What was wrong with my dog?

Turning, I pressed myself to the fence and peered through the slit between two two-by-fours. Her front paws were up at chest height, and she barked hard again and again and again. "Havoc!" I yelled. Her voice hit me over and over, and Valkyrie joined in. I stepped away, slapped my hands over my ears. They sprinted back and forth inside the kennel, shadows flashing between the boards.

I spun on my toes and ran inside, slamming open the back door and not bothering to close it. I dashed into the ground floor bathroom. The adrenaline surge felt like a strike of lightning. My stomach twisted and I glanced at the toilet, but I wasn't that bad. I wrenched the knob on the sink and filled my cupped hands with water. I flung it on my face. The cold shocked me, and I choked in a lungful of air. Long, cool trails of water trickled down my neck, hung off my chin. I closed my eyes. *Havoc.*

Trying to get a grip on myself, I put my hands flat against the wall on either side of the mirror. I blew a long breath and leaned in, all my weight on my arms like I was coming down from a push-up against the mirror. When my face was inches away, I stared at my own eyes. They were brown, with a thin circle of gray at the edge of the iris.

At least, they were supposed to be.

I reached behind me and flipped on the lights. I winced away from the sudden glare but forced myself to lean in again.

Along the left border of my left iris was a very thin strip of bright red. Like my eye was bleeding.

"It could be natural," I whispered to my reflection. My breath fogged the glass. It could have been just like a bruise on my eyeball. Once a kid in my eighth-grade class on the Marine base in Okinawa had been in a bad bike accident, and he'd come to school with the white of his eye bloodred. But the whole side of his face was a giant bruise, too. I didn't have any injuries to my head.

This was too much. Something bad was happening to me, and it wasn't some regular disease. What kind of virus made your devoted dog suddenly turn on you? All I knew was where this had all started.

I only took time to run upstairs for my keys and cell phone before getting in my car and driving west for the prairie.

TWENTY-TWO

It should have been a slow, meandering, peaceful summer; my thriving garden offered more than enough for me to do. And I began experimenting with teas and soap and candles, taking the chore from you because of how much fun it was finding the perfect scent combinations, boiling tallow and dipping wicks, and adding just a hint of magic so that when we went to sell and trade for milk and meat, our neighbors clamored for our wares. I loved having my patient work bring sustenance to the land and our table like that.

As it grew warmer into June, I frequently spent afternoons with tea and a book in the shade of one of the oaks. The only problem was the forest cut most of the wind down, leaving me with only a feeble breeze to wick the sweat from my brow. I decided to plant a linden tree at the edge of my garden, something to give us fragrant blossoms in a few years and shade nearer to the house, where the wind reached.

But one afternoon Gabriel came charging out of the house, the screen door slapping hard. "Arthur!" He yelled, casting his voice over the whole land with his magic.

I was on my feet, stumbling in shock. My book fell to the ground and I ran up, demanding he tell me what was wrong. His dark eyes darted east again and again, then he sneered, not at me but at whatever emotion churned inside him. "Trouble's coming. I can smell her from here."

There was no other warning before we heard tires and the rumble of an engine making its way up the dirt road. We turned together to see a sleek but snub-nosed car push its way up the hill. The woman driving barely stopped the car before flinging open the door and leaping out. She wore an obvious red hat and a white sleeveless dress with red flowers falling down the left hip. Her golden hair curled perfectly under her ears, making me hate her just a little bit, and she tossed her sunglasses into the driver's seat, covering her mouth with a bright grin. "Hello, there!"

I don't think I'd ever seen such a gorgeous, flamboyant woman outside a movie, or anyone less suited to our quiet hillside. There was nothing for me to say, and Gabriel kept to my side.

She took two long steps toward us, strong and graceful as a lioness. "Is that you, Gabe?" Her smile shifted into something sharp, and I knew she didn't like him any more than he liked her.

How could this be a friend of Arthur's?

I lifted my chin. "Introduce us, please, Gabriel."

His fingers were tight on my elbow as he said, "Evie, this is Josephine Darly, a venomous, manic blood witch. Jo, this is Miss Evelyn Sonnenschein."

"What?" Josephine's blue eyes widened. "No epithets for the girl?" She winked at me. "He only doesn't like me because Arthur prefers me."

"Pities you, rather," Gabriel snapped. His entire body was rigid.

My horror at their bickering had no time to find a voice, for you came striding out of the forest, from the barn. You were behind her, but Josephine somehow sensed it, spinning on her toes like a little girl. "Deacon!" she chirped, which was a thing our neighbors called you, too, and then she dashed across the meadow, kicking off her red shoes and throwing her hat into the wind.

You caught her hands with a charmed smile, and I saw something on your face I'd never seen before. Excitement. You were thrilled to have her, eager when she kissed both your cheeks, and you barely waved at us as she tore you away, running and skipping toward the south, past my garden and over the spot I'd imagined for my linden tree. You took her careening down the hill to where the apple trees waited.

I remained breathless and trapped in a sudden stupor. "Gabriel?" I managed to whisper.

He rolled his eyes, shaking himself free of the same stupor. "They'll be back when they're finished." He started back into the house, but I was frozen.

"Finished what?"

From the porch step, Gabriel twisted around. "Devouring the world."

TWENTY-THREE

MAB

While the living crows guarded Lukas as he slept, I brought the body of the dead crow down to the workshop, which was built like a barn, and maybe a hundred years ago had worked as one, too. Bits and pieces of refuge from the land crowded everywhere, piled and shelved and gathering dust. The hull of an old rowboat leaned against a stack of crates, and when I was little it had been my favorite place for watching Arthur create potions and sketch. Every year when we redid the runes on the outside of the barn, I'd drawn charms on the underside of the boat with leftover paint. Once, Arthur crawled inside with me, hunched over to fit his back against the curve of the boat. He'd brought a candle and said it was a good, safe spot. Together we buried a circle of silver wire around it, and sang blessing songs. We wove a mat of cattail leaves and soaked it in milk and blood and honey. "The only thing that would make you safer here," Arthur said when we finished, "is if you had roots growing out of your knees."

At the long table, I set the crow's body carefully down, pinning the wings to the much-marred wood. I plucked out his breast feathers, laying them back in the cedar box for safekeeping. With one of the knives from the butcher's block, I sliced open the chest, glad his fellows had remained behind at the house. They would fly to me if Lukas needed me, and there was no need for them to watch as I carefully removed the long breastbone and cracked back the ribs.

The crow's heart was a burned husk.

I peered at all the little organs, at the shriveled, blackened insides. This crow had died from fire. I would have guessed electricity, except that I remembered Lukas's burning hands and the heat of the black candle rune.

A sad smile tugged at my lips, and I caressed one of the crow's long primary feathers, reveling in the sleek blackness.

I sprinkled salt onto the crow, whispering a song of thanks and rest, then harvested the best of the feathers before wrapping the small body in a red cotton shroud. He would be burned, and perhaps Lukas would like to help me scatter the ashes.

Afterward, I absently drew spirals against the table with my finger, over and over again, as I thought. The wood of the worktable was polished and smooth from years of use. Some bits were stained dark from spilled blood, but mostly it shone as rich as amber.

There had to be a way to remove Lukas's rune safely. Up at the Pink House were books with magical theory, mostly written by Philip Osborn, one of Arthur's very first students. He'd been predominantly a healer, and so perhaps I might find insights in the pages of his rune journals and experiments. The thought drew a sigh out of my belly: I never enjoyed studying, most especially when I didn't know where to begin, and when there was no one for me to discuss the possibilities with. It would be tedious work, but I had to, for Lukas's sake.

Except, I suddenly remembered, Silla had them. She'd asked to borrow all of Osborn's journals last year, before she began writing some kind of thesis.

Sinking to the packed-earth floor, I stretched out on my back. The rafters overhead glowed gently where sunlight found dust motes through the partially cracked southern edge of the roof. A trio of mourning doves nestled together, no doubt grateful I hadn't brought the crows down with me to chase them away.

I shut my eyes and imagined Arthur stood over me, sketching something onto one of his drawing pads. I'd used to sometimes lie here while he worked and ask him questions, staring at the easy slump of his shoulders, the sure way he moved his arms and hands. The scratch of pencil against paper would lull me to sleep, where I'd dream about drawings lifting up to life and flying around me like tiny fairies.

What would Arthur do? I played through everything I knew about the black candle rune, everything I could remember about how they were created. It was a bond between a specific spell or witch and the marked thing. How to get rid of it without hurting Lukas? I could keep him bound, and maybe someday the rune would fade. Or I could change the rune itself, perhaps reinterpret the intention. But burning it away clearly hadn't worked for Lukas.

That single time I'd helped Arthur destroy such a rune, to

protect Eli's friend, we'd gone back after a year and a day had passed to the twisted, dead walnut tree.

Frost had cracked beneath our feet as we stood beside the tree, and the sky was a sheet of thin gray clouds. The tips of my fingers grew numb from the cold as I clutched a bundle of beeswax candles in one hand, a lancet in the other. Arthur faced the tree, where the black candle rune crawled angrily across the bark. Just above, the hilt of a dagger thrust out: we'd stabbed it in the night before, and begun the cleansing spell with a song and the runes etched into the tip of the blade. Though the sky was overcast now, all night the full moon had shone down, and the dagger had leeched its power.

For nine hours, the delicate magic had curled into the heartwood. We were here now to set the final bit in motion.

Arthur said, "I feel it humming inside the tree."

Together we set out the candles in a circle around the tree. Nine of them, spaced equally, and each surrounded by an intricate rune of starlight that we drew with lines of salt.

When the circle was set, we stood across from each other. Holding out our left hands, we cut our tattooed wrists and let blood fall. Pacing one another, we walked sunwise, dripping blood onto the earth in the center of each of the starlight runes. Power slid through my veins, splashing to the ground. The magic rushed together by the time we'd both gone halfway around the circle to replace each other on either side. I smiled at the cutting wind that lifted up pieces of my hair and rattled the dead leaves on the branches above us. Arthur stepped inside and gripped the dagger with a bloody hand. "By my blood," he said, "cleanse this curse."

The surge of magic flared to life deep inside the tree and echoed in my chest. I held out my hands with my palms facing the earth. Arthur held tight to the dagger, and I watched his pale hair whip against his face in the wind.

Fire spat out of the black candle rune in quick, sharp tongues, and then went silent. The tree shook as its branches curled downward. I breathed in long intervals, and watched as the spell tore out from the rune, blackening the tree up and down, turning the leaves into ashes and making the roots quiver.

Arthur released the dagger, and the starlight runes flashed silver. For a brief moment I relaxed, but then I saw Arthur poised beside the tree trunk, fingers tense and his eyes on the ground.

Looking, too, I saw it. The frost melted in a ring around the tree, as if the brown grass cooked from below. Arthur stepped back, but the ring widened, spiraling out slowly and steadily. The dagger spell must have soaked not only into the tree but through the roots and out into the earth. Arthur met me at the edge of our nine-point circle, and we watched together.

Steam rose, thickening the air.

I had assumed the cleansing would only pass through the tree, but this spell crawled through roots and rocks, under the frozen mud.

It slithered under our circle, blackening the ground in its wake, destroying—no, cleansing—everything. If it escaped us, it might travel over the whole blood land, burning away all the magic!

Arthur frowned the same moment I yelled in surprise. I spun around, searching for a way to widen the circle ahead of it, to cast a firm and solid barrier. "Arthur?" My mind whirled furiously. "How do we get our blood around it?"

He watched me calmly. "What would you do if I was not here?"

"We don't have time! We have to save the trees!" I flung my hand toward the living forest, just yards away, where squirrels huddled in their winter nests and a red-tailed hawk gazed at us from the top of a pine, entirely unconcerned.

"Think," was all the Deacon told me.

As the cleansing crawled nearer and nearer to my feet, I slashed my palm with the lancet and pressed the blood over my heart. I whispered, "My familiar," and then "Reese." My blood flashed hot and sharp on my chest, and I flung out my hand so that flecks of the blood arced out into the air.

And he came—all twelve crows exploding over the forest so suddenly and silently the red-tailed hawk startled into the sky, too. It screamed its displeasure, but my crows only barked back and kept winging toward me.

Falling to my knees, I dug a binding rune into the earth with the lancet in quick, slashing motions. Arthur backed away, and the crows landed around me. My breathing was too fast as I pushed again at the edges of the wound on my palm, spilling blood and power into the rune. "Come!" I said, and the crows crowded near me, dipping beaks and the tips of their wings in the pool of blood cupping in my hands.

"Mab," Arthur said quietly.

I glanced up to see the blackening ground edging even

nearer, the steam from melting frost lifting up thinly and delicately.

"Bind the earth, with my blood," I commanded, "bind the sky, with my blood!" The crows cried out in a single voice, and I yelled, "Fly!"

They leapt into the air, the beat of their wings shoving wind at me. I knelt at my rune, pressed both hands down into the earth, and whispered my spell again and again while the crows flew hard and high, spreading into a wide circle. I chanted, and they flew sunwise, around and around. Arthur put his hands on my back and joined my spell, his hands sticky and hot with blood. His power rushed into me and his words echoed mine, over and over and over, a round with no beginning and no end.

The string of my power thrummed between me and all the crows, pulsing with my heart and with their wing beats.

And the binding circle held.

The cleansing curse hit the edge of my magic and died.

I'd crumpled to the side, exhausted, and Arthur caught me, dragging me half onto his lap. He kissed my palm and the cut healed. He brushed a thumb over my wrist and I was whole.

The crows returned one at a time, making hard, tired landings.

"Well done, little queen," Arthur said, with one finger lifting my chin so that I looked. The circle of black earth was contained, but at its center the walnut tree slowly crumbled into chunks of charcoal and ash.

The black candle rune was gone and burned away but had taken everything in a twenty-foot circle with it.

WILL

I drove back and forth along the half-mile stretch of county road I estimated was two miles south of Matt's uncle's lake. But I couldn't find the turnoff to Mab's land.

On my third pass I yanked the wheel. The tires threw gravel off the shoulder as I stopped. I cut my music.

Slowly, the oppressive silence melted into individual sounds. Wind, leaves clapping together, birds chirping—a lot of birds chirping—and . . . nothing else. No highway noise, no distant radio, no conversation or yelling kids or anything.

No dogs breathing down my neck.

My chest felt hollow. I wanted Havoc behind me, dripping drool onto my shoulder as she tried to see out the windshield.

I shut my eyes and imagined flying up into the sky, for that bird's-eye view of the area. In my head, I was exactly where I was supposed to be. There was the lake, and here the slow rolling hills. Dense tree cover, sudden wide-open field gone all prairie and fallow. This road snaking southeast, back toward the interstate.

It should be here.

I jumped out of the car and slammed the door behind me. The bang it made soothed me for a moment, and before the echo died completely I started off. The regular crunch-shuffle of my steps on the gravel was a relief, too.

The trees pushed against each other in a huge mess. No order, no pattern. Just thick trees and thin ones, tall trees with spreading branches, and short, squat little bush things. Fallen logs. Lots of piles of dead leaves from last year. I could only see about ten feet into the woods, too. The trees were so close together, and the canopy kept out so much sunlight. But there was definitely, certainly, no break in them big enough for a person, much less a car.

I tromped on. My girls would've found the path in no time.

About fifteen minutes later, I turned back the way I'd come. After only a few feet, I faced the forest and called, "Mab?"

My voice cracked out like a bullet.

"Mab?"

Nothing. Just the wind in the trees and a lessening of the birdsong. But it picked back up quickly.

"I need your help," I said, but too softly for anyone to hear even if they'd been standing just inside the line of trees.

A crow called. I jerked to attention.

I scanned the trees. It called again, and I saw it. A large black crow perched on a branch about ten feet off the ground. A dozen yards north of my location.

And right beside its tree, the forest parted to make room for a gravel road. It was impossible I hadn't seen it. I'd walked right past it. And driven past it three times.

The crow cawed twice in quick succession. I lifted a hand and jogged toward it, off the gravel and into the knee-high grass. "Thanks," I said, and saluted it. It flapped its wings and took off. I started to yell after it, but it only flew to the next tree, a few more steps into the woods.

It was drawing me inside.

The crow led me for several minutes straight through the dense underbrush. There wasn't any path, and I had to climb over logs and shove through bushes, using branches sometimes for leverage. But the forest barely noticed me. Branches snapped back into place when I passed, birds sang, squirrels ran overhead, leaping from tree to tree. I began to wish I had on long sleeves and boots. My sneakers did okay, but my forearms were scratched up in no time.

Eventually, the trees spread out just a bit. I was on a deer path. The crow overhead was joined by a second and then a third. They darted across the space in front of me, egging me on. The deer path was, like, six inches wide, and my pants brushed up against lush green plants with every step. As I walked, I kept an eye out for poison ivy. I was gonna have to do a serious tick check when I got home.

Sweat dripped down over my eyebrow, and I paused to wipe it away with the hem of my T-shirt. When I raised my head, I saw color flash ahead.

I jogged on, pushing past the crows, and emerged from the trees into a small grove. The grass was as tall as my knees, and totally wild. Little pink and white flowers bloomed in the center where the sun hit, and just past them was a barn.

It had been hard to see through the trees because it was painted gray, but a thick line of red striped the side horizontally, and over the double doors somebody had painted a huge, multicolored pattern. Some sort of star and circle and triangle thing. Bold and fresh—much newer than the rest of the barn. It looked layered, too, like it was repainted every year or so.

One of the doors was ajar, and two crows flew inside. The third waited for me on the ground.

That crow hopped through and vanished into the darkness. I gripped the door and pulled it back another inch or two. "Hello?" I said. No response. "Mab?"

But the crows clearly wanted me inside. I stopped after a foot to let my eyes adjust. It wasn't dark, just dim. Scraps of sunlight shone through the hole in the south corner of the barn's roof. A few little white birds scattered as the crows flew up to the rafters. There was a lightbulb dangling from the center, adding a bit of yellow to the dusty gloom.

Half the barn was full of old crap. Crates, pieces of a rusted tractor, empty gallon jars, feed sacks, and that sort of thing. The other half was more organized, but barely. A long wooden table dominated it, and rows and rows of shelves held boxes, vials, buckets, and I was pretty sure that was a cast-iron cauldron brimming with seashells. The table itself was almost bare. A block of kitchen knives perched at one end. A trunk was tucked under the table, and it was etched with weird old symbols like you'd see in a horror flick.

It all just hit me. Mud monster, too-smart crows, all these crazy dreams. Mab. Holding out that heart. Whispering over it.

Like freaking Gandalf. Or a witch. Only with goggles and a wild smile instead of warts and a pointy hat.

My sneakers stuck to the floor.

"Mab?" I managed.

The crow up in the rafters yelled, dove down to the table. It landed on the edge, scrabbling with its claws. I picked up my feet and made my way around the table. Nearly tripped over

Mab. She was lying prone on the hard-packed dirt, hands folded on her stomach, eyes closed. Her hair sprawled all around her like a Disney princess.

I crouched beside her, a hand hovering over her shin. It didn't look like she was breathing. "Mab?"

Her eyes flicked open.

MAB

When I heard my name, I firmly expected Arthur to be crouched there. Finding Will staring down instead rocketed me back into my body so fast it rattled my teeth.

"Mab?" he said, sweat beading on his forehead.

I didn't move. "Will," I whispered. "What are you doing here?" Surprise was tiny snowflakes melting on my bare arms.

His gaze did not waver from mine as he very simply said, "I need help."

I sat, which put me very close to him. He'd brought the forest into the barn: the scent of damp wood, mud, and blossoming trees. I also smelled sweat and soap made with chemicals that wrinkled my nose.

"Sorry." He stood up, wincing mightily.

"Oh no, I don't mind." I gripped his hand and used it to heave myself up to my feet in order to prove my point. "But some soaps have chemicals in them that could make you infertile."

"What?"

I faced him, not releasing his wrist. His skin was warm under mine, and his frown, his mouth, was level with my eyes, and I couldn't find my voice. In my dream, he'd kissed me, and I'd wrapped myself around him. The memory of it woke something in my belly, a tiny snake that wiggled up toward my tongue and freedom. I parted my lips to allow it out, just a breath, a sigh.

After a moment he said, "Mab, there's something wrong with me." He didn't say it with complaint, or a whine to his voice; it was merely a statement of fact. "I'm not sure what it is, though, or why, or if it's even something you can help me with."

His whole face moved while he talked, as completely animated and changing as water, and beside him, I was a rock grown up out of the ground. I very much wished to help him, and very much wished he'd keep staring at me. "Tell me."

Will opened his mouth again, and I waited, trying to keep my face relaxed instead of displaying the growing delight I felt in my chest.

Finally, he said, "I don't know where to begin."

"What's the most important thing?" I asked softly.

"This. My eyes. There's something wrong with them." Will leaned his face into my face, one eye shut and the other wide. He even pulled down the bottom of his eyelid with one finger.

I let myself put a hand on his cheek. The shadow from the lightbulb overhead darkened his face, though, and I couldn't see anything, so I tugged him around to the other side of the table, where I hopped up to sit. It put me a few inches taller than him. "Show me again?"

He leaned close and tilted his head up. I drew him all the way in to the edge of the table, and his jeans were rough as his hips brushed against my inner knees, pushing up my dress. My breath caught in my throat. Concentrating, with every ounce of resolve I could muster, I took his face between my hands to direct the angle of his head toward the light.

Will looked at everything but my face, blinking rather quickly.

"Will," I said.

He stopped moving and whispered, "Sorry."

I splayed my fingers across his cheeks, reminded myself this was my job, and peered into his left eye.

It was the color of a perfect acorn, with gray around it, and flecks of a paler brown. And there, just at the edge of color, a thin crescent of red, as if his iris were a moon eclipsing a bloody sun.

"It isn't supposed to be there," he said quietly, holding himself perfectly still except for his shaky in-and-out breaths.

"I don't know what it is." I slid my hands down to his neck, and he straightened his head. His mouth pulled into a frown, dragging the corners of his eyes with it.

And then Will sighed in frustration, his whole body melting closer to mine so that he could press his hands against the edge of the table on either side of my hips. I didn't move, or take my hands off his collar.

I could feel the flicker of his pulse under my fingertips.

Will's face was inches from mine, shifting emotions faster than the beat of a sparrow's wings.

I leaned in and felt his breath against my lips. I could so easily kiss him, let myself press closer.

He didn't move at all.

And I was the Deacon. He'd come to me for help, not romance, not this sudden, ridiculous infatuation tearing through me. I shifted away, covering my mouth with one hand as if I could hold inside the air I'd stolen.

"Mab." Will kept his hands on the table beside me, studying me as though I was this amazing, strange thing.

"Will," I whispered back, the exchange of names connecting us.

But.

But the pattern was coming together again. He'd found me in the middle of my land, through the hidden gates, and exactly where I'd been searching for answers. Where I lay under the blood family tree carved into the western wall of the barn.

Arthur once told me that when we worked with magic we were making connections. Between a flower and rheumatism, between water and earth, between breath and thunder. Finding connections and using our blood to make them strong and whole. We didn't make the carrot garden poisonous to deer and rabbits so much as change the animals' association with that patch, by shifting the connection between plant and instinct. Laying ointment on a burn didn't heal it, but reminded the flesh what it wanted to be by reconnecting it to memories. Your blood, and your willpower, had to be stronger than the damage.

It was the difference between nature and magic. Nature found connections, while magic created them.

Now the magic whispered in my ears, *Will is connected to us,* and it sent a thrill through my blood.

WILL

I was barely holding it together.

She'd nearly kissed me. I hadn't been able to move. The thought of it had scorched my skin. All over, making the headache burn behind my eyeballs.

Her hands were cold on my chest and her knees a constant pressure on my hips. I felt dizzy. And soaring. I shut my eyes tight, and then Mab's cool fingers touched my eyelids, soothing away the pain. "Tell me what else is wrong," she said.

"God, I don't know. It's a headache, a tingly, hot headache right behind my eyes." I looked at her, and her fingers fell away from my face. But she stayed so close. Her face was all pieces this close, instead of a whole.

Mab frowned. Her thin eyebrows drew together. "You're sweating," she noted.

"Yeah."

"It's cool in here. And the entire day has been cooler than usual." Mab put the back of her hand against my forehead. Her skin was like ice. I leaned in, it felt so good. "You have a fever."

"Not again." I moved away from her. But I missed her legs around me, and her arms, too. Like she'd been shielding me from something.

"How long has this been happening? You didn't have the blood in your eyes on Saturday."

"I just noticed."

"And the fever, too?"

"No, that's . . ." I thought back to last Monday, when the Internet had told me I was maybe schizophrenic.

Mab hopped off the table and pulled me by the wrist

again. She led me over the dusty dirt floor to a crate. Basically pushed me down onto it. It creaked, but it didn't feel rickety. Mab stood in front of me, all that hair tumbling everywhere in big, fat curls. The light from the open barn doors lit her from behind. Turned that hair into solid gold. "Tell me everything, Will," she said. "I want to help you."

I took a long breath and blew it out through my mouth. I wished for a drink of water. Or Havoc's head pushing into my knee. But that wasn't happening, so I sucked it up and told Mab about the headache, about the bloody nose, even though I wasn't sure it mattered. Though I'd been really hot that afternoon, too. I told her about yesterday's fever and the tight band around my chest. But even though I'd already thought about this being some messed-up magic, it was too nuts. I didn't mention the nightmares.

When I brought up the taste coating my mouth for twenty-four hours after the mud monster, she touched her bottom lip with one finger.

It distracted me.

"Did you swallow some of it?" she asked.

"Uh." I thought back. To slamming down into the mud monster, my fingers sinking into its shoulders. Spitting gritty saliva onto it. The rose petal that had fallen out of my mouth. "Maybe."

"That might be bad," she murmured, her head tilting slowly until she regarded me just like one of those crows. Which, I realized, had left the barn.

"Bad like *bad*? What's going to happen?"

"Is there anything else?"

I hesitated. This was all too weird. But who else was I gonna tell? "I've had more nightmares. Different ones—not about Holly, you know?"

"I know," she said, nodding as if she did.

"I'm drowning in mud, or being strangled by roses, which is the craziest thing ever. Evil roses." I attempted a laugh. Even I knew it was feeble.

Mab's expression darkened. "Roses. I see."

"It doesn't make any sense." My voice sounded desperate even to me.

"It might." She tilted her head and her hair fell sideways in a giant mass. "I need all the details."

I assumed she meant about the dreams, but my hand involuntarily went to my chest, where the bruise was.

Mab noticed and looked at my hand, then back up to my face. The question clear in her eyes.

Trying hard not to remember my brief fantasy of her kissing my chest all better, I raised my T-shirt up under my arms. And stared up at the ceiling rafters. The birds the crows had startled earlier had come back to roost up there again, two of them huddled together. I felt Mab move close to me. Then her fingers skimmed down the bruise. I shivered. Clenched my jaw.

"Will, what happened?"

"The, uh, antler? It hit me there, hard." I swallowed, which was tough given how my neck was stretched.

"What does it feel like?" She put her hand on my chest. The cold sent a shock straight to my heart.

I glanced back down. With her so close and me sitting on the crate, she was taller. Her chin tucked down, and she spread her hand out as wide as it would go. As if she could hold the bruise. "It feels like . . . heavy. A weight there."

"In your heart?"

"I guess so." My voice was quiet and rough. Caught shivering because she had her palm over my heart.

"Will." Mab said my name loud and strong. My gaze snapped up to hers. "Will, do you trust me?"

My mouth fell open.

She only waited, eyebrows up. Frozen like everything about her next move depended on my answer.

I thought of Ben sprawled next to me out at Clinton Lake. *Trust it,* he'd said. And I didn't think there was really a choice anymore. Some part of me had decided on Saturday to believe in her.

"Yeah." I cleared my throat. "Yes. I trust you."

A smile splashed over her face, and she whirled around. She dashed to the worktable and slid a thin knife out of the wooden block. As she returned, she cut the side of her pointer finger. I started to stand, but Mab's hand on my shoulder pressed me back onto the crate. "It's all right," she said, leaning in and touching her bloody finger to my forehead. Then she dropped to the ground and lay down, eyes open and focused on me.

I opened my mouth to ask what she was doing, but—

MAB

There I was, prone on the earthen floor of the barn, my hair as wild as always and my blue dress ruffled higher on my thighs than was probably decent.

And here I was, looking down upon myself through Will's

eyes, my mind spinning, sweat itching in my scalp and down my spine, and this horrible rope of magic around my ribs.

I closed his eyes and stood up in Will's body, noting every sore joint and the tightness of muscles. Oh, did his heart beat hard, and the balance of his body was jarred by dizziness, yet I felt myself settle in his chest. A higher center of gravity than I was accustomed to tilted me as I stepped forward, around my own unconscious body.

At the worktable, I laid his hands flat and stared at them. Darker than mine, with thicker fingers, but also his nails weren't as dirty. I stripped off his T-shirt, dropping it onto the table, and studied the bruise.

From the center of his chest, over his heart, the great yellow rose of a bruise blossomed. Where petals would be, curves of hematoma arched outward, then rays of red and purple stretched toward his shoulders and down his stomach in ever smaller branches. As I breathed, his ribs heaved in and out and I could feel the bruise pulsing in time with his heart.

I crouched uncomfortably and reached under the table for a tin can full of blades. Fishing around, I grasped a lancet. With it, I cut open my own body's wrist at the tattoo, and drained a few ounces of my blood into a small ceramic bowl from one of the shelves. Bringing the bowl to the table, I used the lancet to prick a tiny hole into the center of Will's bruise, then drew a rune of clear shadows around it with my blood. The blood from the tiny puncture dripped out slowly, falling in a line down his skin. It hit the rune mark, and in a flash I felt a pulse of magic ripple through his body.

The pulse left behind a tingling sensation that spread out

from his heart in tendrils much like a tree's roots. The pattern of his bruise was repeated inside his chest, and only from inside his body could I feel the paths it took.

Something had infected Will, and here, possessing his body, I felt exactly where in his blood it lay.

It was my doll's curse, spreading out from his heart like wild rose vines.

TWENTY-FOUR

It was three days.

Three days before you came home with Josephine's hand in yours.

I saw it from my bedroom window as I braided my hair for the night, her white dress mussed by so many hours doing God knows what, but still glowing in the moonlight. All her hair was down and wild around her face. Your fingers laced with hers, casually, intimately. My heart was breaking, and I slid the curtain across the window glass, as if I could pretend it hadn't happened.

In the morning I arrived in the kitchen, tying on my apron, and she was there, lounging at the table with thick-smelling coffee and a slim cigarette. "Morning, Evelyn," she said and, of all things, offered me a drag. I frowned and shook my head, going to get some bacon started, and maybe some oven-cakes. Your favorite, and even after what I'd seen, I still wanted to make them for you.

"Want some coffee, then?" Josephine drawled, and I nodded, thinking I'd better get used to her.

She stood and poured at the counter. I had no idea when she'd brought in luggage, but she had on a new dress, gray-and-pink-checked, all flounce around the hips and knees, with a halter top that tied behind her neck and left her back and shoulders bare to the world. Her lips were painted fabulous red. Up close, I decided she looked only about eighteen, and I wondered if she'd been alive for centuries, too.

"How's your visit been so far?" I asked her, concentrating on cutting slices of bacon.

"Delightful!" She handed me a mug of coffee and then took my wrist. "Don't let's get off on the wrong foot, but come sit with me. The Deacon is still in bed and won't need your slave labor for a while yet."

I pursed my lips and began to tell her I was making breakfast for myself, too. But instead I joined her at the table, sitting tall and smelling the coffee while she began questioning me about my entire history. She hadn't been here in about a year, she said, her eyes darting around guiltily, and obviously a lot had changed! There was no reason to think you hadn't already spilled all my secrets, as close as I thought you two were, so I told her in quiet words about my family and coming here, about the land and garden. She leaned forward on her elbows and asked piercing things about my magic, about Gabriel and you. I tried my best to remain calm and detached, but at the end of that single mug of coffee, she sat back with a triumphant smile and declared, "You're in love with him."

I gripped the mug, then stood as if to refill it, in order to turn my back to her as my whole body warmed and I thought of how happy you'd been when you saw her. Her. But I couldn't bring myself to deny it. I wouldn't betray myself like that, even if you could never know.

She was there, directly behind me, looming over my shoulder in her heels, with all that stature and elegance even in my little warm kitchen. Her breath was on my neck, and I shivered, suddenly sensing danger.

"You should tell him, pet," she murmured.

I shook my head.

"You'll never get what you want if you don't."

"I want a home, Miss Darly. I want to be safe here and continue on. I won't mess that up."

Josephine laughed. "Men are utter fools, Evelyn. Especially men like Arthur."

I spun around and tilted my face up to glare at her. "Arthur's no fool."

Her smile curled wickedly. "He is if he hasn't taken what you'd give. Trust me, I understand what it's like to love and long and want a man. This magic makes it better and worse, because they think they know everything, feel everything. They think it makes us the same, but they're still men, and still thinking of themselves first. If you want him, you gotta take him."

I leaned into the counter, afraid of the sly accent creeping into her words, afraid of the intensity in her face. My head shook of its own accord, denying her. "I thought," I said, "I thought you and he . . ."

Shock parted her lips, and Josephine reared back to laugh. Loud enough I'm sure it's what woke you. "Oh no," she said gleefully, "though I'm sure it's crossed my mind once or twice."

I didn't know what to think. I believed her, but yet, I'd seen your face. She brought you something that no one else did, that I didn't know how to identify. The way Gabriel filled up some part of you, too, and I felt again the weight of all your years, all your friendships and loves that I could never compete with.

The ceiling creaked, indicating you were up, and so Josephine said, "Go on back to your bacon, pet, and think about telling him."

I shook my head again, knowing I couldn't, and felt her gaze tingling into my back until you came downstairs and joined us.

TWENTY-FIVE

WILL

It was like waking up after having been only half asleep. Nothing had changed except that Mab was in the process of sitting up. And a dull burn wormed around in my chest.

She knelt on the ground and put her hands on my knees. "Will?" Her head was tipped up, and I had this sudden double vision of looking down at my hands against the worktable. "What happened?" I asked, rubbing my sore chest. My T-shirt was gone. "What?" I said again, looking down. There was some symbol drawn in blood over the bruise, and a tiny hole right in the center. Had I blacked out?

"I tested your body," Mab said, inexplicably. "And I think I have unfortunate news."

"Wait." I stood up, forcing her back. There my shirt was, in a pile over on the worktable. I went for it. Ignored the spinning in my skull. When I had it, I pulled it over my head and flattened it over the blood mark before I looked up at her again. "Tell me what just happened, Mab." My throat felt clogged up. I didn't know what to do with my hands.

She faced me from the crate, with about ten feet between us. "I used a rune of clear shadows to show me what was going on inside you, under that bruise and around your heart. To discover why your eyes are changing and why your bones hurt."

Instead of rubbing my chest again, I raised both my hands and clasped the back of my head. "Did I black out? You did all that—you took off my *shirt*—alone? And runes? What the hell is a rune? Is this blood on me? Mab, I remember . . ." I didn't want to say. But I was remembering something. It was like I'd dreamed doing all that myself: standing up, walking over her, cutting my chest. Feeling the bruise expand like a slow fire. I shook my head.

"You remember?" Mab closed the space between us fast. She put both hands on my chest, peered at me. "You remember what happened? It wasn't just one moment we were talking, and the next we were talking again?"

I shut my mouth tight and nodded.

She squinted at me, shaking her head in surprise. "That's so strange. You aren't blood kin, and you shouldn't maintain consciousness like that during a possession."

"What?" The word burst out on the tail end of a choke.

"Hmm," was all she said. She massaged her temple absently.

"Mab." I grabbed her shoulders. "What." I hunched over to put my eyes right level with hers. "Are." I pulled her closer. "You—talking—about?"

Mab smiled with her teeth. "Magic."

"Magic," I repeated. I didn't let her go. I was too stuck.

Her grin faded until it was only a pretty smile. Mab cupped her hands between us. "Magic," she said again. And a ball of fire sparked to life in her palms.

I threw myself back, hit the table hard with my hip.

Mab clapped out the fire and said, "That's about all I can manage at the moment."

I gripped the edge of the table, and I believed her.

Hand in hand, we trekked slowly up the hill to Mab's house. She said she needed food and that I did, too. And that there was good tea to make my headache go away.

As we walked, she told me what it was like to possess someone. Or something. She went on about flying, about the slow dance of trees in the wind and running on four feet instead of two. But I just held her hand. Barely heard her, because I couldn't get past *Mab was inside my body.*

There were barely names for what I was feeling. Awe, maybe. Fear. Nausea.

Also this warmth beyond the fever. It was like something inside me expanded a little bit more every time I looked at her.

Crazy. That was a word for it.

It was an Aaron word. Something he'd said to describe the things he wanted. I thought of the last time. At the picnic table in our backyard. His hair still long enough to tuck behind his ears. He'd been poring over a set of maps weighed down against the wind with full soda cans. I'd leaned over his shoulder as he penciled weird places he'd found on the Internet in to the route he and his buddies were taking to the Naval Academy. "Check this out, Will." He poked a spot in Illinois. "There's a huge monument here dedicated to the hippies of the world. Some dude made it, and it's like sixty feet long."

"So you're swinging a hundred miles off course to go see it?"

He clucked his tongue at me in mock disappointment. "Will, Will, Will—what's the point of driving from here to the Atlantic if you aren't going to stop at all the crazy stuff? That's where life happens, man."

And then there was Ben, standing in his dress uniform. Holding open the door to the funeral home. "He shouldn't have driven all around creation. He should have gone straight there."

Ben never did anything crazy.

"This is the Pink House," Mab said as we broke through the circle of trees.

The house was two stories and looked a lot like a giant pink cupcake with chocolate frosting. I couldn't imagine actually living inside it. Flowers spilled from window boxes and hung along the roof of the porch. The grass between me and it needed a mow, but was so thick I thought maybe a chainsaw would work better. There was a garden off to the right that looked like it had come from a catalog, it was so colorful.

"Wow," I said. The crows perched on the roof in a clump. I was starting to think of them as pigeons. Just everywhere. Following you around because you had food.

Mab tilted her head to one side. All her massive hair swung like a curtain. While we'd walked, it had occasionally snagged on a twig, and she'd just kept on going as if it didn't matter. "When we get inside, let's be quiet. Lukas is sleeping."

I reached out and picked a leaf that clung to a curl. "Who's Lukas?"

"A boy who's come to stay with us for a while."

She pulled on my hand and led me inside. It was exactly what you'd expect from a farmhouse. Old wallpaper with tiny flowers, scuffed furniture, family portraits, and lacy tablecloths. Full of light from big windows flung open to the afternoon.

And it smelled like fresh bread. Mab directed me to sit at the round kitchen table while she poured water into the kettle and turned on the stove. Which had probably been in use since the sixties. I studied the scratches on the table. Someone had taken a fork or knife and cut little nicks and letters into the edge. Almost like claw marks. I thought of Havoc throwing herself at the kennel door and stopped breathing. My chest hurt.

Mab came to sit at the table and tied her hair into a knot. Without a band or barrette or anything.

I leaned back in my chair. Watched her. Imagined her getting up and coming over, then sitting down in my lap. Imagined her sinking into my body and possessing me like some ghost. "Mab."

"Will?"

I flattened my hands on my thighs, wiping them as if they were dirty. "Next time, ask."

"Ask?"

"Before you possess somebody." My voice was harsh, because I still couldn't quite get over what I was saying.

"I did ask," she said. Surprise lit her face.

"No you didn't."

Mab reached out her hands, palms up. "I asked if you trusted me. You said yes."

Her hands were there, waiting. Fingers curled up slightly. Her eyes wide open and not hiding anything. "Mab," I said again.

"What is it?"

"It was just so . . . ." I forced air all the way out of my lungs. "Intimate."

She softened her mouth. "Oh." It was a tiny sound. Her eyes swept down my face and my chest, looking at all of me. She leaned onto her elbows. "I wish I could let you inside me."

"Jesus." I covered my face with my hands.

"You'd be able to feel it then, how strange it is in some other person. It's unbalanced and different, like . . . walking on loose stepping stones."

I looked at her through my fingers. Couldn't decide if sitting there was better, or if maybe I should stand up and pace.

Her expression was tender. "I would only learn your body that way if I took time to practice."

Practice. Learning my body. I pushed my chair back and got up. "We should talk about something else."

Just then the kettle whistle began to shriek. Mab snatched it from the stove. Whispered for it to hush.

I took the opportunity to try and steady my breathing. The sloppy way her hair fell wasn't helping. Neither was the way she stood up on her tiptoes to pull mugs down from a cabinet. It made her thin little dress slide up over her body.

I stared hard out the window. Until Mab had poured boiling water into a teapot. She brought it and two little mugs to the table. "It has to steep," she said.

"Great." I returned to my chair. "So. You possessed me to figure out what's wrong. And you did. Lay it on me."

Folding her hands together, Mab said, "There was a curse in that doll. In the homunculus, I mean. That I transferred there from where it had been bound in the roses. I believe some of that magic infected you when you destroyed the doll."

"A curse? Are you joking?"

She shook her head.

"What's going to happen? What's it doing to me?" I pressed my fist into my chest.

"I don't know, exactly. But I know how to help."

"How?"

"A cleansing. It's a ritual, and it will drive the curse out of you."

"How do we start? What can I do?"

Mab pulled the teapot nearer to her and lifted the clay lid. She smelled the steam and set the lid back down.

"Mab!"

"Unfortunately, I can't do it tonight." Her mouth twisted into a sorry frown.

"Why?"

"There's an ointment I need to make and then bless under the moon."

"I don't understand all this." I folded my arms on the table and put my forehead against them. I pressed down. The headache behind my eyes wasn't horrible. But it was easier to think when I wasn't looking at Mab. Not that there was much to think about. It was either believe her or get up and leave.

I didn't hear her stand. Her hand just landed on my back, rubbing cool circles against my spine. "I promise you'll be well. I felt exactly what the curse was doing. I felt where it is, how it's twisting around your heart. You have a little bit of time before it does permanent damage."

One weak laugh escaped.

"Will." She said it firmly. I sat up. Mab took my hands and turned me in the chair so that she could face me. Her chin tilted down, and her hair fell free of the knot. Fear shook through me. I hated that. I wanted to pull on a brave cloak. Desert camo like Ben's.

Mab put her hands on my face. "Listen to me, Will Sanger. I will help you. This is what I do."

I didn't say anything.

"You came here because you thought I could help. Me. Out of everyone you know, you came here. You found this place, because you were meant to." She brushed her thumbs under my eyes. "That red in your eyes is like rubies, Will. It is beautiful, because even when this magic is dangerous or dark, it is also beautiful. And I understand it." Mab took a deep breath, and I suddenly wondered if she was afraid like me.

She said, "It is who I am."

MAB

When the tea was ready, I pulled a fleam off the peg hanging on the side of the refrigerator and, with a tiny tap, cut my thumb and let one drip plunk down into Will's tea. It was willow bark, and hopefully, it would reduce his fever. The bark was part of a batch I'd made up just last week. Fresh and blood-quickened. I whispered a thrice-blessing against the surface of his tea and offered the mug.

"You put blood in it," he said, eyeing it suspiciously.

"To quicken the magic."

Wincing, Will said, "Drinking tea with your blood in it . . . basically goes against everything I've ever learned. About diseases. And cannibalism. And . . . religion."

"My blood already marks your chest, and blood is the element that makes my magic work. If you're squeamish, I don't know if I can help you."

"It isn't about being squeamish. It's just this all takes some getting used to." He didn't look away from the mug of tea.

I took a moment and studied the creasing at the outer corners of his eyes, the pinched skin. This was much to take in, to understand. I'd grown up with it, always believed in the power of my blood. Perhaps for Will, this was tantamount to me being given proof that magic was *not* real, and that my entire outlook on life was skewed false. I wished I could touch his head and transfer the understanding, could help him feel the truth of it.

Walking around the table, I held my hand out to him again, this time the one with the wounded thumb. "Blood is the conduit of magic. It is the house of power." He very gently took my hand and ran his thumb over my palm, examined my fingers one by one. I shivered at the touch, and my eyes fluttered closed of their own accord until Will pressed lightly on the tiny cut I'd made with the fleam.

"That really doesn't hurt?" He kept ahold of my hand, cradling it in both of his, and looked up at me.

"Yes, it does."

He dropped my hand. "I'm sorry!"

I drew it back, and then rubbed the cut thumb against my fingers. "It's just the way things are. Necessary to the magic. You have to sacrifice something to gain something."

Revulsion and fascination twisted through his expression, but he kept leaning toward me. "That doesn't sound very worth it."

"Oh, it is. You only have to adjust to it. Like walking out into a bright afternoon. It might hurt your eyes, but you take it and get used to it and then after a moment you can see all the colors of the world."

"Still. Sucks." Will shrugged one shoulder. "It would be nice if you could just . . . do it."

"Well, eventually you can. If you get good enough at it." I glanced out the window, thinking of Arthur, who never had to bleed for anything.

Will smiled. "Better."

"It's dangerous. You have to work hard to get to that point, and that's as it should be. Nothing should be free. Think about guns. If it hurt you to shoot a gun, don't you think people would think harder about when and where and why they did it?"

Slowly, he nodded. "That does make sense."

I pulled my chair around next to his, and while we sipped our tea, answered all of his questions. I explained to him about the blood kin, about being the Deacon and why I existed. I told him how the blood worked with intention and symbols, but what it really got down to was willpower. About patterns and nature and listening to the whisper of the trees. He wanted to know how I'd learned it all, and so I talked of Arthur more, and of Mother, of the books she'd given me and insisted I read instead of the texts on my homeschooling lists. Not only old journals from other witches but Shakespeare and Milton and Goethe and Malory. Histories of alchemy and witchcraft.

In turn, I asked about him. He told me about growing up in a military family, about their constant movement and all the shifting and change. About wanting to travel the world, see everything, taste and touch all of it. His rootlessness stirred sympathy in me, but it didn't seem to bother him—permanence wasn't something he longed for.

My mug had been empty for nearly an hour when I finally asked if I could have some more of his blood.

"Why?" It was only a question, matter-of-fact and simple.

"To prepare for the cleansing, I need to bless an ointment that's charged to you—to your blood. So I need a few drops. It will work better."

He paused for only a moment before saying, "Yes."

I took the fleam out again and tapped one of the blades into his wrist. His whole face peeled back and he groaned, more from surprise than pain, I think. As his blood spilled into the empty mug, he couldn't take his eyes off of it.

Unable to resist, I scooted the mug aside when it was full enough and healed his wound. It only took a drop of the blessed water we kept in the refrigerator and a small word breathed over his skin. He shivered as the flesh knitted back together and the blood stopped. Only a tiny pink line remained. I smiled up at him, our faces close.

My breath caught as I saw the crescents of red in his eyes.

It wasn't natural, but for one moment it seemed as though it should have been.

He watched me with those acorn eyes, and I was suddenly more nervous than I'd been about anything. His hands were so warm around mine, it felt like the energy might burn up to my elbows. All I thought about for a moment was breathing his breath.

A crow cawed outside and I jumped, squeezing Will's wrist too tightly. "Sorry," I said, and glanced off at the stairs.

Will asked, "Is something wrong?"

"I should check on Lukas. It's getting late."

"What time is . . ." His eyes shot past me to the grandfather clock and widened. "It's after seven. I have got to go."

"Oh." I paused, half twisted toward the stairway, and fought disappointment. "All right. The ointment should be ready to-morrow, but call me if anything changes."

He ran a hand up the back of his neck and into his hair. "I don't have my phone to add your number."

Rushing to the junk drawer, I fished out a dark blue marker and held it up triumphantly. Will offered his arm and, with an air of ceremony, I wrote the Pink House number along the back of his hand. I gave him my hand in the same way, and when he'd written out his number onto my skin, the digits next to each other looked like secret codes in the fading light.

"Wait," I said, and dashed into the pantry for one of our tied bags of tea. "It's willow tea, like you had today. Should keep your fever down." I offered it.

He smiled. "Thanks."

Though I led him to the front door, I was reluctant to let

go of his hand once we reached the porch. "You can find your way from here?"

"If I can't I don't deserve to," he joked. Will didn't move, or let go of me. I watched his eyes flicker between mine, tiny little back-and-forth motions. His lips parted just a bit, and I heard the crunch of tires on the pebble drive.

Donna.

Will turned away, releasing my hand. "Thanks for this." He held up the tea with the hand covered in my phone number.

I waved as he moved across the front yard, paused to lean into the station wagon to greet Donna. Evening shadows stretched from the oak trees and across Will's back. He laughed at something, straightened, and did a little spin in place as he waved back to me. He jogged backward for a moment, then turned again to vanish down the road.

TWENTY-SIX

Gabriel had taken himself off within an hour of Josephine arriving and hadn't come home yet, so that whole afternoon it was you and me and her. To my surprise, you both stayed in the house. You showed Josephine our little blood marks at the windows that could be powered with a whispered breath and made to draw cross breezes through the entire house. She clapped with delight, and began spinning ideas for how it might be improved, how it could be made permanent with additional sacrifice, or perhaps even tuned in to the sunlight or rhythms of air so that it was self-regulating. It was only a conversation about wind and practical magic, and yet both of you lit up like children.

I began to understand. She was obsessed with the blood, with the power it held, in a way I was not and might never be. For her it was the world, it was the purpose. For me it has always been a tool, even when it shows me beauty. She tried a few times to pull me into the conversation, but I shrugged and said a good ceiling fan would do the same trick, out of a perverse thought to differentiate myself from her, even if it wasn't what you wanted.

All day the two of you argued and laughed and drew vast plans up on a roll of paper you had dragged up from the barn. I went about my chores, in and out to the garden and icebox, rolling dough and boiling down lavender. When I made tea for myself, I brought you a pitcher and was shocked to see Josephine crouched on the floor beside a sketch of some complex magical circle, with tears streaking makeup down her cheeks and you softly saying, "He will return, when he's found his peace again."

"He's forgotten all the pleasure in life, Arthur," she hissed, and I took a step back out of the room. But not before she saw me, her blue eyes wild. She stared at me, then at you, then back at me, and smiled.

There was no way I could have guessed what she intended to do.

TWENTY-SEVEN

MAB

The door to Arthur's bedroom was open as I'd left it, and Lukas was on the bed with his eyes shut. He'd kicked off all the blankets and, instead of curling up in a ball, had sprawled across the bed with one arm flopped over the side.

I sat carefully on the edge, smoothing hair away from his face. "Lukas?" I said softly.

His eyelids twitched, and he moved his bandaged hand. I took it, holding it between my hands. I drew circles on the back of his wrist until he slowly looked up at me. "Hey," I said. "How are you feeling?"

"Better," he whispered. He smacked his lips. "Thirsty." His small voice was dry and broken.

From the bathroom, I brought a tall glass of water, then helped prop him up so that he could sip. His skin felt warm, but only from sleeping, not from fever. As he drank, I told him what I'd done to the black candle rune. "He can't hurt you with it now, and I will find another way to break his connection."

Lukas fumbled with the glass because of his bandages, and I gently set it on the bedside table.

"Time?" he said.

"It's evening. Donna's bringing some stew and medicine.

But I think you're doing just fine. You only need to sleep it off, recover your inner stores of magic. Because of the binding, I can't feed you energy, or pass it from the trees."

As he nodded, his eyes drooped. He touched my skirt and I sat again just beside his pillow. Clanking sounds and the light thump of opening and closing cabinets floated up the stairs and through the open bedroom door, from where Donna was putting away groceries and starting dinner. Lukas draped an arm across my lap, holding me very loosely. I put a hand on his head and rubbed circles into his temple, humming Mother's favorite song about the sea.

When he was asleep again, I carefully stood up and went to the window. Through the windowpane I could see the snarl of roses down in the garden. Here I was, Deacon for less than two months and full up with people to aid. It was exhilarating but frightening. What happened to Will was my fault, because I'd chosen not to raze the roses but instead to listen to them. To open the world up to their poison.

How was that different from what Lukas's father had done to him? Intention only. My will to undo it, to change the path I'd wrought.

I pushed open the window, letting in the warm evening breeze. It shouldn't be too hot now that Lukas's fire-fever had broken. I leaned outside, twisting my neck until I saw one of the crows perched at the edge of the roof. "Reese," I said, beckoning with my hand.

The crow swooped down and landed on the sill.

He bobbed his head, and I moved aside so that he could hop over to the roughly carved wooden bedpost. There he clutched, angling his beak down toward Lukas. "Thank you," I whispered.

As I made my way back downstairs, I smoothed my finger over the dark blue marks of Will's phone number. They were both my responsibility now, and I went to ready Will's ointment for setting out under the moon.

TWENTY-EIGHT

I left you both early that night, taking myself to bed, where I read and then slept and dreamed of wandering the house as if suddenly a ghost, with no memory of dying but only knowing I did not belong.

TWENTY-NINE

WILL

With Mab's last smile on my mind, the rush of wind through my open windows was enough to fill the silence in my head. I felt dizzy, as if I'd left my inner ear back in the forest. But about a quarter mile away, my cell buzzed angrily on the passenger seat with a half dozen texts and voice messages. Worried, I slowed down and listened to the first one. It was Dad. "William, where are you? You need to call us ay-sap, boy. Your mother is worried sick." The second was him again, saying the same, only with a tighter grip on his voice that meant he was pissed.

The clock radio said it was 7:52 p.m. I'd texted Mom and Ben that I was running out, and then I'd forgotten the cell in the car. If I was honest with myself, I hadn't even thought about the time or calling to check in.

Instead of returning the calls, I sped up and focused on getting home. The speed blurred all my peace away, and I rolled up the window and punched the radio louder.

It was full dark except for a strip of orange and silver in the west when I pulled up to the house, and every window was lit. I saw a curtain in the front room flick closed. Half of me was irritated they'd been watching so carefully. It made my head pound. I was seventeen. I had my own car. I would have called if I'd been in trouble. As I slammed the car door, clomped up the porch, and pushed into the house, I couldn't even dredge up my usual smile.

The front hall light glared, and I squinted as I shut the front door behind me.

"William."

Dad's voice was firm from the den. I didn't bother dragging my feet. This would be short and to the point.

I rounded the corner. Kept my eyes down. I wasn't sure how easy it would be to see the red in them and didn't want to find out. "Sir."

He stood up from his recliner, hands clasped behind his back. The khakis and polo shirt did nothing to dispel the illusion that this was a military hearing. "You've been gone for hours. And were very sick yesterday. We expected you for dinner."

"Yes, sir."

Dad didn't budge an inch.

"I went for a drive. I've been cooped up and wanted some air."

"You didn't call."

"I didn't have reception."

"Not an excuse."

"Dad—"

"You are not to be out for hours without checking in. That's SOP, and you know it. You deliberately ignored a rule you've always known."

There was no side of the truth I could tell him. I was screwed. "Yes, sir," I said.

Dad relaxed only enough to sigh. "Will. Go see your mother. You're grounded through the weekend. Home by three-thirty every day."

"Dad!"

"William?" His jaw tightened just enough to warn me.

I fell silent, knew my frustration was all over my face, and wished that I could control it better, like all the rest of the men in my family. "Nothing, sir."

"Good."

With a tiny nod, I spun around and left in a hurry. I took the stairs three at a time. Mom would be reading a book in bed.

But Ben stopped me by coming out of his room and putting a hand on my shoulder. "Get off," I said, jerking away. I didn't need him to bitch me out, too.

"Hey." His fingers squeezed.

"Ow." I punched his shoulder, not too lightly.

He caught my fist. "Hold it. I just want to say one thing."

The hall was dark, only dimly lit by the yellow light that had followed Ben out of his room. It made him into this looming shadow, but I could just hear something off in his tone: it wasn't condemning enough. "What?" I demanded, quietly.

"Mom was afraid you were dead."

"What?" I nearly squeaked, and cleared my throat. "I was only a few hours late."

Ben let go of me and crossed his arms over his chest. I could see the perfect V of his shoulders since he was only wearing sweatpants. His muscles annoyed me. Dad was always saying, *If you picked up some weights at school or came to the Y with me, you could be just as strong as your brother.* But I wasn't a cart horse, I'd reply. I was built for speed. For flying.

As Ben continued to not say anything, I rewound through the past five minutes, and it dawned on me what he and Dad were so steamed about. *Aaron.*

I was a jackass. I winced, hissing in through my teeth.

"Yeah," Ben said. "Go apologize." He shoved me on my way and retreated to his bedroom.

Feeling like I deserved to have tiny bugs chomp on my eyeballs, I knocked quietly on Mom's door.

"Come in," she said.

I pushed it open and stepped in. She set the hardcover book in her lap and removed her rectangular reading glasses. A half-empty glass of water sat beside her on the bedside. She kept sleeping pills in the drawer, and I wondered if she'd taken them yet. "Hey, Mama." I crossed the carpet and sat at her knees on the mattress.

"Hi, Will. You made it home safely."

I fiddled with the blanket. "I'm sorry."

Her hands twitched a little, and she pushed the book off her lap. "Come here and tell me what you were doing." She patted Dad's side of the bed.

After untying my shoes and tossing them toward the door, I sat next to her on top of the covers. She leaned her head on my shoulder. "I met a girl," I said very quietly.

"Tell me about her."

I laughed once. "She's incredibly weird."

"But you like her."

"I, uh. Yeah. She's easy to be around." I wasn't sure if I was making it up or telling the truth. Mab was so different. How could I tell my mom that the first time I met her we'd battled a mud monster, and she'd been half covered in dirt and mud? And wearing giant goggles? She had a magic workshop and a life out of some movie. Mom would be scandalized by what Mab wore—or rather what she didn't wear. And the tangled mess of her hair.

"Are you smiling, Will Sanger?" Mom scooted a few inches back to watch me.

"Aw, Mom." I scrunched up my face and looked away. "Stop."

"You should bring her over so we can meet her."

"It isn't like that! And besides, Dad grounded me."

"Ah."

I glanced back. Mom was very innocently reaching for her book again. Face clear of expression. Her wrist bones stood out hard against her skin. Poking up so that they looked painful. I thought I should start pushing half-and-half on her for her coffee in the mornings. "What are you reading?" I asked, scooting close enough to loom over her and pretend to be enthralled.

She told me it was some historical mystery that took place during World War I. I settled in against the headboard while she read a bit from the middle.

A while later, she woke me up and sent me to snore in my own bed.

I dreamed all night about monsters and screaming trees. And Mab, caught in a sticky red spiderweb, struggling to get out, to get to me.

THIRTY

I knelt beside the salvia, tearing out weeds, as the dawn rose behind heavy clouds the next morning. I heard the door open and your footsteps on the porch but continued with my work even as you passed me, paused, and turned back to watch.

After a moment, you said, "Evelyn?"

My first name. I lifted my head and put the sharp bull thistle I'd just torn out of the ground atop the pile of its brothers.

You came to me and stood, frowning slightly in the pale white morning. I got to my feet. "Arthur? What's wrong?"

"Evelyn," you said again, stepping closer and tilting your head, peering at my face as if you'd look through it into my heart. That made me fold my hands under my ribs. You leaned so close there was no room for light between us, and whispered, "What were you thinking, when you kissed me last night?"

I flung myself back, hands clapping over my mouth. You reached out, startled, but I jerked away from you. "What? When I what?" I flew through my memories of the past day, and there was nothing—nothing. Panicked that you or I was running mad, I backed up all the way to the porch while the expression drained out of you, while your fingers twitched and your head slowly lifted until you were staring past me at the house.

Before I could say anything else—I haven't the faintest idea what I might have managed—you charged past me, harder and faster than I'd ever seen you move, up into the house.

Moments later there was a crash, and Josephine shrieked. My boots were tied to the ground as you returned, dragging her in her thin nightgown, out the door and down the porch. You threw her into the meadow. Her shrieks were like an angry cat, her hair flouncing everywhere, and she leapt onto her knees, but you pointed to her car. "Go. Now, Josephine. Before I strip the magic from your bones."

Your voice was red-hot, and you were everything but calm. I shrank away, awed and terrified and with just the beginning of delight because I understood you were taking my side over hers, throwing her out for some sin against me.

She said, "Oh, please, it was nothing."

"It was everything," you answered. Your hands were shaking!

Josephine got to her feet like a queen, despite grass stains and being nearly naked. She glanced at me. "You'll thank me someday," she tossed off, turning and going for her little silver car.

"Ten years, Josephine," you said. "Don't come back."

She gasped, whirled, and began to protest. But when she saw you, she held it back and instead shrugged. "I've been meaning to visit the family in New Orleans," she said, as if it had always been her plan. Neither you nor I moved as she climbed into her car, twisted her hair back out of her face, and left.

We two remained in place long after the noise of her vehicle had faded. I was afraid to look at you and instead stared at the pile of broken thistles.

When you finally approached me, there was sorrow in the hang of your arms. I steeled myself, hoping I could root this out of our home the way I'd rooted the weeds from my garden. "What happened, Arthur? Last night?"

You pressed your lips together and stopped an arm's length from me. You were fully dressed in your daily uniform of trousers and shirtsleeves, despite the heat the later day would surely bring. I wanted to brush your hair off your face, where anger had made it stick.

"You came back downstairs, late, wrapped up in a shawl and your feet bare," you said breathily, watching my mouth instead of my eyes. "You knelt in front of me. I was just alone there, watching the patterns in the fire. You took my hand, touched my cheek, and said, 'I've been thinking, Arthur.' Then—then you kissed me."

I dragged in a shaking breath.

"That was all. You smiled and walked straight back upstairs." Your hands wrapped around your chest now, defensively. "I should have known it wasn't you, Miss Sonnenschein."

"Why?" I said, suddenly furious. "Because you could never imagine me like that? Because I'm not somebody you'd kiss? Somebody worth kissing?" Tears tingled in my eyes like magic in my blood. I wanted to throw a child's fit, to fling myself at you and pummel your chest. To knock my anger and desire straight into your heart.

Your mouth dropped, and you held out your hands. "No, no. Because—because it's easy to tell when somebody's possessed!"

"How easy?" I was not mollified.

"The eyes are all wrong, they're not—real, there's no reflection, no spirit."

I threw up my hands. "So you didn't notice my eyes were lacking spirit. Wonderful."

You closed your mouth, pressing your lips in again. You reached out and touched my hand, then snatched yours back. "I didn't notice because I . . ."

A long silence stretched between us, and my heart was loud as firecrackers in my ears.

You said, finally, watching my lips, "Because I wanted so badly for it to be you."

THIRTY-ONE

MAB

With a shallow bowl under my arm, I carefully climbed out the attic window and onto the flat rectangle of roof where Arthur and I used to watch the stars.

Clouds spread across the dark sky, layers stretched into rippling sheets, overlapping in patterns difficult to understand. As though wind pushed from seven directions, at seven different heights. Some of that wind grasped at my unbound hair, throwing it around like tentacles. I angled my head up and searched for sky—there, and there, in the southwest. Bright, luminous black, and streaks of silver light from the hidden moon.

I crouched and set the bowl where it would catch as much moonlight as possible.

It contained a mixture of Will's blood, dried-fig powder and rue, my blood for power, and five focus stones: obsidian, amethyst, lace agate, moonstone, and citrine. In the pale moonlight, I sketched a circle with chalk onto the roof, adding a rune of focus and a rune of pure intentions. I hummed a discordant tune as I plucked the stones from the bowl and set them around in their proper places in the circle.

It was finished and ready, and I hesitated before saying the words to set the spell. This was the first time I'd been up here since Arthur died.

I remembered late last summer bursting into his workshop with wild magic on my lips. I'd panted in the doorway as he drew a final line onto a piece of red construction paper. When he glanced up, his pale hair swung crazily about his face as though he'd been electrified. I laughed, and he said, "Bit of lightning got loose from its box," as he flicked his fingers toward his bowing shelves. I hopped over to him, flung myself onto the worktable, and whispered my plan. As I spoke, his eyes lit, and he grabbed my hand and together we ran through the forest, leaping like deer, gathering all the excess magic the leaves had to offer.

We flung ourselves out of the trees and dashed through late-summer meadow. We kicked at the grasses and flowers, flinging seeds everywhere. And we danced into the sunflower field, aiming for the center of the riotous tangle of yellow and white.

"They've gone to seed!" I cried, flinging my arms out and spinning. Arthur plucked a single head, and the round flower fit perfectly cupped in his palm. He spat on it and threw it straight up.

"Fly," he told it.

I pulled a pin from my hair and jabbed my finger. Picking a flower just as Arthur had, I dripped three drops of blood onto its face and tossed it high. "Fly!" I told it.

Together we wove through the field, touching flower heads and watching them leap up. The air was full of whirring sunflowers. They darted and dipped, and the crows arrived, laughing their bright, coughing laughs. The crows were black shapes dancing among the flowers. Arthur's fingers wove into mine, and we twirled into a waltz. We tripped on stems and twisting leaves. I called up to the sky, "Shake and shudder! Scatter your seeds! Give back to the garden all that it needs!" Arthur joined me when I repeated the spell, and we sang it again and again.

Petals fluttered down and seeds came raining, a storm of yellow and white and brown. They caught in our hair and in our hands, on our tongues as we raised our heads to laugh.

The crows fed well, making a game of it with open beaks. I was dizzy and happy, and Arthur and I fell back, landing in the scratchy stiff field. Blue sky peeked at us through the deflowered stalks, and some crows landed near. The rest chased each other in a continued contest.

Our heads knocked together, and I sighed as petals fell slowly onto my face.

That evening we'd dragged ourselves back to the Pink House, where Donna and Granny Lyn waited with iced tea on the porch. Granny shook her head and told us we looked like a pair of ragamuffins dropped off a train and left to wander the countryside. Donna only looked sadly at my filthy dress. When Arthur moved to kiss Granny, she pushed at him with her foot, unwilling to touch his dirt. He made kissing faces at her, and so did I, until she was laughing and smacking his hands lightly. Her smile folded the rest of her face into an accordion of wrinkles, and she told him he was old and wise enough to know better.

"Too old to be wise, my love," he said, but winked at me as though to cancel out the silly tone of voice and make the statement true. After our baths we'd climbed up here onto the roof, and I'd asked Arthur what he'd meant.

Stars wheeled overhead, too numerous without a moon. Arthur said, "I'm wise enough to know that oftentimes the best kind of fruit is the freshest."

"Except plums," I teased, and Arthur laughed. He turned onto his side, and I did, too. He put a hand on my cheek and I studied his face, so young and easy and smooth. "That's true enough," he said. "What I mean, plainly, is that wisdom is a habit, and maybe an addiction. We live too long and nothing looks new anymore."

"I'm new," I said, "and you can see everything new again with me."

His smile faded, and he said, "I said something very much like that to Gabriel once."

"Who's that? I haven't met him."

"No, and you won't." Arthur rolled onto his back again and pointed up at the stars. "See the Big Dipper? And the Little?"

I nodded. Of course I could see them—he'd shown me constellations by the time I was six.

"Gabriel used to say he was the bigger, older bear and I was the littler. And now, that is you and me, little queen. Only I am the major, and you the minor."

I took his hand and wove our fingers together. My fingers were nearly as long as his, and I held them up until Polaris was just at the tip of our middle fingers. "Us, circling the pole together, forever!"

Arthur curled his fingers down around mine and said, "For our time, at least."

Less than a year later, here I was putting out an ointment to steep in the moonlight, alone.

THIRTY-TWO

I ran away that day you threw Josephine out, spent it in the western pasture with myself and the flowers and the sun. Gabriel still didn't return home, and I avoided you for nearly a week. I couldn't see you without thinking about everything Josephine had said and done, horrified at the thought of my hands under her control, my voice, my lips. What if you'd done more? What if you only weren't telling me?

Every day I bathed in the Child Creek, pouring the fresh water over my head again and again, drinking it and welcoming it to run through my body, cleansing me of her influence.

It was there you found me on the fifth day, in only my shift, soaked to the bone and cold despite the hot sun sparkling off the water.

I sat up, water streaming down my face and my loose hair stuck to my back, the shift thin and heavy with water. I might as well have been naked. And there you were, leaning your shoulder against a maple tree.

I gasped so hard I choked, covering myself and pulling up my knees so that I was sitting like a duck in that creek. My dress hung from that same maple tree, and my shoes were tucked beside a rock. I'd planned on baking dry in the sun out in the field, but now I was trapped. "Arthur! Get away!"

"It's time," you said calmly, watching my face and careful not to let your eyes trail anyplace else.

"Time for what?" My voice rose near to a shriek.

"For me to show you what I think is most beautiful."

I huffed, "Now?"

You nodded and pushed off the maple. "Come on, quick, or it won't last."

Waiting until your back was turned, I leapt out and tugged my old blue dress on over the shift, even though it stuck everywhere and my hair might as well have been a squirrel's nest. I left my shoes and followed a few feet behind you, not thinking about touching you, not doing anything but watching where you stepped as you led me around south, toward the old grain silo.

You led me to a bower of paper birch trees, all white and gray bark and silvery leaves. Under their branches the world fell away, the air somber and heavier somehow. I wondered if I'd crossed a salt circle. You crouched near the base of two birches that had grown together. In the roots lay a coyote, old enough to sport white hairs on his muzzle. You curled around him, stroked his orange and white fur. He twitched with every slow exhalation. I held back, watching sadly. What beauty was going to be here? The beast was dying.

"May I?" I asked, watching the coyote's golden eyes.

"Ask the old man yourself," you said.

I crouched and put my fingers to his muzzle, and he creaked open his jaw. Many of his teeth were missing, but his tongue curled out between yellowing fangs, and his nostrils quivered as he smelled me. He sighed heavily, and I put my palm under his jaw to scratch gently.

You cut your finger with the fleam you always carried in your pocket, and drew a triangle against his forehead. You whispered into his huge ear, and I felt the blanket of magic slip around me, too. What the coyote felt, we felt. Its bones ached, and pulling air into its lungs took too much concentration.

"Oh, Arthur," I murmured, glancing up to see the sorrow coating your eyes.

"Stand back." You lifted up onto your knees and put your hands on the coyote's ribs.

The world shivered and the coyote's mouth yawned open. Its fur rippled and its paws splayed out. A strong wind rushed over the ground, scattering leaves and strips of fallen birch bark. The wind peeled the fur away from the coyote, tossing it into the air like dandelion seeds! The coyote's skin sank down, sucking close to bones. The skull and ribs and sharp shoulder blades stood out. His eyes melted, and so did his tongue. Bones crumbled, sounding like tiny hail slapping down through baby leaves. From his eye socket a thin green stem grew, like a pointing finger, and blossomed into a tiny, perfect violet.

You laughed. It was a soft, happy sound. You said my name, Evelyn, and I couldn't feel my own body suddenly. My heart had vanished into the earth along with the coyote's spirit. I was overwhelmed, and tears made my vision waver.

You stood up and grasped my hands. "Did you see?"

"I've never seen anything like it." Your skin was hot, and I put my hands on your face.

"That is my most favorite beautiful thing," you said. "Not the sunrise or flying with the wind. Not any of it but this: death and life, and this moment when they are the exact same thing."

It was so quiet in the grove, with your face in my hands. Your voice was low, and the death energy continued to resonate around us, but softly. Gently.

And I knew you, in that moment. Love seemed too small a word for what I felt, what I understood. I knew you, Arthur. And I've never stopped.

THIRTY-THREE

MAB

All night, Lukas screamed with nightmares.

I crawled into bed beside him, humming and singing all the lullabies I knew from Mother and Granny Lyn. When he was awake I used a pen to connect his burn scars with smiling faces and elephants to make him laugh. In the morning I strengthened my binding and gave him a draught of magic to keep his body relaxed. I asked him to tell me exactly what his father had done, what was the spell he'd needed the black candle rune for.

Lukas curled his feet onto the sofa, leaning away from me and into the corner, and said, "I don't wanna say."

I crawled nearer, sitting with my legs tucked up, too, unthreatening, kind, young as I could be. "It was not your fault, Lukas, I promise. You couldn't have stopped him, whatever it was."

His fingers made dents in the sofa cushion because he gripped it so hard. Behind him a fire crackled in the hearth, because although it was hot today, Lukas couldn't get warm. Donna had brought hot chocolate and tea, offered him medicine and soup, suggesting he was only sick from his hard work.

But I knew, and he knew, what was keeping his energy and temperature down now.

I put a finger on his knee, traced a protection rune there, though it would do no good without blood. "It may help me to know why, the particulars of it. Even if you don't wish to talk about it. And when I can remove it, you won't need to be bound."

"It's cold," he said.

"I know."

"Have you ever—have you ever been . . . like this?" Lukas caught my finger and held my hand achingly tight.

My eyelashes fluttered. I didn't like to think about having my magic bound. "I did it to myself once, after my mother died. To know what it felt like."

"Why?"

I scraped my teeth over my bottom lip, pinched it. Thinking how to explain. "For . . . solidarity. So that I would feel how she felt when she died, so that I could carry that memory with me forever."

He said very quietly, "My dad sells curses sometimes. Things so, like, a farmer's fields go all to rot or—or once so a man stopped breathing exactly when Dad wanted."

"It isn't your fault," I said again. "Come on."

I took him down to the workshop, and while he explored the barn, I shifted the stacks of drawing paper and can of colored pencils off my worktable. I moved a pile of my raw rubies onto the ground and the plastic bin with the remains of my doll, too, until the only things left were the butcher's block of knives and a can of blood-letters. "Hop on up here," I said.

There was plenty of room for Lukas to stretch out, and I helped him remove his shirt. "Are you warm enough?"

"Mm-hmm," he said, closing his eyes and pressing his cheek down onto the old worn table.

Rummaging around in one of the wooden boxes on the uneven shelves off to the right, I pulled out an old pair of Josephine's glasses and brought them back. "I'm just going to look, all right, Lukas? But let's ground you so you're safe."

With one of the small pins from the butcher's block, I jabbed his wrist as quickly as possible. He did not even flinch as the blood trickled into my palm. "We feed you, Earth," I said, "that our magic may come full circle," and dripped his blood onto the earthen floor of the barn. With the final drop, I dotted his shoulder and then his forehead.

I slid the blood-sight glasses over my ears, and immediately my vision reddened. I saw my binding spell like a circle of calm around his center, and the curling magic of the black candle rune carved into his back. Its sickly red wavered gently like grass in a slight breeze, and tendrils of it doubled back to sink into his flesh, while others reached up into the air, up and up through the roof in thin strands. All the way to his father, no doubt. The dots of blood on his shoulder and forehead shone brighter, newer.

It was going to take effort to destroy the black candle rune without hurting him. But I couldn't let him go on with these nightmares, and with that fierce, uncomfortable binding. Lukas didn't deserve that sort of cold, that rope imprisoning him away from the magic of the world. I'd find a temporary fix to hold him while I hunted for the permanent solution.

"All right," I said, removing the blood-sight glasses.

He rolled over and sat up, hugging himself. His hands were healed, though the burns had left tiny pink scars almost like caterpillars creeping around his knuckles and across his palms. I took one of them and said, "I have an idea."

THIRTY-FOUR

You showed me the rest of yourself that summer.

Our mornings we spent separate, working around the house and land. But in the afternoons, you would come find me and take my hand and lead me on long, meandering walks, stretching for miles. And you talked. You answered any question I thought of, big or small. You told me all the same stories Gabriel had, but in every detail, with tangents and looping philosophy. Sometimes Gabriel joined us, interjecting his version, which was usually more audacious and amusing than yours. We laughed, all three of us, and I have never been so happy.

As you wove history for me, I felt again that overwhelming sense of age wrap around you, but it was not oppressive, it was freeing. Because as you gave me this gift, I began to realize that you could have been doing anything: traveling, adventuring, living anywhere and loving anyone.

But you chose to spend your time holding my hand.

THIRTY-FIVE

WILL

It had been a very long day, thanks to a bad night and having to face the growls of my dogs when I fed them that morning. Havoc's curled lips stuck with me all through school. I'd been too swamped, trying to catch up with my teachers since I'd missed Monday and finals were next week, to hang in the halls. Or even eat in the cafeteria. So it wasn't until after final bell that I tracked Matt down in the locker room. He flipped me shit about getting grounded. When I told him I'd been with Mab Prowd, he hit me on the arm. Called me a secret agent. Which made about as much sense as anything he ever said. Matt refused to let me go until I coughed up details. I walked him out to the practice field and told him a condensed, incredibly edited version of how I met her and why we were hanging out. He said we should all four of us, him, me, Mab, and Shanti, go to a movie when my sentence was over.

I really hoped we got this curse taken care of so that I'd have a chance to try and convince Mab it was a great idea.

As we hit the sunlight, I noticed him peering at my face. I remembered the red in my eyes and said, "Shit, I'm late," before peeling off for the parking lot. The blood color was tough to see in most indoor lighting at this point. But the sun seemed to narrow in on it like a spotlight.

Mab called just as I walked in the door. I smiled through my hello. Tucked the phone between my ear and shoulder while I grabbed a mug out of the kitchen. She said everything would be ready the next day for my cleansing ritual. I broke the news that I was grounded, and all she said was "Hmm. Well. Drink the tea. I'll think of something and let you know."

"Should I—" The dial tone interrupted me.

Being left hanging like that didn't do wonders for my headache.

As I pulled my steaming mug of water out of the microwave, Ben clapped me on the shoulder. "Hey. What's up with all the tea drinking?"

I shrugged him off and dropped in the little paper bag of Mab's tea. "Tastes good."

"You used to be as coffee-blooded as the rest of us." He headed for the fridge. Cold air puffed out as he reached in for a soda.

Ben leaned against the kitchen counter, giving me that superior officer dress-down look. I stood with my arms crossed. Chin down slightly so that it was harder for him to stare right into my eyes.

It stayed like that between us until I hooked the teabag with my finger and dropped it in the sink.

"Let's take it outside," Ben said, jerking his head toward the sliding glass door that led to the backyard. He grabbed my mug and propelled me forward. He slid the door back and basically shoved me out onto the concrete steps.

Ben sat down on the top step, stretching his legs out in front of him. He handed me the tea and cracked open his pop-top. "God, smell that! Smells like summer. I can't wait for the rain."

Reluctantly, and avoiding looking at the kennel, I joined him. I grunted instead of responding. I guessed the mountains of Afghanistan were pretty dry compared to Kansas in May.

Neither of us spoke for a while. The incoming storms had started to push out a lot of the heat and humidity, so it wasn't too stuffy, but so far there was just a little wind and a couple of clouds breaking up the sunlight. I imagined flying straight through them, toward the sun. The wind in my ears would be so loud.

"Let's go get the dogs and bring them around for some fetch." Ben set his soda can on the step with a clang and stood.

"Oh no, I'm—uh . . ." I didn't know what to lie about. I pushed to my feet. "I'm not really up for it, but you should take them for a walk or something if you want. They could use the exercise."

Ben planted his hands on his hips. "What the hell is wrong with you? Not up for fetch? That involves about two points of effort."

We were the exact same height, but I stood up on the step and he was in the yard. He looked one part annoyed, three parts baffled. I avoided his eyes. Couldn't take chances in the sun. I glanced at him and away, sure it was making me seem even more guilty.

"I knew it," he said. "Tell me now what you're into. Drugs?"

"Jesus, no!"

"Then what?" he stepped up so our glares were level. "You're not yourself. Avoiding eye contact? Fevers? Running off like last night? You used to have ambition! Drive! You're acting so different, Will, and I don't like it."

"What would you know about how I act?" I wrapped my arms around my chest, fingers pressing into my ribs. "You've only seen me twice in two years. One of which was a *funeral,* and you were only here for three days before they packed you back off again. You haven't been here."

"I know that." He jabbed a finger down in the air.

"For a whole long year, it's just been me and Mom and Dad."

His lips flexed and he shook his head. "I'm here now. I'm not going anywhere."

I laughed so I wouldn't sneer. He'd only be here until the Marines snapped their fingers. "You can't just fix things because you want to."

"Tell me what's broken so I can try."

"No." I shook my head. Bent to pick up my mug and go back inside. "You don't get it."

"You're my only brother, and I'm not going to just walk away."

"Again, you mean."

"I was fighting a war, Will, not off on a pleasure cruise drinking martinis and ignoring my family. I was doing my duty."

"Not to us."

"Will." He shook his head disapprovingly. "Is this about that girl? This secret girlfriend of yours? She's getting you into whatever it is?"

I never should have even mentioned Mab. Everything was a weapon to Ben. I shoved away and spun to go back in. But he caught my elbow.

His fingers tightened. "Remember that last time, right before I shipped out. Remember? Down at El Dorado."

I didn't want to, but it was plastered in my memory with superglue. Me, Aaron, Ben, with a cooler full of beer and soda and sandwiches, out camping at the big old reservoir in southern Kansas. We'd only just moved to the Midwest after a two-year tour in Japan. I was prepping for my sophomore year—my first at a regular high school instead of DODS—Aaron was about to be a senior, and Ben had his marching orders and was only a few months out from his first major action as a lieutenant in the United States Marine Corps. I barely knew Ben then, either. But at least he'd been my supercool oldest brother, off learning how to shoot rifles and jump out of planes.

That night he and Aaron had even let me have a beer while we built up the fire for hot dogs and s'mores. There'd been so much laughing and joking around, and all my clothes were wet from me being dumped into the lake. They steamed when I got close enough to the fire. I remembered telling Ben that I was gonna be just like him, and Aaron would, too. And even though they'd never let us all serve in the same platoon, it would be like we were superheroes secretly working together across the world. Ben would come up with the crazy world-saving plans, Aaron would MacGyver some used car parts into a special weapon, and I'd deliver it with perfect, last-minute timing.

There'd been bright stars, howling coyotes, and the crackling fire. I'd smeared melted marshmallow on Aaron's face in revenge for him throwing me in the lake. Ben taught us an awesome bingo game involving little pocket-cards with sex acts drawn on them with stick figures.

I stared at Ben now. He'd probably thrown those cards away a long time ago. "It doesn't matter," I said. "We're all different now."

Both.

I should have said we were both different, since Aaron didn't get to change anymore. I jerked my elbow out of his grip.

The sun came out from behind a cloud and made Ben squint at me. He said, "Different doesn't have to mean separate."

Wasn't I supposed to be the one coaxing him back toward brotherhood? He was the one who'd been to war, who should have post-traumatic stress. I shrugged unevenly. The center of my chest itched like something was alive under my skin. "Sometimes it does."

He stepped up onto the top step, close to me with his hand on my shoulder. "Mom and Dad need us, Will. If you won't tell me what's wrong for yourself, talk to me for them. They're worried. Mom is worried."

"I'm fine," I whispered.

My brother's fingers tightened on my shoulder. "I don't believe you."

"You said I have to trust this thing, and I'm trying. Can you trust me, too?"

He sucked in air through his teeth. "Will, do you remember what we said that night? Around the fire?"

I lowered my head in a nod. My chin nearly touched my chest.

"Don't forget it," Ben said quietly, before jogging off toward the garage.

I escaped upstairs, but watched from my bedroom window as he romped around with Havoc and Valkyrie. Everything was squeezing me out. Out of my body, out of my place. I used to know. I used to know everything. What I wanted to be, *who* I wanted to be. Who my family was and what they'd do for me. What I'd do for them.

I rubbed the pink scar on my wrist where Mab had cut me, bled me, and healed me again.

At El Dorado reservoir, Ben, Aaron, and I had all three cut our hands and bled together into the fire. A dumb kids' trick. Ben had said "Always faithful." It was the Marine Corps motto. *Semper Fidelis.* We'd repeated it over and over again while drops of Sanger blood splattered into the flames.

THIRTY-SIX

It was a cool reprieve in the middle of August, the hottest month. I'd been eighteen for three weeks, though you didn't know my birthday in those days.

I'd gone down to the meadow near your favorite oak tree with a basket to gather flowers for drying into tea. The meadow spilled violet with verbena and phlox, and I settled down in the sunlight, where the wind ruffled the prairie grass and the blossoms bobbed. The beauty of the afternoon distracted me, and I unpinned my hair, leaned back on my hands, and watched the clouds roll by.

You couldn't have been watching for more than a few minutes before I noticed you, leaning as you always did with your shoulder against a tree. Cradled in one arm was a pad of sketching paper, and you delicately held a thin lead pencil. Your eyes darted to me and down, back and forth, as lazy as the wings of the monarch butterflies spinning around the phlox.

Slowly, you set down your drawing and came to me through the tall grasses. They whispered against your knees, and I shivered, though the sun filled the glade with golden warmth. Just before me you knelt, and you took my face in your hands. You said, "Evelyn Sonnenschein, may I kiss you?"

I turned my head and kissed the ball of your hand, then gently took your wrists and led your fingers into my hair. The motion pulled you closer, and I said, "Please."

THIRTY-SEVEN

MAB

The gathering storms lent the air a quality of anticipation. I felt the hairs on the back of my neck rise as I chalked a complex rune of stalwart action into the grass atop our hill. At every point I placed a black candle to absorb the aftershocks of the cutting I planned. And in its open center, I drew a black candle rune to match the one on Lukas's back.

Donna watched from the porch, holding Lukas's hand. Her chin was up, and she would help because I'd explained to both of them and Lukas had agreed. It was going to hurt, but in the end, his father would have no more power over him. The rune would still be there, and there would continue to be danger, but the immediacy of his suffering would be gone.

I was dressed in a long white skirt and a shirt Lukas had chosen from my closet—his favorite color of green, he said, and it was for him to focus on. To remember me for the long moment when I ripped apart the black candle rune's connection to his father and fed it into the earth instead.

First we all three stood at the edges of my ten-foot rune, and together each cut our wrists to drip blood and ground the magic. "We feed you, Earth," I said, and Donna finished it with me, "that our magic may come full circle."

Immediately I staged Lukas in the center, walking him over the lines of my rune so that none of it was disturbed. I put him on his hands and knees, and pushed up his shirt. "Are you ready?"

His back quivered, and I saw his fingers dig into the grass on either side of the black candle rune there. "Yes," he said, and I touched his spine gently. Proudly.

With a thick but sharp dagger, I rebroke the skin of my wrist and quickly drew a blood circle all the way around his black candle rune. I crouched, finding a strong stance, and took a deep breath. I dripped my blood onto the rune of stalwart action marking the grass, and the earth shivered. Wind picked up, tossing my curls around my face.

Donna said, "I'll catch what falls," and reached into the circle to hand me the blood-sight glasses.

I smeared my blood up and down the blade of the dagger, whispering that the blade should slip between worlds, be sharp against skin and air and magic, too.

Then I took it in my fist and, with no warning, slashed down Lukas's ribs, cutting through my day-old binding and waking his power.

Lukas cried out, but did not fall.

The braided ribbon slipped away from his waist, and through the blood-sight glasses I saw my day-old binding break. The sickly red tendrils of his father's magic flailed like tentacles, and I sliced through them with my dagger. Each was cut apart but stuck to the blade, twisting and burning up the steel and into my hand. I gritted my teeth and hissed, my breath as sharp as the knife.

Lukas whimpered. His fingers dug into the earth.

Dropping the blade, I quickly clapped my bloody hands together and activated the tiny runes of entrapment I'd drawn on each of my fingers and my palms with a marker. I reached out and gathered the swinging tendrils of magic in the basket of my fingers. If we didn't do this fast, the magic would only reconnect to his father.

"Now, Lukas," I said, and he rolled down and onto his back. I moved with him, stretching the tendrils and slamming their ends into the ground. Into the earth.

The rune of stalwart action flared into a red so brilliant I winced away, wishing I could throw off the blood-sight glasses.

Lukas groaned, and I whispered his name, and I yelled a blessing to the earth, a song to link them together. He sang it with me, tuneless and hard, and the wind tore over us.

The glare of magic faded.

I shivered and said, "So it is done, and Lukas is familiar to the blood land."

Overhead, thunder cracked. Rain poured down and I lifted my head, tossing aside the blood-sight glasses. Warm water slipped down my face, streaming down my neck and plastering my clothes to me.

Donna joined us, and we helped Lukas sit. He hugged me, and leaned in to Donna. The three of us remained, exhausted, in the open yard as the rain washed us pure, the sky blessing our magic.

THIRTY-EIGHT

We stole kisses every chance we could, but when Gabriel joined us on our walks or after supper for hot chocolate by the fire, we hid the truth of the thing blossoming between us. For my part, I reveled in the secret and wasn't ready to share it with him. I expected he would be sarcastic or hurtful, and perhaps even jealous. I never knew why you were as willing to keep secrets.

To my mind, all three of us were happy. With each other, with our home, with all the possibilities of the future.

And then an old paramour of Gabriel's called him to Washington late that winter. He enjoyed making a nuisance of himself to the FBI so well that he chose to stay for a bit of time. You and I were alone and free to be in love.

Gabriel sent us a curling love letter of his own tucked into the pages of that novel, 1984. And every few days another letter arrived, filled with adventures and protests. We both read them, but I dismissed the events he discussed as if they had no effect on me. What did I care for Communists or South Korea or earthquakes in Ecuador? Neither you nor I had been reading the newspapers or magazines much, because it had always been he who'd bothered to purchase such things when we ran errands in town. For us, the land was a sanctuary apart from politics and civilization.

It was heaven.

THIRTY-NINE

WILL

Thanks to a particularly intense nightmare that woke me up yelling and the low-grade fever that came with it, Mom freaked out. She let me go to school after I argued for about ten minutes that I had reviews for finals next week, that I obviously wasn't contagious since nobody else in the family was sick, and managed to get Dad on my side with a well-placed line about soldiering through hardship for success. But the price was leaving two hours early to see a doctor.

At lunch I was so nauseated I only managed to choke down the to-go mug of Mab's tea I'd thought to brew this morning. Cold, it tasted vaguely like dirt. Matt slid in next to me on the bench. He thumped down his giant paper bag of food. "You on some weird power diet?" he asked, jerking his chin at my tea. "Or just charging up?"

"It's tea. My stomach hurts."

"Try some ginger," said Shanti as she and Lacey joined us.

"Where's he gonna get *ginger* in the cafeteria?" Matt asked. He paired it with a smile and a quick kiss on her cheek.

From across the table, Lacey pointed at me with her fork. "I like to suck on mint when I don't feel good."

"That's what Dylan said about you," put in Austin as he sat on my other side, smirking.

"Ugh." Shanti rolled her eyes. "That doesn't even make sense."

"Besides," Lacey said lightly, "Dylan doesn't taste that good."

It even got a laugh out of me. For a moment I forgot to pay attention to where I was looking. Lacey frowned and leaned toward me so that her gold crucifix tapped against the table. "What's wrong with your eye?" she asked.

I looked down, winced. "Nothing. It's just . . . ah." I shrugged. Glanced around at the curious faces. "I was roughing around with Ben and he accidentally threw me into the fence. This is just some, uh, hemorrhage from the blunt force trauma."

Thank God for online medical diagnosis. Of course, it had also suggested that a change in eye coloration could be a tumor. I wasn't looking forward to the doctor's appointment and whatever they'd tell Mom. The situation was pretty messed up when you started hoping you were cursed by blood magic.

"Jesus." Matt offered me half his sandwich. It was as big as his hand. "You should eat some real food."

"Yeah, thanks, but no." I could barely choke down the simple tea.

Austin shoved his shoulder into mine. "Matt says you're missing practice because you stayed out all night with some girl."

"That isn't what I—" Matt leaned around behind me and punched Austin's arm.

"Mab," I said. She wasn't some girl.

Shanti lifted her dark eyebrows so high. "Mab Prowd, who kidnapped you from the farmers' market?"

I nodded.

One of her eyebrows stayed up. The other lowered. "The one whose family is some hippie cult out on the prairie? Who doesn't come to school because they don't believe in traditional education?"

I didn't know that was the reason for sure, but I nodded again.

Shanti's lips pursed, and I got the distinct impression I was being judged. I focused on my tea. How did Matt kiss a girl who could pin you down like that?

A quick glance up showed her looking over at the lunch line, where Holly was paying with her punch card. But to my surprise, Shanti said, "Well then. You should introduce her sometime. Officially." Her voice was nice. Sharp, but nice.

"Sure," I said. At her side, Lacey seemed as surprised as me.

Matt swung an arm around Shanti and tugged her right up against him. "That's my girl."

"Your girl?" she said coolly.

"My *woman*," he corrected. Her face broke into a smile. She kissed him full on the mouth. We all looked away. Austin muttered something unflattering, Lacey dug into her salad, I managed to finish the tea.

And sitting in the cafeteria while my friends were just being my friends, I started tipping in favor of all Mab's magic being totally insane. I had some crazy disease, and was only believing her because she was new. Exciting. Because I wanted to kiss her. And because she said she could help me.

Suddenly I couldn't wait for the doctor's appointment. But I wasn't sure if I wanted him to know what was wrong or be totally clueless.

MAB

Lukas slept through the night without any dreams, and woke refreshed enough to join us for a hearty breakfast. Even Donna seemed cheerful after aiding us with such a powerful spell. Magic sparked inside me so bright and ready, I wanted to drive out and pick up Will first thing, to bring him here regardless of his being grounded and cleanse the curse out of his blood.

But he surely had school, and I'd been neglecting my own schoolwork long enough. To show Lukas a good example, I spread out with a pile of algebra worksheets at the kitchen table for a few hours. They weren't my favorite, but solving for missing numbers was remarkably like putting together patterns of magic, and so I didn't despise it, either.

By early afternoon, I decided I'd waited long enough, and gathered up all the things I'd need for the cleansing into a woven bag. I'd have preferred the blood ground for this, but because of the rains last night, the world remained damp and muddy. And so I left everything tucked away and ready in the barn, then returned to the Pink House for the car so that I might go claim Will from his imprisonment.

Sunlight smeared when I emerged from the shade, and Donna waved from the edge of the yard. She had on thick gloves and was raking old leaves out of a garden box. Lukas crouched next to a tent of sticks, and when he saw me he jumped to his feet. "Hey, Mab."

"Lukas." The skin under his eyes was a little hollow, but he didn't move at all like he was still in pain. I smiled, thrilled that redrawing the lines of magic from the black candle rune seemed to have helped so well.

He stuck his hands into his pockets suddenly. "Will you start the fire for me?"

I glanced past him to his tent of sticks, then to Donna, who raised her eyebrows noncommittally. Sighing very gently, because I knew he feared to try his magic and feared fire even more, I said, "Lukas, there are matches in the kitchen, next to the silverware drawer."

His hands fisted in his pockets, but he nodded, then raced barefoot over the grass and pounded up the porch.

Donna made her way to me, boots brushing loudly through the tall grass. When she reached me, she put her hands on my cheeks and said very seriously, "You be gentle with that young man today, Mab."

"I am." I frowned, realizing she meant Will and not Lukas.

She shook my head very slightly. "I mean it. He isn't part of this, and his newness reeks off him like he was a fresh head of garlic."

"He's strong."

"I believe you, but he's also not you. He isn't somebody who lives and breathes magic, little queen. He's from out there— from the rest of the world."

I pulled away from her. "I know it, Donna."

"It's scary stuff."

"Will isn't afraid." Anger coiled in the palms of my hands,

and I curled my fingers up into loose fists in order that nothing spilled out.

"Perhaps he should be, a little."

"Because you always are." I tightened my fists and then let go, wiping my palms against my dress and staring into Donna's eyes.

Her lashes fluttered, but she never looked away. "I am."

Guilty, and thinking of her magic last night, I touched her wrist, just at the end of her sleeve. "I know you have reason. But I don't. We don't."

Donna smiled. "Sure you do, you just make different choices about it."

WILL

Dr. Able was Mom's primary care doctor, so she swung right in. Chatted up all the nurses and told me not to slouch in the waiting room chair. I flipped through a *Highlights* magazine and tried not to rub my chest. Mom didn't even know about the bruise.

I got called back and Mom, thank God, stayed behind.

Dr. Able seemed used to guys like me who didn't really want to be there. He was in his fifties, with rimless glasses and a tiny green frog sticker randomly stuck to the shoulder of his lab coat. He kept his smile on and didn't make me talk other than to tell him my symptoms. I stuck to the physical, focused on the frog sticker.

We did the usual regimen: height, weight, temperature, blood pressure. Turned out my vitals were just fine. He wasn't happy about the bruise, but since it didn't hurt, hadn't even been an open wound, and wasn't hot to the touch, he said we'd only have to keep an eye on it. He prescribed some antibiotics in case it *was* cellulitis. Told me to keep hydrated. Drew some blood. Promised if it didn't get better in a couple of days we'd do an X-ray and explore other options. If I got another fever or the bruising started to get any infection streaks, I should come back in. Probably, I'd gotten food poisoning or a fast virus and the bruise was unrelated to the fever and vomiting, since it was three days later and I'd been mostly fine since. I joked about getting it from the farmers' market.

My eyes, that was something he recommended I go to a specialist about. Could be trauma, like I'd told Matt, could be a genetic thing. Since my vision wasn't affected, it could be nothing, but the headaches meant it could be worse. I asked if I should be worried, and he said he didn't think so. I didn't really believe him.

He explained everything again to Mom, and she frowned at me like she was disappointed I hadn't told her about the bruise. She asked for his penlight so that she could see the red in my eyes. "Oh, Will," she said, her thumb on my cheek.

On the way home, Mom took a hand off the wheel and skimmed her fingers through my hair. "I'm worried about you, baby boy."

"I promise I'm okay, Mom." I looked over at her. In profile, she seemed exactly how she'd always been. Proud. Pretty. Gentle. Like the last year hadn't happened, and she'd never been delicate enough to need therapy. Her hair was in a simple ponytail, with fancy clips holding shorter strands off her face.

Mom offered me a lipstick smile. She'd rarely worn makeup until recently. To hide the sadness, I thought. She said, "I know. Why don't I drop you at home and go pick up this prescription and some of that fried chicken you like so much? Dad should already be there."

"Sure." I gave her a smile back, then leaned my head against the window. My head was aching a bit, behind my eyes. I didn't want to tell her, though. I just needed water and ibuprofen.

And the second we got home, I was calling Mab. If I had to, I'd sneak out tonight, but we were doing her cleansing. No more delays. I had to, either so all this would clear up and Mom could stop worrying, or so I'd know it was . . . something else.

But when we arrived and I dashed upstairs to my bedroom for some privacy, there was no answer.

The phone at her place rang and rang. Apparently they didn't even have an answering machine.

I hung up and tried again. Same result.

The headache behind my eyes burned. I squeezed them shut and put my hands flat against the wall. Taking long breaths, I did a few push-ups. Slow and measured. After about twenty, I just leaned my forehead in. The wall was cool. What was I gonna do? I guessed just keep trying. Maybe go up there tonight anyway, if I could get away.

Outside my window, I heard a car door slam. Probably Mom leaving for my prescription. I spun around and dug my iPod out of my backpack. Jammed the earbuds in and hit play.

Two minutes later I was sitting at my desk with my physics textbook out. At least I could study. My pen tapped against the paper, though, in time with the hard music beat. I immediately started doodling next to a picture of Max Planck.

The iPod was set loud enough I didn't hear Ben knock or open the bedroom door. He had to shove my shoulder and tug one of the earbuds out. It popped away, and his voice interrupted my music with "—is here."

I turned to find him staring down at me with an alert, expectant expression. But it was tough to focus through all the layers of tired. "Who?"

"Wiry thing, strong, curly blond hair?"

"Mab?" I swung the chair around.

"That's her name. She seems sweet. Can't imagine what she sees in you."

Sweet. That wasn't exactly a word I'd used to describe Mab ever. I shoved Ben back. "I'll be right down." I scrubbed my hands down my face in relief and turned off my iPod. "Is she okay? Everything's okay?"

Ben shrugged as he ducked into his bedroom. "Far as I know."

Downstairs, just as I was coming around the corner into the dining room, I heard Mab say, "I asked him not to tell anyone, but I'm very sorry it caused trouble."

I paused, fingers on the wall as I leaned as close to the doorway as possible without revealing myself. Hopefully, I could pick up on whatever she was saying so we wouldn't get our stories crossed. I mean, she couldn't possibly be telling them the truth.

"We certainly understand that, Mab. But it is very important for us to know where our son is." That was Dad.

"Yes, sir," she said. "It's truly not far from here, if you'd only let him come for the evening and help us."

I pushed my forehead against the cool wall to calm my headache. Was she so worried about this curse that she'd come all the way out here to convince Dad to let me go with her?

"What sort of project is this?" Mom asked. She must not have made it out yet.

"Grafting. We've got some old apple trees on our property, and I'm learning to graft. It's part of our homeschooling biology curriculum to do the project and present it to a special panel at a summer camp in July. We combined with some students from Will's high school to help us with social integration."

I couldn't stop my mouth from opening. She said it so smoothly I wondered if she'd practiced the whole way over. *Social integration?*

Ben's footsteps sounded behind me in the upstairs hall. I quickly turned the corner into the dining room. Mom and Dad sat in their usual spots, Dad with his summer-afternoon iced coffee dripping condensation onto the busy tablecloth. Mom had scooted her chair so near him Mab must've interrupted her telling him everything Dr. Able said before going for the drugs.

And Mab was in Aaron's seat, her back straight, hands loosely gripping a glass of water. Her hair was in a braid, so the curls didn't look like a haystack. She'd put a cardigan over her dress. I stared. It made me think of that old story about Pecos Bill, who lassoed a tornado.

"Good afternoon, Will," Mab said, following it with what was, in fact, a sweet smile.

She so didn't fit against the backdrop of the dark wood of

our dining room. The ship's clock gonged its 1600 hours bell. It took me a second to find my voice. "Hey," I mumbled.

"William, good, you're here." Dad nodded firmly.

Mom smiled, and met my glance with a secret nod.

"I was just telling your parents about our science project," Mab said. "The trees very much need to be grafted now that we've had rain, or it might be too late."

I nodded and winced, as if I had any idea about trees.

"It's so nice of you to be helping her," Mom said, standing up. "Would you like some coffee?"

"Uh, water's fine."

Mom went through into the kitchen and pulled down a glass. Filled it with filtered water.

Dad tapped a finger against the table. "You should have said something, son."

"Yeah, punk," Ben said, coming in behind me and knocking his shoulder into mine gently. His tone was playful, and he pulled out the chair beside Mab. "Don't know what you see in this guy."

It wasn't really a question, but for a moment uncertainty filled her eyes. And that was horrifying on several levels. Then she glanced at me and smiled. "He makes me laugh, and is so kind."

I sank down into a chair. Fought not to put my face in my hands.

Ben laughed and shot me a look of incredulity.

"Here, Will." Mom set the water down in front of me.

"Thanks," I managed.

Dad sighed. "Drink up so you can be on your way."

My head jerked up. "You're letting me go?"

"The doctor said there's no immediate danger, if you're feeling up to it. And we aren't going to punish the young lady for your inconsideration."

"I am so sorry, Mr. Sanger." Mab's hands tightened around her glass and her eyes drooped. Where had she gotten to be such a good liar? "Like I said, we were out in the orchard and the time just flew by before we knew it."

Dad grumbled but nodded.

I downed my water and ran upstairs before they could change their minds.

MAB

While Will dashed to get his shoes, I offered the Pink House phone number and told them a little about Donna, as if she were officially my stepmother. She'd done my hair for me, combing it wet and plaiting it into some semblance of order. And reminded me that I should put on a bra and wear sandals instead of galoshes.

Mrs. Sanger took the number down in a delicate, swooping hand. Her fingernails were painted a very soft pink, and I noticed that she wore a ring next to her wedding band that was lined with tiny emeralds. A gem for powerful love and positive energies. She had an easy smile like Will's, but something about the way she held herself reminded me of Granny Lyn in the last months; like something inside her hurt so much she had to be deliberate and move only when necessary.

Will's Dad was more of the pillar holding up the ceiling. Strong and solid like Will, and with the exact same haircut, but his edges were sharper. He would keep down a storm with one hand. I liked him.

But Ben reminded me of Silla: forcing himself into the world so hard because there wasn't anything but a big hole in his heart. He was the one who grilled me on the land and my family and the way homeschooling worked. I told him mostly truthful answers, keeping my voice light.

Will came back downstairs in a different shirt, with thick black and white stripes. It said NORTHERN ROCK on the front and S. TAYLOR 27 on the back. I stood up and took his hand. "Ready?"

He wove his warm fingers with mine and nodded. To his parents he said, "I'll call if it gets late. I promise."

"Make sure you do," Mr. Sanger said.

"It was lovely to meet you, Mab," added Mrs. Sanger.

I smiled at them, and at Ben, who offered me a painted-on smile exactly like Will's. It made my own smile wider.

Will took me outside, and we got into the station wagon. I'd left all the windows rolled down, and Will leaned back in the passenger seat with his arm hanging out. His brow pinched as if he was in pain. I backed out, twisting around to look behind me, and said, "I like your family."

He seemed startled, and stared openly at me until we were a block away. The sun was bright all around us, and I could see the freckles under his eyes as well as the red burning in them.

"What?" I asked lightly.

"Just . . . nothing. I'm glad you like them. I do, too, most of the time. Do you have a radio?" Will reached toward the dash.

"It's been broken since nineteen eighty-seven."

Will laughed, releasing the last of the tension he'd carried out of his house, as if it had its own voice. "Damn. How'd you know where I live, anyway?"

I gestured to the map and silver hand mirror in the backseat. "I used the last drop of your blood for a location spell."

"Of course. That explains everything."

My fingers tightened on the huge steering wheel, but he was grinning wryly at me. Relief spilled down my arms and I slid one of my hands onto my thigh.

Will reached over the gearshift and carefully wove his fingers through mine, stroking my thumb with his. It sent tiny shivers that felt almost like blood magic tingling under my skin.

We drove in silence through the sticky afternoon, the tires splashing water from the highway, until I pulled off the county road and through the gateway to our land.

"I still didn't see it," Will said as we started along the pebbled drive up the hill. I smiled and started to tell him about the wards that kept the gateway hidden, but his hands suddenly gripped his own knees. "Whoa."

I stopped the station wagon and pushed it into park. "Will?"

His eyes squeezed tightly shut and sweat beaded at his hairline. I clambered out of the car and ran around to his side, jerked the door open, and knelt with my hands flat on his thigh. "Will!"

"Just . . . just massively dizzy. Give me a sec." His voice was breathy, and he pushed one hand flat against his chest. "My heart is, like, burning."

I pried his hand away from his heart and put it against my cheek. He was on fire.

Out of nowhere, the crows dropped down and landed on

the roof of the station wagon. I gripped Will's hand, closed my eyes, and imagined strength from inside me flowing out through my skin and into his hand. It would run up his arm and feed his heart. With my free hand, I dug through the glove box for my emergency pocketknife. I unfolded one of the blades with my teeth and pricked the tattoo on the wrist of my hand that held Will's to my face. Dropping the pocketknife, I smeared the blood over my other fingers, then put that hand against Will's cheek to complete the circuit of energy. Face to hand to face and back around, magic tingled in pulses of heat.

Will sighed through pursed lips, and his eyelids fluttered. "That's better," he whispered. "It was, like, I don't know, Mab, something was pulling at this bruise. That wouldn't happen if it was a tumor."

"What?"

He shook his head. "Ugh, I am so glad we're getting rid of the curse."

I pressed his hand to my cheek. "We are. Today. I need to know, though, if it's been building all day, or if it just happened when we crossed onto my land."

"Definitely just now." He sat up farther and gazed out over my shoulder at the trees. "It's been itching, and my head hurts. But it was just now that I got dizzy and it all tightened up."

I released him, reluctantly, and stood. "Come on."

Dashing into the woods, I found a redbud tree with low enough branches I could use it as a ladder into one of the taller cottonwoods. After taking too long to unbuckle my sandals, I scrambled up. Drops of water rained down on me as I shook limbs, and when I leapt across to a gray branch of the cottonwood, I heard Will call out in shock. I was only about ten feet high, but off the ground and in the lattice of trees like this, the forest came alive in a myriad of new layers. Birds fluttered everywhere, and butterflies, too; squirrels ducked into their nests when they saw me, tails twitching; a raccoon stared from a hollow halfway up an elm. The trees shifted in infinitesimal motions, swaying not to the wind but to the turning of the planet.

I closed my eyes and put my cheek against the cottonwood's trunk, where it shimmered with invisible magic. Strings of power lined everything here, and I could just feel the threads unsettle, the pull of strangeness, a shift in the pattern. Was it because of what I did to Lukas, grounding his rune to the land like that? Or because of what was happening to Will? Did the blood land recognize the roses' curse?

"Mab!"

I glanced down to where he stood just under me, face lifted and wide with shock.

"Are you feeling better?" I asked him.

"Healthy as a horse."

"Good." I smiled at him and took a deep breath. "Catch me."

WILL

Her body relaxed as if she fainted. In slow motion she slipped off the branch and fell toward me. I cussed and held out my arms. She landed hard against my chest and right shoulder, staggering me to my knees. Her arms and legs fell limp. Her head lolled back, and all that yellow hair streamed around me. I yelled her name, shook her, and set her down. The ground under her was muddy and covered in a layer of leaves. "Mab."

Nothing. She didn't respond at all.

I saw thin blood all over my hands. Holly's slack mouth.

Cawing crows snapped me out of it, and I yelled, "Mab!" I put my ear to her mouth and scrambled to find a pulse under her jaw. It was there; she was breathing. Calmly, like she was asleep. "Mab," I said again, pleading with her to wake up.

She didn't so much as twitch. I touched her cheek, her lips, her chin, and ran my hand down her arm. No blood. She was warm. Just asleep, I told myself.

No. *Possession.*

She'd left her body, and I remembered that double-vision memory of stepping over her prone form on the floor of the barn.

An owl swooped past my face, its white feathers flapping silently as it sped through the branches. The crows cawed at it, and about half of them took off after it. The others hopped down to me, circling around us.

My heart thudded hard and fast.

Do you trust me? she'd asked. I'd said yes without even knowing what it meant. Without asking her the same. But now, here, was her answer.

I lifted her into a sitting position, and scooted behind her. She slumped against me. I wrapped my arms around her. Her shoulder pushed into the bruise. I ignored it. Her hair tickled my neck. The damp ground soaked into my jeans. All around me the crows watched, wings spread. When they flapped those wings, I smelled thick rainwater and mud.

Catch me, she'd said. And hadn't even considered that I wouldn't.

FORTY

Once, you said to me, "I love you because you're part of the world."

FORTY-ONE

MAB

The trees tried to whisper to me, but I couldn't understand. I flew through the topmost branches, beating silent white wings, and listened with the owl's ears, but to no avail. I leapt into a sparrow and rode its tiny mind through the trees until there was a pair of blue jays shrieking at me. Taking them both, I spread out. Reese joined us, and we were a flock of black and blue, spreading a net over the land. As we flew past squirrels and a family of foxes, I snatched them up, too, throwing myself into more and more small minds. I let go of my name and became the forest. I listened, I watched, I felt and sensed and smelled, and all of it rolled into a giant ball of knowledge I could almost parse.

The wind shook branches, and I crawled over roots, I scampered up through twigs, I skimmed wings across the canopy and yet did not understand. Even when I pushed toward the roses, when I felt the energy of them, the message was garbled.

I was the skin of the forest but could not touch its bones.

And so I turned toward my body at the base of the hill, and let go some of my little souls.

First a raccoon and then the sparrow, and soon I released more. The squirrels and the owl, the blue jays, the rabbits racing from bush to bush. Until I was only a red fox, running head-long through the rain-soaked underbrush. I could smell Will, could feel where he'd passed, for it had left a red-hot mark on the earth. There he was, cradling my body. I let go of the fox's mind and dove home into myself.

Oh, it was grand to lie there on the warm, wet earth with my eyes closed and feel my heartbeat. I did not move but breathed in a circular pattern my mother had taught me for reconnecting with all the tissues of my body, for helping what I had seen and heard and smelled in different tiny animal minds coalesce in my own mind. It needed a long moment to process, to transform from animal memory to my own. Too fast and it was all a black blur, confusing and maddening. Force it, and it became a blank palette to imprint your own assumptions upon. *You are only a different kind of animal, pet,* my mother had said when I was small. *And you only need give your blood and your power time to convert beastly knowledge into your own.*

Heat flooded me, from Will's arm. His fingers lined up against my ribs, his thumb over my sternum. I felt pressure where his other hand twisted in my curls. A small smile turned up my mouth as I nestled closer.

"Mab?" Will whispered.

I opened my eyes.

His eyes were right there, big and dark and edged in blood.

"Will," I said.

"Mab." His breath puffed over my cheek, and I touched his face just under his eye.

"That red is darker," I murmured. "And I couldn't discover what exactly made your curse flare up."

His lips pressed together, pinching his whole expression. "Are you okay, though?"

"Yes." I pushed gently off of him and stood. My skirt was muddy and stuck to my thighs. "Let's get to the barn."

Although the blood ground seemed the most logical place to cleanse away a curse, the barn would do, not only because it was drier than the rest of the world but because the wards painted around the outside made it into a permanent working circle. The curse could not escape these solid pine walls.

While Will fidgeted over near the family tree, I dragged the basket of purity stones out from under a pile of old rugs and set them onto the dusty floor next to a short cast-iron fire pit. I spread out a thin red cloth for him to lie on, and another for my tools: a fleam, a crow-feather fan, and six little bowls of herbs I'd ground down earlier that afternoon. From outside, I fetched a wide and shallow stone bowl that had collected rainwater overnight, and as I carefully walked it to the fire pit, I noticed Will running his finger along one branch of the family tree.

I'd always loved the mural. Arthur's name created the darkest lines of the trunk, and we were all there, our names and birth dates penned in blood ink. Every branch led up and away from him, out to the dozens of cousins since his son was born in 1887. There on the left was the unrelated Harleigh line, ending with Nick, and just below him, Donna. And far across from that, a lonely branch named Josephine Darly that stretched up thin and winding to my name. We did not know where our bloodline came from, and now that she was dead, we never would. Maybe Mother had been an orphan from a known line, lost to time, and maybe that's what Lukas was, too, for we had no records of family settling in the Ozarks. The nearest were the Yaleylah witches, of Arthur's own direct line: Silla's family, where Arthur had drawn Reese's death date below his name, as well as the silhouette of a flying crow.

That was the branch Will touched, tracing the line of the crow's wings.

"Will," I said gently, and he turned to me, his shoulders twisting and his smile in place. "Can you build a fire?" I indicated the fire pit with a slow wave of my hand.

"Of course." He joined me, and I showed him the old newspaper, bundle of dry logs, and long matches.

He crouched and got to work twisting paper, and I turned my attention to the purity rocks. Each was marked with a strength rune so that it would not crack in the heat, and a rune of holy rain so that it might carry only the clean magic we wished. With the fleam, I pierced my tattoo, letting a single drop splash onto the center of the runes. Lifting each of the nine stones to my mouth, I breathed life into them and set them in a small pile.

The fire danced up from the tent of sticks as Will's newspapers caught alight. Sweat glistened on his forehead, and he lifted the hem of his shirt to wipe it off.

I gasped when I saw his stomach.

He froze, shirt halfway down again. "What?" His voice rang with alarm.

I reached forward to lift the hem of his black-and-white-striped shirt higher. "Take it off," I whispered. Lines of angry red cut down from his chest, just under his skin, streaking like blood poison.

"Jesus," he said, standing and stripping off the shirt. It fluttered to the ground, and he pushed his fingers into his chest. "It was not this bad two hours ago."

"It must have been when you stepped back onto the blood ground. Here is where the curse originated, so here it is stronger." I skimmed my fingers along one of the largest blood branches, and Will shuddered. "Take deep breaths. In, count to five, out, count to five."

His breathing remained shaky, but he got it under control as I traced my finger along the lines. I stepped in close and put both my hands against him, covering the center burst of the bruise gently. It radiated the tingling heat I knew to be magic. Glancing up at him, I said, "It will be all right, Will."

"Oh yeah?" He was hoarse, and he tilted his chin down. My eyes were only a few inches from his. Even in the shade of the barn, I could see the red around his irises had bled inward, stretching thin fingers toward the black of his pupils.

"I promise," I said. "Now take off the rest of your clothes."

He started in surprise, and I hoped I'd calculated right.

It only took a second before Will laughed a little bit. I kept my hands on his chest, and his merriment didn't last long, but when he covered my hands with his, he wasn't shaking anymore. He wasn't holding himself so tightly he might explode.

WILL

Turned out, she hadn't been entirely kidding. Mab dug through a cardboard box of clothes and pulled out a pair of dark blue drawstring pants. Apparently, jeans weren't going to cut it for the cleansing ritual.

I was glad to grab onto the slight embarrassment of ducking behind a stack of crates to change into some incredibly hippie-looking pants. Embarrassed was better than scared. I rubbed my hand over the bruise. The hard weight pushed into my chest. I remembered looking at it in the mirror this morning, when it had been free of red streaks and just a bruise. And I remembered the sharp compression when we'd driven onto the land, when I'd been dizzy and hurting and felt like somebody had dumped a bucket of hot coals over my head. If it had been like this at Dr. Able's, he'd have hooked me up to an IV of antibiotics and I'd never have escaped.

This had to work.

I came out, leaving the rest of my clothes in a pile. For a moment I watched Mab kneel and set the last of her rocks in the fire. She seemed calm. Certain.

"Will. Come lie down." She patted the red cloth beside her.

I obeyed. The floor of the barn was flat enough. Not super comfortable. Mab leaned over me, positioning my hands at my sides, palms down. She'd taken off her cardigan, and her hair was loose. It spilled all around her, falling onto my shoulders and face. I closed my eyes. The fire crackled. Wind blew through the rafters. But there was no other sound. My lungs squeezed. I was supposed to be calm, but the silence was making me crazy.

"Mab," I said into her hair. It tickled my mouth, sent a buzz down my whole body.

"Oh, sorry." She gathered it in one hand and tossed it over her shoulder.

"No, it isn't that."

"Yes?"

With her face tipped down, it was hidden in shadows. "It's just so quiet. I relax better with noise."

Mab sat back onto her heels and folded her hands in her lap. Her hair was like a thick yellow cape. "I'll hum, and sing a little. Will that be all right?"

I squeezed my eyes shut.

She put her hand on my chest. It was cool compared to me. "Will?"

I took a deep breath, expanding my lungs all the way, and let it out slowly. Mab shifted her hand so it was directly over my heart. "Why don't you tell me about the quiet, Will." She kept saying my name, like it would make things better. "You can relax into it a little? And letting it go will be part of the cleansing."

I curled my hand around hers. Hadn't ever told anybody about this. It wasn't the kind of thing Matt would ask. But with the warm fire, the weight on my chest, and Mab's hand, I realized I wanted to tell her. "It's just that the quiet makes me think of the night we found out my brother was dead."

We'd been at dinner. Dad was grilling me on the hours I was working. Mom put in a few words every once in a while, keeping the mood light. I cleared my throat. Squeezed my eyes shut. "He—Aaron—had been on his road trip for five days and called every night just before our dinnertime, which was precisely nineteen hundred hours. He was late, though, and when the phone finally rang, I just remember wanting to give him a hard time. But Mom shushed me back into my chair, saying I didn't get to escape so easily. She picked up the phone, and I leaned over my plate, trying to hear. Dad wanted to know how it was going, too, so he didn't bother talking. It was really quiet." Except for the ticking ship clock.

"She said, 'Sanger residence' like always, and then 'Yes, this is Mrs. Sanger,' and 'Yes, Aaron is my son.'" I opened my eyes. Mab was there, bent over me. She didn't move and kept her gaze on mine. Not making any expression, just witnessing.

I said, "Then the phone fell. It was this incredibly loud plastic crack on the kitchen floor. Dad and I were up and squeezed through the kitchen door at the same time. He went for the phone, and I went for Mom. She'd sunk down onto a chair at the breakfast bar, staring out the window. Dad said some things, while I held Mom's hands. His voice was low, and I don't know how long it lasted. All I could hear was Mom's breath, panting out of her open mouth. Nothing else in the whole world. Like there wouldn't be noise ever again. Then suddenly Mom stood up, walked to the TV, and turned it on. She put the volume all the way up. I went with her from room to room, turning on all the TVs and the stereo, opening all the windows to let in noise from outside. It was almost enough."

Tears stuck Mab's lashes together. She wiped her finger under her eyes, and put it against my chest again. She drew a simple rune, and it should have been a little gross to have a girl drawing on my skin with her tears. Instead it made me feel better.

She whispered, "I am so sorry about your brother."

"It was a car accident." I sighed loudly. "Stupid luck, they said. He hadn't been drinking or anything. No rain, no bad conditions. Aaron just lost control, and we don't know why. There were skid marks, so maybe he was avoiding a deer, but . . ." My throat clogged. I gasped, remembering my dreams of choking on roses.

Mab leaned down and kissed my forehead. Her lips were cool against my fever. She said, "Put your head on my lap, and I'll sing your curse away, Will Sanger."

I let her direct my head to her thigh. A great open feeling settled in my stomach. One hand of hers rested on my chest. I tilted my chin back as far as it would go to see her use barbecue tongs to grab one of the hot rocks and set it onto the barn floor. She lined up three of them. Then scooped water out of a bowl and poured it over them. It vaporized with a hiss.

She pinched brownish powder from one of the tiny bowls and sprinkled it over the rocks, too. The steam instantly smelled sharper and burned my nose.

"This will only hurt a very little," she said as she showed me a small silver knife. When she cut my chest right at the center of the bruise, it was more of a relief than pain. A quick burn, and the weight lifted just a little.

Mab said, "I'm only adding the other herbs to the fire next, and then a little blood. You don't have to do anything but try to relax."

I focused my gaze on her face, on the triangle of shadow under her chin, on the single long curl falling over her shoulder. With that as my last sight, I shut my eyes.

Into the darkness came a soft sound. Humming. Mab was humming. The vibration of it traveled down into her leg and brushed my neck. I didn't know the song, and maybe she was making it up, but it turned around and around on itself as though she was singing a chorus only, over and over. I heard her rustle, heard the hiss of steam, felt her shift occasionally under my head. Her finger smeared something onto my chest again. I began to sweat, and Mab's humming sped up. She put her hand on my forehead, stroking in a spiral.

My bones turned to hot water and my muscles loosened. My skin vanished, became mist. All I knew was her touch on my forehead, her voice in my ear.

MAB

I bled onto the stones.

My blood became fog and hung in the air. I diffused it with water, and gave it power with my song. I traced runes of wellness and purity into Will's slick skin, pushing all my hopes into the music and into the runes. With the crow-feather fan, I blew the steam against him, into his face, across his chest. I brought in the rest of the rocks, swaying in rhythm with my heartbeat and Will's. I poured water; I breathed thick, hot air laced with sage and dandelion, garlic and milk thistle. Also lavender for peace and skullcap for relaxation. Sweat poured down my face, and my hair bounced up into tangles of chaos.

I was light and tethered to the earth only by Will's heavy

head on my thigh. I breathed. I drew in long strings of air and let them out with music.

Magic rushed from my center, spilling out over Will with a burn. He winced, and I brought my singing ever so slightly louder as my power burned his curse away.

A tiny breeze moved into the barn, gathering up stray wisps of steam and carrying them out.

Bending down to peer at Will's chest, I saw that the branches of angry blood had faded, and there was no yellow rose. I sighed, relieved, and tickled his cheek with the tips of my hair.

As his eyes opened, I took his face in my hands and tilted it this way and that, inspecting his eyes. Flecks of red held on to the brown irises, but I wasn't worried. They, too, would fade as the bruise had.

"Mab?" he whispered.

I was all curled around him, smiling down. "I pronounce you cleansed."

FORTY-TWO

Gabriel came home early that summer. You went to pick him up at the station, and when the two of you climbed out of the Pontiac in front of the house, all smiles, I threw my arms around him, glad to smell that sunny aftershave lotion again and not even minding the stiff hold of his hair. He returned my embrace and said, "More enthusiasm than I expected," with a low chuckle. I took his hand and led him inside, where there was a pie from the last of our winter preserves and roast duck just for him. Do you remember how excited we were? How we'd looked forward to him being there, the long summer evenings by the fire, him reading to us like he'd always done, telling funny stories from his time away? How I'd spent the week cleaning the house, fluffing out my garden, and you painted the trim around the windows and the whole porch? How we planned the exact moment you'd tell him you'd asked me to marry you?

There were a few moments of awkwardness, because you and I had lived alone for almost a year, and we knew exactly what space we had, how we moved inside it, when to slide past and steal a little kiss or brief touch of fingers. And here was Gabriel again, a lost piece of the puzzle, so we all needed to rearrange. I remembered vividly how it had felt to be the odd one, and went out of my way to stand so he was as close to you as to me, and to hold myself as if I didn't constantly think about slipping my hands inside your jacket. We ate that duck and laughed and Gabriel regaled us with tales of Washington rallies, snotty wives, and elegant parties. I told him about my soaps and how popular they'd become, and you said you had started a project where the Child and Mighty Creeks came together to enspell the ground so that it was always protected for permanent magic. We ate nearly that whole pie, and as we lolled like cats in the parlor, you took my hand and Gabriel's, and with your fingers twining with mine, said, "Gabriel, Evelyn has promised to be my wife."

He grew as still as a hunted rabbit, then his eyes flicked to mine. I smiled, making my whole face and body as happy-seeming as I could. I squeezed your hand and added, "But Arthur insisted on waiting until you came home."

At that, Gabriel relaxed, sinking into the wingback chair with a laugh. "Well then," he said, glancing at the ceiling in relief. "And here I'd been worried about you two finding more than three words to say to each other."

"Talking isn't much of what we do," I said impishly, and you blinked in astonishment while Gabriel crowed. He tore into the larder and brought out a dusty bottle of brandy. That night we got drunk, all three of us, dancing and laughing and singing—even you. I remember imagining years ahead of us, many celebrations, children shrieking, Christmases and birthdays and merry fires.

Gabriel was in all of those dreams. Always with us, our brother and friend, uncle to our children. We should have been so happy.

FORTY-THREE

WILL

Mab helped me sit, and ordered me to stay still while she picked things up. "You need to rest, let your body adjust."

I watched her put out the fire. My head swam, but not in a sick way. More like after shooting a winning goal. Looking down, I saw that my chest was slightly discolored, but the red infection lines had all pulled back. I touched it. The skin there wasn't any hotter than the rest of me. I smiled. It had worked. Even my headache was gone. I smelled smoke and those sharp herbs. Fresh wind from the wide-open barn doors. Laughter shoved my smile wider.

Mab knelt beside me with a platter of cookies and sliced meat and cheese. Also a big cup of water. "Go slowly," she said.

I concentrated on sipping the water she handed me. My stomach growled, and I dug in. Mab only touched my hand to slow me down once or twice. She ate, too, and together we decimated the picnic. I couldn't wait to show my mom I was fine. To prove it to Ben. But first thing when I got home, I'd go out with a peanut-butter bone and say hi to my girls again.

With food and water, I felt completely myself, and completely revived. I leaned onto my hands. Breathed deep. Mab pulled her knees up to her chest and watched me. When she didn't glance away, for lack of anything better, I grinned. She smiled back and said, "I want to show you something."

Getting up, she went to the row of crowded shelves against one wall. She brought back a basket of what looked like toys. "Pick one."

"What for?"

Her smile was mysterious. "Just pick."

Blowing breath up my face, I leaned over and carefully rummaged through. They were wooden carvings and glitter-encrusted ornaments. Little figurines, metal shapes, origami flowers. I pulled out a small plastic statue of a running horse with a jockey stooped over his back. A little ring came out of the horse's head. Mab tied a red string through it.

"Great," she said. With the horse in one hand, she offered me her other.

Mab took me around the west side of the hill, through a meadow. We were both barefoot, and carefully avoided blackberry vines hidden in the knee-high grasses. She pointed out different plants with names like dogbane and compass leaf. The sun shone down, prickling my bare shoulders. Wind blew gently.

I told Mab that knock-knock joke where it's always "banana" until you break it up with "orange you glad I didn't say banana," and even though Mab laughed so brightly it drowned out the singing birds, I realized *magic* had made me stupid giddy. But I didn't care. Just held on to her hand and let my head be a hot-air balloon sailing off to the clouds.

At the south side, we were confronted by a field of waist-high stalks with big leaves. I asked if it was corn, but Mab gave me a funny look and said, "Sunflowers!" before diving between two rows. I ran after her, and the leaves slapped my stomach and sides. It was like hurrying past the other team at the end of the game, shaking and slapping hands without really looking at any of their faces. I slowed to my favorite jogging pace, barely noticing the uneven ground. Ahead was an old silo that glared orange in the light. Mab made straight for it, crossing a field of very short purple flowers. She didn't even try to step around them.

At the silo, Mab grasped the rickety-looking ladder. "Afraid of heights?"

"Not that I know of," I said.

She started up and I went right after. Made the mistake of looking up. Her skirt was flowy enough around her knees, thank God. I paused, gripping the ladder, and waited until she was to the top before continuing. The ladder shook with my weight, but not terribly. Several of the rungs had been reinforced recently. The rust wasn't too bad.

Up top, I rolled over the rim and onto thin grass, surprised it wasn't a built-up roof. A tree grew out of it, too, shading most everything. It dripped with ribbons and ornaments like some crazy summer Christmas tree. Mab waited with a smile, her hip pressed to the lip of the silo "Welcome to my tower," she said, throwing out her arms.

"It's great." I angled my head back to look up through the tree branches.

She asked me to pull a branch lower so she could tie the

ornament onto it. When she released it, the snap made all the little silver bells ring out. Wind picked up the crazy song, and Mab dragged me back to the edge.

We were at least four stories high, and from here could see out over miles and miles to the east. The hill was to the left, with no sign of the house visible through the leaves. I could make out the country road only by the break in the trees. Everything else was rolling prairie and forest, all green and dazzling. I walked along to the south, where the view was mostly the same, with more cultivated farm fields, a checkerboard of green and gold grass.

"Our land goes to the end of that meadow there, where the line of poplars is." Mab pointed with her left hand, and her front angled against my arm. I wanted to move it out of the way, so she'd lean into my chest. "We have it mowed for hay every other year," she continued, "and trade out with the west field, which you can't see because of the tree and the Mighty Creek back there."

I shifted my arm. Mab moved in naturally, head tilted up for my reaction.

"It's incredible," I said. Her hand rested on my side. And her hair prickled my skin. I basically never wanted to move again.

Mab pushed gently away from me and walked back to the tree. The spot where her hand had been was cold. I didn't follow.

From the shadows, Mab said quietly, "I haven't brought anyone up here before." She sounded surprised.

I winced. "I can go, we can do something else, or—"

"No, no," she took one stilted step back toward me. "I didn't mean . . ." Mab sighed. "I was only realizing it, not regretting it."

I smiled. She smiled.

To break the moment, before I started feeling too awkward again, I pointed at the meadow. "Could I bring my dogs out here sometime? They'd love it." Thinking about Havoc barking happily, and Val bouncing all around, made my smile expand until I thought my face might break. I couldn't wait to see them again.

Mab made a serious face. "If they promise not to charge at any of my spells again."

"Hey, now," I picked my way closer, and returned her look. "That wasn't their fault. And besides"—I paused, standing just out of reach of her. I felt soft, suddenly—"all things considered, I'm pretty glad it happened."

"Me too," she said, a smile cracking through.

MAB

Having someone else atop my tower should have made it smaller, but instead it felt expansive and new again. I sat back against the trunk of the redbud, hugging my knees, while Will stretched out in the sun with his arms folded under his head. The crows joined us, settling into the tree and causing the bells to ring and the leaf shadows to shake. The patterns dappled across Will's face and chest. I could see the shadow of the yellow-rose bruise, but it was nearly vanished.

Relief seeped down my body, relaxing me. Now that the curse I'd released from the roses was cleansed away, any rampant strands of magic should fade. I'd have time to fully remove Lukas's black candle rune, safely and certainly. Everything was falling into place.

I leaned my cheek onto my knee and watched his eyelids flutter as his eyes moved under them. "I'm not sure I'm going to be able to climb back down," he said softly, surprising me.

"How come?" My words sounded skewed because my cheek was pressed into my knee.

"Too comfortable." He stretched, arching his neck and reaching with his arms back toward me. His fingers splayed and so did his toes, like a big dog just waking up.

I curled my toes into the grass. That was how I always felt up here, too. "A little sleep would probably be good, after how hard we worked."

"I just lay there. You did all the work."

"It's my job." I lifted a hand up and skimmed a finger along the bottom of a low-drooping leaf. "And I can gather energy back up to me from the land."

Will's eyes opened, and he looked at me, craning his neck a bit. "Oh yeah?"

"Yeah."

"What else can you do?"

I smiled secretively. "Anything."

"Walk on water?"

"Oh." I pursed my lips. "I've never tried, but I bet Arthur might've."

He laughed and shook his head. "Was he your dad?"

"No." I hugged my knees together.

"How'd you end up here?"

"The way all the magic does. Someone brought me. My mother did, when I was almost two years old. Old enough she decided I didn't need her all the time, she said."

Will's smile died. "That sucks."

"Oh, it was true, though. I had Arthur, and Granny Lyn, and several frequent . . . cousins, I suppose you'd call them. When I was younger, there was a boy named Justin here, and for five years a couple lived with us named Faith and Eli, and they had two children. Mother came and went, and when she was here she loved me fiercely." I shrugged. "I haven't felt neglected or abandoned, if that's what you're thinking. My family is here."

"Non-trad, huh? I guess normal isn't really something that applies to many families these days."

I nodded. "And now I have Donna. She's been here since I was eleven, just longer than my mother's been gone. Her son, Nick, treats me like a stepsister most of the time." I thought of Silla. I wasn't sure what she was to me. What she wanted to be. I'd have liked to call her sister. *Sister-in-magic,* perhaps.

I glanced up at the crows roosting overhead. "And them," I said.

"The crows?"

"They're my family, too." I looked back at Will. He was watching me instead of the crows. "I was up here, you know, when they first came. I was tying a charm into the branches." I twisted my body and pointed up. "That one, the little wooden bear. I was on my tiptoes, and the ribbon kept slipping because it was stiff and new. And then a crow landed right on the limb, put his claw against my knot, and held it in place while I looped the bows. I said, 'Thank you, sir,' and he bobbed a little bow for me. I was so delighted, I plucked a few hairs from my head and braided them together." My eyes drifted closed as I remembered. "I offered the braid to him, and he took it delicately in his beak as if it were more precious than gold."

"You talk like they're human."

I blinked. "Oh, well. They were."

"What?" He sat up.

"They're a boy named Reese. He lived in Missouri, and just before he died he threw his spirit into one of the crows, so that he wouldn't be dead. Possessed them. And he lives on, flying and free, and he's here with me and safe. We're friends." I smiled up at the nearest crow. He ruffled his neck feathers.

"That's amazing. Like being immortal, and being able to fly." Will sounded wistful, half dreaming and full of faith. He understood.

I crawled the handful of feet to where he sat, and when he glanced down at me, I touched his chest. Slowly, I flattened my palm against it, near his shoulder, where on the first day we met I'd left a bloody handprint. Will's breath brushed against my temple, ruffling my hair. Shifting even nearer, I tilted my head and touched my lips to his cheek.

One of his hands lifted to my jaw, and his fingers caressed just under my ear. Neither of us moved otherwise for several shaking moments, until Will turned and kissed me.

It was his lips on mine, unmoving, only resting together so that if we held still enough we'd melt into one.

I leaned my chin away, to breathe him in, all my blood

atingle, and it put my face even nearer to his, so that when I blinked, my lashes swept along his cheek.

"Mab," he whispered.

Smiling, I looked into his acorn eyes, at the glints of red like broken glass. There was a line of magic between us, and it hummed.

FORTY-FOUR

You wanted your oldest friends to meet me, to come to our wedding, and for me to have a chance to know them. So many weren't available by telephone or even mail—you had to leave and track them down. Your old apprentice Philip Osborn, who'd vanished into the Rocky Mountains after the Second World War; the German twins; and Earnest Harleigh in particular. Gabriel said, "Go, man, I'll make sure no dragons devour your princess." I said I was dragon enough to fight back myself, and Gabriel tugged my braid like a ten-year-old boy, and you were comforted that we'd be all right.

The first few days passed as normally as ever, though I missed your touch, especially first thing in the mornings. Gabriel slid back into farm life, taking up the slack you left, and being, I must say, more appreciative of my baking than you ever were. As the sun set on the third day, he brought me tea as I watched the sky change from pale blue to purple from the front porch. He claimed it was a tea he'd found in New York, from a tiny yellow flower we didn't have on the prairie. I took it and drank it. The cloying flavor was covered with mint, and overall quite delicious.

But it was not merely tea. It was poison.

FORTY-FIVE

M A B

Because it was getting to be evening time, I took Will back to the barn for his clothes, then we circled around to the car. As much as I wished for him to stay, we climbed into the station wagon and headed into town. Halfway to his neighborhood, Will got out his cell phone and texted his parents, then put a hand on my wrist and said, "I don't want to go home yet. How do you feel about concretes?"

I hadn't the first idea what he was talking about until he directed me onto an appallingly commercial road with fast food every five feet and giant superstores. We pulled around a drive-through at a building with cartoon cows painted on all the awnings, and Will ordered a strawberry ice cream for himself. After peering at me for a moment, he asked for another, flavored mint chocolate chip. I tried to pay with a couple of hastily transformed leaves from the glove compartment, but Will snatched the fake money from my hands and dug his wallet out of his jeans. As we drove back toward the real world, Will balanced the two Styrofoam cups between his legs and popped open the glove compartment. He pulled out every last leaf and tossed them all out the window. They floated in our wake. A couple of crows dropped down from the sky to catch at them.

Content to follow Will's directions, I turned us into the parking lot at his high school. There weren't many others near at this hour. I supposed most of their after-school activities were just finishing up, and students trickled through the cars. We got out at the far corner, near the football stadium. Holding the cold, hard ice cream in my hand, I climbed up the concrete bleachers. It was like an ancient coliseum, all stone and cement surrounding the green playing field. The white stripes were freshly painted against the grass, like runes, and a ring of bright pink track surrounded it. "It's like a giant magical circle," I teased. And Will said, "This is *my* silo, Mab," with a smile.

It entirely made up for being trapped in town, without the comfort of dirt under my feet.

Overhead, the clouds had vanished along with most of the humidity, leaving the sky a solid blue. I sat beside Will, the setting sun shining on us from low above the trees, and curled my legs up under me. The crows landed around us, bobbing around as they hunted for old crumbs and bits of trash.

"I don't think this is real food." I pushed the plastic spoon into the chunk of frozen dessert.

"It's custard." Will offered me his spoon. "Taste the strawberry?"

I considered the rock-hard ice cream in his hand. "The only food that should be that pink is steak."

"You're staring at that like you want to turn it into a frog," Will said with a full mouth.

I tasted mine. The mint was surprisingly refreshing, and I

let it melt over my tongue, leaving the little flake of chocolate behind.

"I knew you'd like it."

He was half finished with his, and I gave in, digging into the custard. We didn't have ice cream very often, and I'd never had this flavor. I ate about half, too fast, and when a burning cold headache bit into my forehead I gasped and pushed it away. As Will tried to muffle his laughter, I lay down and put my cheek to the hot concrete step. The heat radiated up into my whole body.

Will sat on the row below me, his back against the vertical stair, so that his shoulder rested a few inches from my nose. I opened my eyes and stared at the scatter of freckles drifting down from his hairline to vanish under the collar of his T-shirt.

Reaching out, I skimmed my fingers there. Will jerked in surprise but settled back again. I set my hand on his shoulder, just where it met his neck. His skin was warm from the sun, and his shoulders rose and fell as he breathed. "Is this where you play soccer?" I asked.

"Naw. Practice sometimes. But soccer needs a wider field. We play over there." He pointed south. "See the goal nets?"

I didn't look, but murmured my assent. He lifted his hand to cover mine, and I was content to soak up heat from the stadium and watch the way his jaw moved when he talked, the way the muscles connected down his neck and the very slight motion of his earlobe.

Several rows below us, a little gray and brown sparrow landed, only to hop nervously away from the crows that had spread themselves in a wide arc up and down the stone bleachers. The sparrow had a large chunk of bread in its tiny beak. My eyes fluttered closed as the rush of town traffic filled my ears. I smelled the city's summer cocktail of exhaust, mud, and sweet rotting trash. The heat cooked my skin, and sweat prickled along my spine. But I didn't want to get up and go. There was something shocking and easy about being under such bright, harsh sun. Anyone could see me, could see all of me, and Will's hand in mine.

He asked me, quietly, "What do you want, Mab?"

I leaned up so that I could look at him. His face was scrunched as he tilted his head at the sun. A slight glint of red still winked at me from the edge of his iris. "Want?"

"Yeah. You know. From life."

"Oh, well. To be what I am, who I am. The Deacon. Magic. Living and breathing the land and its energies. Helping people, binding curses. It's what I'm meant for."

Will's smile twisted on one side, hinting at bitterness. "That must be nice."

I shook my head. "It's hard."

"But at least you *know.*"

"You don't?" I brought his hand into my lap, held it in both of mine. "You told me you want to travel. To visit beautiful places and fly across the ocean."

"That doesn't mean anything, though. It's just—it's just running away." Will stood up, pushed his hands into his eyes. With his back to me, he said, "I only really know what I don't want. I don't want to be a Marine. I don't want to do everything my brothers did and my dad. I don't want . . . I don't want to be what they think I'm supposed to be. Aaron followed that path, and it killed him. For stupid reasons." He made a strangled noise. "It was like this wake-up call, you know? Telling me that there were other roads, but when I opened my eyes I didn't see anything."

I climbed to my feet, too, and stood on the edge of the step so that my stomach was level with the back of his head. "You saw me," I said gently.

Will turned and looked up. "I do see you, which is making it worse, somehow. You know. You're so sure of everything, and it makes me crazy, but it's also what I want. To be sure."

"I'm not sure. I don't know exactly what to do all the time!" I laughed helplessly, thinking of how I'd only come up with a temporary patch to help Lukas. "I'm still learning."

"But you know who you are," he whispered.

The despair layering in his voice tugged at me, and I reached out. I pulled him against me until his face was buried in my stomach. His arms went around my hips. "I know who you are, too, Will," I whispered back. I'd seen and tasted and transformed his blood. It was impossible not to know someone after that. I curled my body down over his, as if I could protect him from the world.

Will pushed away from me to crane his head up, though his hands stayed firm on my hips, the grip burning through my dress. "Who am I, then?"

"I can't just tell you. That would ruin the magic of you discovering it yourself." I said it with a quirk of my mouth, to show him I only teased.

He laughed. A soft, high-pitched laugh that sounded more

sad than happy. "I can't believe I'm talking about this. It isn't something real people talk about, you know?"

"No, I don't know that."

"That's probably why it's happening." Will tugged me down onto his level, and I slid against him, our bodies pressing completely together. I gasped, catching the breath under my heart.

"Hey, Will!" yelled someone.

Will jumped back from me, turning and throwing a hand up to block the sun. "Matt!" he called back.

I wrapped my fingers into the hem of Will's T-shirt, in the small of his back. The crows took flight, soaring up to find higher vantages.

The other boy—Matt—took the bleachers in flying leaps, so that his backpack thumped against him and his flopping hair fell into his face, and every other step he shoved it away.

"I thought it was you," he said as he joined us halfway up the side of the stadium, "though supposedly you've been *grounded.*"

Will grimaced. "Mab sprung me."

"Damn," Matt eyed me with mingled suspicion and respect, and once again brushed his hair out of his face. "You must have some kind of magic charm to get past his dad."

It startled me, but Will immediately laughed and pulled my hand away from his shirt, though he kept it tucked into his own. "She does. She really does," he said. Turning the smile on me, he introduced Matt as the captain of his soccer team. "And Matt, this, obviously, is Mab Prowd."

Wishing there was a thing softer and more natural than concrete under my sandals, I removed my hand from Will's to offer it for a shake. Matt took it, and I kept my gaze firm, my expression as calm as I could, until it occurred to me that Will would smile. I tried it, and Matt instantly responded, shaking his head slightly as he did. "Nice to meet you finally," he said.

"Finally?" I glanced questioningly between the two of them. "It's hardly been as long as all that we've known each other."

"Yeah, but"—Matt leaned into me so that our shoulders nearly touched, and turned to face Will, effectively putting him and me on one side and Will on the other—"this jackass got himself in trouble twice over you. So it might not have been long, but obviously it's been real."

"I wasn't sure, for a while, if it was," Will admitted, and I felt a little bit lost between them. And so I merely nodded. If only there were wilderness here to bolster me instead of this sterile stadium!

"Wait," Will added suddenly. "Twice? What?"

Matt widened his eyes but failed to appear remotely innocent because of the crooked tilt of his lips. "Shanti only mentioned something about you abandoning them at the farmers' market."

Will's face scrunched up. "They didn't even want me there."

"Oh, well." Matt shrugged similarly to the way I'd seen my cousin Justin gesture before, always when talking about women.

"I should be getting home soon," I said, unwilling to share my time with this boy, and not just a little sad Will and I had been interrupted.

Sighing, Will said, "Me too. I'm not totally free."

"That's incredibly stupid." Matt stepped back from both

of us. "You guys should come get dinner. We'll swing around to grab Shanti." He nodded to Will. "Like we talked about. I know for a fact she's dying to hang out with Mab."

It filled me with discomfort, around my stomach like hot water, to imagine other people my age, out here in the civilized world, talking about me or thinking about me at all. I wasn't for them or their world.

Will paused, but then he saw me and read the uncertainty I'm sure painted my face. "I can't. But," he flicked his eyes at me and back to Matt. "We should. Like, after finals." The last was said with a tiny uptilt to it and directed mostly at me.

I firmed my resolve and said yes.

WILL

It hadn't been a lie when I'd said I wasn't free. I'd texted Mom, but it was good Matt had given us an excuse to head home.

I directed Mab how to drive to my house. She concentrated on the road. After a couple minutes of silence except for the chug of the engine, I said, "Thanks. For being cool with Matt."

A smile flashed on and off her face. "Of course. He's your friend."

"I just don't want to push you into, ah, anything you don't want."

Mab didn't say anything until we rolled to a red light. Then she looked at me, and if I wasn't crazy, she looked shy. "I don't mind going out with you and your friends."

Out the window behind her, the sun was setting. The particular orange light reflected in through the windows and somehow found just her lips.

All I could do while I watched them was nod.

She smiled and kept driving. I relaxed back into the cracked bench. Warm air poured in through the slightly open window.

Mab said, "I was thinking about what you said earlier. About not knowing who you are. And I was wondering who you want to be."

I sucked a deep breath. "I don't know. I should, though. Everybody else does. Doctors or lawyers or marine biologists. Soldiers, writers, accountants. Everybody I know has a plan."

"All right. Tell me what you don't want."

To let you drop me off at home and go days without seeing you again. I cleared my throat. "I don't want to join the military. I don't want to do anything just because I'm supposed to or it's expected of me."

"Okay," she said. "Start with that."

"It isn't much. It's a nonanswer."

She glanced quickly at me before looking back at the street. "Sometimes when I don't know what choice to make, I think about what my mother would have done, and then I do the opposite."

I winced. "Was she that bad?"

"She killed Reese. She killed his parents."

The way Mab said it, almost casually, made it more horrible and less at the same time. "I'm sorry."

"I didn't know the worst of what she did until she was gone. To me, she was powerful and beautiful and sharp. I loved her, even though she was always leaving." She sighed, and blinked several times. "I used to think I wanted to be like her. Before I knew she broke everything she touched. She forgot about connections. About how our magic isn't about ourselves but the world. I don't ever want to forget that. To act on purely selfish impulses. My magic is for the good of the world."

"You're trying to fix what she broke."

"Yes, I suppose. But more than that."

"You can. I know you can."

"And you can find your own destiny, Will." Mab smiled.

I smiled back. This was definitely the most wild, embarrassing conversation I'd ever had. But Mab turned everything a little wild, even this old clunker of a car.

A few minutes later, she pulled into my driveway. With a jerk, she put the car into park. Turned to me. "Here you go."

Instead of making a move to get out, I stared at her. I'd never admired somebody my own age before, but Mab, she wasn't just gorgeous and weird, she was confident. And knew herself. I wanted that.

I leaned across the bench. It creaked under my hand, but Mab met me halfway. We kissed. It was just like before. She smelled like fire and herbs, and her hair scratched the hand I slid behind her neck.

It was only a few seconds, but my ears roared. I smiled into the kiss, and Mab pulled back just a bit. Her animation eyes were so huge and blue, right there. Her cheeks were flushed. If we hadn't been in my driveway, I'd have grabbed her again. Kissed her as hard as I was dying to.

She curled her fingers against my chest.

"I'll call you, okay?" I whispered.

Mab only nodded. Her lips closed tight, and she nodded

a second time. Put both her hands on the steering wheel and gripped.

The tightness of her fingers whited the knuckles out, and made me think she was as desperate as me. I grinned. Was able to push out of the car and slam the door. Happy, I stood there while her station wagon backed away.

Before she vanished, she pressed her palm against the window. As she drove off, the flock of crows shot swiftly after her.

FORTY-SIX

The poison Gabriel fed me was not a fast one, or one to kill me. He was putting his own magic into it, drops of his blood to invade my own, to slowly, slowly creep inside my veins and transform me.

For two days I shook with a fever, sweating and whimpering, caught tight in my own blankets. The magic made my bones ache, my head throb, my fingers tremble. I thought it was influenza, and as I seemed to get better with Gabriel's ministrations, what else could I have suspected? He did everything for me, and I blessed him. I remember taking his hand the morning I finally pulled myself out of bed to kiss his cheek with thanks. He put his arm around me and was so, so gentle. Oh, Arthur, how could I have known?

I was weak, but capable of going about my business, and it was not until I was dressing to go into town on Sunday, pinning my hat into place in the mirror, that I saw the glint of red in my eyes.

FORTY-SEVEN

WILL

Music played in my head as I threw open the front door and strode into my house. It was eight in the evening, and I'd just been dropped off by the craziest, most beautiful girl in the universe. I put my hands on my hips, leaned back, and yelled, "Hello, Dad, Mom, Ben! I need to call a family meeting!"

Mom was the first to respond, gliding in from the kitchen. "Will?" She smiled curiously. A flowered apron tied her waist in tight, and she had a towel in her hands.

"Hey, Mama. Do you have a few minutes?"

She nodded. "I just finished filling up the dishwasher."

I walked forward and kissed her cheek. "Are Dad and Ben here? I saw the cars."

"In the back, sharing the sunset."

"Great, this won't take long. Come out back?"

"I'll just get the washer started."

I went out through the sliding screen door. The yard was dim, thanks to the sun having fallen down past the neighbors' roof. Dad and Ben lounged in two beat-up camp chairs, soda bottles dangling from their hands. "Evening, kiddo," Dad said. He had on his favorite T-shirt: a knock-off Hard Rock Café Bahrain one a buddy had sent him from the first Iraq war.

"How'd the grafting go?" Ben asked.

"Huh?" I was too busy scanning the yard for my dogs to process his question.

"The trees? The reason you were sprung from prison this afternoon?"

I swung back around. "Oh. Right. It was great." I smiled widely. Tried to look innocent. Ben didn't buy it. "Mom's on her way out. I need a brief family meeting."

Dad lowered the Coca-Cola from his mouth and frowned. "What's wrong?"

"Absolutely nothing." I shot Ben a glance. "I just want to tell you something about my future."

Before either of them could reply, I stepped off the patio and jogged toward the kennel. I'd spotted Havoc's coloring through the slats. I unlocked it and crouched. I held out my hands to my dogs.

Valkyrie hung back, tail low. Havoc walked to me. Her fur bristled, but she kept coming, not baring her teeth or growling. I kept my hand steady and reminded myself to breathe. Havoc stopped two feet away and stretched out her neck, reaching to put her cool black nose against the tip of one of my fingers.

I was shaking from the effort not to move.

"Will!" Ben called.

Havoc jumped back, but her ears were high. "Hey, girl," I said softly. She cocked her head to the side. Relief made me laugh. She was being cautious, sure, but herself. "I'll be back with some bacon or something for a real treat, okay?"

At the word, Valkyrie's tail shot up and she stood at attention.

"I promise, Val," I said, laughing again. It had worked. Mab's magic had worked.

Backing out of the kennel, I left the door hanging open so the dogs could join us if they wanted. Mom waited with Ben and Dad on the patio. She'd taken off her apron and stood with her arms around both of their waists.

My heart hammered in my neck. I rubbed my hand just under my jaw, pressing where my pulse tried to rapid-fire its way to freedom. Then I went to tell my parents I was ditching their plans for my life.

MAB

The moment I was alone in the car, I kicked off my sandals to drive barefoot. The station wagon rattled as I pushed it faster across the highway overpass, and two crows shrieked at me through the windows. I stuck my hand out and felt the hot, strong wind, letting it surge in through the car and sweep away the sudden giddy laughter bubbling up from my heart.

I hadn't felt this light in so long. Not since the last time I danced with Arthur and Granny, just before she died, when we set that huge bonfire next to the garden to burn all our wishes up to the stars. Donna and Faith and Eli and their children had come, and even Nick and Silla were there, because it was their college's fall break. The whole world had smelled like apple cider and sharp wood smoke, and I remembered laughing hard enough that I was nearly unable to speak the next morning, my throat was so raw. I'd taught Hannah how to read her name in the changing patterns of the red and gold maple leaves, and when the sun had set, Nick passed around his flask of whisky.

He made a toast to Reese on the fifth anniversary of his death, and the burn of the alcohol made my eyes water. All the crows spun around us overhead, and Silla spat her mouthful into the fire. When it flared, she reached out her hands and caught the flames, pulling them like a rope, then tossing it up to her flying brother.

It had been hard for everyone, because of the weight of history there, because my mother was the reason we all knew each other, but her name was never spoken when Silla came.

The crows had spiraled out with the rope of fire, and had each taken a strand, splitting it off into twelve threads that they wove into a web before dropping a piece down to each of us. Even little Hannah, who knew already to cover her hands in dirt before catching it. The web of thin flame connected us all; its burning magic shot straight through my palms, through my heart, and out my feet into the earth.

My family had been all around me. I could have leapt off the ground to fly with the crows.

As I drove past the acres of our blood land and came to the hidden gate, I decided to send invitations out to all the kin, bringing as many as would come to the new Deacon's blood ground. We would have a long summer party, bask in the sun, and grill and play games and laugh.

I'd ask Will to come, too. Maybe his friends.

The station wagon rolled to a stop in the driveway, and I climbed out, trying to formulate exactly how it would be best to ask Donna if she knew how soon I should or could call him. I didn't want to seem desperate or uninterested, and I hadn't the faintest idea where that line was.

I came into the house and stopped. Donna stood in the hallway, staring at the telephone. It hung heavy on the wall, the old rotary dial with its numbers worn away by years of fingers, and the polish rubbed off the hand piece. I kept still, waiting.

She held her hands lowered at her sides, and the long linen sleeves of her shirt fell nearly to her knuckles. Her hair was braided down her back, and she was wearing her favorite loose jeans with the holes in the knees and gardening boots. As I watched, she reached for the phone, clutched the hand piece in her fist, and drew it to her. But she paused with it halfway between the wall and her ear. The cord jiggled; everything else was frozen.

Finally, Donna set it back into its holder and spun around to stalk into the kitchen.

I padded after her, sparing a sorrowful glance at the phone. With one hand relaxed against the arch between kitchen and hallway, I softly said, "Is everything all right?"

She whirled around, butter knife in hand. "Oh. Mab. Yes."

"Where's Lukas?"

With the knife, she gestured at the ceiling. "Bathtub. We got all the leaves burned out of the side garden, and he was a mess."

"What can I do for dinner?" I went to the sink and washed my hands, wondering how to bring up her near miss with the telephone.

"I thought we might grill shish kebabs with these tomatoes and green peppers and the leftover stew meat."

Out the window, the yard darkened in creeping fingers of violet. "I'll set out some mosquito wards." As I dried my fingers on the towel tucked into the oven door handle, Donna stepped up behind me.

"Silla's graduation is this Sunday."

All the lightness I'd felt as I drove home rekindled. "That's right! Are you thinking of going?"

"I could go up tomorrow on the train and help them pack up their apartment, organize things for the move to Oregon." Donna kept her expression light and her eyes trained on me.

I glanced at the phone over her shoulder. "You should definitely call. There are a few things Silla has that are Arthur's, that I'd like to make sure we get back here before she leaves. And"—I popped open the refrigerator to pull out the carton of tomatoes—"I want to have a party—a summer event for all the blood witches, to introduce them to their new Deacon." Tilting up my chin, I spread my smile out wider.

"So I could bring Nick and Silla back with me, to swing by on their way out of Kansas."

"Exactly! I'm sure Nick will want to see how Lukas is doing."

"Hmm." Donna shifted away, glancing toward the telephone. She cocked her head as if she were just thinking about this now. "I want him to know I understand why he's going." She took a few steps back toward the phone. "Why don't you and Lukas come with me?"

I tapped my fingers on the plastic carton of tomatoes. "I don't think I should take him off the land so soon after reworking the black candle rune. He needs to settle into it; he and the land need to find each other's balance." Raising my face, I looked up as if I could see through the plaster ceiling to where Lukas was. The singing of the pipes told me he'd let the drain go. "We'll be all right. It'll be good for us, even, to have time to study and brainstorm ways to free him completely."

"He's so young," Donna frowned. "Maybe I should stay."

"No, too late!" I danced around her. "I like this idea too much. Lukas and I won't cook or clean, and we'll sleep out under the stars like regular heathens." I skipped backward nearer to the phone. "It'll be a long weekend of camping, and so if you don't call Nick, I will."

Laughing, Donna caught my hand. "Oh no you don't. I can be brave, Mab Prowd."

"I know!" Stepping onto my tiptoes, I kissed her lightly and dashed for the front door, calling, "I'll set the mosquito wards!"

WILL

The sun set behind the neighbors' house, but the sky remained blue. Mom and Dad talked softly at the patio table over the remains of a tray of caramel brownies. Ben had a fireplace match and was very slowly lighting the wicks of some bamboo tiki torches around the edges of the patio to keep the mosquitoes away. At his heels, Valkyrie gripped her favorite neon ball, waiting for him to throw it for her again. I sat on my butt against the house, legs stretched out in front of me. With Havoc lying three feet away. She'd inched closer every few minutes since I sat down.

It had all gone way better than I'd expected. Ben clenched his teeth and kept quiet while I told Mom and Dad I wasn't applying to the Naval Academy, or any college, because I wanted to take a year off to work and travel. Mom asked me where I wanted to go. Dad very calmly said that he was glad to know what I'd been considering but that really, taking time off was not the best plan. Although I wasn't sure, I stuck to the New Zealand idea. Mom covered her mouth because it was so far away. And I told Dad I didn't need the best plan, just one that worked. That had gone down like battery acid, but I held up my hands and said, "I don't want to discuss it, Dad."

"You called this meeting, Will," he reminded me. "It wasn't just a memo. At meetings we discuss."

But Mom touched his wrist and said, "We should sleep on it, though, Dan. It's a very big idea, and it will take some getting used to."

Dad shot her an indecipherable look. She lifted her eyebrows, and he nodded. "All right. It'll be a Sunday afternoon conversation." He smiled at me, that hard-boiled smile I knew meant he was working on a steel-tight counterargument. My insides turned hard. I wasn't giving in on this. Dad could come up with all the rational arguments he wanted. Like Mab had said, I was starting with what I knew I didn't want. And at the end of the day, I'd be eighteen and they couldn't make me do anything. I just really, really hoped they wouldn't try to.

Afterward, I'd gone back inside with Mom to help her slice tomatoes and lettuce for the burgers. She didn't bring up anything I'd said outside, only quietly asked me for the pickles or mustard jar. As I passed her, she touched my shoulder, brushed my back. Little possessive gestures that she'd always done. It meant that she, at least, wasn't angry. With the radio turned to an evening game show for background chatter, I'd managed to relax and just do what she asked me to. Without thinking too much about the future, or even the past. Or even of Mab.

But post-dinner, post–mostly easy conversation that involved questions about my final exams and summer soccer practice, post–kicking the ball with Dad and Ben, and post-brownies, I could think about her all I wanted. With Havoc scooting ever closer and the humid evening breeze making me sleepy, I shut my eyes. Leaned my head back against the house. Thought about kissing her again.

"So." Ben dropped down next to me. Stretched his legs out. Valkyrie panted over and collapsed, too. "Tell me what happened to you today."

"Huh?"

He crossed his arms over his chest and waited with his eyebrows up.

Havoc lifted her head and put the edge of her chin on my knee. Scratching her ears gave me something to focus on.

"You changed. Stuck up for yourself."

The total lack of accusation in his tone made me look at him.

"It was the girl, wasn't it?"

I shrugged uncomfortably.

"Are you in love with her?"

"Man." I scrubbed my hands over my face. "I don't . . . It's . . ." The thought made me fidgety. There was this dumb, warm glow. I felt new and open and like I was waiting for something. Anticipation stuck in my chest like a magnet.

"You're smiling."

I was. I wiped it off, but it crept back. "Look, Ben, I don't want to talk about it. That might ruin it."

His face scrunched up. "That's the dumbest thing I've ever heard you say."

"I doubt it."

Ben laughed, and I opened my mouth, not sure what to add. "I only just met her, like, two weeks ago. The day you flew home."

"That was fast."

"It isn't like that. She's so wild and strange. Beautiful. We didn't even . . ." I blew out a hard breath and admitted, "I only kissed her today."

"And yet she managed to convince you that you can throw off all our traditions?"

"Ben!" I started to get mad. Then stopped. "Yes. Yes, actually. I've seen some incredible stuff recently, because of Mab. And this feels right. Real."

His frown seemed less angry and more uncertain. "Tell me."

"You won't believe it."

"I believe a lot of things I didn't used to."

I shook my head. "Like curses? And magic? I don't think so."

"Magic."

"See?"

"You're talking fantasy, Will."

"No, that's not it." My agitation made Havoc prick her ears back. I tried again. "Mab talks about patterns, connections in the world that most people don't see. Things happening for a reason, because they were caused by something. And we might not understand that cause, but it's still real. It was still the cause. That's what Mab's magic is."

Ben's arms relaxed, and he clasped his hands in his lap. Stared down at them. "I'm pretty sure that isn't the generally accepted definition."

"What would you call it?"

"I don't believe that things happen for a reason. Not a supernatural one. At all."

"Why?"

He turned his head just enough to nail me with his eyes. "Because I've killed people."

I tried to hold on to his gaze but couldn't. I looked away. Off at Mom and Dad still chatting quietly at the picnic table. At Havoc's worried ears. How did I argue with that? It made everything I'd been through seem kind of useless and petty.

Ben drummed his fingers on his legs. "That wasn't fair."

"I don't think fair and killing people are usually anywhere near each other."

"Yeah. Well."

We sat there against the house in silence for a bit. Just us and Val's occasional snorting as Ben rubbed down her belly. I listened to the traffic from out on the main street. The crickets. Mom and Dad. Finally, I said, "Remember that girl you told me about? Your reporter?"

"Yeah. Lauren."

"That's magic."

Ben's eyes tightened.

"You said you didn't understand it, but you just knew it was right. It was going to happen with her."

"I did say that," he muttered.

"That's how I feel. I don't get this. But Mab—and her magic—I know it's real. You just have to take my word for it. Trust me." I thought of Mab, falling out of that tree. Knowing I'd catch her. That's what I wanted from Ben.

He studied me for a long moment. "Okay."

"Really?"

"Yeah."

I watched him carefully. Waiting for a sign that he was blowing smoke. "You believe me."

Tilting his head back, Ben stared up at the indigo sky. "I think I'll try to."

MAB

Halfway through setting the mosquito wards, the crows chuckled loudly at me, landing in a wide, perfect circle, and I realized it was more than time for me to talk to Silla.

Dropping my fleam and rushing back up the porch into the house, I found Donna leaning in the hallway with the phone cord wrapped around her forefinger. She straightened fast. "Mab, are you all right?"

Paused, trapped in a moment of uncertainty, I very slowly nodded. "I'd like to talk to Silla when you're finished, please."

Watching me with concern pressing down her lips, she relayed my request. I backed into the kitchen to wait, putting the kettle on to boil, but it wasn't more than a minute before Donna called me.

I drew myself up and walked steadily to the phone, thinking of Will and the lost look in his eyes when he said he didn't know who he was. He was so correct that I did know, in detail, who I was and who I wanted to be. That person, the blood keeper, as Lukas called me, would never have shied away from the difficulty of balancing her responsibility to the crows and her need to care for her whole extended family. I took the phone from Donna, who quickly untangled her hand from the cord and withdrew.

"Silla?" I said into the mouthpiece.

There was a crackling pause, then her voice answered me. "Hello, Mab."

I slid down the wall, curling my knees up to my chest. "I wanted to apologize," I said softly, then imagined that perfectly cool expression Silla got any time my mother came up. The still, stony frown and lofty eyebrows. "I shouldn't have said what I said about Reese."

She didn't answer for the longest time, and while I waited I stared through the archway into the sitting room, tracing with my eyes the long lines of rusty pink and orange vines on the antique rug before the fireplace. Finally, she said, "He chose."

"He wasn't choosing against you."

"I did—I do—want him back. That will never go away." Her voice wavered, making me sit up straighter. "But he gets to pick what his life is, even if it isn't . . . if he isn't the same Reese I loved."

"Everyone changes."

Silla laughed, but only once, and quietly.

I didn't know what to say that could remove the grief from

her heart. To me, transformation was very much better than death, but it might not have made a difference to her.

"Thanks, Mab," she said after a moment. "I know you're better than her. Arthur raised you, not Josephine."

She couldn't even say Mother's name without a quiver of anger, after so long, but I didn't blame her. "I hope you'll come back with Donna after graduation. I'm going to have a summer party, my first as Deacon, and it would—would mean a lot if you could attend." I closed my eyes at the stilted, too-formal words.

"We will," Silla answered right away. "If I have to drag Nick by his—um, ears."

I smiled to myself, thinking of Nick and Donna together for days on end. "Donna will need plenty of tea to cope."

"Send it with her. We mostly have coffee and vodka left over from my thesis writing," she admitted, the answering smile perfectly apparent in her voice.

The shared moment worked nearly as well as any blood magic, reuniting us through the phone lines.

FORTY-EIGHT

I went to Gabriel, heart fluttering, and asked if he'd seen anything like my illness before. He smiled softly and nodded. "I know exactly what to do," he told me, taking my hands. "You go sit in the parlor. I'll get everything ready."

I waited an hour, eyes closed, praying. There was no way for me to contact you; I couldn't fly across states and mountains, I couldn't walk into your dreams the way Gabriel could. I had to rely on him, trust that he would purge this sickness from me.

We went together out to the garden, "where you'll be comfortable," he said. He'd dug a circle into the earth just beside the roses. Big enough for me to lie down in and for him to sit at my side. He took off my shoes and hat, the armored ring you'd made for me so that no one could possess me again the way Josephine had, the pearls from my ears that I'd put on because it was Sunday. My dress was simple and the color of spring leaves, with short sleeves and buttons all the way down the front. Gabriel spilled his own blood into a bowl of ink, whispered words into it, and set it over a tiny flame. He put his hand on my forehead and told me to close my eyes. It was a cleansing, he promised, a spell to draw out all the illness inside of me.

I relaxed against the earth. Overhead, the clouds gathered nearer, preparing to storm later that evening. Wind blew hard through the trees, as if to protest his magic. My roses bobbed their tightly knotted buds, and I closed my eyes. Gabriel's circle was warm and safe. I trusted him.

He used a tiny paintbrush and began tracing lines onto my arms with his bloody ink. From both my palms up to my shoulders. He rolled up the sleeves of my dress and unbuttoned the top so that he could paint across my collarbone and down to my heart. The warm ink tingled on my skin, and I remember smiling as he connected all the lines, as he sang a very quiet song in French. It lulled me—more than it should have, I know now. He stole away my awareness, teasing me with magic and song into a light sleep so that I did not know all that he did.

I dragged open my eyes once, when he paused in his tracing. The dark clouds made the sky like dusk, and I lifted a hand to brush hair off my mouth. But I saw the runes he'd put there, in my palm and encircling my wrist. They were familiar. I blinked heavily, slowly understanding that my dress was unbuttoned to my waist, and the tingle of magic curled down my breasts and ribs, crawling along my belly.

They were the same marks tattooed into Gabriel's skin. The tattoos you told me hold him into his body. And there Gabriel was, mixing more ink in his charmed wooden bowl.

"What are you doing?" I whispered, feeling like the words were dragged out of hell.

He looked down at me, shirtless, his tattoos glowing against his body like embers. "Transforming," he said, and then, regretfully, "I do like you, Evelyn."

"Gabriel." I struggled to sit, but my bones weighed like lead, holding me against the earth. "Gabriel."

"I'm sorry," he said. And he sounded wistful. "But you'll only go to sleep, without pain, and your body will be mine."

FORTY-NINE

MAB

Friday was a rest day.

Donna packed her things while Lukas and I read the first half of *A Wrinkle in Time* out in the garden. I eyed the roses between chapters, growing slightly bored and distracted from the book as I wondered how deep I'd have to dig in order to root them completely out, but Lukas was so enamored of Charles Wallace I couldn't bring myself to stop reading.

In the afternoon we went into town for a rare meal out and so that Donna could purchase a graduation gift for Silla. We chose a small necklace from a local artist, made from blown glass that matched the deep red of her favorite cowboy boots.

And that night, for the first time in what felt like months, I went to bed happy.

First I set a silver bracelet that my mother had given me on the windowsill, to soak in blessed water infused with anise and white clover. The moonlight would spill onto the water for three hours, and in the morning it would be fresh and open and ready for me to reach in and draw out her blood to the surface. To make it sing.

It was going to be a protection amulet for Lukas, something to give him comfort and to spread soothing magical shields around him so that it would be even more difficult for his father to reassert any control. I planned to give it to him tomorrow, after we dropped Donna at the bus station. We'd finish our book, have a picnic, and I was going to ask him to help me purify the bracelet with a tiny bit of fire, to walk him through it.

But as I lay with my cheek on the pillow, listening to the frogs outside and the wind jingle the leaves, I was thinking about Will's laughter. The way he expressed so much with it. Other people had many faces, or ways of talking or gesturing. But Will had shades of laughter. I fell asleep imagining the various parts of his face sliding around a laugh. Pretending I could catch the noise in my hand and transform it into bells.

My dreams, though, were not happy.

I dreamed of the roses sucking me down, dragging my feet into the roots, twisting hard around my ankles and knees until the bones cracked. I screamed, and leaves dove down my throat. Vines tangled in my hair, my arms were pulled apart, my muscles tore, and my joints snapped. Mud flowed up my thighs and hardened around my belly. It slicked up my ribs one by one, and I was encased. I couldn't breathe! Lungs clogged with cracking leaves, and my chest squeezed tight. The forest pulled and pulled. My back arched, and my heart broke into a dozen chunks. Everything tore free in a shower of blood and dirt: arms, hands, legs, and eyes flying out in an explosion. The forest gathered the pieces and consumed them.

I died in my dream.

WILL

I had a normal day at school on Friday. Took crap from Matt and the others. Met with a counselor about deferring college and whether I should still plan to take the ACT in the fall. Caught up with a few teachers about reviews I'd missed. Even went to soccer practice, because Ben had argued my side. He showed up halfway through, and the guys made him join us. We kicked the ball around, and he watched me carefully, but seemed to decide I was good. Better than good. I thought about calling Mab, to ask her out. But surely she needed some breathing room. Of at least a day.

I didn't get to bed until late, because Ben and I hooked up the computer to the TV and streamed some old Nickelodeon cartoons. Then early Saturday morning, a full thirty-six hours since the cleansing, I woke up cracking with pain.

It was a jolt that arced through my chest. I clenched my jaw—which hurt—and sat up. Blinking, I tried to force my eyes to adjust faster. There was enough light from the street lamps outside to let me easily see the faded green numbers on my alarm clock. Five a.m. *Begin morning nautical twilight.*

Silhouettes came into focus: the computer, the chair rolled into the middle of the room, my soccer bag. I slowly climbed out of bed, feeling a hundred years old, or like I'd been hit by a steamroller. My chest had turned to fire. The ache bit through to my spine, and I ground my teeth harder. I shambled down the hallway like a zombie. It felt like my skin was expanding, like my muscles were twisting all around. Braiding into knots. My knees shook, and I clutched at the bathroom door. I managed to swing it shut behind me and flipped on the light.

I threw up a hand to block the sharp glare, wincing. My head pounded, and I leaned it against the cold tile wall. After a moment I opened my eyes, squinting at myself in the mirror.

Shock knocked me back against the wall, as far from the mirror as I could get.

Lines of dark brown and red scoured my chest, shooting out from my heart. In patterns I recognized from my dreams. They were like detailed tattoos, but pushed up from my veins. Twisting out from a center point on my chest, spinning down my arms and stomach. I shoved forward, gripped the sink. My eyes were pure red.

As red as Crayola markers.

I felt faint. Too much time in the sun, too little water. A hit to the head, a concussion. A fall from an airplane. The floor swirled around beneath my feet.

I dug into one of the drawers for a razor. My fingers shook as I snatched it up, and I tried to breathe deeply and calmly but couldn't. I was gasping. Choking. I put the razor against one of the tattoos on my forearm and sliced.

Blood slipped out instantly, hot red. Instead of dripping onto the porcelain, it wove itself darker and wound around my wrist again and again in tinier strings. Soaked back into the tattoos.

The razor clattered to the floor.

What could I do? I thought of Ben first, but he'd probably try to shoot me. And Dad and Mom . . . What would I say? I'm not a monster, I just have evil tattoos? What if they tried to take me to a hospital, where they'd only try surgery or some crazy chemo—it would cost thousands of bucks we didn't have, and I'd be ruined for soccer and miss all my finals and probably be screwed for life because this psycho disease would always be on my record.

And doctors and expensive tests couldn't help me anyway. I had to go to Mab, right now. Crazy pain doubled me over, and I pushed my fists into my gut, crouched low to the bathroom tiles. This would kill Mom. Me disappearing, with no word— what would she do? Or think?

I couldn't breathe.

"Will?"

It was Ben. Voice muffled through the wood of the door.

"No," I said, leaning into it so that he couldn't open it. He couldn't come in.

"Will. Are you sick?"

I managed to climb up the wall and grab a robe from the hook next to the shower. I got it around me just as Ben pushed in. But I couldn't stop hunching over. Couldn't raise my eyes, because then he'd see the blood in them.

Ben grabbed my shoulders. "Jesus, Will, what's wrong?"

"Just . . . puked," I said. Head down. Pain rocketed out from my chest again. I shuddered. Eyes tightly shut.

Putting his arm around me, Ben helped me out into the hall. The light was off, so I looked at him. "Ben, don't wake Mom and Dad. I just need . . ."

"You need to get to the hospital," he hissed. "What's wrong with you?" His frown pulled his whole face down. "Drugs? A reaction to those antibiotics?"

Nausea twisted up my throat. My knees shook. I had to lean on Ben.

"Sit down, I'm getting Mom."

"No." I gripped his wrist tight. I tugged him onto his knees with me. We faced each other in the dim, narrow hallway. The only light came out of his open bedroom, a yellow line pointing at me. I said, "I know what I need, and it isn't doctors. I need to get to Mab."

"She did this to you?" He angled his head, staring at my eyes. "I thought you were fine; you said—"

"You can't do anything. Only she can."

"What did she do to you?" Ben's voice rose.

"Quiet," I begged. "Please don't wake them. Just let me go. It's not that bad."

"Are you insane?" His fingers bit into my forearms. I felt my hard heartbeat where he touched me. Pounding in my head. I really was gonna puke now.

"Ben, please."

"What's wrong with your eyes?"

I shut them. I took a long, deep breath. "Ben. It's the magic. You have to trust me. You said you would."

Silence. His hands didn't loosen at all. I held on to him, too, as my head swam and I fought swaying there in the hallway. "Trust you," he said, voice low.

"Yes. Let me go."

"That is never going to happen, you stupid ass. Get up." He struggled to his feet, dragging me with him.

"Ben, I won't—"

He jerked me up and said straight into my face, "I'm driving."

FIFTY

Gabriel explained as he painted how in three hundred years he'd had five bodies, possessing them completely, stealing them, according to his own fancy, or sometimes, yours.

I cried, fearing you'd known all along, that you'd let me think you loved me when it was only this shell you wanted, this body of mine, but with Gabriel in it.

The tears burned down my temples, and the ground shivered under me. All I knew was that I had to get away. I wouldn't die like this, becoming a marionette for Gabriel to play with. But I'd only get one chance to escape, I knew. Gabriel was old and strong. If I didn't surprise him, I was doomed.

I focused on moving one hand in tiny increments, nearer and nearer to his bowl of ink as he painted around my ankle, tickling with his brush against the sole of my foot. I breathed slowly, gathering my little strength, and curled my fingers around the bowl. "Gabriel," I whispered, and the moment he turned I flung the ink into his face.

He yelled, and I scrambled away, into my roses. I clutched them, splitting my skin. My blood burned out, and he yanked my ankle, throwing me forward. A hundred tiny rose thorns slashed at my bare skin, and I jerked away from him. But Gabriel was too strong. He cried out a word, and my body caught fire from the tattoos. They tightened around me, and

I shrieked with the sudden pain. I dug my fingers into the ground, dragging and pulling, but he was there on top of me, shoving my head into the earth, scratching my face on the roses.

The only thing that saved my life was an old trowel, the one I'd forgotten a month before when you surprised me with tickets to a traveling musical and we had to leave suddenly for Kansas City.

I grasped it, and as Gabriel flipped me onto my back I stabbed it into his neck.

Blood cascaded down onto me, choking me, and he reeled back. I scrambled after him, terror stealing away all my hesitations. I stabbed him again in the chest as he scrabbled at his throat. His eyes were wide, and his lips splattered red.

I grabbed my roses, whispered to them, and with my blood dripping down their stems, they wrapped around Gabriel, piercing him a hundred times.

FIFTY-ONE

MAB

Dawn brushed the car with gentle fingers as Lukas and I returned home from dropping Donna off at the bus station. We'd had to be up hours ago to make the 5:27 a.m. pickup, but that hadn't been difficult, because my nightmares had brought Lukas running into my room to take his turn holding my hand and soothing me back into wakefulness.

Now I distracted both of us from heavy eyelids by telling him the story of how my mother had given me the silver bracelet I was charging for him. It had been an armoring bracelet, and her lover had created it for her with a drop of his blood and a drop of her own, in Paris in the 1930s. Lukas said his dad had armor like that, but made from leather and wood rings. We were so involved in discussing the relative strength of silver armor and wood that I didn't notice the crows' changed behavior until we were a hundred yards up the pebble road and the entire flock shot across our path with raucous shrieks.

I hit the brakes, and the station wagon skidded to a halt, nearly swerving off the road.

"Mab?" Lukas said, leaning forward to stare out the windshield and up at the frantically circling crows.

My palms tingled as I gripped the wheel and closed my eyes,

listening to the wind and the whisper of the trees. I pushed open the door and got out, crunching barefoot up the road. The door slammed behind me, and all the crows dove at and around me, their wings snapping at my hair and face.

Falling to my knees, I dug my fingers into the raw earth and felt nothing unusual. Everything was quiet.

Lukas ran around the car and gripped my arm. "What's happening?"

"Are you all right? Do you feel anything strange?" I looked into his summer-green eyes for any sign of pain or magic.

He shook his head and his curls flounced. "Just tired. Kinda heavy."

The crows batted at both of us, but more gently, and half of them took off up the hill, darting between branches straight for the Pink House.

I said, "All right. Let's go see what they're fussing about."

Together we stepped off into the forest, following the crows. Through the soles of my feet, I felt the earth more firmly, felt the familiar hum of the blood land. It was charged and ready, but not crying out.

And as we came out of the woods onto the lawn, I saw Will's brother Ben, in jeans and a dark T-shirt, leaning over the open passenger door of Will's truck.

"Ben?" I called.

His shoulders flexed as he pushed away, turning sharply. "Get over here," he yelled in a panic, but I heard Will say from inside the car, "Is that Mab?"

Releasing Lukas's hand, I hurried forward, opening my mouth to ask what was wrong, then Ben jerked back from the car, and Will crawled out. He fell to his knees, and Ben knelt instantly to help him, but Will shoved him back. He lifted his head; from halfway across the yard I saw his eyes.

Red as blood, through and through.

My heart expanded in shock, and I ran forward, sliding to a stop in a scatter of pebbles and collapsing next to him. "Oh my God, Will," I breathed, pushing the collar of the bathrobe he wore off his neck.

His skin was dark, and rolling with red and brown blood marks.

"Holy shit," Ben whispered.

The marks rose off his skin like long, boiling scars, like tree roots or rough vines wrapping his shoulder and trailing down to his chest under the robe. "Will." I breathed his name, aware of a sensation washing through me I'd never known before, a gasping sort of half pain, half violent emptiness. "Will!" I gripped his shoulder so hard flakes of blood broke off and crumbled.

I tugged my hands back and said his name again.

His lips moved, and nothing but raspy air came out. The second time he tried I heard "Mab." His eyes were flecked with a hundred shades of red.

"What did you do to him? What's wrong with him?" Ben demanded, pushing my shoulder roughly away from Will. Anger painted his voice, and his teeth were bared.

I said, with the calm of a thorough lie, "Help me get him into the house, and I will help him." But I had no idea what was doing this to Will, why he suddenly was twisting in pain when yesterday I'd cleansed him, yesterday he'd been fine!

"Tell me now!" Ben said. "He needs a doctor, and I don't know what kind of drugs and bullshit you're growing out here, what you fed my brother, what these abrasions are from, but you're going to tell me now so when I call an ambulance I know what to tell the police, too."

I smeared my fingers down Will's shoulder, and new, fresh blood slipped out. It glinted scarlet on my skin.

"Trust me," Will choked out, one hand grasping Ben's T-shirt.

The sun lifted over the trees, beating down with the promise of a hot day, and Lukas held back tentatively but with one hand out toward me as if to align himself.

Will's brother glared. "I promised I would, and that's the only reason we're here. His story is insane—everything he told me on the way over . . ." Ben trailed off, looking between me and Will and back again.

I flattened my hand on Will's shoulder. The crows landed around us in a wide circle, and I said, "He's cursed. It's a curse, and you cannot call the police or hospital. They can't help him."

"Bullshit."

The blood on my hand tingled with power. It was Will's blood burning with magic, and I clapped my hands together.

Fire exploded in the air, knocking Ben back two feet to hit the ground. Will winced away, and Lukas cried in fear; the crows jumped as one back into the sky. And I knelt with a rainbow of brilliant fire balanced between my hands—the same trick I'd shown Will, but fueled now by drama and need. "See here," I said, holding my bow of fire toward Ben. "This is my power, this is why Will is here, because I can help him. It's magic hurting him, and magic that can heal him. And I will not explain more until he's in a bed, and resting."

Sweat slicked down my neck, and the skin of my face tightened from the heat. My fingers ached, and any second now they'd burn, the skin would blacken, because my heartbeat was too erratic, my own blood was not in control. The curse in Will raged between my hands and all around us.

I snuffed the fire with a clap and glared at Ben, then ducked down and helped Will get his arm over my shoulders. My nose and mouth were overwhelmed by the scent of wet stones and rainy leaves and blood, and the hazy ozone smell of fire. I struggled to my feet with him beside me, leaning into me. Will's breath rattled in his chest, and where my hands touched his waist he felt as hot as the silo's orange tiles at the end of a long sunny day.

Then Ben was there, lifting Will from the other side. "I've got him," Ben murmured as he took Will's weight. Together we hobbled up the porch steps.

"Lukas," I called, "tear up three of the coneflowers down by the well, and bring me their roots as soon as you can." The boy only grunted, and I heard his feet shuffling fast through the tall grasses.

Inside, I told Ben to get Will up to the second floor, the first door to the right. He obeyed, and I ran into the kitchen for a wide bowl to fill with water. I sprinkled in willow bark and wished I had time to dig up fresh acorns to grind, but first I had to get Will cool, had to get this fever down that was eating him from the inside, wrapping itself around his bones and heart. I grabbed an envelope of boneset powder from the pantry and stirred it into the water, then I cut my wrist with the fleam and let three drops of blood spill in, all the while whispering a song for cool cleansing, for peace and gentle rain. Then I tucked the fleam into my bra and gathered the bowl against my stomach.

I had to balance the bowl carefully up the stairs, and it gave me time to center my energy, to calm myself on the outside. Even if my insides were a raging summer storm.

In the bedroom, Ben was stripping the robe off of Will, jaw set fiercely, hands moving quick and certain. He did not look at me as I entered. I pushed a cluster of dried butterflies off the bedside table, smearing pollen and flecks of their wings everywhere. I put the bowl down and sat on the bed, edging Ben away. He leaned over me, breath hard and uneven, but he didn't say anything.

"Will?" I brushed his hair with my fingers. Sweat glistened on his temple, and his eyelids parted.

"Mab."

"I'm here. I'm going to try to cool you down." I wetted one of the cloths and wrung it out. The cold drops of water splattered onto his skin, and I scattered the water down his chest. Will shivered, and I dripped it out over his ribs, over his heart and up to his shoulders. But the blood marks twisted all around his body, raised against his skin like huge, dark welts. I'd never seen anything like them. My fingers moved over them, rubbing in the boneset.

Ben paced behind me, slow and steady from one end of my bedroom to the other. His footsteps lent a rhythm to my heart, and to the motion of my hands as I covered Will with cool, soothing magic.

When the water had all been transferred from my bowl, I pricked my wrist with the fleam and drew a rune for balance as best I could over the uneven surface of Will's chest. Ben stopped me with a strangled noise, and I said, "Wait outside, Ben Sanger," hoping the invocation of his full name would compel him.

Helplessness cut through his dark brown eyes, so like Will's had once been. Sorrow was thick in my throat as I saw the battle in him, as I remembered the way Will had listened to me and decided to believe what I was telling him about my homunculus. This man would not be so quick to choose my side, with his narrow pressed mouth and hard cheekbones. He was at once the same as Will and oh so different. I held his gaze, willing him to go, to let me do my job so that I could get Will to rest and then have a moment to *think,* to figure out what had happened.

Ben looked past me to his brother, to Will's slow but finally measured breathing, and I saw the moment he let himself take in the blood roots, the intricate patterns of them, so unlike anything remotely natural. His face loosened as I watched, falling into a distant expression like nothing I'd ever seen: haunted, remote. Filled with helplessness. "You have fifteen minutes," Ben whispered. "Then I'm taking him to the hospital, no matter what."

I nodded, though I knew I'd have to think of some way to delay that again, to convince him to listen to me. For now, though, it was enough that he was leaving me alone with Will.

After a long, despairing look, Ben slipped out of the room and shut the door.

There was no moment of relief for me. I leaned over my rune and whispered against it, asking Will's body to remember what it was, to know its strength and power. "Will," I whispered. *Will*. A name, and so much more than that.

His hand found mine, and I gripped it. I held it up against my heart.

WILL

Everything was warm, and I felt like I was melting, but Mab's voice never faltered.

I came to on a mattress, a cool washcloth on my head. Mab was there. She rubbed my chest. Made me drink water that tasted like she'd soaked pennies in it. I cracked my eyes, slowly falling back into my body from wherever I'd been. Long rainbow-colored scarves were pinned to the ceiling. It was like a circus tent. Cluttered shelves lined all the walls, closing in on me.

Mab's hair tickled my side and my left arm. Tilting my head, I saw her, kneeling on the floor with her arms folded on the bed and her head down against them. Her words were quiet, but the sound of them was familiar. A rhythm I knew. I opened my mouth. Pulled my tongue from the roof, where it was sticking. "Are you—" I asked. "Are you praying?"

She raised her head instantly. "Will. Are you feeling any better?"

"Sure. I can see. And I can move without it hurting." I closed my eyes. I felt empty, drained, and sore, as if I'd spent a hundred years puking my guts up and slept hunched between the toilet and the cold tile of the bathroom floor. I took a deep breath. My throat was thick, as if the same branches winding outside my body wound inside, too. Air rushed out of me, and I coughed.

Mab got up and sat on the bed, one hand on my chest. What was left of my chest. Her lips pulled down, and her whole face screamed worry.

I cleared my throat. It hurt. "Where's Ben?"

"Pacing in the hallway."

"Is he okay?"

"Oh, Will." A tiny smile flashed on her mouth. "Don't worry about him."

I tried a smile, too. It stretched my face painfully.

There was silence. My insides were hard as rocks. My skin was on fire. My head pounded, and even just the light from her window shot through my eyes like ray guns. I was in deep trouble. And I wasn't sure she could help me.

All my fear must've been playing on my face, because Mab shut her eyes tight and a tear fell out of each corner.

"Hey, stop." I caught her hands. "I'll be fine. You'll fix me up."

Mab pulled her hands free and wiped them across her cheeks. Then she pressed her palms to my heart. Compared to me, her hands were frozen. "Will, I don't know what's wrong, so I can't fix it. If you had a cold, I could force it from your lungs. If your bones were broken, I could knit them back together. If you only had bruises or the flu or anything I understand, I could change it. I could remind your body what it's supposed to be. But this . . ." Her hands were a cold weight against my heart. "I don't understand it. I've never seen anything like it before. I know it's in your blood, but it's too deep, because the cleanse didn't work. It only . . ." Mab's eyes widened, and she glanced at the window. "Oh no."

Struggling to sit, I followed her gaze. The window was full of light, and on the sill a shallow bowl of water glinted. Something silver rested at the bottom. "What? What?"

Mab gently pushed me back down. "I have an idea why this got worse so quickly. You rest, Will. I'm going to go outside and get help. I will be back very soon."

My tiredness pinned me to the bed. I grasped at her hair, caught a curl in my fingers. I tugged gently. "Promise."

"I promise," she whispered. And then she was gone.

MAB

My shoulders knocked into the wall, I hurried so fast, ignoring Ben's call. I barely touched the stairs, flew down the hall, and fell out the door and down the porch steps. I landed on my hands and knees in the grass, gasping for breath.

It was my fault ten times over. I'd cleansed Will, but the magic that consumed him had been so deep, so much already united with his blood, that all I did was clear the path. Just as I'd set Mother's bracelet out to purify under the moon, so that I could draw the power freshly to the surface, so I'd prepared Will.

I'd leapt at the first solution, instead of exploring deeply enough, gathering all the knowledge and whispers. I'd shoved forward, as if there were a race or a prize to win. And now if

I didn't discover a means of rescue, Will would die! He was changing, transforming before my eyes. Becoming the forest.

I pushed to my feet, wiping dirt from my hands and knees. Donna had warned me to be careful with Will, but I hadn't listened. I'd thought I was too strong, too powerful, too much a natural part of magic to make such mistakes. I didn't deserve this power.

The crows circled overhead, spiraling down to land around me, and I wished they could talk to me, wished they could help me figure this out.

And I realized there were nine of them.

Only nine.

WILL

It was too quiet. Quiet like dawn. Quiet like a cemetery. Quiet like the beat right when you answer the phone before anybody says anything.

The worst kinds of quiet.

Until I heard my name.

Will.

From the air itself. The wind blowing in through the window.

Will.

MAB

I ran forward, calling to the crows, and Ben was right behind me, grasping my elbow tightly. He spun me around. "What are you doing? I want real answers right now."

I spread my hands as dread piled around me, weighing me

down. I opened my mouth to say something, anything, but a scream shocked through me, high and hard, coursing up from the dirt and clenching its fist around my gut.

It sounded like Lukas.

"What?" Ben shook me, and I clasped my hands over my ears, but he couldn't hear the scream, even as the prairie wind snapped into a fever, throwing the oak trees into disarray.

Lukas's scream bellowed up from the earth.

Tearing free of Ben, I ran toward the well, around the west side of the house where the garden was, and when I came around the corner, I flung myself back.

He was there. Lukas. Held high in the center of the swarm of roses, their vines holding his wrists and ankles firmly. Blood dripped down his arms and legs, and the roses shook with it, the scarlet painting their leaves with power.

"Lukas," I yelled, running toward him, as Ben cussed behind me, running after.

The scream cut off, and Lukas's body fell slack.

Will called my name from the front porch. His voice strong and clear.

I froze, and Ben said, "Will?"

Will stood on the porch, shoulders back and head high. His bare chest was smooth and free of the blood roots but marked with dark red tattoos. Pajama pants hung off his hips, and he grinned so widely it was a crack in the world.

"Mab!" he called again, laughter in his voice.

Confused, I stepped forward to meet him. He put a hand on the porch rail and, easy as cake, swung over it. His bare feet hit the grass, and he crouched, then stood tall and strong. The change in him was complete, with no sign of sickness or weakness, only power.

I could not move, and Ben cursed again, standing so close behind me I could feel the pressure of his energy against my own.

Will jogged to us, ignoring Ben entirely. He crashed into me and gathered me up into an ecstatic embrace. He lifted my feet off the earth. Gasping, I clutched his shoulders, dizzy and stunned, and he set me back down. Before I could do anything but think his name, he tightened his grip on my shoulders and kissed me.

It was wild and hungry, and I dug my fingers into the muscles of his back to stay afloat. He pushed open my mouth and I shoved him away, falling back against Ben.

"What the hell?" Ben asked, catching me. "Will, what is your *problem*? Are you okay?"

Will continued ignoring his brother and licked his teeth strangely, then tilted his head in thought. "That taste of mint and blood, is it my mouth or yours?" he asked.

Cold weight settled around my ribs, compressing them until I couldn't draw in breath. Dappled shadows danced over Will's face as the oak trees bent in the wind. I clutched my hands to my chest when I realized there was no light reflecting in his ruby-red eyes.

"Who are you?" I whispered.

His smile curved in a way I'd never seen before, because it was not Will. The voice was the same, though, and it cut gouges into my skin as he said, "Your humble servant, little Deacon."

"You were in the roses," I whispered.

Ben's hands tightened on my shoulders. "Cut it out," he said, moving around me. Will snapped something in another language, pulling his hand into a sudden fist, and Ben blanched, doubling over and coughing onto the ground.

I dropped with him, hands on his face, trying to tell him to breathe, frantically trying to understand how the *thing* in Will used magic without blood, who he was, what he'd done to Will—but then he was there, shoving Ben and me apart. He flung Ben onto his back with easy strength, and roots burst up through the lawn to wrap around Ben's arms and legs.

Lukas screamed again, his pain echoing up through the soles of my feet.

That was where the power came from. I'd offered the power of Lukas's black candle rune to the earth where this curse waited!

I spun and ran for the roses, ran for Lukas. Grabbing rose stems, I pulled, but they broke open my hands and Lukas groaned aloud. I couldn't tear him free without hurting him more, without ripping my hands to shreds.

Bending, I began to draw a rune of release into the earth with my bloody finger.

"None of that, little girl," Will said from right behind me.

I did not stop, and he reached down, grabbed my hair, and jerked me back.

"You should behave yourself," he said. "You freed me, after all. Everything you've done helped me a little bit more."

I clutched at his hand, trying to drag it away, and saw the exaggerated pout spread over his face. It was the opposite of everything Will. "No," I said. "Let him go."

And I dropped Will's wrist, bringing my hands around. I clapped them together and opened my mouth to yell a word that would send him flying back.

But he hit me across the face.

My head burst, and heat wrapped around my eyes as I fell back, onto my hip, retching and unable to look, to move. The world was sharp knives, shoving at me and turning in fast circles.

"None of that," the thing inside Will said.

I rolled, crawled away, but my quivering, reeling stomach took charge of the rest of my body and nothing worked, I couldn't even think past the swirling nausea.

The last thing I knew was his hand twisting in my hair again, and my helplessness as Lukas's scream ripped through the hill.

FIFTY-TWO

Gabriel died quickly.

Numb and weak, I got to my feet. Thunder tore across the prairie, and I stood over his body.

I used the roses to bury him. They twined around him like a shroud and drew him into the earth. I put salt around the whole of them, flicked my blood in benediction, and bound him there forever.

By the time the rain came, there was no sign of Gabriel, of the thing he'd tried to do. I waited through the thunderstorm, standing in the middle of the yard, and let God do the work of cleansing me.

FIFTY-THREE

MAB

Darkness pressed all around when I opened my eyes. My head throbbed, ears ringing as if surrounded by a thousand tiny bells. When I breathed, pain cut up my side, and tears prickled in my eyes. Through the smear of water, I stared up at the sky: orange and pink at the western edges, making fiery silhouettes of the oak trees. A bright planet poked through the twilight, a single beacon high overhead. I focused on it, smoothing my breath, drawing up cool energy from the hill below my back.

Wind churned the trees, brushing my face with warmth. I slowly sat up, alone in the yard of the Pink House.

Yellow light spilled out from all the first-story windows, and jazz piano, slick as syrup, flowed gently on the air. It had to be the thing in Will. But there was no sign of Ben. None of Lukas, either, or his screams.

But the roses were there. I had to find Lukas first, no matter how I wished to go to Will, to tear that thing out of him. Lukas was my charge, and he needed me.

I crawled to my feet, breathing in through my nose, out through my mouth with every step. Evidence of my attention to the roses spread about: a discarded blue glove, a dirt-caked trowel, a pile of uprooted rose stems. None of the salt circle from two weeks ago, none of the runes I'd gouged into the earth. Rain had taken care of that.

I knelt before the wild roses and raked the earth with my fingers. "Lukas," I whispered. The ground tingled with power, burning the tiny cuts on my palms from when I'd torn at the roses earlier.

"Lukas," I whispered again.

The roses trembled.

A sob shook free and I let it out, gasping at the pain in my ribs, one arm wrapping protectively around myself. I closed my eyes against the throb of blood through the left side of my face. It was hot and swollen.

And this was all my fault.

Why didn't Arthur tell me *why*? Why I was supposed to destroy them? He should have known me well enough to know I'd choose otherwise—choose to explore! How could he not have known?

I pushed forward on my knees. My forearms tangled in the rose vines, and I gripped one, tore it free with all the weight of my body. Pain shot up my arms as my palms and wrists were shredded against the tiny thorns.

I took that pain and fed it back into the roses, my blood connecting us. Long cuts bloomed up my forearms, just like Donna's scars. Then, dripping blood, I went for the trowel. I stabbed at the base of a rose plant, the blade hacking in, ringing off the hard wood. I cut at it again and again, mindless of the shaking roses. They vibrated and danced, and the more I disturbed them, the harder they thrashed. Their stems whipped my shoulders, gouging me. Every prick like a sharp kiss.

I bled from a thousand tiny wounds and let it flow into the earth. I forced my will, hissing that the roses should wither and rot.

Slowly, some blackened. I tore them free. Petals cracked, turned to ash.

In the center was a cocoon of vines and round red blossoms.

Peering through the tightly wound vines, I saw a coppery curl. And his brown skin there—a finger, a brush of his thigh. With my blood, I parted these vines carefully, until I found his face. His lips were cracked, but air moved over them, fluttering the leaves hanging just against his cheeks.

He was held by the roses, a foot off the earth, and a half dozen vines crawled up and into the black candle rune, sucking power from it, from him.

"Lukas?" I whispered.

There was no response. Not a flicker of his eyes under closed lids, not a hint in his breath that he'd heard me.

Bloody footprints marked my path up the porch stairs and into the Pink House. Pain and anger, all my spirit, seeped out through my skin as blood dribbled from the myriad of cuts on my body. I was left with numbness, as though everything inside had crystalized. Quartz was hard and cold, one of the most abundant minerals on earth. Best for magnifying power and clarity. My vision was clear: rip this thing out of Will's body, free Lukas. I was the Deacon, I could do it.

He was in the kitchen, frying a grilled cheese sandwich. His hands moved deftly with the spatula, and he'd cut a tomato and butter with one of the butcher knives. A small smile tilted his mouth as he hummed along with an old record of Granny Lyn's.

I sighed loudly enough for him to hear over the sizzle of butter in the frying pan and the jazz.

Will's body turned smoothly, a ready smile showing his teeth, and he said, "You know this was her favorite . . ." His ruby-red eyes widened into circles. "My God, what have you done?"

Blood dripped off my finger and splashed onto the kitchen tiles. I didn't answer but only stared. He wore an old shirt of Arthur's, unbuttoned because his shoulders were that much broader, and a pair of ritual pants like the ones I'd cleansed him in. It was Will's hands and face and hair but nothing of Will in the carriage and movements. I'd never noticed how uncertain Will had been, until I watched this new creature stride over, calm and confident, a frown of concern aging his face.

He stopped before me, and I put my bloody hands on his chest. With all my pent-up fury and power, I said, *"I banish thee from this body."*

My magic surged hot as a geyser, pushing into him with all the strength of my heart.

I saw it flare in his tattoos: the red lines turned orange as melting iron, shimmering with heat.

But Will closed his eyes and sighed as if my power were a kiss. He put his hands on my shoulders and said, "You'll not be rid of me so easily, Mab."

I tried again, pushing this time, but nothing happened. My hands slipped against his bare chest, my injured ribs sliced into my breath and I couldn't speak. The third time I only hissed

"*Banish . . . ,*" and the thing in Will shook his head slowly, gathered up my hands in his, led me to a kitchen chair, and sat me down. My thighs squished against the wood because of all the blood. He knelt before me and drew healing runes onto my knees, into the palms of my hands, and onto my forehead. He muttered to himself, working his mouth as though he tasted something unpleasant. I understood: the blood smell filled my mouth and nose, as well.

A tremor of magic traveled from the crown of my head to my toes, and he asked me to whisper healing words with him. I did, barely moving my lips, and the flash of power that mended my wounds was so strong and hot I fainted.

It must have only been a moment, for I came to still in the chair, and he was saying, "You silly, wild thing."

I sat up, stared at him. My ribs ached only dully, and my face didn't hurt when I opened my mouth. "I will destroy you," I said.

"You'll forgive me," he said, trying to put an earnest expression on Will's face.

I laughed at the sheer ridiculousness of that sentiment. I thought of Arthur laughing as rain poured in through a leak in the roof. Of Donna laughing at a TV movie. Of Mother laughing for no reason but being alive. And of Will laughing, giddy on top of my silo.

All their laughs clogged my throat now, and I covered my face with my sticky, bloody hands.

"As mad as your mother," he muttered, pushing away from me to return to the oven. I seethed behind my hands, and all he did was flip over the burned cheese sandwich. The acrid smell drew a smile back to my lips. I stared at his back, at the tight, angry jerks his hands made as he created a new sandwich. The record buzzed between tracks, and I knew this song, too, because Granny used to sing it: "Our Love Is Here to Stay."

"Tell me who you are," I said as I smoothed my torn and bloody dress over my thighs.

He spun smoothly and bowed his head. "I am Gabriel Desmarais, and I have lived in and on this land longer than you can imagine, little Deacon. If you go clean yourself up, and allow, perhaps, a brief truce, I shall tell you quite the story."

FIFTY-FOUR

MAB

I huddled in Arthur's preferred wing-back armchair in the parlor while Gabriel leaned Will's body lazily back on the rug beside the fire. The tea went cold in my hands as he spoke, and I searched for signs that Will was still in there, was still aware of me, looking out through his own eyes.

But there was nothing. I only had faith on my side that Will himself survived.

I hardly listened to Gabriel tell of generations of his life: from a beginning in Paris nearly four hundred years ago to meeting a boy named Arthur in New York. He spoke of traveling through the Old West, of the Civil War, of the first railroad, and all of it with Arthur. He told me about settling in Missouri together and of children they'd shared, and even through Will's voice I felt the truth of Gabriel's love.

He told me about the first time he met my mother, and about the last time, coyly complimenting me on taking after her in looks. I didn't give him all my attention until he finally offered his version of how he'd become trapped in the roses.

Granny had hated him, Gabriel said, for being the focus of Arthur's love. She'd attacked him, easily bested him because he'd never suspected her of ire, never thought for a moment she was jealous enough to curse him.

Yet curse him she had. She'd planted him in the roses, and twisted their roots and their magic so firmly he could not even get whispers free to warn Arthur.

Eventually she died, and her magic began to weaken. Gabriel, who had lived in an endless dream state, knowing but not knowing where or who he was, slowly woke. He could not reach Arthur, who was caught in his own grief, and then I was there.

"You, Mab," Gabriel said, his smile as smooth as a purr. "You were there, listening to me, coaxing me up through the roots with your smile and your power and your gentle hands. You tore my magic off the roses for it to work itself into this body. To prepare him for me."

He put a hand over Will's heart.

"You can't have him." I set my cold tea down onto the round sofa table. "His body is not for you, Gabriel. I am sorry for what Evie did to you, no matter how much of what you're saying is or isn't true. I am sorry you were cursed, and sorry you lost your life. But." I stood up. "You cannot have Will. You must let him go. You must free Lukas."

Gabriel spread his hands and said, "This body is mine now. There is no returning it. I have transformed him into a vessel of magic, down to the essence of his blood. This"—he stood, brushing his hands down his chest and then gesturing wide with his arms out—"this is Gabriel, not Will. That boy did not want it hard enough to hold on the slightest bit."

Stepping nearer to me, Gabriel allowed sympathy to run

down Will's face. "I am sorry for your loss, too, Mab. But *you* are the one who cannot have Will."

He was wrong—I would fight that until I died; there had to be a way. I lowered my eyes, fluttered my lashes, and prayed he would think I fought tears instead of fury. It was not Arthur's power I needed now, or Granny Lyn's patience, or Donna's practicality. I needed my mother.

And her lies.

I let my breath shake, which wasn't difficult, and wrapped my arms around my ribs as if weaker than I was. My mother had done everything in her power to get what she wanted, and I had that in me, too.

"You're tired," Gabriel said.

It was oh so true, and I nodded, letting my eyes fall shut completely. There was nothing I could do tonight, not with my energy so low, not without understanding better what Gabriel had done. Those tattoos held him firmly in Will's body. And so long as he had Lukas and the black candle rune to strengthen himself, I couldn't simply overpower him.

"Gabriel," I whispered, feeling him stand close to me, lean in.

"Yes?"

"Let Lukas go. He's just a little boy who's been abused his whole life."

Gabriel sucked air in through his teeth. I peeked up at him, and saw regret twisting his mouth. "That I cannot do," he said. "Yet," he added quickly, when I began to protest. "I will, and I assure you the boy lives, but I need him." Gabriel carved a smile into Will's mouth. "I am no fool, Mab. I know how strong your mother was. How strong the Deacon is. If I lost Lukas as my familiar, you might stand a chance against me."

I made fists with both my hands, and hit them firmly into his chest just over Will's heart, where the tattoos swirled together most intricately. Gabriel caught my wrists, and I didn't struggle. I looked up at him, into those bright, brilliant red eyes that used to be Will's. That I used to think were beautiful.

"Don't make me bind you, little Deacon," he said. "I don't want this to be your prison as it was mine. This is a home—our home."

"Home." I stepped back, tugging away. As Gabriel let his hands fall to his sides, I slapped him as hard as I could. My hand burned with the contact, and Gabriel's head knocked around. He slowly put a hand against the flare of red on his cheek.

We stood, staring across three feet at each other. I knew he would not leave, because of Lukas, because he thought he belonged here. And I knew I would not leave, because I was the Deacon. Because everything I loved was here.

Until I could rip him out of Will and scatter his soul to the four winds, we were trapped with each other.

FIFTY-FIVE

MAB

An arrhythmic thumping woke me, vibrating up through the frame of my bed. If I stared at the scarves draped across my ceiling, I could just make out the very fine shiver. The whole house seemed to tremble.

I pushed away my covers and got up carefully, listening to the rush of blood in my ears. My fingers and toes were cold, but I was no longer light-headed or overtired. Blue dawn crept in through my partially open window, along with a thick breeze that smelled of mud and roses.

Wiping my hands over my eyes and then back through my hair, I went to the door. Through my bare feet, I could feel the thumping more clearly, a rough punch spreading from some-where below.

As I opened my bedroom door, Will emerged, too, from Arthur's room at the end of the hall. My heart surged when I saw his hair tousled flat on one side, and the pillow marks pressed into his cheek. But the euphoria died in the moment of its birth, as Gabriel's frown drained it away. "I should have turned him into a stool," he muttered, seeing me.

"Ben?" I'd forgotten about him entirely, and spun in place

to go toward the stairs, before Gabriel's hand was hot around my wrist.

"I'll take care of it." He tugged me back, and my shoulder fell against his chest. I closed my eyes as my skin touched his and the tattoos flared softly red. Tilting up my head, I studied the blood flecks overwhelming the brown of Will's eyes. They shone angrily. Would they ever fade now? As Gabriel filled the body out more firmly and completely, would the outward signs of trauma vanish?

I wouldn't let myself find out.

"No, Gabriel. Let me. He knows me, and what would you say to him?"

His smile only covered half his face. "Oh, I wasn't thinking I'd say anything."

"We need him—you need him." My imagination spun furiously, hunting for a convincing argument. "You only must convince him that you're his brother, and he'll be able to help you settle into life."

Gabriel's fingers tightened around my wrist, and he leaned to hiss in my ear, "You don't plan to let that happen yet. So you need something better to persuade me with, Mab."

I sighed sharply through my nose. "Fine. Well then, let me have him anyway. I . . ." Flattening my free hand against Will's chest, I paused, struck by a moment of genius. Below, the thumping picked up again with a giant crash like breaking furniture. Ignoring it, I stroked my fingers down the center, gently as I could, then traced along one of the tattoos that curved around his ribs. "I am interested in what you did to Will's body, even if I don't intend to let you keep it. You know . . . you know I've been working with the crows as my familiar?" I glanced up at him with my chin low.

His face softened just a fraction as he watched my eyes. "Yes."

"They used to be a boy, did you know that? Used to be a young man my mother cursed so that he's trapped in the birds' minds."

"Did she, now."

"Yes, and . . . I've always felt," I looked down, hoping I seemed ashamed. "I've always felt guilty. Responsible, even. As if I should have stopped her. Let me have Ben, and see about doing to him what you did to Will."

Gabriel released me. He watched me with narrow eyes, and his head crooked curiously. Slowly, his mouth twitched into a smile, and then he laughed. It was a deep, amused chuckle, and I fought to keep my hands at my sides instead of wrapping them around myself. He was dark and sardonic and everything opposite of Will.

"Mab, you're good," he said. "But I knew your mother, and you're not as good as she was. Josephine never fooled me the way she fooled so many others. Try again. Third time's a charm, they say."

Fury sparked in my stomach, and I shoved my fists onto my hips. "Just give him to me, Gabriel. Because I want him, because I'm asking you." Stepping forward once, I reached up and touched his face, cupping one cheek in my hand. It was the same one I'd slapped, the one with the pillow creases. "As a sign of faith," I added quietly.

He regarded me, and we stood like that through a long

string of thumps, hammering under our feet. Gabriel lifted a hand and covered mine with it, tenderly. "That's all you had to do, Mab. Ask."

I withdrew my hand and turned away. We both knew that was a lie, too.

Before I could slip back into my room to get dressed and brush my teeth, Gabriel said, "Don't do anything stupid. I'll know. Through Lukas I feel the whole of the blood land, Mab. So I'll know if you work heavy magic, I'll know if you pull just the slightest."

Pausing with my hand on the door frame and my back to him, wishing he'd let me go so that I could get to Ben before he hurt himself, I said, "I have to touch the magic. It's who I am."

"I know." He was just behind me, and I gasped. He put his hands on my bare shoulders, thumbs over the thin straps of my nightgown. "Just like Arthur."

His words made me shiver. I'd always wanted to be just like Arthur, but not because someone like Gabriel said so. "Let go," I said.

He did, but remained close enough that I could feel the heat coming off his body, like tingling magic. "I'll be near, love. All day. Getting to know this land again, with my own two feet. Don't call for help, don't tell anyone what's happening here. In a few days, we'll break the news to the family. Until then, anyone else who steps foot on the land I will kill. And if you try to leave, I'll have no reason to keep Lukas alive."

Instead of frightening me, his threats only offended me. "Save your threats for someone who's afraid of you," I said. Then I stepped into my bedroom and firmly shut the door. A spot of daylight warmed the rag rug, and I walked into it with my arms held open: the brightness soaked into my face, and I prayed the sun would keep me bold.

Ben Sanger waited at the top step of the cellar, and the moment I opened the door he charged out. I touched his bare arm with my hand, gripping him tight so that the blood rune I'd drawn in my palm connected.

And then I was both of us.

Disorientation drove me to my knees—both my body and Ben's.

We did not move, and I spread my will through both minds, putting both of us down on our hands, and shifting my own body nearer so that my shoulder brushed his. Physical contact made it easier and faster to slip between us, to overwhelm him with my magic. Nausea clawed up both our throats, and I was twice as weak, but my mother had taught me to do this, to close my eyes and shift into two bodies: two heads, four hands, four feet, two hearts.

As the rhythm of our blood moved into alignment, I focused on breathing, on opening Ben's eyes. I didn't need to know anything about him except how to get to his feet. I breathed in and out, walking up the porch in two bodies, going for the telephone. It was a simple thing to reach into his memory to dial his home number, to tell the woman who answered it—who he recognized in a distant echo as his mother—that me and Will had dropped everything for a spur-of-the-moment camping trip. I didn't give her time to argue, only saying I was sorry with Ben's voice, only saying I loved her and we'd be home soon.

Then we went, both my body and Ben's, two steps at a time down the dark hill to the workshop.

I released him and fell to the ground beside him, shaking with exhaustion beside his unconscious body.

After I don't know how many minutes, I got to my feet and went outside into the meadow of red clover. There I collapsed again, rolled onto my back so that I could watch the sky for the first sign of crows.

FIFTY-SIX

MAB

For lack of anything better, I used blood to coax roots up through the floor of the barn and into a cage to contain Ben Sanger.

He woke from my possession and raged—at first trying to break through the bars with sheer strength. But my roots lived, and they were solid, hearty wood. Ben's groans of effort and yelling and cursing filled the barn with noise I was certain it had never before known. This was a place of beauty, of magic and peace and family, yet here I'd brought a prisoner to keep.

When he accepted that brute force wouldn't free him, Ben inspected everything carefully, paying particular attention to the base of the roots. He hopped up to grab two of the bars, then swung himself higher, pulling himself hand over hand toward the center. The branches bowed slightly under his weight but did not break. They wouldn't, and even if they could, I'd only need to grow replacements.

It was a losing battle, and that wasn't something I believed Ben was used to at all.

I watched from the far corner, mostly concealed by shadows and a green tractor so old I'd never seen it move in all my years. When Ben had been quietly standing in the center of his cage for quite some time, I slowly emerged.

Instantly, he leapt to his feet, grabbed two of the bars, and demanded I tell him what the *hell* was going on, and where Will was.

Holding my hands out, fingers splayed wide, I said I'd explain it all, if only he'd sit.

We stared at each other for a moment, and Ben crouched. It wasn't sitting, but the angle of his chin told me it was the best compromise I could possibly hope for. Backing away, I sat against the worktable, with my spine pressed into one of the legs. I hugged my knees against my chest and explained everything to Ben. He gripped the rough wooden bars of his cage and watched me so closely I hated to move. Every shift, every sigh, every flutter of my hands drew that sharp gaze.

Ben said nothing, but I said everything. He had to understand. I told him about the blood magic and the Deacon, about the far-flung blood kin, about Eli and Faith, Gabriel and the crows and my mother and Silla. About Donna, Nick, and Lukas. About how I'd met Will and everything I knew that had happened to him.

I talked until I was hoarse, until all I could manage was a whisper and my bottom was numb from sitting, my arms tight from how I held them so close around my knees. The sun lowered enough that it pierced straight through the hole in the southwestern corner of the barn roof, lighting up the rafters and showering us with golden motes of dust.

There was silence for a long stretch after I finished. The quiet lasted so long I began to think he would never acknowledge me, never let go of the bars of his cage. I let my knees stretch out and sighed hard, rubbing the heels of my hands into my eyes.

It would be better if only the crows would come, I thought. If only I had them near me, could hear the familiar swish of their feathers and the comforting barks of their play.

Another minute slipped past, and I used the edge of the worktable to climb to my feet. Standing, I pressed my hips into the table and turned to Ben. His face was drawn, his knuckles white where he gripped the cage. Something desperate shone in his eyes, and I felt like I was walking a precipice on a thin strand of rope. When it snapped, he would either pull me to safety or watch me drown.

I didn't have any idea what else to tell him, though, because I'd said everything. All the truths laid out for him in the best words I knew. My confession. I needed him to believe me, the way Will had.

But unlike Will, there was nothing welcoming or ready in Ben's expression.

Closing my eyes so that I would stop seeing his accusations, I grabbed a lancet from the coffee can under the table and went to the overflowing shelves of potions and boxes and knickknacks.

I rummaged through them, hunting for the crayons I knew were hidden somewhere. I shuffled aside old bank documents; I moved a pile of river-bored stones; I tipped upside down a woven basket of seashells and twenty-year-old plastic Happy Meal toys. There it was—the crumbling box of crayons that had been tucked behind a ceramic piggy bank. Taking it and the lancet, I grabbed loose drawing paper from the worktable and knelt an arm's length away from Ben's cage.

Without glancing up at him, I drew a colorful butterfly on the blank paper. I heard his breath hitch and then the shuffle of movement as he crouched to get a better look at what I was doing.

When my blue and pink and yellow butterfly had antennae and a long swallowtail, I took my lancet and pricked my wrist. A long drop of blood slipped out, spilling onto the crayon butterfly. I bent down as if bowing deeply and breathed my mother's favorite spell.

"Become," I whispered, channeling the tingling magic from my heart, through my blood, and into the drawing.

The paper fluttered, and the butterfly snapped up and away, flapping its rainbow wings in dizzy spirals. It bounced toward Ben, and I leaned back onto my heels, watching him.

His fingers uncurled and he reached to touch it. It skimmed along the back of his hand, and he turned it over to cup the little magic creature delicately.

Then he began to shake his head, pulling his hand back, making a fist. I said, "Will would love that spell. He believed me."

Ben met my eyes, and finally he spoke. "He cared about you. I don't."

Swallowing a surprising hurt, I said, "That isn't why he believed me, though. He believed me because magic was the only answer that made sense. Not because he—he cared."

He laughed once, bitterly. "What does sense have to do with it? I've been places and seen things that didn't make any sense at all. But that didn't make them less true. Sense and logic and truth don't have much to do with each other." His low voice was as calm and certain as mine had ever been. "Just because I think I see that butterfly, or that—that fire, doesn't make it more likely. Just because I don't understand and you say you do . . . that isn't how the world works."

My hands were limp in my lap. I'd never had to convince anyone of this before, who didn't believe what they saw. "You don't want to believe me."

"No shit."

"Why not?"

"Are you kidding?" Ben gripped the bars again, shook them. "If I believe you, then there are people who have so much power and they're sitting in Kansas gardening instead of using it, for starters."

I opened my mouth but wasn't sure what to say.

Ben kept going. "And worse, if I believe you, then my brother isn't just on drugs but *some other person stole his body.* How is that something I'd *want?*"

"Because I can fix that!" I leapt forward, grabbed the bars just below his hands. "I can save him, if it's magic!"

He moved his hands onto mine, crushing them into the wood.

"You're hurting me," I said.

"I know." Ben put his face inches from mine. "Let me out of here."

I pulled back with all my weight, but he held tight. My fingers pinched, and I felt heat in my palms. "Stop, let go."

"Let me out and I will." There wasn't any emotion in Ben's face. Just calm, hard certainty.

"Please, Ben, Will believed me," I gasped as he tightened his grip. "You said you trusted him."

"And then he punched you in the face."

"It wasn't him, *I told you*." Desperate, I put my feet against the bars, but Ben was that much stronger than I was, trapping me. "Please." I closed my eyes and tried to relax. The bones of my hands crunched together.

Crows dove down at us, cawing as loud as firecrackers. Their wings flapped between us, slapping the cage, batting at my face. One clawed at our hands.

He let me go.

I fell back, scrambled away, then curled my poor fingers into my stomach.

The crows landed around me and around the cage. All remaining nine and relief blossomed cool and gentle in my chest. "Hi," I whispered to them. One brushed my cheek with his wing. The tenderness sent a shiver through me, and I felt tears pinching my eyes. At least I still had someone.

I bowed against the dirt, smelling the dusty barn floor, huddled there, drawing strength up through the earth just a little, but not enough that Gabriel might notice.

"Mab."

Ben's voice was so soft it took a moment for it to register that he'd said my name. I pushed up to sit, and one of the crows hopped onto my lap. His claws scratched my leg through the thin dress. I looked at Ben, and he was staring at the crows, who all nine cocked their heads at him in the exact same moment, in the exact same way.

"Look." He shut his eyes, and I saw the shudder pass down his body. "Look." He pressed his hands flat to the dirt a few inches from the nearest bar of his cage. His eyes snapped open. "If you want me to trust you, you have to give me something. You have to let me out of this. So long as I'm your prisoner, I'm your enemy."

I watched him, studying his face, wishing I could read it. But he was solid and unflinching. How did I know he meant it at all? That he wasn't lying to me in exactly the way I was lying to Gabriel?

One of the crows hopped through the bars and into the cage next to Ben. He flapped up and landed on Ben's shoulder, who leaned away and grimaced as the crow's claws cut through his T-shirt until little pricks of blood seeped into the material. Ben turned his head and stared at the crow, and the crow stared back.

I supposed that trust should be a mutual gift, and Ben was right that I needed to offer first.

I reached forward and picked up the discarded lancet, cut my palm, and pressed it into the cage bar. Closing my eyes, I breathed through the magic, and the tingle of power spread into the cage. Two bars grew out, bowing until there was room for Ben to slip through.

The crow on his shoulder pushed off him, flying out and up past me. The wind of its passing ruffled my hair, and the crow on my lap leapt up, too, until all nine spiraled over us in the air.

Ben climbed out of the cage and stood, stretching tall. I

looked up at him from the ground, waiting. The barn door was open, and he could get to his car, because I wouldn't chase after him, wouldn't stop him. He glanced at the wide-open doors, at the sunlight and the red clover, at the hint of green from the forest. His eyes narrowed as if he was seeing something he didn't like, and he lifted a hand to the back of his neck.

A heavy sigh settled his shoulders, and he dropped down to crouch in front of me. "All right. Tell me your plan."

Once he turned his attention to believing me, Ben poked holes in all of my ideas. *What if this? What if that?* he asked again and again. I put my head on the table and thought, *If only he'd been around to destroy my plans before I lost Lukas and so perfectly readied Will for Gabriel's magic.*

By the time the sun had set enough that it was difficult to tell the crows from the shadows up in the rafters, I was thoroughly frustrated and said, "But I have to try something!"

Ben tapped his finger on my worktable and shook his head. "Being patient is sometimes the best offense. You have to make sure your intelligence is the best, and that you know as much as you can about what's around the next corner."

"The longer Gabriel has Will, the harder it may be to get him out."

His eyes narrowed again like he was peering into the sun, an expression I was learning to interpret as Ben weighing options that he didn't like. "Better it be harder than we screw it up."

That was true, and stabbed at my guilt. I nodded and took a deep breath.

"I won't give up, Mab," he said, almost gently. "And I think you're as stubborn as anybody."

"I should go back up to the house, before Gabriel comes looking for me."

Ben sighed through his teeth. "Back into the cage for me."

"I'm sorry."

He nodded and said, "I'm gonna go . . . outside for a second."

I watched him, hoping he was enjoying enough wide-open freedom that sleeping in the cage wouldn't make him angry again by the time morning came.

While Ben was outside, I dragged the plastic bin with all the remains of my homunculus away from the wall and dumped it out. I spent a few moments arranging it, setting up some old sketches of regeneration runes and my notes from last month when I'd begun to create the doll—in case Gabriel came down when I wasn't here, he'd have evidence of what I was supposed to be doing.

The crows hopped around me and the remains, nudging at them with their beaks and claws. I said, "Stay here with Ben, keep him company. I know even your strange presence will be good for him—so he doesn't feel alone."

Two crows angled their heads up at me, questioning.

"I'll be fine." I offered a smile.

"Are you talking to them?" Ben asked from behind me.

Turning, I said, "Of course, and you can, too."

"Hmm." He frowned, and reluctantly climbed back into his cage.

After I re-formed it around him I promised to bring food and more water at dawn. He held on to the cage as he had earlier that afternoon, but loosely, and leaned his forehead against one of the bars. "Be careful," he said.

It felt like he was only protecting an asset, but I smiled just a little before I left him.

The forest was all purple and midnight shadows as I walked up the hill. I skimmed my hands along tree trunks, reached up to cup leaves and say hello. We whispered to each other, me and the trees and the wind, and I tried to imagine it was all as it should be for a moment: all of us connected because I was the Deacon and this was my land. I knew the roots, and I knew the patterns here, but where I should have been joyously diving my energy into the earth and drawing back out rejuvenation, instead my thoughts were sorrowful. I wished to reach in and find Lukas's spirit, surround him with myself and promise he would be free, but Gabriel would know. Gabriel would sense it the moment I neared the garden, and I did not want him to shield Lukas, to cut the boy off completely from the rest of the world.

I paused, wound my hand around a thin birch branch. How was Lukas receiving sustenance? Gabriel would have to answer that, or I'd poison everything he ate, lay sleeping traps in all the corners of the house, until I managed to knock him out and dig Lukas free. And then I'd either have to leave Will to Gabriel while I ran with Lukas, or—or—I didn't know.

The birch branch snapped, and the force shocked up my arm. Biting my lip, I moved on through the darkness, and with every step my heart told me that Will would say I should save

Lukas. That I should let Will go, if I could free everyone else. He'd never let me choose him.

I didn't want to choose at all.

There had to be a way to free Lukas and Will both, to best Gabriel at his own twisted game. Gabriel had taken it all from me in one move, and I would take it all back from him the same way. This was my land. My responsibility.

I broke out of the forest in a burst of energy, and there he was: Gabriel, standing in Will's body, directly over Arthur's grave.

Only dim white stars and the lamps from the parlor lent any light to the yard, but as I approached, I saw the glint of tears on his cheeks. He saw me, and one half of his mouth quirked up. "Amused, Mab?" His voice was hollow.

Standing beside him, I kept my eyes on the roots of Granny's linden tree. "Never here. The two people I love most in the world rest in this earth."

"Two?" He made no motion to hide his tears or wipe them away. Nor did he look at me.

"Arthur, of course, and Granny Lyn."

"Together even in death," he said with a bitter cast to his frown.

I cupped my hands around my elbows, shivered as an unusually cool breeze slipped down around us. "You could always join them."

Gabriel smiled.

"He wouldn't approve of what you've done," I said. "If you love him so much, you're disappointing him."

"What makes you think that? Arthur knew me in a half dozen different bodies, and loved all of them."

The thought was a snake curling around my heart. "I don't believe you."

"Believe what you will." He shrugged, a careless, lazy gesture that did not suit Will's shoulders. "I loved him, and Evie took that away."

"I love Will, and you've taken him from me." I said it breathlessly, and fixed my eyes on one knot halfway up the linden's trunk. My knees weakened and I felt myself trembling as I thought about what I'd just said, and about how close he was, how near to my bare arm Will's arm was, how easy it would be to lean in and touch it.

But Will was not here.

Gabriel sighed sorrowfully. "Mourn him, Mab, because he is gone. There is not a whisper of him in my mind. The boy did not even hold on for a single day. Save your love for a worthier man."

"No." I stepped away from him, hugging myself. I wanted blood covering my hands. I wanted to tear into Will's chest and hold his heart until I found him.

"Eh. As you will." Gabriel knelt and put his hands against the grass. "Do you have any bits of him left, Mab? Of Arthur? Or is he all transformed into the world?"

I dragged myself away from hurting, shut my eyes tightly. "Tell me how you are keeping Lukas well, and I will give you an answer."

"Bargaining now, are we?" Gabriel looked up at me with Will's red eyes.

I waited.

Standing very near to me, Gabriel murmured, "I keep him well alive, as I kept myself alive. Energy from the sunlight and rain, through the roses. His body will live for months like this. I know."

"You're certain."

"I give you my word. I need him that way, or what kind of familiar would he be?"

Eyes shut, I nodded. "I'll give you what I have."

Granny had been gone for six months when Arthur came out of the Pink House just after dawn and found me eating a breakfast of almonds and dried apricots with the crows under her linden tree. He was naked except for a pair of drawstring pants, with his hair down about his face and the thin blood tattoos encircling his wrists just like mine, bright with fresh magic. He knelt beside me, and I offered him my handful of almonds, which we shared in silence.

In the quiet morning, we listened to the wind whisper through the forest, to the early songs of bluebirds and chicka-dees. After I'd flung the last of the nuts up for the crows, Ar-thur slipped his hand beneath mine. "I'm leaving, Mab," he said softly and simply.

I knew he meant more than a drive to the ocean. This had been coming, building up in his every action and expression, for weeks. Without looking at him, but squeezing his hand, I asked, "Why?"

With his free hand, he smoothed the wild curls back from my face. "I've made all my mistakes, and lived all my conse-quences. I've loved and lost, and felt the long pain of betrayal.

And I finally have you, who will make different mistakes, who will be beautiful."

"I don't want you to go." A great emptiness opened up beneath me, and we sat at the edge of it, just Arthur and I.

"I'll always be a part of the land, a part of you."

"She wouldn't want you to stop living."

"Ah, Evelyn. Yes, she would want me to listen to my heart."

I tugged my hand out of his. "I don't believe your heart is telling you to leave me."

Arthur's voice shifted, became hollow. "All the people I've loved in three hundred years are dead. All my long family, gone. Vanished forgotten into the world, or died, or killed each other."

"I'm here! You love me."

"I do."

"I'm not ready." I clutched at him again, at both his hands. The crows flapped their wings angrily as my emotions translated.

"You are."

"Arthur!" Tears smeared my vision until he was only a point of light in the shaded morning. I dashed them away.

"I am tired, little queen."

A sigh rattled out of me and I shut my eyes.

"It is time for me to be with all of them again," he said, spreading a hand to indicate the earth. "The blood is yours now, Mab, all the beauty of the world. Take it."

He kissed me gently on the lips and on the forehead. He pulled me to my feet and added, "And please destroy those roses, for your granny's sake."

I wished now that I'd asked more, pressed for answers—why didn't he destroy them himself? What did they have to do with Granny Lyn? Could he truly not have known about Gabriel? But in that moment, I'd been losing my Arthur, and nothing else mattered.

For him, I had spilled blood into my palms. Arthur spread out near the linden tree and let go of all his long life. I pressed handprints into his chest, and whispered his name as my blood darkened against his skin. From those two points, death spread across his body. The flesh sank into his bones, and his bones turned to dust. They sank into the earth, and tiny violets sprang up, facing the sun.

The final spark of his power made the wind howl, shaking the circle of oaks, and I felt it burn inside me. I bent to the earth and kissed it; I lay down and felt the hill tremble. The earthquake ripped outward, marking Arthur's passing like the world itself cried.

Nine days later, the violets had begun to wither, and so I gathered all of them into my skirt and carried them into the house.

A quarter of the flowers I baked in the oven, gently, to preserve as much color and scent as possible, later to be crushed into powder for spells. The second quarter I boiled, throwing in ginger and a vanilla bean. Drops of the mixture went into all manner of tonics. Lotions and soaps, too.

A third quarter I put into a basket and took onto the roof that night, where Arthur and I used to watch the stars. I cradled the basket in one arm, and with my other hand lifted out handfuls of violets. I offered them to the wind and they were snatched away, tossed up in curlicues, just specks of pale purple against the infinite sky.

The last of the violets I kept.

I pressed them between the pages of books in the parlor: *The Complete Works of Walt Whitman*, *Paradise Lost*, *Beloved*, and *A Wizard of Earthsea*, because they'd been Arthur's favorites. He'd read them out loud to me when I was a girl, sitting on the edge of my bed, making different voices for all the characters and pausing to explain how Ged's magic was or wasn't like ours. Mostly while he read I imagined other things, and always fell asleep quickly, eager to escape to my own dreams. But I'd never asked him to go. I drifted away best to the rhythm of his voice, no matter what words he spoke.

It was into the parlor that I took Gabriel. I pulled down *Paradise Lost* because it seemed the most appropriate, and held it out.

He took it in Will's hands, brushing a finger along the embossed title with more reverence than I'd seen anyone show a book. With a little sigh, he opened it up, and the pages parted with a quiet creaking. Three violets, flattened and pale, stared up from the poem. Gabriel lifted the page to his face and breathed in.

"There is nothing of him here," Gabriel said, closing the book. "All the magic is gone."

All the magic is gone.

I stared at Gabriel as he pressed *Paradise Lost* to his chest like it was the most precious thing.

I stared, because I suddenly knew how to destroy him.

FIFTY-SEVEN

MAB

The next morning I went to the barn armed with water, cold chicken, and bread, as well as a pile of clothes to offer Ben. My plan had rolled through my head all night; I'd examined it from all sides, pulling it this way and that until the first rays of sunlight slipped through my window. But the more certain I became, the more sure I was that this was the path, the more a tiny part of my heart hoped that Ben might find a flaw.

I nudged open the barn door with my hip. "Ben?" I called as my eyes adjusted to the dimness.

His answer was quiet and strung with tension. "They're up to something." He stood up at the front of the cage, hands encircling two of the roots loosely.

I put the plate of food and pile of clothes down atop a crate and followed his gaze.

Five of the crows waited on the worktable, watching me with their heads cocked at the exact same angle. Four hopped anxiously on the ground beside the earthen remains of my homunculus.

"What are you doing?" I crouched beside them.

All nine gave an agitated squawk.

One of them on the table scratched the wood with his claw.

I glanced up. He stood beside the can of pencils and blood-letters. Delicately, he tapped the tip of a lancet with his beak. "Blood? You want blood?"

As I stood, Ben said, "They stood around that dirt all night."

The crow carefully bit the lancet and drew it out of the cup. He flew to my shoulder and landed as gracefully as he could. His claws punctured my skin, bringing familiar pain and causing blood to trickle down my arm. I held out a hand, and the crow dropped the lancet into it. It was a steel medical lancet, plain and sharp.

As I contemplated the blood-letter, all nine crows met on the ground, surrounding the pile of dirt that had been my doll. The one who pushed off my shoulder landed in the center before turning to me and holding his wings out wide; exactly the pose of the crow I'd pinned to the doll's chest with the antler.

"You want me to stab you," I whispered, feeling for a moment as if my heart stopped pumping and the world stopped turning.

None of the crows moved. There were only nine of them, and in the past two weeks they hadn't added again to their number. How could I kill another one now? When they dwindled so?

Behind me, Ben shook his cage. "Think about this."

But I suspected the crows already had, all night even, and just as I'd given Ben my trust by opening the cage, I needed to prove to the crows the same. So I knelt, pinching the lancet in my fingers, until the blood from my shoulder slipped all the way down and smeared into the metal. "As you wish," I said.

The crow's wings shook, and I could hear the roar of blood in my ears. I didn't know what they were doing or why they were asking this of me, but I trusted them, and did not hesitate as I jabbed the lancet into the crow's breast.

All nine cried out as one.

I pulled out the lancet and backed away as the crows leapt together. They brushed their wings across the bleeding chest of their fellow, dipped beaks into it until they were a teeming mass of black feathers, making small sounds of anguish, little barks and purrs, and then they all cried out again. A shiver stole down my back, lifting the hairs along my arms.

The crows seethed together, and I wasn't certain what I was seeing, until they weren't nine crows any longer but a single large body covered in feathers and wings and beaks and claws.

My hands pressed against my mouth, and I heard Ben's strangled grunt. The crows were transforming! I smeared my bloody shoulder and flicked tiny drops of my powerful blood over them in benediction. I said, "Take my power, friends, become what you dream, bone to bone, feather to flesh."

The body of feathers rolled like boiling water, and behind me Ben whispered a stream of the worst words I'd ever heard.

And then a man's body lay there, dark as the bones of the earth, with feathers for hair and fingernails as black as a crow's claw. Not fully human, but with arms and legs, lips, rounded ears, Adam's apple, chest and shoulders, hips, and everything in between.

I fell to my knees at his head, my hand hovering just over the delicate-looking feathers that sprouted from his temple. "Reese?"

His eyes snapped open, bright blue turquoise like the stones I'd chosen for my homunculus, and a hand grasped at mine.

WILL

The image-memory looped in the back of my mind like a scratchy old radio signal or SOS.

The air under my wings was thick with summer. Her hair shone like a piece of the sun had broken off and fallen to earth. The crow part of me forgot everything else for a moment and zeroed in on it. Shining. Glowing. I fanned out and surrounded her with all my bodies. Landed in the tree at the top of her tower. She turned up her face and spoke. I opened all my mouths and spoke back.

When she offered me a strand of that hair, I was hers.

I was hers I was hers I was hers.

My body hurt all over. Hit by a car and left on the side of the road hurt. I should've been used to it.

The last thing I remembered clearly was the quiet in Mab's bedroom. Only then I'd seen my body on the floor, crumpled up to be tossed out with the trash.

I was hers.

Images flashed one after another: the ground far below, a graveyard, Mab looking up into the branches of a tree, me kissing her—only not *me*—a white farmhouse with a tree out front, a teal truck, the graveyard again. On and on until I was dizzy with them. A girl with blue eyeliner, an old man in a baseball cap, my body—my body—*my body with bloodred tattoos I knew from my dreams.* Mab's yellow hair. Pulling me down.

Mab said, "Reese."

I opened my eyes.

She leaned over me, joy spread across her face and her hair falling everywhere. Normal. Her touch on my forehead was tentative. As if she thought I might break. "Mab," I managed to say, but my tongue stuck.

Her smile sweetened even more. "You need fuel. That transformation must have taken everything out of you."

I tried to sit up as she stood. The rafters overhead told me we were in her barn. My vision went out of focus, and I saw the barn from, like, ten different angles simultaneously. The ground spun and I closed my eyes.

"He's my familiar; this will make everything better," Mab was saying to someone else.

Before I realized who she was talking to, I managed to sit, and saw my legs. Shock slammed the breath out of me. My legs were black. And not a natural, human brown that looked black, but like I'd been roasted alive and come out shiny and black as coal. My hands, too—I held them out, and they immediately began to shake. Everything was wrong. This wasn't my body. Where light caught my skin, it glinted purple and blue and gold like spilled oil.

Dazed, I touched my thigh. My forearms were streaked with tiny soft feathers instead of hair. I was fascinated. Then it turned over in my stomach and became horror and nausea. Feathers trailed down my chest a little, too, and along my belly.

I was naked.

Only it wasn't *me*. It wasn't right.

Mab knelt next to me with a plate of food. I drew up my knees and tried to make my nakedness as inconspicuous as possible. I stared at her, wide-eyed. Why wasn't she horrified, too? Why wasn't she afraid or even concerned? Instead something like happiness pressed out of her smile. There were a million questions beating each other up to be asked first, but I couldn't get them out.

Mab was holding out the plate. The smell of meat hit me, and I was starving. My stomach growled louder than I'd ever heard it.

"Here, Reese," she said. "Eat."

I was hers.

"Oh my God," I choked out. "Mab."

Someone from my left called, "It talks."

I knew that tone of voice. I pushed the plate of food away and was on my feet in an instant. I swayed, but found my balance, and stumbled to my brother. "Ben! What are you doing in there?"

The rough wooden bars of a cage separated us. Ben drew away before I could touch his hands.

"Ben?"

His lips curled back, and I recognized the expression of about-to-fire anger. "Whoa, back off."

I gripped the bars of the cage and stared at my brother. Flashes of memory punched me: Ben catching me in the hallway, driving the car, Ben pulled to the ground by vines. I shook my head as if I could rattle the images out.

"Reese?" Mab's voice was soft. Her fingers dug into my arm.

I turned to her. "Why did you put my brother in a cage?"

Her hand fell away, and she stared up at me. Dirt was smudged under one big blue eye. "Will?"

"Will," Ben repeated.

"Yeah, of course," I said.

Mab's face split into shock, and she flung herself at me.

I staggered back, arms flailing for balance. She held on, pushed her face into my neck, arms wrapped what felt like five times around me. Her hair scratched my cheek and chin. And her feet knocked loosely against my shins as she dangled. I put my arms around her, slowly. I was stronger than I should have been. Mab felt as hefty as a paper bag.

Mab leaned back and grasped my face. "Will," she said again.

I tightened my arms around her. "What happened to me, Mab?" I whispered. "What happened to my body?"

But Ben shook the bars of the cage and yelled, "Let me out of here."

Both Mab and I turned our heads to him. I didn't let go of her. "Ben," I said, not knowing where to begin.

She wiggled to get down. I stepped toward the cage and heard Mab scrambling behind me. Wrapping one of my large black hands around a bar, I tugged. It bent, but no more than a thick tree branch would've. Ben stared at me, eyes wrinkling. I didn't know if I looked like me but with black skin and feathers, or if I was totally unrecognizable. Ben shook his head, a hand coming up as if he would brush me away.

And Mab was there, pricking her finger with a tiny metal thing. She skimmed blood against the cage and shut her eyes briefly. The bar shivered and bowed out. Ben climbed free, moving his body to completely avoid the possibility of touching mine. He stood next to Mab, facing me. Said to her, "What is it?"

She reached out and touched my stomach. "It's Will."

I remembered I was naked. Jerked away from her. "Do you have some of those pants?" I asked in a stupid high voice, just as Ben said, "Bullshit it's Will."

"Yes," she said to both of us. Spinning on one foot, she dashed over to a crate. Left me staring at Ben.

"Ben," I said.

"You're . . ." He shook his head. "No way." Old sweat and mud streaked down half his forehead, and his eyes were tight. It was the expression he'd worn the whole weekend of Aaron's funeral. "I'm not dead," I said.

"You aren't Will, either."

Out of habit, I wiped my palms on my thighs as if they were sweaty. The feathers instead of hair were too weird. But I couldn't let myself freak out about this new body thing. I was me. I pushed the heels of my hands into my eyes and tried to think of something to convince him. I said, "I am. I'm your brother." I looked at him. "Remember in sixth grade we had this assignment to write a story about somebody we admired, and I wrote about you? Called it 'American Hero.' Mom mailed it to you, didn't she?"

I waited. The barn was so quiet I could hear the whine of an airplane flying over some field far away. Mab stood behind him with clothes in hand, not moving. I really wanted those pants. But didn't move, either.

Ben ran his hands up over his face and back through his regulation-short hair. "I still have it."

"Really?"

He looked like he'd eaten lemon peel. But it wasn't hostile anymore. "It tucks real nice into my boot," he admitted.

"Ben." I moved as close as I could until he leaned away. "I'm sorry."

"For what? Turning into whatever the hell you are? Or for letting me think you were doing drugs? Pretending I was the douche bag when you really were into some heavy shit?"

Shrugging uncomfortably, since I couldn't really deny any of the charges, I said hopefully, "You kiss your mother with that mouth?"

His expression darkened again. "You gonna kiss her with that one?"

I looked at my hands, so totally not mine. My mouth hung open, and Mab tossed the pants at me. They smacked into my chest and I grabbed them. Turned around for no good reason to pull them on. The drawstring barely tied around this newer, broader waist. Irritably, I thought, *I finally have a body more like Ben's.*

"How did this happen?" Ben asked.

As I turned, I realized he was asking Mab. Looking at her with something a lot like trust. She pointed behind her at a plate of chicken. "Will, you eat that, and I'll explain what I think. And how we're going to get out of this."

I shoveled the chicken in, sitting knee-to-knee on the floor of the barn with Mab and Ben.

Mab gave me an abridged version of what had gone on since Saturday morning. Then, studying me with a half-calculating, half-awed look, she said, "This body was my crows' doing. They're my familiar, the way Gabriel is using Lukas as his, though more voluntary—we have no runes linking us. Only intention." She sucked in a deep breath and skimmed her hand down the line of feathers on my forearm. "They knew what I needed, knew I needed them more than ever—a familiar to balance out Gabriel's power. And not one that's scattered as they were, as a flock of crows, but one as strong as a human familiar." Her eyes shut, and she put her clasped hands against her heart. "So they transformed themselves."

"But I thought Will," Ben frowned at me, "was overwhelmed in his own body."

She looked at me again. "The crows caught you when Gabriel took your body, didn't they? They were right there, and they caught you, pulled you up into them the way they'd escaped their own death. Do you remember?"

Uncomfortable, I thought about what I remembered. Flying. Mab's hair. Disjointed images. "Yeah. Yeah, I think so," I agreed. They weren't all from yesterday, or my life. I'd seen things from his old life, too. Reese's. "What happened to him?" I stabbed my fingers into my forehead. "Reese. Is he here?"

Mab paused with her mouth slightly open. Her lips were pale around the edges. "I don't know," she murmured. "Do you feel anything?"

"Like what? What would it feel like?"

"A buzzing in the back of your mind, a song stuck in a loop. Something like that. Niggling and strange."

"Everything about this is strange," I said, spreading my

hands, and looked down at this dark body. Nothing in my head made me think of Reese anymore. It was just me in here. "I don't think so."

She nodded, but I noticed her hands pressing hard into her thighs. I reached out and took one fist. Pulled the fingers out one at a time and wove our hands together.

Ben grunted. "So. What are we doing next? To get Will his body back. And save your kid? And plant this jackass into the ground."

I was impressed how well Ben was taking all this. I said, "You're being so compliant."

He half smiled at me, which looked a lot like a threat. "It's willing suspension of disbelief. Don't take it personally."

Mab squeezed my hand and climbed to her feet. "Come to the worktable; I'll sketch out my idea so your brother can poke holes in it." She shot a wry smile at Ben, who bared his teeth.

I'd missed a lot.

Just as we were getting up with her, I heard *my voice* call her name outside.

Mab froze for a split second, then shoved at me. "Hide," she hissed. "Don't come out no matter what."

I whirled. Ben already was jumping back into the cage. Just as I dove behind an old overturned rowboat, the barn door shoved open.

MAB

I was a whirlwind of hot and cold emotions, panic flapping hard as a crow's wing in my chest as I forced the cage closed around Ben. He glared out at the doors, and I turned my back, praying fast and silently that Will was hidden in shadows, just as Gabriel entered.

"Ah, Mab," he said with a slick smile. "There you are, and your new pet, as well."

He wandered in, hands clasped behind his back. I'd noticed that yesterday, while I'd talked to Ben for hours, he'd slashed the tires of all our cars and cut through the phone line. He was pretending to give me space, to trust me, but it wasn't real, and we needed to be more careful now that Reese didn't have many eyes to look out for him.

I said, "What do you want, Gabriel?"

"To visit, is that not enough?" He smiled at me, a very not-Will smile filled with sarcasm.

"I'm busy."

Heaving a dramatic sigh, he said, "I thought I felt some magic pulling at the roots of the hill earlier."

"As I said, I've been working." I swept around him to the worktable, and pushed around the papers I'd used to diagram ideas for Ben yesterday. "I need to focus."

"Well then. Tell me if you know where Arthur kept his drawings." He fiddled with one of the old pencils in the coffee can on the table. "I went through his bedroom and found nothing. Nor in the den where he used to keep them in the footstool."

My back tingled as he neared me, as I imagined him ransacking Arthur's things. I shuffled through some of the rune-circle sketches I'd made, folding them into piles. "He kept them in an accordion file over there." I nodded at the crowded shelves. "Take them and go, if you would."

Gabriel wandered to the shelves and ran his hand over the wooden front of one. It was difficult not to hunch my shoulders against his presence, and I reminded myself to keep my mother in mind. With her easy living, her flamboyance, she'd have adapted quickly to Gabriel, I was certain, flirted and teased until she had him in the palm of her hand. I took a deep breath and imagined myself in a flared red dress, low-cut with thin shoulder straps, and my hair styled, my lips painted.

But the little purring noises he made when he discovered something of interest and his sighs of dismay distracted me. When he glanced at me through the corners of his eyes, my cheeks filled with heat and I glanced down. I was not Mother. I couldn't flirt with anyone, much less Gabriel looking at me from Will's body. Especially while Ben observed from the cage with a dark frown.

"Ah!" Gabriel turned abruptly, his hands full of old sheets of parchment he'd pulled out of a stiff accordion file. The portrait on top was of Granny Lyn, when she'd been young and first married, in a field of verbena and prairie phlox. She'd posed for Arthur with only a shawl draped around her bare shoulders. Every pencil stroke was a long caress, and when I was little I'd traced them with my finger as I recognized the shape of her eyebrows and the secret little smile she reserved for him. Her hair had come loose from its bun and fell in soft waves around her cheeks as she held her chin low.

There'd been one of my mother, too, face alive with laughter and hair in a short bob. I'd taken it up to my bedroom and hidden it in a drawer. He'd drawn Donna in the garden, her hat pulled low to cover her identity unless you knew the shape of her shoulders. Faith in her overalls, Eli folding butter into croissant dough. Justin with his new eyebrow ring, Silla with her face a study in pain as she fed the crows. And me—well, I never would sit still unless I was practicing my runes, so all the sketches of me had my brow low and my lips pressed together in concentration. Arthur always shook his head and told me I didn't really look like that, but he wasn't skilled enough after a hundred and fifty years to capture it.

Arthur had collected portraits, the way I marked all the blood kin who passed through our gates with a charm tied to the branches of my redbud tree.

I drew a calming breath as Gabriel put the sheaf of pages down on the corner of the table. "So take them, and go," I said.

He shrugged one shoulder and walked lazily toward me. "Here." Gabriel smoothed his hands over the top sketch, then held it up by the edges. It depicted a young man in a long coat. A rifle was slung over his shoulder, and his hair was braided back with beads and charms. His smile curled up, and he slouched on one cocked hip as though he needn't be prepared for anything.

I took it, bringing it close. It was a familiar drawing, of course, though I'd never thought much about it before. The edges of the man's left boot had smeared, and I noticed he held a small bouquet of flowers in one hand. They might have been violets. Overall, it was a crude drawing, and it had to have been old, before Arthur gained skill. Turning the portrait over, I saw the single tiny word in the bottom corner: *Gabriel.* No date, but a tiny preservation rune and a brown blotch of blood.

"Not many of the others are meant to last. He wanted to remember me," Gabriel said quietly, coming up beside me. He breathed against my neck, and I shivered.

"That's nice for you," I whispered. "Keep it. Take it and let me do my work."

"You don't need to hate me, Mab." Gabriel put both his hands on my shoulders, leaning close to my back. "In time, we'll forgive each other, and think what a home we could fashion here."

I forced myself to keep breathing, though he smelled spicy like the earth and my lavender soap and sweat. Like Will, but more a part of this land. "Maybe," I lied. "Maybe you're right." Turning in his arms, I touched his chest and firmly pushed him back. "But not yet."

A scuffling noise had him glancing swiftly behind me. "What was that?"

"Crows," Ben called. "Picking around in that back corner."

Gabriel let go of me and strode to the cage. Ben backed up as far as he could, until his shoulders hit the opposite bars.

"Let him alone, Gabriel," I said. "I don't need him worked up. It ruins what I'm doing."

Running a finger down the root bar nearest him, Gabriel smiled. "I think getting him worked up would help the magic quicken."

"Let me have this place to myself!" I cried, rushing forward and grasping his wrist. I pulled at him. "I need a refuge, Gabriel, or I will lose all my patience to stop fighting you."

"You can't fight me." He pressed close to me, taking my

hands and holding them tight between us. "I will defeat you because I hold all the power of this land behind me, through little Lukas."

I rose up onto my tiptoes and said, with my mouth a breath from his, "I will hurt you beyond repair even as you destroy me."

"So like your mother," he said, then nipped at my lips with his teeth. I shoved away, and he pushed me, too, so that I stumbled back and hit the floor hard on my hip.

Gabriel stepped over me, sneered down. "I always hated that bitch."

He left the barn then, left me with the shocking memory of such disgust seeping out of Will's own face.

WILL

I was on my feet, running for her, the moment he was gone. "Mab." I lifted her up. "Are you all right?"

My skin rippled. I squeezed my eyes shut and grit my teeth. I'd had a hard time breathing the moment that guy walked in wearing my body. Now it felt like my chest was falling to pieces.

"Will?" It was Ben. His hand touched my shoulder, fast, like it burned him.

"What's wrong?" Mab frowned at my chest, ran her hands down it. I shuddered and wrapped my arms around myself.

"I'm coming apart," I said through my grinding teeth.

Mab pulled me to my knees, put her hands on my face. "Breathe, Will, calm down. You're too upset."

My heartbeat was loud as a helicopter. I wanted to fly—no, I wanted to be here. To be. Here.

"What's wrong with him?" Ben asked. I heard the cage creaking.

Mab kissed me.

She clutched my shoulders and pushed her mouth against mine. Opened up to me.

Everything lasered in on that.

On her lips.

Not moving, just being there.

"Will," she whispered. "Don't lose hold of this."

Cupping her face, I kissed her again, ignoring my brother, ignoring everything but Mab. My chest fit back into place. The terrible fluttering in my skin slowed. Mab slid closer, wrapped her arms all around my head until my cheek was against her neck. Her heartbeat filled my ears, and she ruffled her fingers in my feather-hair. "What happened?" she asked.

"It was—it was my body." I twisted my fingers in the ends of her yellow hair. *I was hers,* that voice said again. "I want it back."

"Good," she soothed.

"No." I pushed away. Stood up. "Not good. That's *my body* and I *want it back.*" I bent over, braced my hands on my knees. "I have to get it back. It's mine." Every time I shut my eyes, I saw it stalking around Mab. Grabbing her shoulders. Shoving her down. Laughing and frowning with *my face.* I scrubbed these black crow-thing hands over my black crow-thing eyes as if I could block it out.

Mab stood, too. Her hands set firmly on her hips. "It is good, Will. Because I know how to do it."

FIFTY-EIGHT

MAB

It had only taken an hour to explain my plan to Ben and Will, even now that it had been altered to fit both of them into it. Ben had asked a few questions, and I'd had answers for all, until he was satisfied that it was dangerous, but possible.

Everything revolved around the countercurse Arthur and I had used to destroy the black candle rune on that walnut tree last year.

I'd use the same curse on Gabriel, and it would burn all the magic out of Will's body—Gabriel included.

The spell required two steps: Getting the initial magic into Gabriel in order to open him up to the countercurse. That I would accomplish from the inside: just as Gabriel had poisoned Will's blood, so would I poison his now. Then, nine hours later, it was a matter of activating the countercurse by delivering the second rune—in our case, by way of an inscribed dagger that would be stabbed directly into him.

Because magic is a dance of balance, there were also two complications. First was breaking Lukas free of Gabriel's control, and second was preventing the countercurse from tearing loose to destroy everything in its path.

The first I would solve by using a black candle rune of my own. The second had a solution, but not one anybody would like.

The only sound was the scratchy old ballad singing out from Granny's radio. I'd called for Gabriel, then hitched myself onto the counter with the bottle of charmed wine tucked in my lap.

From my perch I could see through the archway into the main hall and on through to the living room, where Gabriel was settled with Arthur's books. "Coming," he called back to me.

I crossed my ankles, held my heels against the cabinets, and folded my hands around the neck of the wine bottle. I'd thrown open the windows to let in the warm night wind, grossly aware of how quiet it seemed without the rough calls of my crows.

All my life had centered in this kitchen. I imagined Donna washing dirt off her hands in the sink. Granny Lyn patting a stool in the corner so that I'd come and let her trim my hair. Mother dancing down the hallway in a two-step, arms up to embrace an imaginary partner. Justin carving letters into the edge of the table with his dinner fork. Faith and Eli huddled over the newspaper, pointing out ads for free kittens because Hannah was begging for one.

Arthur stood across from me, under the arch of the door. Staring back, not doing anything but looking at me. I wanted to smile, to promise him I was holding the land together. He said, "The blood is yours now, Mab, all the beauty of the world. Take it."

I closed my eyes, and when I looked again through a film of tears, he was gone.

All the beauty of the world.

In order to stop the countercurse from destroying the blood land, I would have to anchor it to myself as well as Gabriel. Giving it a second point of origin would force the magic to spiral away from both of us, but toward the other. Only we, and everything between us, would fall under the curse.

This world, this land, was my home, and I could not let the burning fire of the countercurse ravage it all. I could not create ripples of power the way Arthur had when he'd gone into the earth. That single act had drawn Will into all of this, and I would not let anything slip through my cracks, to draw more people into danger. There would be no holes in this plan. No homunculi run amok, no earthquakes, no mistakes. Even if it meant I gave up everything else.

This curse would begin in Gabriel, and end in me.

All the beauty of the world.

My breath was so shallow and fast.

Come to dinner, Gabriel, I begged silently, *before I lose all courage to do what must be done.*

When I was a little girl, and afraid, I'd run to Arthur or my mother. Or I'd tug on one of Granny Lyn's long silver braids until she let me onto her lap, and there she would put her arms around me and pray.

Now I couldn't turn to Arthur, not even to put one of his dry petals onto my tongue, because Gabriel would smell it. If my mother were here, she'd have said, *Throw that wine away and embrace your new life with Gabriel—take what he's offering, pet, and never look back.*

And so I clasped my hands more tightly together around

the dark glass bottle. "May I live by thee, oh God," I whispered, and felt a ghostly dry touch against my knuckles, as if Granny Lyn stood before me, holding her hands over mine. "Support me by the strength of heaven that I may never turn back. May I find the grace sufficient to all my needs."

"Are you praying?" Gabriel asked, lounging indolently against the archway.

Will had asked me, too, and sounded just as surprised. "Why shouldn't I pray?" I set the bottle of wine a little too hard on the counter.

He slunk nearer, grinning. "Oh, only because we have no need for God here. Because I expected you to be far beyond such needs. But I suppose you are young yet, and perhaps Arthur put strange ideas into your head."

I shrugged one shoulder. "Prayer is like magic. Ordering words to put a call out to God."

"Yes, but when you were calling out to magic," Gabriel put his hands on my knees and parted them so that he could slide up against the counter and say, with his lips very near mine, "you were calling out to *me*."

His power curled around me, a living thing, with roots and tendrils of its own, petals blossoming against my cheeks. I raised my free hand to his neck and rested it there. His pulse thumped under my finger. The rhythm of magic. Oh God, how I'd miss it.

Gabriel nipped at my nose and then pulled away with a smile. "Have you forgiven me for being cruel this morning?"

I summoned up a light smile and offered him the wine. "If you've forgiven me for the same."

Taking the bottle, Gabriel held my hand as I hopped off the counter. Together we sat at the fully set kitchen table. Roasted peppers, stuffed with paprika and ground beef and peas, steamed from our plates. A recipe Granny had taught me, and I wondered if he would know it.

He did, shooting me an amused look as he poured us both wine. He lifted his glass. "To friendship?"

"To the past, and the future," I answered, raising mine as well. "But Gabriel, there is magic in this wine."

He paused with the rim against his bottom lip. The purple wine glittered richly through the crystal, as deep as his red eyes. "Magic."

I smiled. "Only a potion of sharing. Of gentle connection and forgiveness."

Skepticism narrowed his eyes, and so I let all the wine in my glass pour down my throat for him. The power tingled, stretching through me to my fingers and toes, wrapping gently around my heart.

WILL

The moon was this tiny sliver just over the trees. We tried to draw a picture with salt and wax in near pitch darkness. Ben held the paper with the rune Mab had sketched. He loomed over me as I crouched, trying to get the salt circle right. Or the wax curved without burning my fingers off. Or setting these crazy feathers on fire.

Our mission, while she distracted Gabriel and poisoned his blood, was to make this giant magical circle around the rosebush. We wouldn't complete it. But everything except for the final line would be ready for Mab in the morning. It was a nine-spiral rune, she'd said, and apologized for the complicated angles we had to make nine times as evenly spaced around the circumference as possible. This was how she'd suck Lukas up from the roots and sever his ties to Gabriel. With power from the sacrifice of this body I was wearing, because it was all that remained of her familiar now.

The timing had to be perfect, or I'd die and she'd fail.

Ben nudged my shoulder and pointed at a spot I'd missed. We tried not to talk at all. Quiet, buzzing jazz music filtered out from the open kitchen windows on the front of the house.

Working with these hands was easier than it should have been. I thought about it. Focused on it. Instead of worrying about Mab inside with that psychopath.

Frogs screamed from the forest. Clouds rolled in just enough to hide the stars in the east. I shuffled along, pouring salt. Ben muttered as he counted steps around the circle and marked the best places for the nine runes.

And finally, we were done.

Ben and I stood side by side, looking at the house. The music continued, but we were more overwhelmed by the wind in the trees and those damn frogs. Crickets, maybe. Ben said, "You should get going. I'm going to use that tree there," he pointed at a large one, with a branch low enough he'd be able to climb up easily.

"Yeah." I didn't move.

The wind blew lightly at us. It ruffled the feathers on the back of my neck. On my forearms. I shivered and remembered flight.

"Better not rain," Ben said. His eyes pinched as he looked at the distant clouds. "That would really screw all this up."

I still didn't move. Didn't say anything. My bare feet felt rooted to the ground.

Ben turned abruptly and clapped his arms around me. "Be careful, you jackass."

My fists dug into his shoulders.

"I wish I could do this for you." Ben's voice was hardly even a whisper.

I whispered, "You can't."

"I know. Don't be stupid. Don't be . . . Just be a Sanger."

Be a Sanger. I shook my head. "I wish I knew what that meant anymore, since Aaron died. It's like the world ended."

Ben pushed away, just enough to grab my face. He had to tilt his head back, because in this body I was taller. "It didn't."

"The world where I had two brothers did."

He didn't like that, but he pushed his eyebrows together. "Maybe," he admitted after a moment. "But not the world where you have one brother."

I started to say something, but Ben gripped my head hard enough I felt a feather behind my ear snap. "Not the one," he said, "where *I* have a brother. You're going to survive this. Both of us are. And that's gonna be a world we deal with."

Pulling away, I bent to pick up the bag of supplies we'd brought from the barn. A knife jutted out against the plastic. I took it and cut my hand, gritting my teeth at the sting. Then I offered the hilt to Ben.

Solemnly, he cut his hand, too. He held it out. I took it, and our blood smeared together.

Gabriel drank the entire bottle of wine, because I continued pouring it into his glass, sipping along with him. Will's face popped pink in the cheeks, and Gabriel swayed. He laughed outrageously, delighted, he said, at the low tolerance of his brand-new body.

I turned the music up as loud as the little radio would go, and Gabriel cheered, picked me up, and whirled me around in a jig. Our hands twined together; we cavorted into the parlor, kicked over stacks of books, and scattered Arthur's drawings to the corners of the room. The bottle of wine rolled over the rug, under the sofa, anointing the house with its sharp aroma. Gabriel sang an old French song, grinning his never-Will grin, and I let my head fall back and closed my eyes as we danced and twirled. I was dizzy, and the magic pushed against my mind, Gabriel pushed there with his power. I welcomed it, I let my blood burn with his, and as we danced the potion seeped into our bones. Our magic reached for each other, and suddenly all the communion I had ever known while racing over the land, touching the power of the trees, rushed through me. My bones rang with it; my skin burned with the power. Oh God, I would miss it! Would miss the magic.

My back hit the wall and Gabriel held me there, my feet off the ground. He kissed my neck, pressing the whole of himself against me. "Gabriel," I said, struggling away.

He laughed and caught my hand as I dashed down the hall, gave a sharp tug and spun me back into a dance.

I swam through it, the earth turning under me and the music all around. Just those little sips of wine and the potent magic in them set my head spinning. I danced with him, knowing this was the last night of his life, of my magic. For these few moments I would give in, I would swell with the power, our power. And always, throughout the rest of my life, I would have the memories of it burned into my imagination.

WILL

I flew down the hill toward Mab's silo. Crashed through the trees once I was far enough away from the house. I let go and ran.

If something went wrong tomorrow morning, I was going to die. When the magic ripped through this body, if I couldn't hold on to my real one, that would be it.

Poof.

No more Will Sanger.

So I flew.

My bare feet knew the way, and I dodged branches like I'd been running these woods my whole life. In this body, I heard everything. Wind rushed past my ears. I remembered the sound of flying, too, all roaring air and wings beating louder than any heart. Even now the world had come alive for me. Insects, night birds, frogs, and the constantly shifting leaves. It was so loud. So awesomely loud.

I didn't want to go back to the quiet. To the scratchy white noise that had been my life as Will Sanger.

I don't want.

I don't want.

Always what I didn't want.

What did I want?

I stumbled and fell to my hands and knees in a slick patch of cold, dead leaves. I clutched at them, digging my strange black fingers in. I thought about what Ben had said. The weight of a year without Aaron pushed into my back.

And with it, Reese's memories: dead mother, dead father, anger so hard it broke walls. Fighting for life and failing. Death. Death. Death.

Then flight.

I rolled over onto my back, wiped at my eyes. Overhead, the trees rose up, winding limbs together into a net of black. Through leaves and twigs, the sky was only more black and tiny, tiny stars.

In my daydreams I was always flying away from things. From Aaron's death, from the Naval Academy, from Mom's silence. From Dad's expectations and honor. From the sheer awesomeness that Ben wanted to trust me. And even when I had a destination, it was only that distant promised land. Not anything real. Not a future or a destiny. Not even a job.

Like I was the one who'd died. Been cut off from the life intended for me.

But I wasn't dead. Not yet. And it was moronic to stand still just because Aaron didn't get to go forward.

I was going to get my body back. Live my life—not anybody else's but mine.

Because I wanted it.

FIFTY-NINE

MAB

Arthur's ceiling had a skylight, roughly cut out and paned with a single piece of glass. Through it, I watched the stars move, while trapped under Gabriel's arm. He'd passed out singing, holding me with him. I should have slept, too, but couldn't bring myself to close my eyes on my last night with magic in my veins. Gabriel's breath pulsed slow and steady against my cheek, and my heart fell into rhythm with it.

But late in the night, so late it was nearly morning, I slid out from his embrace.

"Where are you going?" he whispered.

"Seven-day binding, and to watch the dawn." I brushed my fingers on his forehead, skimmed one along his cheekbone just under a bloodred eye. I thought of the black feathers cresting along Will's new cheek. "If you feel any magic, that's what I'm doing. Don't worry, and I'll return as soon as I can."

A sweet smile edged his mouth as he drifted back to sleep.

As I watched, I felt the lines of my face harden. Now was the time.

In my own bathroom, I bathed quickly and slipped into a pale lavender dress with a low-cut back. I braided my hair with purple and black ribbons for strength, power, and binding. A single red ribbon wound around my left wrist. Mother used to say it was best to dress the part, and that was the only thing she and Granny Lyn ever agreed upon. I smeared my hands with oil of yarrow and rue, rubbing it deep into my skin, and pulled the wax-sealed box out from under my bed, for it held the things I required.

As I made my way down the twisting path toward the sunflower field, I reached out and skimmed my fingers along leaves. It was dark, but they knew me as I knew them. So many hundreds of times I'd done this as I walked, but now, this, this was the last.

I paused in a shady grove of elm trees, beside a cluster of evening primroses. I gripped a dagger in one hand, dangerous and bright, and the other hand I held out, palm up and fingers curled loosely. As I quieted myself, I listened to the beat of my heart as it pumped magic swiftly to all my capillaries. I stared at the lines of my hand, the rough pink pads of my fingers, the bluish veins hiding under the most delicate flesh spreading from between my thumb and forefinger.

Wind brushed through the narrow elm leaves, sending several to flutter down. Predawn birdsong and the distant tinkling of bells from the charms atop the silo sounded like giggling.

Gently, I plucked a primrose. The four brilliant yellow petals matched my hair. I wanted more than anything to prick my finger with the tip of the dagger, to send the flower flying up as a butterfly, to perform one final tiny act of beauty before my magic went dark.

But I could not chance altering the fragile magic infusing

the blade. All I could do was listen to the sound of the magic rushing through my body, and pray I wouldn't forget it when it was gone.

WILL

I waited for Mab at the foot of the silo.

It was her hair I saw first, bobbing at the edge of the forest. I stared at it as she waded through the low sunflower plants, thinking about Reese.

She emerged like a queen, her purple dress spreading around her knees in the wind. Dark ribbons blew over her shoulders to slip along her arms and chest like rivulets of blood. She held a flower in one hand, a knife in the other. Totally weird, just like the first time I'd seen her. In a tree wearing goggles and combat boots, with blood smeared over her mouth.

This was just as strange. Just as wild. But normal now, too.

"Mab," I said, walking out of the shadows.

She lifted her face. "Will."

I climbed up the rickety silo ladder first, and Mab behind me. We spilled over the side onto the dark, sparse grass. Under the leaves of the tree, the shadows felt deep. Mab immediately went to grab her tackle box from the roots and began setting up a spell. All she'd said to me was that we needed to do this so that I could be her true familiar. Could channel magic to her, and from her.

She laid out a circle of black ribbon, and two thin candles. Onto a scrap of paper, she drew an angry-looking design. It spidered out from a center point. Mab offered it to me. "Do you think you can replicate this?"

Nerves tickled in my stomach. But I nodded.

"Good." Mab picked up the dagger she'd brought with her and offered that, too. Kneeling on the ground with her back to me, she said, "Carve it into my back."

I dropped the weapon. "What?"

Twisting her neck around to look at me over her bare shoulder, she repeated herself.

I crouched behind her. "Mab, no way. How can I do that?"

"Carefully but quickly."

"I can't cut you."

"Then this will not work."

"Mab!"

She turned completely and snapped, "I told you about magic, Will. Nothing is free. Sacrifice! Balance! That is the essence of what we do."

It was as close to anger as I'd ever seen in her. Pressed lips, brow wrinkled. I picked up the dagger. Looked at the discarded drawing she'd given me. "What is it?"

"A black candle rune. It will tie our power together completely. You'll draw from me and be able to begin the spell when you stab Gabriel. And I, in turn, will be able to draw from you, because you will be connected to me as my true familiar." Mab glanced up at the charms dangling over us, bobbing in the light breeze. They were only hanging shadows because it was still so dark.

I took a deep breath, deeper than I was used to because of this strange body. It reminded me suddenly of how Mab had said possessing another body took getting used to. I didn't want to be used to this. "Okay," I said, shakily.

"Thank you." Mab turned back around and took a deep breath herself. It lifted her shoulders and then sank everything down. I positioned myself just behind her. Her lower back was pale even in all these shadows. The sun didn't touch this skin often. I gripped the dagger and spread my other hand out. So black against her, like a hand-shaped hole.

I had to pretend it wasn't real. It wasn't her skin. This open back was just paper. Mab tugged the straps of her dress to the very edges of her shoulders. But it wasn't necessary. She'd picked the right thing to wear to give me all the room I needed.

This was me stalling.

I clenched my jaw, glanced a final time at the drawn rune. Put the tip of the dagger against her back.

It made me sick to my stomach when the sharp blade slid through her skin. So easily. Mab made no sound, and didn't flinch. But I froze, and she whispered, "Don't stop, Will."

I wanted to shut my eyes but couldn't. I wanted to go faster but not screw it up. My tongue was dry, but my hand was surprisingly steady. That was probably shock.

There was only enough light to see the lines of red blood. They marked my progress. I started kind of panting. Mab reached her hand back and touched my knee. Her fingers dug into the pants, gripping me.

I gritted my teeth so hard my head began to hurt. But I kept going. Cut lines and angles. Jagged spider legs.

Finally, it was done.

I pulled away. I said, "Okay."

Mab rolled her shoulders. Hissed quietly. "Good," she whispered.

Wind ruffled the tree over us, tossing the charms. I found the little horse and jockey I'd picked. It leapt like it was actually galloping.

"Your turn," Mab said, turning on the ground. "Give me your back."

Heat spread down my whole body in a weird combo of relief and fear. But I bent over so my hands were flat against the rough ground. Mab left the drawing next to me and knelt beside me. "I'll be quick, but brace yourself," she warned. Then the knife was in my skin. My back was on fire.

I shut my eyes. Curled my fingers into the ground. The pain was so focused, right where Mab cut. It followed her knife like a spotlight: cold, burning pain moving down my back in a straight line. Then across. In a sharp V. It hurt more over my shoulder blades. Hot blood trickled around my ribs. It almost tickled. At one point high up, the pain flipped some switch and I almost liked it. I let out a kind of puffing laugh. Endorphins.

"Hold still, I'm nearly finished," Mab said. Her breath was warm on my back. Brought the pain straight to life. I winced and kept still. Little shivers crawled up my spine, dragging pain with them. It all settled in a little fire at the base of my skull.

Then it was nausea. Awesome.

She stopped cutting and put down the dagger. I leaned up, felt a slick of warm blood slide down my back. It soaked into the waistband of my pants.

"Now." Mab took my hands and we stood together. "We get into that circle, backs together. I will say words, and you repeat them. Then we say them together. And you focus on that candle, on letting the magic spin through both of us. It'll be like fire spilling into your back from mine, into your heart. You draw it out and use that to light the flame."

"You want me to light a candle with my mind."

"And my magic." Mab smiled sadly.

"I guess all the cool witches can do it."

She clearly didn't get my joke. Just nodded. And led me into the ribbon circle.

We turned our backs together. Mab stepped back into me, and even though I was a good half foot taller than her in this damn big body, the moment her bloody back squished against mine, the power slammed us together.

I gasped. Mab clutched at my hands. "Don't let go, and don't fall, Will," she said.

It was so hot between us. The slick blood filled all the spaces between the shadows and leaves with its smell. I tasted it on my tongue, gagged at the memory of the mud monster in my mouth.

MAB

The black candle ritual did not look like much from the outside. We were only two people back to back, whispering words and waiting for candles to light. A scared girl and a crow-boy with feathers cutting up from his cheekbones and down his spine.

But from the middle of it, there was a rage of hot pain and exploding power. It was give and take, pushing and pulling. It was a rainbow of fire.

I said the words to bind myself to Will, and gave them to him. He repeated them, and we said them together.

Your power become mine. Your blood my blood. The mark of my strength on your flesh, forever. Reflecting power into power like a flame in a black mirror. The mark of my strength on your flesh, forever.

The chant wove around us, a tight band of air circling again and again, linking us together. My back shivered and writhed as tendrils of my blood flowed out of the torn skin and pushed for Will's. His blood reached for me. Our blood coiled together like scarlet worms.

Sharp nausea circled my thighs, weakened my knees. I held on to Will's hands so tightly, focused on the building power between our palms.

And the moment the runes snapped into reality, I felt it. Will jerked and so did I. My heart pounded, and we breathed simultaneously. Drawing my eyes to the wick of the candle, I blew a narrow stream of air.

It flickered to life.

Will's candle did, too, and the flames made the heart-shaped redbud leaves into ripples and layers of shadow.

WILL

We watched the sunrise together. Mab leaned against my shoulder. I leaned against the trunk of the redbud.

My back didn't hurt at all. And Mab's rune had scorched into dark scar tissue. I only assumed mine was the same. It felt just like a sore muscle.

Mab's braid hung over her shoulder between us. Scratching me when she shifted. As the sun came up, it turned the curls into gold. Here under the tree, with the wind making the silver bells and wind chimes shake, I could only think about the crows. How they'd seen her here first. The sharp image-memory of her hair. Of being hers.

I turned my head and put my lips against her hair. Breathed in the smell of blood and green things. My back flared a little, and Mab said, "My granny used to tell me that all the magic in the world was right there in the sunrise."

Looking out through the leaves at the spread of colors on the horizon, I could believe it. Especially feeling the echo of Mab's power in my heart. It was like the mud monster's poison—Gabriel's poison—tucked into my chest. Except not heavy. Not scary. It tingled more like when my foot had been asleep and started the process of waking up.

If only I could keep hold of this when I took back my real body.

I said, "I think I don't need any more magic but this." I held up my hand, with her hand in it. Our fingers together.

Mab raised our hands up to her mouth. She kissed the shiny black knuckles, then smoothed her cheek against the tiny feathers scattered across the back of my hand.

A hidden fear slipped out of her heart and into mine. I didn't understand it. "What's wrong?"

"I'm scared, Will," she whispered.

"What?" I scooted around, pulling her to face me. "This is going to work, Mab. You are so strong, you know what you're doing. It's a great plan."

"I know." She blinked fast. Drew her legs up so that her knees were against her chest. "I know it will work. That's what scares me."

I put my hands around hers. "Why?" I rubbed my thumbs along her knuckles.

Her forehead lowered until it touched our hands. She took a shuddering breath, then looked directly at me. "This is going to cleanse all the magic between us. Between me and Gabriel."

"I know. That's . . . the point. To burn him out, all that magic out of my body."

"Yes." The first full rays of sunlight reflected in her eyes. And tears made them shine.

I turned over what she'd said. And realized what she meant just as she said in a shaking voice, "I'm going to lose my magic, Will."

"You can't!" I squeezed her hands. "Mab!"

"There's no other way. I have to seal the countercurse. I can't let it go raging off to burn the whole world. It's my job to bind it. It's what I do. I keep curses." She shrugged, looked off past my shoulders. A little line appeared between her eyebrows, and her lips turned down with determination.

Shaking my head, I tried to imagine her like a normal person. All schoolbooks and—and cheerleading. No blood or knives or air-into-fire. "There has to be another way."

"No," she whispered. "I can't think of anything. Not that promises Lukas will be safe, and you."

"I'm willing to risk it!"

"I'm not." It sounded so simple when she said it. "And Lukas is depending on me, too. I don't know how long he'll survive. There isn't time to go through this all again and again. We have one chance, and it must be now."

It was impossible to argue with that. I opened my mouth and closed it.

She touched my face. "This is how it has to be. I'll do this final spell, and then . . . I don't know. I don't know who I'll be."

Those were my own words. I thought of the times she'd told me that she *was* magic. When she'd sat on the concrete stadium step and said, *It's what I am meant for.*

I stood up, pulled her to her feet. Putting my hands on her face, I looked straight into her eyes. Said, "I know who you'll be."

Lifting up onto her tiptoes, Mab kissed me. I pushed into it, my hands on her hips. The feeling between us heated up, centered in my back and shooting through my heart toward her. Gasping, Mab put her forehead against mine. "You taste like wind," she whispered. "Did I tell you?"

"Mab." I kissed her again.

Mab closed her eyes and put her hands flat against my chest. Over my heart, where in my own body the antler had bruised me, where all the magic that brought me to this had begun. "Will Sanger," she said, breathy but certain, eyes still closed as if she was picturing something in her mind. "As long as you kiss me, I will always remember that magic lives in the world outside my blood."

"I promise I will." I tightened my hands on her hips, tugged her closer. For just that moment, nothing else mattered.

SIXTY

MAB

We met, the three of us, as the rising sun bathed the oak circle and the Pink House in soft golden light. Ben dropped down out of one of the far trees and loped over to the rosebush.

"He hasn't moved at all," he said quietly.

I scanned the rune-work they'd done, nodding my approval. It was quite good. Taking the knife that had been stabbed into the ground and waiting, I pricked my wrist. "Ben, I need your bare chest."

He hesitated, frowned at Will, but then quickly stripped off his shirt.

With my blood I painted a rune over Ben's heart. "To hold your body firm against Gabriel's possession," I said.

"That's really pretty nasty."

Will smiled. "You get used to it."

Ben touched my wrist, smeared the last drop of blood there. "Are your tattoos like his?"

"Yes. Blood tattoos, runes worked into my skin as permanent magic . . . *Oh.*" All the air rushed out of my lungs. This countercurse would strip my tattoos out of my flesh, the tattoos Arthur had given me, that we'd painstakingly diagrammed and spent long mornings under the sun pricking into place.

I'd always believed I'd have that piece of him forever. Indelibly marked into my skin.

Tears washed my eyes, but I ground my teeth, pushed my tongue against the roof of my mouth, and sucked in air through my nose. Will touched my cheek, his thumb on my lips. I nodded against his palm and blew out a harsh, strengthening sigh. Ben touched my shoulder, though I could see in his face that he didn't understand. He didn't waste time with questions, either.

I said, "Will, when you stab the knife in, I'll feel it, and I'll immediately begin pulling on your power to disconnect Lukas."

"I know."

"And then you just concentrate on your body." I took his feathered hand in both of mine and gazed up. The sunlight turned his skin oily, a blue and violet and golden sheen through the feathers. It was beautiful, especially with the turquoise eyes peering down at me. "This one will fall to pieces, and you must hold on to your body. Want it more than anything."

He brushed stray curls off my face, and I wished my hair could just stay where I put it sometimes. "I know, Mab. I know what to do."

"We both do." Ben stepped in to make us three points in a small triangle.

"You remember Faith's number and address?" I flicked my eyes at him, unable to stop fretting, unable to move on with this last act of magic.

"Yes." Ben rattled off the information, and I had to nod. If things went wrong, if Will was injured, or I was, or even Lukas needed healing, he would go for Faith. I wouldn't be able to help.

Ben squeezed my arm and backed off, while Will glanced over his wide shoulder toward the house. He looked back at me, and I only stared at him for a long moment, reveling in the colors and crow remnants. There was nothing left for me to say, and Will gave my hair a final little tug before going with Ben.

I watched them approach the porch, then turned around to kneel at the unfinished edge of the salt circle.

WILL

Ben and I paused on the porch. He set his closed fist against my shoulder. I nodded. Our plan was simple. He was the distraction. I would come up behind my body and jam the dagger in. Hopefully missing all major organs. Since it was my own body. That I was about to mutilate.

Better not to think about it.

My brother gripped the door, popped it open, and strode inside.

I counted one-Mississippi-two-Mississippi up to twenty, with my forehead pressed into the door frame. Listened for his voice. For any yell for help.

Then in I went.

The windows had all been opened, and the temperature in the house matched the outside. A little humid. A little breezy. No lights were on, and everything was grayish and lit with the morning sun. I heard my voice from the right, and crept slowly forward.

My body had its back to me, hands on my hips, and he was saying to Ben, ". . . letting you get out too much."

Ben stood near the open window, having maneuvered so that there was a sofa between him and my body. A curtain flapped against his elbow.

It was this easy.

I stepped forward, out of the hallway and into the den.

Gabriel stood loosely, hip cocked. It was so not like how I imagined myself. Even from behind. He was shirtless, wearing slept-in pants. The blood tattoos had mellowed into a rusty, dim shadow of what they'd been before. Old. Like they were totally a part of him. Of me.

"I called the police," Ben said, edging nearer to the window.

"I cut the phone cord two days ago. Stand still, or I'll turn you into topiary." But Gabriel didn't sound at all concerned.

It was impossible to move. That was my body. My skin. I clenched the dagger in my hand that I was supposed to drive into it. My mind whirled. I tried to recite the magic words to myself. Tried to use them to force my feet forward.

"If you're gonna do anything," Ben said to Gabriel, but his eyes flicked back to me, "*then do it,* damn it."

I leapt forward and drove the dagger into my own shoulder.

MAB

The shock of Will's spell burned in the center of the black candle rune over my spine. I sliced open both of my palms and placed them at either end of the broken line of salt, completing the circuit with my body. "Unmake," I said, "your power severed. Your blood unbound. The mark of his strength on your flesh, shattered. The mirror cracked, this reflection sundered. The mark of his strength on your flesh, shattered."

The words were the reverse of the black candle binding.

Beneath me the earth trembled.

WILL

Gabriel jerked and cried out. He staggered, but caught himself on the back of an armchair. Turning, he tried to reach around to pull out the dagger. But he faltered as his knees gave out. He fell hard, and blood streamed down his back in a fresh assault. From his knees, he glanced up at me, horror dawning on his face. My face. "The bird boy," he whispered.

I stepped close again. Reached to touch his blood, to start the spell. But he grabbed my wrist. "Don't. I'll make you so much more powerful than she has."

Ben clocked Gabriel in the head with his elbow. He toppled to the side, and I jumped with him. Landed on my knees, and as Gabriel groaned I smeared the blood from the dagger into a circle and said, "By his blood, cleanse this curse."

"Mab!" Gabriel screeched. The tattoos on his skin flared as red-hot as fire. He dove forward and hit me with both hands. We collapsed back. My body slammed on top of me. Its blood dripped hot onto my chest.

The rune on my back exploded in power.

A strangled cry burst out of my mouth. Gabriel gritted his teeth—my teeth!—and said, "She can take Lukas from me, but this body is mine now."

"No, it's mine," I managed. It was like looking up into a mirror, only with no expression I'd ever make.

"William!" He laughed, hard and ugly. My hands slid in the blood as I pushed at him. All his muscles trembled and shook, and the skin was on fire. His face flushed, his lips almost purple.

He rolled off me. My chest was falling to pieces again. All the skin sloughing around, the feathers shaking. I couldn't breathe. I was dying.

Ben stood over us both, and he used his foot to knock Gabriel back onto the floor as he tried to get up. Gabriel coughed, and I straddled him, pinned him down.

The ground bucked under us.

Gabriel choked on his own cries, writhing. I held on to his shoulders, spread my weight down onto him. "Stop!" he screamed. "Stop, I don't deserve this!"

"It's my body."

"This curse will destroy you, too!"

"I know." I ground my fingers into his shoulders. Felt my own blood slick under my hands. And the burning magic breaking me down. Tearing through this crow body. Spinning in a ball of fire, a supernova, in my heart. I closed my eyes and thought of myself. Gabriel screamed, and I screamed, too.

Ben yelled my name.

I refused to let go, even as his blood tattoos turned to acid, even as the body around me tore apart.

This was mine. Mine. My body. My life.

Mine.

M A B

My familiar exploded in a flare of magic so bright my vision whited out and it was all I could do to channel it into this unbinding.

Fire tore through the black candle rune, burning my throat, shaking my bones so high and fast it felt like they shattered into a million pieces. I dug my fingers into the circle, focused, focused, focused while I burned from the inside out.

The inferno raged, louder than anything, roaring until I couldn't hear my own screams.

And it vanished, sucking into the earth as the salt circle held.

The roses had turned to ash, and Lukas lay prone in a bed of it, everything burned away but his body.

Struggling, I crawled forward, shook him. His skin burned me, but I shook harder. "Lukas!"

He opened his eyes and sat up. "Mab." His voice sounded weak and dry.

I smiled, my lips cracking painfully. "Go. Get out of this circle," I ordered.

"But Mab." His eyes were sunken into his face, his cheeks hollow. But he lived.

"No, go. I am . . . not finished."

The earth had not stopped trembling.

"Get out of the circle, Lukas!"

He tripped to his feet, falling over himself, but managed it. The burn of the countercurse tingled my feet as I stood, too—I had to, or this magic would tear everywhere, destroy everything, including Lukas, including the whole blood ground. Everything.

Grasping my knife, I held out my hand and put the dagger's tip to the tattoo on my wrist. I pricked it deeply, letting the pain become a sound on my tongue, and I walked to the nearest of the nine spirals. "By my blood, cleanse this curse!"

WILL

I was nothing but fire.

And my name. *Will.*

Wind tore through my feathers, I couldn't control it. I couldn't fly. I was falling. I was—

Will.

MAB

The first drop of blood fell. I felt the ripple as it awakened my rune.

The second drop at the second spiral sent a shiver of pleasure up from my toes. *Ah, magic!*

The third tore at my heart.

I dug the point of the dagger back into my wrist. The fourth and fifth drops of blood weakened my knees. The sixth clogged my throat, and the seventh brought tears to my eyes.

The eighth cracked my bones.

The ninth hit the rune, and the immediate magic flung me to the ground.

I landed on my hip and bleeding wrist, cried out at the snap of pain that whipped up my arm. "Cleanse this curse," I commanded. "By my blood, from his blood. Cleanse this curse. Cleanse this curse."

Wind screamed, whipping the circle of oak trees, tearing at the roof of the Pink House. Lukas yelled something but kept back.

The nine spirals glowed, and I stepped into the center of them.

Sudden, eerie silence permeated the hill. Sunspots danced in my vision as for one moment the wind froze, and everything was still.

WILL

I opened my eyes. My head pounded, my heartbeat slamming my ribs. Ben bent over me. "Will?"

Slowly sitting up, I spread my hands on my chest—my chest! Even my bones hurt.

Black feathers floated everywhere, dancing in the wild wind that shot in through the window.

"Ben!"

He grabbed my hands, and said, "Will?"

"Semper freaking fi," I said and he dragged me to my feet.

Together we stumbled outside into a storm of leaves and ashes.

I held up my arm to shield my face. There was Mab, standing where the center of the rose garden had been. And Lukas crouched next to a box of some flowers that snapped hard in the wind. He was totally naked, but his eyes were wide and alert.

Mab screamed.

She stood there, in a glowing circle, the nine points flaring silver and shooting out light straight up to the sky, and straight into the center. Into Mab.

I ran for her.

MAB

It began in my fingers and toes, but quickly swirled into my palms and the soles of my feet, spinning, burning, sucking at my magic. I ground my teeth and let my head fall back, spreading my arms out, welcoming the sweep of magic for the last time.

A shock of fire hit my middle, doubling me over. I screamed, clutching my stomach, and my knees hit the ground.

Oh, the fire! It gnawed at my liver and chewed through my intestines and lungs, turning my breath to jagged needles.

Then someone wrapped around me, saying my name again and again.

As the magic was flayed from my bones and boiled from my blood, he huddled over my curled, shaking body as if he could protect me from the pieces of the falling sky.

SIXTY-ONE

Arthur. I am so sorry.

I killed him, the man you'd known and loved for centuries. And then I went inside and waited for two weeks until you came home. I thought of running, but I waited. I had to know if you knew. If you'd expected to return to find him inside of me.

It was a devastating, sticky afternoon, when the leaves hung limp on the oak trees and even the sparrows were too hot to sing. You drove up in that old Pontiac, and I stood on the top step of the porch in my favorite dress. It was peach colored with small oranges embroidered at the hem, do you remember?

You hopped out of the Pontiac, and there were two folks with you, Jessica and Dietrich, both dripping from the unaccustomed heat. You bounded across to me, smiling, and even though I said nothing, made no gesture of welcome, you kissed me and held my hands. You put the whole length of your body up against mine, and you breathed my name into my ear.

"Evelyn."

And I knew. I knew he hadn't told you anything. I knew you expected me to be well, knew you wanted me here and wanted to marry me and wanted to spend our lives together. I knew you loved me.

And I knew I could never, ever tell you what Gabriel had done.

SIXTY-TWO

MAB

It was the day of my summer party.

I straddled a branch of the tall sycamore just to the north of the Pink House, tying long purple ribbons and crow feathers into the leaves. Silla sat below me, braiding the feathers individually with silver bells and little blue beads the color of Reese's eyes. She finished one and glanced up, shading her eyes from the ripples of sunlight. The rings on all her fingers glinted bright. "Ready?" she called.

"Always."

With a gentle kiss, Silla sent the feather floating up to me. It trailed ribbons and tinkling bells. I caught it gently, and stretched up to tie it over my head.

We'd gathered the feathers in the aftermath, and now more than three hundred feathered charms circled the house and yard. Everywhere I looked, Reese's wings fluttered in the wind.

Laughter poured out of the house, where Faith oversaw Lukas and Nick as they angled chairs carefully out the front door to set up around the long picnic tables spread across the front yard. Donna was in charge of the meat, over with Eli at the grill. Hannah and Caleb played with chalk against the garage doors. They'd drawn a huge pink and red tree full of stick figures and what might have been dogs.

Over the past two weeks, most of our extended blood family had come home. Some stayed to help rebind the curses that I could not, or to strengthen the magic of the trees. Others stopped in for a few hours, to pay homage to Arthur, and occasionally to Granny's linden tree, as well.

Mostly, though, they came to see me.

The new Deacon.

They didn't know my magic was not everything it had been. Even I didn't know if it would ever be the same. It had been Silla who'd turned over my arm, inspecting the smooth, unmarked skin where my tattoos had been, and suggested my magic hadn't vanished completely. That in time it might replenish itself the way our blood was constantly reborn.

She and Nick had returned with Donna the day after I'd burned up my magic and freed Lukas, in a pickup truck full of suitcases and cardboard boxes. Nick had helped Donna level rose ashes, and then gone into town for truckloads of volcanic stone and slate to spread out into a multihued rock garden. Silla and I had gathered up all the crow feathers, and I spent most of the first days holding them for her as she set them with preservation spells. She took me to town for a manicure and haircut, and for the first time in our acquaintance told me stories about Reese when he'd been her brother.

That night I had stood up and walked down the porch steps so that I could see the stars. Thick summer wind lifted my hair, and I listened to the quiet. Frogs chirped, and the million cicadas screamed their songs of desire, but the trees no longer whispered to me. I'd burned their voices out of them, destroyed the man at their heart.

I'd looked back at the remains of my family sitting on the porch, Lukas using the tip of a small dagger to carve his name into the railing, Silla writing slowly in a leather journal, Nick flipping playing cards against the porch boards, trying to convince Donna that she really did want to play a hand with him and bet a flight to Oregon on the outcome.

I had thought of those kin slowly trickling back, and of Arthur and all his violet flowers. Of Gabriel and how passionately he'd loved and hated. Of Granny cupping my hands to pray. I'd thought of my dozen lost crows, and I'd thought of Will. I had so very much wanted him there, with me on the land, when there was nothing to fear and nothing to keep us from laughing.

Despite losing my magic, despite perhaps not being a very powerful Deacon, I decided to throw my summer party.

And here we were, expecting all sorts of people we knew, most of whom had never been to the land. The house had been scrubbed bare, most obvious magical paraphernalia tucked away, until it was only a farmhouse my family had owned for a handful of generations.

Ostensibly, the party was for Nick and Silla, who'd be driving out to Oregon in three days. But I knew, and they knew, that we were inviting life back into our forest. That we wanted to cover up the scars with new patterns of friendship and goodwill.

I climbed down from the trees after hanging the final crow

charm, and Silla and I stood together as the wind lifted them, spinning the feathers in tiny spirals.

Silla whispered, "Fare thee well, great heart. This earth that bears thee dead bears not alive so stout a gentleman."

"Is that a prayer?" I asked, taking her hand.

She eyed me. "It's Shakespeare, you heathen."

With a laugh, I pulled away and went inside to bathe.

I took my time in water steeped with violets, pinned my hair away from my face, and slipped into a bloodred dress we'd found in Mother's things. It fell from my shoulders in diaphanous layers, and everyone agreed it made me appear older even without any shoes, which I refused to consider.

With nothing else against my body, no rings or barrettes, no makeup or bra or necklace, I went into the kitchen for a silver cup. I filled it with cold water I'd infused with anise and honey, and carried it onto the porch.

Lanterns had been strung overhead, and torches set out for when the sun set. I smelled burning wood and greenery, saw squat vases of pink and white coneflowers set out on all the tables.

Donna came over, and I offered her the cup. She sipped, and kissed my cheek. I went to everyone, offering water and blessings. Little Caleb spilled it down his chin, and Lukas dipped in a finger and flicked some back at me. Nick suggested a nip from his flask might improve the flavor—and the magic. Faith and Eli drank together.

When all my family had imbibed, I waited at the edge of the driveway, and every guest who came was given my cup from which to drink. The butcher, our neighbors from the farmers' market, the old couple who sold us sweet wine. Everyone who helped us survive, helped the magic survive even if they didn't know it, had been invited. And I presented them with my cup. Most were surprised, and laughed it away, but no one refused. They made their offerings in return: we had music and plenty for the grill, colorful pasta salads and fruit Jell-O.

Our lands were admired, the pink color of the house exclaimed upon. Kids danced through the rock garden and played games in the azalea bushes. All of us caught up in conversation, about Arthur and Lyn, about old memories and the goings-on out in the world. A perfect cadence of chatter, enough to hide the silence of the trees.

I had long since retired my cup to the porch when Will and Ben and their parents arrived. I didn't even see them at first, but Silla found me and whispered in my ear. I grabbed Donna and pulled her through the crowd of new and old friends. We met the Sangers at the edge of the crowd. I barely refrained from throwing my arms around Will, but he grinned at me all the same. His parents knew me, of course, but I introduced them to Donna, and I dragged them around to see where the food was, the coolers, and point directions into the house if they needed the toilet. All the while I stole glances at Will, my breath speeding up when I caught him looking back. My stomach twisted, and I feared suddenly that there would be distance between us.

But he was polite and as charming as I imagined a boy could be to so many strangers. He wore jeans and a green T-shirt that hugged his shoulders in a way that tightened my stomach. Silla came over to us, and he seemed at a loss for words until she smiled sadly at him. He said, "I saw you in his memories," and she rescued him by asking after his dogs, who she'd heard so much about, and then we were surrounded by others.

Lukas came to drag Will off and I almost died, but there were so many people, and I kept myself smiling and talking, remembering this party was a spell of its own, and just as important as any. I ate and I drank, I danced with Caleb on my hip.

The mosquitoes appeared, and there was much slapping and annoyed laughter, until the torches were lit and I saw Nick surreptitiously casting antibug wards all around the yard with Hannah's help. The air tingled when they popped into effect, and the mosquitoes forgot about our guests' blood.

It was sunset, and I desperately hunted around for Will. I found him at the front of the house, against the porch rail, talking with Eli and Ben and a man named Winchester who worked the stall beside ours at the farmers' market. They were arguing through smiles about professional soccer teams. I leaned over the rail from behind and whispered into his ear, "Knock, knock."

Tilting his head around, he said, "Who's there?" Eli and Winchester gave us a knowing smile.

"Banana."

Will's eyes creased as he laughed, shaking his head, too. "Please, God, don't remind me of *that*."

I held out my hand. "Excuse us, friends," I said. "I have business with Will Sanger."

WILL

Everything about the last two weeks had been slow. Mom and Dad had forgiven us for our impromptu road trip. Probably because Ben covered for us with seamless lies. I'd passed all my finals—barely. And I snuck Havoc and Valkyrie into my bedroom every night. Set an alarm to get them out before Mom woke up in the morning.

Dad and I had a long discussion about the practicalities of me taking some time off before "furthering my education," but I had a year to convince him before I graduated. It didn't seem hopeless. Especially now that Ben was on my side. He argued that when it came down to it, I'd make the right choices. That Dad should trust me.

To make up for stressing Mom out, I looked up lavish recipes on the Internet that we spent hours on together in the kitchen. Seeing Mom and Dad relaxed after a great meal with smiles on their faces and their hands woven together when I came out of the kitchen with an experimental zucchini cake made life worth living.

We'd gotten the invitation in the mail just a couple of days ago. A little blue envelope with a postcard inside of a field of sunflowers. It said, KANSAS GOLD. On the back was a short message: *Please join us for a barbecue at five p.m. on the twenty-first, a going-away party for Silla and Nick. All family welcome!—The Prowd family.*

I showed it to Mom, who pursed her lips and stared at me thoughtfully for a moment before saying, "I'll speak with your dad about it."

Mab took me down through the forest, past the wide field of sunflowers, and to her silo again.

In the sunset, the tiles glared dark red and orange, like a pillar of fire. She stood before it, facing me, and her dress made it look like she'd walked out of that fire, all crackling with energy.

I didn't know what to say. I could hardly breathe. "Come up with me?" she whispered.

I nodded, and Mab tucked that red dress up around her thighs to climb. If I'd had any doubts I was firmly back in my body again, they flat-out disappeared as I watched her move gracefully, dangerously, higher.

When she reached the top of her tower, she leaned back over and beckoned me. "Aren't you coming, Will?" Her hair caught fire, and she was the sun. It flashed as the real sun sank lower, casting shocking color toward us from the west.

I gripped the ladder and climbed to her, head craned back, unable to take my eyes off hers. She took my hands as I arrived, and pulled me over and into her arms. Vertigo swept the hills into a spin, but I held on to Mab and focused on her. She smiled and started to talk, but I stopped her with a kiss. She tasted like the cherry dumplings someone had brought to the party: sugar and cinnamon, with a burst of hot red fruit at the edges.

Mab laughed. She wrapped her arms around my neck and lifted up off the ground. I closed my eyes, hugged her so hard her spine cracked. She squeaked, and I started to let her down, but she shook her head and gripped tighter. "Not yet," she whispered.

I held on to her, eyes shut, breathing through the scratchy

curls that swarmed around my face. They'd picked up the smell of the grill, all smoky and delicious. I could feel her warmth through her thin dress, and had the urge to turn her around and move her hair. To kiss her where the black candle rune had been. Where I'd carved into her skin.

"I have something to show you," she said, gently pushing away.

MAB

I'd found the stack of papers in Arthur's room, when I'd gone through to tidy everything Gabriel had pulled apart. It had dropped behind his bedside table, the little pile tied together with a yellow ribbon. Written in Granny's hand.

This is a love letter, it began. *And a confession.*

Sitting in the center of Arthur's room, I'd read straight through the account, then clasped it to my chest and ran here to my silo, to hide it from the world. All the world except for Will.

I lifted it out of the hollow I'd created between two of the redbud roots, unbound the ribbon, and offered it to him. He knelt with his back against the rim of the silo, shuffling through the papers. Slowly, his eyes widened, and I found myself searching for little flecks of red. But there were none to be found.

He didn't speak as he read, didn't move as the sun set and he drew the letter closer to his face in order to see. I wished I could light a fire in the palm of my hand.

All around us the breeze blew, making music from the chimes and bells in my tree.

I closed my eyes and recalled the final page of the letter,

which I came up here to read again and again over the past few days, until it had seared into my imagination.

You always wondered why I didn't let you near the roses. Why I kept the little ones away, why nobody could help me tend them until Donna came with her hard scars, keeping magic out of her skin.

Because I dream of him, Arthur. He comes into my dreams and I don't know if he's still alive somewhere under those roses or if I'm imagining it because of all this guilt piled up. When you went away for any amount of time, I used to dig into the flowers and try to find his bones. But the earth had swallowed them whole.

And you always wondered why I stopped using my magic. It wasn't that I stopped, but that I channeled all of it into keeping him bound. Keeping Gabriel prisoner in those thorns. I had none left to spare. And yet I did not miss it at all. I had you. I had our beautiful family.

Now I am dying, and I cannot go to God with this in my heart alone. I hope you can forgive me. I hope you can look back at our years together and agree I did the right thing, that I could only defend myself and live.

And I hope that someday when you grow weary of your long life, that you will come to me, and perhaps he'll be waiting, too. All three of us will have a chance again, to laugh and dance together.

I love you.

WILL

Evelyn Sonnenschein's last words echoed in my thoughts as I put the papers down and looked up at Mab. She was on her knees before me. Hands clasped. Big blue eyes worried. And sad.

Before I could change my mind, I got up. I moved around behind her and crouched. Pushing aside her mass of hair, I slid a finger under one of her shoulder straps and pulled it off. Mab breathed quickly, and I slipped the back of her red dress down.

Gripping her around the ribs, I leaned in and put my lips against her skin where the rune had been. I closed my eyes and listened, breathed against her as gently as I could. She wrapped her arms around her stomach so her fingers could brush mine. And she sighed.

There it was. Her heart.

Just under my mouth.

I turned my head to the side and put my ear where my lips had been. I didn't move as I listened to her blood pumping, to her lungs whispering like the wind through leaves. Then I pulled her back into my arms, hugging her. The place where the black candle rune had been pressed up against my chest.

Mab said, "I think it's time to say goodbye."

Shock turned me cold. I jerked. "What?" I tightened my arms around her.

She twisted enough to smile quietly. "I didn't mean goodbye to me."

I let go. Mab crawled back to the base of the tree and lifted a basket of ribbons and beads and slim black crow feathers. Her expression softened, turned almost shy, and she offered me the basket. "They're charms for my redbud tree. Will you help me hang them?"

My throat tightened. I nodded at Mab, and she drew one feather free of the others. Blue ribbons and little silver bells dangled from it, catching the very last rays of daylight.

She showed me how to tie it on, and together we filled her tree with wings.

ACKNOWLEDGMENTS

I'd like to thank the following people, who made *The Blood Keeper* possible:

My partner, Natalie Parker, for every day, for pretending to love my crazy.

My early readers: Maggie Stiefvater and Brenna Yovanoff, for holding me to my best and being mean. Myra McEntire and Robin Murphy, for helping me to make it stand alone.

Laura Rennert, for working on Sundays.

Suzy Capozzi, for saying there should be more kissing and letting me rewrite it all.

All the copy editors, library and marketing gurus, publicity whizzes, and sales geniuses at Random House, especially Jocelyn Lange and the subrights team, for selling the book in eight territories before I'd even started writing it. No pressure! And Nicole de las Heras, for a cover I can't look away from.

Robin McKinley, for writing about roses and beasts and transformations. Pieces of this book have been in my head since I was ten years old.

Melinda Harthcock, for helping me understand what turning into crows might do to a boy's dreams.

My family: Dad, for reminding me that Marines are not soldiers and soldiers are not sailors, and for being my hero. Mom, for the T-shirts, and for being like Evie on the outside but loving as fiercely as Josephine. Sean and Travis, for making sibling rivalry a thing I write about but don't really understand. And Adam, for being my proof that war can break you, but you can heal.

The members of the U.S. military—all of you I know and love, and all of you I've never met and never will. Thank you for being brave.

STARS AND STRIPES . . .
AND VIKING GODS
Welcome to the
United States of Asgard!

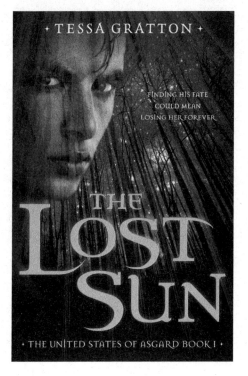

I N AN AMERICA where the president rules alongside
a council of Valkyrie, a young warrior and a teen
prophetess take off on a road trip to find a missing god.

ONE

MY MOM USED to say that in the United States of Asgard, you can feel the moments when the threads of destiny knot together, to push you or pull you or crush you. But only if you're paying attention.

It was a game we played during long afternoons in the van, distracting ourselves from Dad's empty seat. Mom would point out a sign as we drove past—WELCOME TO COLORADA, THE CENTENNIAL KINGSTATE, bright green against a gray backdrop of mountains—and she'd ask, "Here, Soren? Do you feel the threads tightening around you?" I would put my fingers to my chest where Dad used to say the berserking fever stirred. "No," I'd say, "nothing yet."

And Mom always replied, "Good."

We both dreaded the day Dad's curse would flicker to life in me.

LEAVING WESTPORT CITY—COME AGAIN! "I hope it wasn't back there, my little man!" "No, Mom, I doubt it." CANTUCKEE: HOME OF BLUEGRASS. "Soren, do you hear the clacking loom of fate?" "I couldn't hear anything over the banjos."

But I have felt it, four times now.

When I was eight years old, standing in a neon-lit shopping mall, and my ears began to ring. My breath thinned out and I ran.

Again five years later, when Mom stopped the van for gas and we happened to be across the road from a militia station. The sun was just barely too bright, cutting across my cheek. I knew what I was supposed to do.

Six months ago, I was in the dining hall about to take a long drink of honey soda when the air around me turned cold. I had time to get to my bedroom before this jagged hot fever began to burn.

And today.

It's Tyrsday afternoon, and so I'm in the library reading the thickest section of the *Lays of Thomas Jefferson* for my poetry and legends class, trying to ignore my excited classmates as they whisper back and forth about the famous new student arriving any moment now at Sanctus Sigurd's.

Perrie Swanson and her roommate huddle over a copy of the winter issue of *Teen Seer*, which isn't the sort of magazine I normally pay attention to. The headlines tend toward fashion and boy hunting: "Top Ten Ways to Make Runes Sexy" and "Dating and Prophecy: Things He Doesn't Want to Hear."

I definitely don't want to hear. But the cover features a girl my age against a shocking orange background, her eyes sad. Curls like licorice twists surround her face, and there's a necklace of large black pearls at her throat. Her hands are up, gripping ropes as if she's been caught on a swing.

The headline reads: "Astrid Glyn—Seventeen and Ready to Change Your World."

I stare back at her, as if she can see out from the glossy cover. I hear my mom's voice echoing against the metal roof of that old Veedub, *Is this the sound a knot in fate makes, little man?*

A commotion at the library window has Perrie on her feet, and she races over with her roommate stepping at her heels. I slowly stand, waiting until I'll be the last to arrive. Over the bobbing heads, I look through the panes of glass toward the front gate of the school as a silver town car pulls through, its windows tinted so dark the sunlight vanishes against them. The girl in front of me holds up her cell phone to take a picture, and on the ground outside, students pause on their way between classes to stare.

It isn't that Astrid has done anything remarkable on her own, but we all know of her mother. Astrid grew up traveling the country, like me, but she wasn't living in trailers and the backs of old vans. Astrid is the daughter of the most famous seethkona in a generation—a prophetess who read the fate of the president himself, and had private rooms in the White Hall in Philadelphia. But Jenna Glyn vanished one night about five years ago from the South Lakota plains, setting off a days-long search that eventually recovered her body. Astrid was on TV at the time, small and sunken and alone, and I'd wanted to send her a letter because I knew what it felt like when your parent died in front of the world.

I turn away from the library window and go back to the

Lays. It will not be me who makes her feel like a specimen on her first day at a new school, no matter how my blood is rushing in my ears.

But the next afternoon she walks into our history classroom and stops beside me. She looks less glossy in real life, with messier hair. But the black pearls are the same. I stop breathing as her eyes level on the spear tattoo cutting down my left cheek. She might stare forever, and I might let her, if not for her roommate Taffy, who tugs Astrid into a desk.

All through Mr. Heaney's lecture I feel her watching me, feel the fever churning in my chest. It's good I've done my own reading on the Montreal Troll Wars so I don't have to worry about missing anything vital for the test.

When class ends I wait, as I usually do, for all the other students to file out so I can slip through the narrow aisle by myself. But Astrid remains, pushing Taffy on with a silent wave.

Even Mr. Heaney leaves us alone. He pulls a black cigarette from his pocket and marches outside to indulge in that particularly Freyan habit.

I slowly stand. Astrid's eyes are washed brown, the color of very old paper. She reaches toward me, her finger aiming for my tattoo. I don't move. If she touches me, I'll let her. I even want her to—a thought that makes me hot all over—and tell myself it's only the berserking fever, not hormones or wanting.

But she doesn't. Astrid only holds her arm out and turns her eyes to mine. "I dreamed of you," she says in a voice as distant as clouds. Then she spins and is gone from the classroom.

The words sink down through my skin and embed themselves in my bones.

It's the end of my Thorsday morning run, and I'm coming into the courtyard in the center of campus, where a statue of Sanctus Sigurd himself rises out of a fountain. My eyes are on Sigurd's spear, which he lifts in a stone hand to defeat his dragon. Directly behind him the sun rises, split in two by the shaft of the weapon. I'm already slowing on the cobbles when I realize Astrid is there.

She sits on the marble rim, trailing her fingers over the thin layer of ice.

"Soren," she says without looking up.

"Astrid." I pause a few steps away. My breath hangs white in the air before me.

"Everyone here is afraid of you."

My stomach tightens, and I'm glad she doesn't follow the seethers' tendency of being long-winded. "Yes."

"Because of your father."

There's no reason not to be honest. I know who her mother was; of course she knows of my father by now. "And because of my tattoo and what it means."

Her gaze narrows to the rune she draws over and over again on the ice. She begins to smile, then stops, leaving only the promise of it in the corners of her lips. I wish suddenly that she would give that smile to me. "Doesn't it mean you'll be a great warrior, strong and sworn to protect New Asgard against her enemies?"

I could say, *That's what my father was, and it didn't stop him from murdering thirteen people and only falling when the SWAT team shot him.* Instead I roll my shoulders.

She looks up at me with the same mysterious not-quite-smile. It throws me off guard, not knowing what to expect. Which, I suppose, is exactly what I should have expected. If Astrid is a seethkona like her mother, she's devoted to Freya, the goddess of magic and fate, and of course she's so mysterious. So beautiful and alluring. It's in their nature.

"The seethers say," Astrid tells me, "that before the world existed there was only darkness and ice, and cold nothing waits for us when we leave behind the sun and stars to venture into death. That there is no light, and all is chaos. And a slice of that cold chaos is what lives inside berserkers. Lives in you, as it lived in your father, his father, and his father's father, all the way back to the times when Odin Alfather, King of the Gods, gave a bear spirit into a man that he might become a perfect warrior."

She speaks in a hushed tone, too intimate for two people who've only just met. I shut my eyes. For six months I've felt the frenzy burning, cutting up against my heart and keeping me from sleep, making my skin hot to touch. For six months I've struggled to lock it away. Yet here is Astrid Glyn summoning it with a few words—pulling on me. I don't know what to tell her, how to protest, and when she's next to me I'm unsure that I even want her to stop. "It doesn't feel like cold nothing in my chest."

Behind me, the dormitory doors open and footsteps tap lightly down the sandstone stairs. Astrid stands, ignoring the students who slow nearby, as if she knows they won't interrupt us. She says, "Tell me what it feels like, then."

She touches her own chest, low over her diaphragm, which is exactly the place on my body nearest to the fever. As if she knows, as if she feels it herself. And I remember suddenly that Odin stole his mad magic from Freya. If Astrid has the gift for grasping the strands of fate, for dancing in wild circles and asking question after question until the universe talks back, maybe she actually can understand. Maybe that's why I feel this way around her. Maybe it's worth it to tell her. I say, "Most of the time, like a million tiny flames. A fever."

Astrid smiles very softly and nods as if it's exactly as she expected. Then she walks around me, just like that, to join the group of girls who've been heading for the dining hall and breakfast. She doesn't look back. After she disappears through the heavy double doors, I have to tear myself away from the fountain, where my feet have frozen to the earth.

The best thing for me to do is go about my routines. To ignore the way I catch my breath when she passes, and the thoughts that shoot up about touching her hand. Nonengagement is the way to avoid getting upset, which can trigger the berserking, and once it finally overtakes me I'm stuck with it forever. I keep myself out of fighting, out of situations where most boys my age throw punches. I avoid falling for girls—until now they've made it easy by avoiding me right back. If I hold the madness off, maybe it'll fade. Maybe I can squash it, bury it for the rest of my life.

Only that won't happen so long as Astrid is making me feel this way.

I have Anglish and biology on Freyasdays, and as Astrid comes into biology carrying a brand-new elf anatomy textbook, she notices me. She sits only two desks over. I stop breathing.

In lunch period, I glance across the dining hall to see her fingers at her chest, rubbing tiny circles against the button of her cardigan.

And my fever burns hotter.

The bench creaks beside me as my former roommate London slides in and slaps his laden tray onto the table. "You're staring," he says, digging into mashed red potatoes. He's a hand taller than me, and his skin is even darker than mine. I used to think it was the reason we were originally dormed together— Sanctus Sigurd's two charity cases—but he was quick to tell me his grandfather was the king of Kansa for one term, despite their race and allegiance to Thor Thunderer, the least diplomatic of all our gods.

I look back at Astrid, who's in the middle of a circle of admirers, with Taffy at her right hand. "Not at your girlfriend," I say to London as I push ham around on my plate. I stab two chunks and eat them.

"I'm not worried about you and Taffy."

His mouth is full as he says it, and I make sure to swallow before answering. "What are you worried about?"

He picks up his mug of honey soda in one big hand. London is the only student on campus stronger than me, but we'd still had to quit sparring when the fever started keeping me up at night. He'd thrown a fit worthy of his patron the Thunderer. But it hadn't done any more good than when his parents requested that he be removed as my roommate. "The match," he admits.

I clench my teeth against regret. Last year we were co-captains of the school's battle guild, re-creating famous battles for competition. Next week is a campaign against one of the big Westport City public schools. Very calmly, as if it hardly matters, I ask, "What's our team's role?"

"The horde of greater hill trolls that swarmed into Vertmont ninety years ago."

"The Battle of Morriston."

"I'd love to go over some tactics with you."

"You know where I'll be."

"Staring at Astrid Glyn?"

I snap my head toward him.

With a great laugh, he says, "Soren, I think you'd blush if you could."

Swinging my leg over the bench, I stand. "I'll be in my room after devotions if you want to bring by the tactical map." And I go, forcing myself to keep my eyes on the path ahead, to not look back at her.

Fortunately, I have private lessons on battlefield history with Master Pirro all Freyrsday. He's a retired berserker who served in the president's personal bodyguard at the White Hall until a wound from the Gulf conflict gave him a limp that relegated him to teaching. Because he'd volunteered to act as my custodian when everyone else refused, the kingstate of

Nebrasge agreed to subsidize my tuition here. Sanctus Sigurd's is a humanities academy, privately owned and meant for the kids of people who can afford to keep them out of apprenticeships while they're still young. If not for Pirro, I don't know where I'd be.

Anytime my focus drifts away from the immediate lesson, Pirro slaps a gnarled old hand against the desk between us. The backs of his knuckles are crisscrossed with scars. "Soren," he says in his gravelly way, "is the fever stronger? Is that what's distracting you?"

I can't imagine telling him I'm thinking about a girl, and only stare at the sharp blue of his eyes. They droop at the corners. He should have glasses, but he says that if a berserker can't do it with his own body, he shouldn't do it at all.

After a moment, he coughs and orders me to write out the best strategy for defending the city of Chicagland against siege.

It's nearly two hours before he's satisfied and I'm free. On my way home to my dorm, I hear Astrid call my name.

She stands in the arched doorway of the chapel, one hand on the edge of the heavy wooden door. Beyond her, the glow of candlelight transforms the edges of her hair into a halo. Taffy's there, hip cocked impatiently, along with two other girls from their year, waiting to begin their evening devotion. Last year Taffy's parents won a civil suit in the Nebrasge king's holmcourt that meant Sanctus Sigurd's had to put a Biblist cross up in the chapel for her to pray. But I hadn't heard of Taffy herself ever bothering before.

Astrid gestures for me to go into the chapel with her, and I almost laugh. But it would be a bitter, ugly noise, so I just shake my head and move off on my way. There's only one thing I've ever prayed for: to have this fever pass me by. Every Yule and Hallowblot, and every Disir Day since my father died, I've lit candles and made sacrifices to Odin that his particular curse not fall onto my shoulders. But my prayers never mattered. The Alfather didn't listen, and the madness curled its fingers through my ribs, clutching tight. It will never let me go.

"Soren." Astrid dashes across the lawn to me, making Taffy's and the other girls' eyes go wide.

I wait for her, unable to turn away when my name hangs between us.

"Do you ever come in?" Instead of reaching for me, she folds her hands together before her stomach.

I focus on them, on her small wrists. If I lost control here, with her, it would be so easy to break her. "Praying won't make my life better."

"That isn't what praying is for."

Because we have an audience, I don't ask what she thinks it *is* for.

Astrid goes on when I don't. "Your berserking is a gift. We need your strength to protect the people of New Asgard. To defend our values, our freedom against our nation's enemies."

It sounds as though she's been reading pamphlets from the Hangadrottin War College. Why is she challenging me like this? Why does she care that I don't join in evening devotions? Can't she see the fear and mistrust engendered by this tattoo on my face? With half our year slinking out of the chapel to watch our encounter—some excited, some hostile, and one dashing off, probably to get a teacher—it should be impossible to miss.

"That is what they say," Taffy adds, coming up behind Astrid to take her elbow. "But not all the Alfather's berserkers can keep themselves from brutal murder."

Astrid, instead of shaking Taffy off as I suddenly want her to do, turns to go with her roommate, saying only, "Soren, you should come to my room tonight. I'm throwing runes, and I want to see what future is in yours."

I stand there, gutted, colder than I've been in a half year, as Astrid goes inside with the others, as the crowd melts away.

I tell myself I don't need to know my future. I won't go. I can't go.

I know exactly what she'll see.

My room is sparse: the walls empty, the floor bare, with only a trunk of clothes and a desk that should have pictures and mementos but doesn't. My father's sword, sheathed and silent, leans against a corner. The second bed was removed last year along with London, so I have space for indoor exercise. It's what I usually do, and will all day Sunday, too, as it's our break day from classes.

But tonight I only lie on the hardwood, staring up at the ceiling, thinking about Astrid and my mom's destiny game, about how angry I was when I realized we'd been running away from the world ever since my dad died. Mom wasn't helping me listen for my destiny so that I could find it, but so that she'd know how to steer me away. I left her because I refused to run anymore.

If Astrid can read my future in her runes, how is it brave

to ignore her? She might tell me the berserking is inevitable. But there's the outside chance I'm right, that I can fight it, and maybe Astrid will confirm that. She'll see me grown and free, living my life apart from the berserking bands, liberated from battle and killing and this always-present fever. Then I'd know I'm on the right path, that I'm doing what I need to.

I get to my feet and pull a school hoodie on, scrubbing a hand through my short hair. It's been about a month since London buzzed it, and it feels shaggy. The second I notice I'm worried about how I look, I frown. Astrid is making me crazy.

It's a quick walk between dorms, and early enough that I can walk straight past their RA's open door without checking in. Thanks to London, I know Taffy's on the third floor in a corner room, and I take the stairs three at a time, in large, slow steps.

The hall is brightly lit, with fewer scuffs on the walls than in the boys' dorm, and a newer carpet. All the doors hang open, but I don't glance in. At the far end, students overflow from Taffy and Astrid's room, their backs to me as they peer inside. I smell honey and candles, and am vaguely surprised at the hushed atmosphere.

A small girl leaning on the doorjamb, probably a second-year, notices me first; her shoulders jerk in surprise. She knocks into her neighbor, whose painted mouth makes a wide O. I keep my face solidly expressionless and stand in the doorway so I'm clearly visible.

At least twelve people are crammed inside, all on the floor but for Astrid, who's on the center of her bed like a queen, and

Taffy, who's perched right on the corner. Taffy purses her lips, but Astrid smiles. "You came."

I tuck my hands into the front pockets of my hoodie and wish I hadn't. Light flickers on the ceiling from the candles stuck to the windowsills and desktop, overpowering the dim lamps. A bottle of honey mead is being passed around, and it occurs to me that I'm the only boy here. The other guests are in pajamas, sitting on their own pillows or wrapped in blankets. I tower over them all, and can't see a path I could pick my way through in order to get to Astrid. I study her, seated with her legs up in the middle of a web of red yarn and dark scattered runes made from sticks and bones and rock. She's got dark writing on her palms, and she's staring back at me.

For just a moment, we're alone. It's only the two of us, and in my mind I can hear her whisper, *You're a berserker, Soren. Fate is inexorable.* That's all she'll read in my future.

Several girls shift away from the door, away from me. They don't want me to brush past them, as if even that quick exposure might be deadly.

"I shouldn't have," I say, and Astrid's smile fades. Like I'm a child who's done something disappointing. A sick feeling sinks down through my stomach. I gesture toward her company, wanting to say I can't let this happen with so many witnesses. But it's a ragged motion. Astrid nods sadly and I leave as quickly as I can.

It doesn't matter what she might see in her runes. My fate is sealed.

AND DON'T MISS THE EXCITING SEQUEL!

About a young girl who
wants to be a Valkyrie,
and the boy who
changes everything